The Wendover Whale
A Nautical Tale from the Great Salt Desert

The Wendover Whale
A Nautical Tale from the Great Salt Desert

James R. Lane

SHARED VISION BOOKS
Distributed by
Wilshire Book Company
12015 Sherman Road
North Hollywood, CA 91605

The characters in this book are fictitious,
and any resemblance to actual persons, living or dead, is purely
coincidental. Only the fish-lizard is real.

First Edition – August, 1999

Copyright © 1999 by James R. Lane

LIBRARY OF CONGRESS CATALOG CARD NUMBER
99-95119

Lane, James Richard, 1953-

The wendover whale / James R. Lane

p. cm.

ISBN   0-87980-443-2

Cover Design by Jimes_Art

This book is dedicated
to my friend, Delia.
May she find the library
in Heaven always open.

PART ONE

ANCHORS AWEIGH

"With ordinary talent and extraordinary perseverance, all things are attainable."

Sir Thomas Foxwell Buxton

ৰ্জ্ঞ LITTLE KNOWN DATES IN PREHISTORY

On July 4th of the year 180,378,011 BC, an act of independence took place. That it was also an act of sheer and utter stupidity was the consensus of those lower life forms that observed it.

A fish-lizard, going by the name Ich, attempted to subvert evolution by taking matters into his own hands, make that, fins. His race of beings had for millions of years been confined to the great inland sea that occupied major chunks of real estate in the area not soon to be known as Nevada, Utah, Colorado, Arizona, etc., etc. Suffice it to say it was a big puddle of water.

Not content to be a little fish lizard (at 18 feet long) in a big puddle, Ich had somehow gotten it in his mind that his future lay in something more solid than salty water. Land. He glimpsed this strange world when he poked his snout above the surface of the sea and looked shoreward. To his simple mind, a dry unknown was much, much better than a wet boredom.

Ignoring the pleas from his mother and father and the dire warnings of the other water-locked denizens of the deep, Ich chose the simplest route to becoming a landlubber. He mustered all his strength and courage and then swam as fast as his tail and fins would allow on a beeline for naked land. At the last possible moment, he headed heavenward, driving out of the water and into the air—the Earth's first flying fish-lizard. His brief moment in the loosely populated air molecules would certainly have accorded him a spot in the Guinness Book of Records. Alas, neither Guinness nor his fellow beer-drinkers were around to observe prehistory in the making.

Ich's execution was flawless. The feeling of being unshackled from the water pressure was exhilarating. Unfortunately, gravity, a concept and physical property unknown to scientific-minded fish lizards of the Jurassic period, jumped into Ich's flightpath to anti-evolutionary immortality. At this very heavy (gravity-wise) moment in time, Ich's life took a decided downturn. A course correction that Ich never recovered from.

Ich's snout reached the apogee of flight just as the bulk of his body passed over the demarcation between sea and land. This spot became known in history as 'the point of no return' for reasons that became abundantly clear to the fish lizard. Ich hit the ground with all the force of a watermelon rolling off a table onto the floor. It didn't sound good and, like the split watermelon, didn't look too good, either. While evolution had yet to give Ich a set of lungs to replace his gills, his lungs were meant to handle oxygen replacement in an environment that didn't know the meaning of dry. Perspiration was an alien word to animals that lived in the sea.

It didn't take long for Ich to recover from the shock of impact, only to realize that he was in a whole bunch more trouble. He drew a breath of hot, dry air and it tasted like no other breath he ever drew. He felt the air go into his lungs but there was no force of life in the air. Like pouring a cool, refreshing drink into your parched mouth only to have it spill out a hole in your throat before it gets to your stomach. Most unsatisfying. He panicked and started hyperventilating. No matter how hard or fast he breathed, those important little oxygen molecules never made it into the blood stream. His mind told him that this 'land thing' was a bad idea and he needed to retreat back to the water. He tried pushing off the soil but flippers trained in an aqueous environment are 90-pound weaklings on land. Thus, he was anchored to the land, bonded to his new home.

And in that milli-second before his brain stopped functioning, he had a thought that allowed him to die with a smile on his fish-lips. 'I have lived the rest of my life, however short it was, on land, as I promised myself I would.'

Born. Lived. Died. That is usually how the story goes, even for courageous beings that buck the tide of times. But Ich's tale didn't end on this Independence Day. Even as time marched on and the Inland Sea gave way to the Great Salt Desert, his spirit hovered over the site of his corporeal demise. He stayed put because he had achieved all he ever hoped to achieve; he was home.

ҨѲ WEIGHING ANCHOR

There was a small hill to the east of Wendover that afforded a marvelous view of everything in the Great Salt Desert including the faded black paint line which separated the small towns of Wendover, Utah from Wendover, Nevada. The hill was equally marvelous for its view to the east into the nothingness of the desert. It was precisely for this reason that thirteen-year-old Jeff Cutter sat on the hill facing east, away from the two towns, toward the shimmering ribbon of gray known as I-80. He turned his back, both figuratively and physically on the towns that harbored him for all thirteen of his years on Earth.

With junior high school ended on this particular day in time for the entire summer, Jeff had made his almost-daily pilgrimage to this spot to look at Nothing. Unusual, since he would save both time and walking if he stayed in Wendover, either the Utah side or the Nevada side, and seen Nothing there. But Jeff was not the kind of kid who chose the easy way in anything. He felt it was a great cosmic mistake that placed him in Wendover in the bosom of the Cutter family and his only mission in life was to rectify this mistake. Which was why, today, he trudged up the sandy hill, plopped his thin, under-sized body on the ground and waited for a sign. A sign he knew wouldn't come from the towns themselves but from somewhere out there.

Sometimes squinting his eyes in just the right way, combined with the sunlight bouncing off the desert sand, resulted in phantasmagorical images leaping and splashing in the heated air currents. Jeff imagined them to be the land-locked equivalent of dolphins at play, although he had never been to the ocean to observe this phenomenon first-hand. He saw it weekly on the TV show, "Flipper," so it must be so.

Against the advice of the school nurse and the strong threats of his parents, Jeff sometimes let himself get dehydrated, forgoing the juice packed in his lunch bag and the milk cartons at school nutrition, hoping that his hallucinations would gather in strength on the salt desert, leap into the reality and rescue him from his hilly outpost. To date, this effort resulted in his illusionary allies seeking refuge someplace cool and comfortable leaving Jeff with a headache strong enough to kill any dreams. Except the ones dreamed by this small boy.

His dreams lived on. He moved through his days in Wendover with his head bent and shoulders scrunched down as if barricading his internal organs from the relentless attack of complacency; no-no-no to accepting a future of eternal and insufferable life in Wendover. There must be an exit; a window or doorway of opportunity that would allow him out.

After several hours of waiting, and watching, Jeff sensed that today was not THE day. No propitious signs from the heavens, no phantasms dangling keys. Even his friends, the elements, conspired against him. The clouds, great assistants in forming apocalyptic images, left the skies seeking greener pastures. The sun was moving west looking for a nice beach in Southern California to spend the night on, leaving Jeff to watch his shadow (and unfortunately not his imagination) lengthen on the hillside. And the wind picked up, disrupting his last chance to catch some frolicking transparent images waltzing on the heat waves.

"Damn you, wind." He threw a handful of sand over the desert and watched it slowly drift back down to Earth. He got up and slumped his way back toward the town. The wind kicked up the sand around his feet and swirled it into little dust tornadoes. By the time it settled, Jeff had disappeared from his lookout.

৩৫ FLOTSAM AND JETSAM

This same breath of wind blew through the window of the shack, brushing past a pair of tattered BVDs substituting for a curtain. A scrawny mutt, of indistinguishable parentage, pretending to be man's best friend lifted his snout and let out a mournful yowl.

"Not now, Salty, can't ya' see I'm busy?" This rebuttal to the yowl was issued by the master of the shack—a gruff, sandpaper-skinned old geezer bent over a pile of rocks, carefully scrutinizing each and every one with a dime store magnifying glass.

Salty staggered to his feet and stretched. Then he padded across the dirt floor, weaving his way between the odd collection of desert cast-offs that inhabited the one-room palace. He carefully avoided the scabrous looking mattress, finally coming to a stop inches away from a pair of ripped and gloriously faded denim jeans. These jeans, the much-too-small chambray shirt that matched it, a pair of work boots sporting more hole than leather and a rakish looking but filthy cap from the Long Beach Yacht Club were the sole garmental possessions of Cap. No witnesses have come forward willing to testify to Cap's preferences regarding undergarments. If Salty knew, he wasn't doing any barking about it. Though he was willing to let out another yowl in case Cap didn't get the message from the first.

"It can wait, there's ancient fossils to be found."

In what could only be described as a pitiful gesture, Salty grabbed hold of Cap's pant leg and gave it a yank. Not much of a yank but enough to enlarge the rip across Cap's knee by several inches. Cap pushed Salty away from his leg but Salty, the ingratiating and starving guy that he was, nuzzled against Cap's hand.

"Salty, my mate, haven't you learned anything since coming onboard? Feed the mind first, the stomach second." Cap gestured at his noggin to make the point. Even if his gut, straining to break the thin threads holding the buttons on his shirt, suggested otherwise.

Salty, being more hungry than polite, barked at his master. A literal translation, sparing the subtleties of dogese, would go something like this: 'get off your fat human rump and get me some grub.' Cap, having mastered only the rudiments of canine conversation, was not offended by such demands. He moved across the room to peer at a wall rack of dented and crushed food cans perched above his butane two-burner stove. Pickings were slim, leaning more toward Del Monte fruit cocktail in heavy syrup and Rykoff green beans than the Dennison's and Dinty Moore's that made Salty salivate so profusely. "You wouldn't settle for some creamed corn? Good for the waist line. Besides, veggies are brain foods."

Salty turned on his heels and walked out of the shack into the desert. Vegetables? He was a dog of the seventies but he was still a dog whose ancestors had tracked down wild beasts and savaged them, ripping out the raw flesh to have for midnight munchies. No creamed corn for this little guy.

Cap watched his four-footed carnivore leave. He picked up his threadbare rucksack, adjusted his yachting cap on his head and followed Salty out the door. The bright sun made him squint as he searched for his pal outside the shack. There wasn't much to see. The shack was built in the shadow of a small hill. In lieu of a rolling green lawn, Cap had several creosote bushes and a stunted Joshua tree. Landscaping by God with a soft spot in his heart for xeriscapes.

He finally made out Salty ambling around the side of the hill, making a beeline for Wendover and, more specifically, food for his empty stomach.

"Wait up. No sense rushing into town now. If the spirits haven't seen fit to drop off a government check, well, you're wasting both our times."

Salty continued onward. The grumblings in his stomach drowning out the pessimistic voice of his master. Besides, he'd rather be hungry close to food than stuck in the shack. His parents may have left him to fend for himself in the desert but they didn't leave him with an empty head.

Cap caught up to him on the outskirts of town. "Maybe you know something I don't. The Indians say that animals carry the spirits of wise men." Salty didn't respond, knowing that humans who spend too much time alone in the desert are prone to fits of inane babbling. Besides, dogs know that it is the graceful Native American who carries within himself the spirits of wise and virtuous canines.

"If you're right about the money, we could do with a little celebratin'," Cap volunteered as a peace offering to his dog. He began to salivate at the thought of spending the evening getting blissfully drunk while telling his life story to an eager audience. Not wanting to seem over-eager for his debauching, he smiled a crooked grin. "Of course, we have to stop at the grocery first." Salty barked to confirm agreement with this last statement.   Cap smiled beatifically, and thought how easy it was to pull the wool over Salty's eyes.

Salty glanced up at Cap and shook his head. It was amazing how simple-minded some humans could be.

ଥ୵ BEACHCOMBING

Not wanting to waste any opportunity, Jeff strolled along the shoulder of I-80 West, head down searching the ground for signs of the unusual. He was focused, both his eyes and mind were narrowed to a single beam seeking out the Strange, the unwendoverian. A battered hubcap lay half-buried in the sand. Countless beer and soda cans, crushed flat by the eighteen-wheelers and the Winnebagos sparkled in the receding sunlight. Jeff continued his search.

Even while his attention was drawn to the ground, his ears picked up an unusual sound, not quite recognizable, like the sound of sails being snapped in the wind. He shook his head just enough to make the sound vanish, and then it came back even stronger. Definitely the snap of sail as the wind pulls on it one way and a sheet pulls it the other. He covertly glanced over his shoulder, hoping not to frighten this sound away. He succeeded.

The tip of a wood mainmast rose from behind a small dip in the highway. Jeff sucked in his breath as the mainmast rose higher and higher displaying more and more billowing sail. Other masts, both fore and aft of the main appeared carrying their own sails. Jeff slowly turned to catch a full view of this magnificent sight—breath taking in its majesty—the clipper ship S.S. America had made port in Wendover. Totally awestruck, Jeff could not move fearing this image would vanish. The bowsprit rose above him; the salt spray whipped off the acres of sail stung Jeff's eyes. He tasted the salt of a thousand ocean voyages and he smelled the pitch in the hull boards. The ship was almost upon him, the strong following winds driving this wooden apparition straight toward him. A drag rope was dangling from the cheek of the bow beckoning him to grab on for the sail of a lifetime. He leaned forward tensing his body for the leap that would lift him up and away from the ground and his grounded life. His muscles ached as he awaited the proper moment, how excruciatingly long it took for the rope to swing close. So close it swung, he could see the carefully braided hemp ending in an artfully woven serving.

The squeal of tires and the invasive bleating of a truck horn snapped Jeff's head around. A '67 Ford pick-up brodied to a stop in front of him. A mass of human arms, legs and torsos jumbled together waved, squid-like, at him from the bed of the truck. Then he remembered the sails, the beautiful ship, and his ticket out-of-here. He spun around and found only an empty highway. He turned back to the "ship-killing" pick-up truck ready to vent his anger on anybody and everybody associated with this vehicle, this gas-powered, smoke-belching demon from the hellhole of Motown.

"Hey, Jeffery." Mary Gilliam, schoolmate and secret heartthrob of Jeff's, leaned out the passenger side window. To a smitten Jeff, she was almost as breathtaking as the vision on the highway. Not quite. "You dummy, school's out for the WHOLE summer. You should be celebrating. With us. In Tooele. At a movie. Not alone. Out here." Mary talked in short breaths, perhaps a result of a breathing problem she had as a baby or that stringing ten words together was a task not quite in reach for her mental faculties. No matter, Jeff had blushed down to his jockey shorts just from the brief attention.

Just as Jeff mustered enough courage to wittily respond to Mary, the driver of the truck, Steve Bergstrom, leaned across the seat. "Like to help you out, Jeff-E-RY, but we ran out of space in the back," Steve's voice was devoid of any of the warm human emotions that Jeff equated with Mary's voice. But then Jeff was never certain if Steve belonged to the same animal species that included man. Steve slipped an arm protectively around Mary's shoulders and smiled a smile at Jeff that withered weaker souls. "Maybe next time, Sport." He withdrew his death's head countenance from the window, ground the truck into gear and whipped it back into the east bound lanes long before Jeff could come up with a savage and biting response to Steve's. Jeff's thought processes flooded; first, with an overdose of pubescent testosterone dead set on capturing a girl's heart (and really, primarily, her body) with verbal swordplay and, then, with a lethal injection of boiling rage. But he could only splutter out some inappropriate mumblings. Then with a resource that is second nature to all American-born thirteen year-olds, Jeff fliped off the fleeing Ford. "Screw you. Screw all of you to a doorknob!" And with that scintillating retort, Jeff headed into the sunset. Physically and figuratively, since all good guys return to fight the battle another day.

৩৫ WENDOVER'S GREEK CHORUS

A town's progress or regress, growth or decline, is not measured by the travelers passing through it nor is it evaluated (in the true senses) by the social historians and statistical geographers who map its undulations through time. A town is most often and most accurately put under the microscope by its own ancient inhabitants, a judge and jury, self-appointed and imbued with the mortal-given rights of self-judgment and self-criticism. No matter that myopia or glaucoma generally blurred Wendover's majestic magistrates' unerring view. No matter that their thought processes evolved in a time best known for mustard gas and flappers. These men who have lost hope (and a few of their proverbial marbles) sat and waited to pass judgment on those who had the misfortune to cross their paths.

Court was in session at Simon Locke's Dry Goods Store, a prehistoric vision of a 7-Eleven store—long before the tide of immigrated Iranian clerks and corner mini-malls. A two-room wooden storefront with an authentic sit-and-gab-awhile porch overlooking all four lanes of the highway. All rose until the judge, one Amos B. Gottchalk, had taken his seat and released a spray of tobacco juice and saliva over the railing of the porch. Amos was an imposing man—imposing his opinion on each and every person within earshot. Physically, he bore a striking resemblance to a California raisin on a hunger strike. Having made it through 78 years on the blessed Earth, most of them within tobacco-spitting distance of the porch he now sat on, he bore the mantle of a man who knew.

Eager to receive his Talmudic (scratch that, make it Talmuddied) wisdom on this afternoon, four elders of Wendover arranged themselves in four broken down rockers graciously provided by Simon Locke. They tensed and leaned forward, eager to see and hear more pearls of wisdom roll off Amos' tongue and out his mouth. Amos surveyed his crowd, licked the spittle off his lower lip and sat back in his chair. Apparently his cognitive juices had yet to start flowing.

And this day might have passed into Wendover history un-noticed and un-commented upon, like so many in the past, except that Cap and Salty had the misfortune to wander into range of Amos' half-shut eyes. Man and Dog's route to the bank made them a target, dead ahead and point blank range, for a forward gunner like Amos B. Gottschalk.

"Look what the cat just drug in." As if it weren't obvious, Amos pointed out the only two breathing creatures within eyesight that weren't seated on the porch. "Tain't seen him in quite a spell."

One old geezer cleaned his glasses and squinted forward. "That ain't no cat, Amos, that's a dog sure as I'm sitting here."

Amos launched a stream of tobacco juice at the geezer's foot hoping to force the man back into the catatonia he came from. "Listen, shit for brains, that's an expression. I know the difference between a cat and a dog as sure as I know a mouth from an asshole. Although in your case, I think you got your pants on the wrong end."

Simon Locke stepped outside in time to catch the last bit of vituperative babble from Amos. Simon looked old beyond his 48 years, like he had heard and seen everything twice but didn't plan on wasting the energy to get excited about it should it come around a third time. He put his hand on Amos' shoulder to cool him down. Amos brushed it off like a fly just shit on his shirt.

"The mans' got a right to go to the bank, just like you and me." Simon gave a brief wave to Cap, hoping this small sign of friendship might get Cap to spend a little of his money at Simon's store.

Cap didn't return the greeting, continuing on into the bank. Salty waited obediently by the bank entrance, knowing full well there was no rear exit for Cap to escape through.

Amos checked with his sycophants to make sure he hadn't lost them to the wry observations of Simon. "That old fart is a burden on our government. He does nothin' but waste his time in the desert looking for cockamamie dinosaur bones. Then he comes down here, collects his government check, drinks it up and staggers back into the hills. "No self-respectin' American man can do that. Right, Boys?"

"Amen."

"Anything you say, Amos."

Amos hadn't carefully nurtured his "chorus" for all these years for nothing!

Simon sadly shook his head and retreated back into the store. "Right as always, Reverend Gottschalk. Let me know when the next exciting thing happens out there. Nothing smaller than a car overheating..."

With Cap in the bank and Simon hiding in the store, Amos and his crew settled back into their own special indifference. The salt and sand seem to settle into the very folds of their weathered faces as they waited. Like Jeff Cutter, they're waiting for the different to happen, but rather than seeking it out to embrace it, these relics from the present are prepared to destroy the different, to abort the unexpected.

ᘰᙡ AVOIDING THE TYPHOON

Cap stepped out of the dusty cool of the bank and into the bright sunlight. He carefully folded the money into his back pocket and faced I-80 like a man who owned the world rather than one who barely owned the clothes on his back. As a sign of ample largesse, he bent down and gave Salty a perfunctory pat on his head.

"Salty, my boy, its time for a little celebration. If you would be so kind to follow me, we'll adjourn to the nearest dive, for a drink or two." He stepped off the bank porch and moved toward the Nevada side of town. Salty stood his ground and barked a not-too-altogether-friendly bark. Cap stopped, but didn't turn around. "We will be getting your food in the morning. Now just keep your yap shut."

As Cap got further into the sunshine, he pushed his filthy yachting cap to a jaunty angle and adopted the stride of a man about town. "It is going to be a fine evening. Yes, Sir, a very fine evening." He caught a glimpse of Amos and his gang out of the corner of his eye, and moved away from them. He listened to Amos rant and rave enough on his last hundred visits to the Wendover that he didn't feel it necessary to give him one more chance. His hide was tough but no use putting yourself in for extra abuse.

"Did I ever tell you about the time when me and whatshisname were in Singapore?" asked Cap.

Salty barked an even more vicious bark. He just didn't want to listen to foolish sailor stories all night long just so he could have some dry Kibble in the morning. Salty had begun to think this dog's life was not all it was cracked up to be. He followed Cap, but a reasonable distance apart, in the hopes that he wouln't have to listen to every single exaggerated phrase.

Amos watched them ramble off but couldn't shirk his self-imposed responsibility as God-incarnate in Wendover. " I tell you, that man has struck a deal with the devil! He is going to hell. "

His vehemence carried his words into the store. Simon's rusty laugh tumbled back at the open door. "No he's not, Amos. He's going to the Nevada Bar. And he'll be there all night, if the devil really is looking for him."

Amos was totally shocked. The color drained from his face leaving him looking like the ghost of Christmas passed-out. "And how would you know, Mister Locke? Are you consorting with that fruitcake after hours?" A surprising and misleading statement since it didn't take more than a mental midget to keep tabs on the private lives of all the residents of Wendover—both NV and UT. And the mental midget known as Amos Gottschalk knew that Simon Locke's life ended every night when he locked the doors to his store.

"Because half your so-called friends tell me so. And they're the one's buying him drinks to make sure that he don't leave. And speaking of leaving," Simon leaned back out the front door, "I think it might be time for you-all to be thinking about heading home."

Amos and his friends staggered to their feet. Simon had said the magic words and Amos knew his exit line. "We'll see you tomorrow."

"I'm sure you will, Amos. Have a good evening."

"We'll say a prayer for you."

Simon couldn't resist the one-upsmanship. His head bobbed back into the doorway. "And one for Cap..."

Amos spat violently. "No, that bastard's going to have to take care of himself."

҈ A FAMILY CAST ADRIFT

Norman Rockwell might have painted a picture of the Cutter home if he wandered far enough west to catch the particular and peculiar form of Americus Normalus-Wendover style. The Cutter house was a small wood frame affair only minimally encroaching on the Salt Desert, occupying a spot equi-distant from I-80 and the Santa Fe railroad tracks. It was a decidedly middle-class modest home certain not to make the transient, lower-class of the area, like Cap and Salty, jealous of the Cutter lifestyle. But it was enough of a home to make Elise Cutter proud to own it and reside there with her husband and son. Or in the vernacular of the 1970's, a home sweet home.

This evening Elise was less concerned with the sodium levels in her homemade soup she was stirring on the stove and more concerned with her son. When she saw him, which was infrequently, he appeared distracted and always on his way to doing something else. His greeting this evening, like most, was a casual flick of the hand as he headed toward his room in the hinterlands of the house.

"Jeff?" Elise put down her stirring spoon, denoting an important conversation was about to take place, whether Jeff was ready for it or not.

"Yeah, Mom." He stopped his momentum and turned toward her. He loved his mother dearly and didn't mean her disrespect but she was only a bit player in the grand play of his future life.

"I was worried about you. School's been out for a couple of hours." Elise fretted. Maybe she should leave him alone. After all, there are not many dangerous activities that a boy gets involved with in Wendover. And Jeff wasn't the kind of boy to get involved.

"Sorry, Mom. I should'a left you a note or something."

"Where were you?" she asked casually picking up her soupspoon and pointedly looking into the pot.

Jeff laughed a quiet laugh. "You know me, Mom, nowhere special. I just took a walk down the interstate."

Elise sampled the soup, frowned, and added some salt to the broth. "See anything special?" Perhaps a faint glimmer of hope caressed the question.

"The usual, salt and sand, sand and salt," Jeff hesitated before finishing his answer, "and a beautiful clipper ship sailing up the I."

Too late for any good response from his mom. Her nose was back in the cookbook looking for the missing seasoning link to change her meal from a hot soup to a haute cuisine. "Well, never mind. Your dad's already home and growling for his supper. Why don't you go wash up and we'll eat?"

Jeff just shrugged. It happened before and it would happen again. His mom was sweet and cared but she just didn't KNOW. "All right...sorry about this afternoon, next time I'll leave you a note."

Elise sprinkled in a generous portion of Lawry's Seasoning salt and sampled her brew once again. She smiled, perfection attained. "Forget about it. Summer's here, and you should have the time to do what you want." Jeff pushed through the kitchen door trailing a thank you in his wake.

৩৫ CHAINED TO THE MOON

Salty only wished his mother was around to engage him in petty conversation. Instead he was forced to hunker down in the shadows close the Nevada Bar, alternately watching the sun set and the moon rise. Neither natural wonder was enough to keep his canine intellect sharp. Cap had deserted him in favor of more human, less perceptive, company in the dark regions of the bar. To Salty, Cap's inclination to tip a few drinks was less a fatal flaw in his character and more a quirky habit that gave Cap an opportunity to drop down the social ladder and engage in sordid human behavior. In other words, even if Cap wanted Salty to accompany him into the bar, and Ike, the bar owner was willing to let him in out of respect for Cap, Salty would still prefer the company of the Sun and Moon., Laughter rolled out the door as another patron entered the bar. Salty whined and pawed his way deeper into the rough soil of Wendover, "Oh what fools these mortals be," he groaned to himself.

ꝏꝏ SHIP SHAPE

The Cutter's dining room would have made *House Beautiful* quite proud. It certainly made Elise Cutter proud. Although at this moment, with her husband, Ken, engaged in a shouting match with her son, stuffed lions' heads and stretched zebra skins on the walls would have been a wasted touch.

Ken, a plain looking man even when he wasn't flushed with anger tossed his fork down into the remains of a perfectly cooked country-style meatloaf with oven roasted potatoes and frozen peas with minced carrots.

"No, no, no! That is an absolutely ridiculous idea." He accentuated his point by pushing his chair back from the Lemon-Pledged table and slightly scuffing the Simonized floor.

Jeff was also flushed but the redness of his face seemed to focus his features. "Mom said that since it was summer, I could do what I wanted."

Ken turned on his wife. He was a man who broached no insubordination from anyone of lower rank, including his wife and everyone who didn't sign his paycheck. This had the smell of a family rebellion and he would stamp it out before it ever gets started.

"You didn't really say that, did you?"

Elise was frantically trying to remember how *Redbook* said to handle family squabbles but her mind turned blank under the fiery glare of her hubby. Perhaps it was time to serve dessert—a raspberry tri-level Jello.

"Not exactly. I told him that he could have some time to do the things he couldn't do during school."

Ken's face moved beyond the darker shades of reddish indignation into the purple hues previously unexplored. "Then you agree with his crazy idea to spend the summer in California?"

"No, we didn't specifically talk about that."

Ken interrupted, "He's only thirteen!"

It was time for Elise to put her foot down and act as the mediator that wives and mothers are supposed to be. Or so said *Ladies Home Campion*. "I agree with you, Ken," she said speaking calmly and patiently, "I don't think that he is old enough to go by himself."

Jeff slammed down his Welch's jelly jar water glass in his passion. He pleade, "But, Mom, I can't stay here in Wendover the whole summer. There is nothing to do here. I'll be bored to death."

Ken cooled momentarily. His son was now acting like a normal, spoiled 13 year-old. In his best patronizing voice, he said, "You are talking silly now, young man. There is plenty to do here. You've got friends."

Jeff, having learned his "passionate argument" lessons from his father, interrupted. "They're boring! Like the rest of this stinking place."

Ken's face atomically exploded from the purple hues of mere anger into pure animal rage, raising the temperature in the room by several degrees. "That is enough! I made my decision. No California. You'll stay in Wendover this summer, and every summer until I say differently."

"You can't make me stay. I'll run away." To accent his point Jeff rose from the table and glared at his father. "I will."

His father started to point a menacing finger at Jeff but Elise pushed it down, skewering a small glob of mashed potatoes on Ken's fingernail. Elise forgot the myriad of articles she read dealing with these father-son crises and let the inner mother spin out. "Now you're acting like a child. We are trying to treat you like an adult, so the least you can do is start acting like one."

Jeff's mouth dropped open in utter surprise—stabbed in the back by his own mother. He anticipated his father's knee-jerk reaction but his mom was the one person he counted on to back him up. That mistake will not be repeated. "I get treated like dog, worse than a dog." He dropped his paper napkin as he stormed out of the room. The napkin fluttered down onto his plate gracefully covering the remains of the last peaceful family supper for a good time to come. A shame, too, the tri-level Jell-O dessert might have made everything right.

Not one to miss an opportunity to make a bad thing worse, Ken drew his finger through the mountain of mashed potatoes on his plate, creating two separate mounds with a large chasm between them. "It won't work this time. Running to his room is going to get him nothing, I mean nothing."

Elise eyed the spud sierras on Ken's plate; visions of fried mashed potatoes and bacon dancing in her mind. "I agree."

"No, you don't," he answered calmly, almost resigned to the conversation about to follow, "you're as bored as he is."

Elise jumped to her feet, hoping to get the tri-level pacifier before everything got totally out of hand. Unfortunately, her reflexes were slowed by years of too many mornings lingering over coffee and magazines. Ken's words caught her before she could get to the kitchen door.

"I'm not that blind. I can see it every night when I get home." An honest moment for Ken, one of possible many if he just loosened the tight controls he placed on himself. But what 35 years had wrought a single thought can't undo.

Elise gave up the Jell-O panacea and turned back to face her husband. "I'm not complaining." Those same long years have taught Elise that this was a moment to comfort not to contradict. Her lot might not be the best with Ken in Wendover but definitely would be worse with no Ken in Wendover.

"I never said you did." As Elise came back to the table, Ken took her hand. She ignored the potato-proffered hand and sat next to him. "If I could get the time off, and we had the money, I'd take you both to California. But the sad fact is I'm not up for time off till next year, and my wallet isn't exactly bulging with extra cash."

Elise took her husband's hand in both of hers, "We aren't blaming you."

"Jeff is," he said but he was thinking how much Jeff was hating him for—a boring summer, a boring town, a father with not much time or inclination to spend with his son and the distinct possibility that the future wasn't going to get any brighter. Hey, life doesn't always give you Beverly Hills, or even Salt Lake City. And you take what you get and accept it, no use fighting against it.

Elise was trying to read the message behind her husband's suddenly defeated looking eyes. All she was got was dark glimpses of a sad soul and she wasn't sure if she was seeing into his spirit or seeing the reflection of her own. "Jeff's not blaming you. He'd yell at anyone who was keeping him here. There just doesn't seem to be many things to keep him occupied."

The truth, or at least a portion of it, sat midway between the two of them, gently floating on the greasy surface of the gravy boat.

Ken capitulated, or at least offered a small peace offering. "Maybe I can spring for a three-day weekend, in a couple of weeks. For some hiking or something."

Elise's body ached to not say what it was about to say but the truth ball had started rolling down the potato mountains and, once started, was difficult to stop. "I'm sorry, Honey, but I don't think one weekend's going to do it." Pain welled up in Ken's eyes and burst out, a long-simmering pot overflowing its top. Elise had to find a verbal Band-Aid to close the wound. Not used to pure, intense, inter-personal dialogue, she resorted to placation until she could find something better. "We'll work it out, Honey. I know we will," was all she could muster on short notice. The words took a steep dive as they left her mouth and sank what remained of the truth floating in the gravy boat. All souls were lost as this ship went down.

ᏽ TALES IN THE "HIGH" SEAS

Ike Barstow, proud but tired owner of the Nevada Bar shifted his weight off his severely flattened feet by leaning his sagging belly against the scarred wood bar. To keep from nodding off on a particularly slow night in his tavern, he focused his attention on Cap. He forced a small smile onto his face but he knew a much more genuine smile would leap onto Cap's face to reward the gesture. For Cap loved, more than anything else, an attentive audience who responded to a good storyteller, er, make that 'reliver of history.'

Cap caught Ike's half-hearted smile like a trout leaving a winter-long fast in favor of some juicy hellgrammites. The few bar patrons listening took Cap's pause as a God-given opportunity to put some space between themselves and the spinner of tall tales. Cap broke his stare at the bartender and glanced around only to find he lost most of his audience. No matter. One person was as good as a crowd as long as they were receptive to what Cap was saying.

"You don't remember this, Ike, but it was reported in all the papers," the words slipped through Cap's well-lubricated mouth without making the required detour through his brain. Cap was on auto-story, somewhere the far side of a drunken autopilot with a programmed mission to tell all or crash.

Ike was on auto-listen since he had heard this story many times and never, ever, saw it reported in the papers. He set another shot glass down in front of Cap. "Do tell," he offered up to Cap. And Cap snatched it like a suicidal moth catching sight of an argon laser.

"We was pounding some rivets on a cruiser," Cap paused briefly to make sure that all who might listen knew he was talking about the Big War and then he continued, "when I look up and there's this big ol' Nip Zero coming at me, both guns spittin' bullets at me." With a flair that would make Laurence Olivier jealous, Cap paused to savor the bouquet of the cheap whiskey and allow his audience to hang on his next word.

Ike, never one to miss an opportunity to step on another man's chance at the spotlight, asked, "where'd you say this happened?" He even managed to replace his boredom with a sense of skepticism.

Cap took up the challenge after finishing his whiskey. "Ain't you been listening, Ike? Wax in the ears?"

Ike shrugged, "Had to serve some other customers."

"Well, as I said before, this was when I was workin' the Navy shipyard during the war, down in San Pedro, California. And this Zero comes down on us like he meant to put us out of business."

Another old man, mistaking the repartee between Cap and Ike as a license to butt in, did just that. He good-naturedly slapped Cap on the shoulder. "An' you ran like shit for cover."

Cap gave this intruder the hairy eyeball and said, "Hell, no, Boy, we started throwing rivets at him." He demonstrated his throwing technique, almost bopping the old man in the mouth. Perhaps a less than subconscious attempt to silence his skeptic. The old man seems much more attentive after he checked to make sure the few teeth he had were still in his mouth. "Well, he keeps on coming, til' I kin' almost smell the Jap pilot's bad breath."

As Cap relived this "riveting" tale, a large and downright ugly trucker-type stepped up behind Cap and signaled for Ike's attention. He towered over Cap and the old man, treating them like beer suds on the wooden bar. In a voice displaying all the sensitivity of a man driving a thousand miles on a bumpy road with a bad hemorrhoid, he yelled over Cap, "Can I get another damn beer?"

More than a bit miffed at this intrusion at the most critical stage of his presentation, Cap straightened up to his full diminutive stature and half-turned to face his antagonist. He was looking at a very dirty, very red neck. Ike stepped into the breach, "Hold your horses, I'll get it in a minute. Go ahead, Cap, I'm listening."

The trucker was feeling every inch of the road dust covering his taste buds. "But I'm thirsty, now!" Said with the assurance of a man used to getting the finest service at the worst dives from coast to coast. He leaned over Cap to make sure that Ike heard him.

Ike had. And Ike was used to giving the worst service to the best customers from all over the States. "And I'm saying, sit down, and I'll bring it to your damn table. No charge. Comprende?" He hadn't balked at the behemoth in front of him. The trucker sensed that he had met his match for the moment, and retreated to his table. Besides, what the hell, it was a free beer.

Ike savored his own little show and wiped down the bar. "I'm so sorry, Cap, go 'head with your story."

Cap picked up the thread of his story as if he were never interrupted. This was the mark of a great story teller, or at least one who spent much time being bothered by Cro-Magnon types, who thought that can openers were man's first great invention. "Like I was saying, this Zero's almost sitting on our faces, when I hit the propeller with a couple of them rivets, danged if I didn't knock the thing out of whack." He paused for a lick of his now parched lips and then continued, "the plane goes shooshing down over our heads and crashes smack dab in the middle of the harbor. His hand did a swan dive until it met the polished wood of the bar. "Wanted to give me a fool medal but I told them to shove it up their rear ends."

The old man nodded in approval or, maybe, he had just nodded off. Ike was in awe—how could one man tell the same story over one hundred times and still make it sound like it was the first time? He cracked an enormous grin and gave Cap the thumbs up. "That was beautiful, Cap. You're one hell of man," he said, all the while thinking that if he weren't a steady customer, and a paying one at that, Cap would'a been history a long time ago.

Cap rose from his barstool and pulled his pants away from his crotch, giving the area a bit more breathing room. He grinned back at Ike, "And right now I gotta' take one hell of a piss. S'cuse me." He swaggered across the floor much like a young sailor on his maiden voyage through a North Atlantic storm. He bounced off the jukebox on the far wall and caromed into the men's bathroom—a perfect billiard shot except he missed knocking into the Mormon cowboy at the bathroom entrance by inches. He gave the Mormon the once over and fell into the bathroom.

These peregrinations were watched closely by the red neck pretending to be a whole human being. He took the exit of the human cueball as his opportunity to slacken his thirst, er, chug another brew. He carried his empty beer mug to the bar in front of Ike, making sure that any innocent who crossed his path on the way left the bar with more bruises than he came with. The neck, when he responded to a name, was called Charles. Not Chuck, not Charlie. Able-bodied men who had made that mistake were now selling rabbit-foot keychains from wheelchairs. Charles set his mug down on the bar in a none-too-genteel fashion. "If it ain't too much trouble, I'd like that beer now."

Ike was unaware that he was addressing a Charles and forgot to ask if he preferred the imported rather than the domestic variety of hops. He good naturedly responded, "Sure 'nuff. Sorry about the delay, but it was rude not to hear old Cap's story. He tried to take Charles' mug away to give him a new one but Charles held the mug firmly in place on the counter.

Charles smiled the smile made famous by bloodthirsty guillotine operators during the French revolution. "How come you listen to that old fool? It's nothing but pure bull shit." Sounded like fighting words to anyone within earshot. And like the extras in every 'B' Hollywood movie, they started edging toward the door. Ike being neither a fancier of westerns nor a Marie Antoinette type smiled back at Charles.

"Maybe so," he said, slow and steady, "but it don't do anybody no harm listening to it."

"It makes me sick," and as Charles said this he leaned forward as if to retch in Ike's face.

Cap chose this rather awkward moment to carom back across the room. Apparently the leeching off of some of the whiskey through urination had not reduced his blood alcohol level far enough to keep him from listing. He tried to shimmy by Charles, which was not an easy thing to do when you're shaped like Cap and your motor skills aren't fully functioning. To Charles, "S'cuse me, Boy. That's my special seat over yonder."

Needless to say, Charles didn't move. If he couldn't provoke a fight with Ike, the least he could do to preserve his self-esteem (which was already becoming quite important on his truck routes through California) was to punch Cap's lights out. He cupped Cap's sagging jaw with his pineapple of a hand so that they were looking eye to eye. "Don't you know the new rules here, don't allow no liars to sit at the bar."

Cap was bewildered by this declaration, after all, he lied and sat at this very same bar for the last ten years. He threw a dazed look at Ike hoping for some rules clarification. "That ain't so, is it, Ike?"

Ike lost a bit of his composure but he was still playing it cool, like any bartender should. "He's just funnin' you, Cap. You can sit anywhere you want."

With that small problem cleared up, Cap tried to move around Charles to get to his stool. Charles leaned from the hip, effectively blocking his way. Charles said, as quietly as he could, "I disagree." He looked down at Cap and forgot for the moment about Ike.

Ike didn't forget about him. He raised his voice so that there was no mistaking the threatening sound, "I don't give a turd whether you agree or not. It's my bar."

Without taking his eyes off of Cap, Charles responded, "Why don't you let me and this old goat settle it ourselves?" He pushed up against Cap, and Cap's watery eyes get a wee bit more watery.

Over his shoulder, Charles heard the sound of something solid dropping onto the bar counter, and he heard Ike say the magic word, "no," which meant at least he'd be fighting someone before the night was over. He pushed Cap away and turned to face off with the bartender. Only he couldn't quite see the bartender's chicken shit eyes since the ugly end of a sawed off shotgun was blocking his view.

Ike pulled the gun back a little so that Charles could see the nice scrollwork on the stock if he had a mind to at this point. Ike gestured with the gun toward the door, "I think it was time you found another bar. There are plenty, just pick one that isn't mine."

Charles noticed the scroll work at the same time he noticed the gun was cocked and Ike's finger was resting (but not asleep) on the trigger. Being a redneck, beer guzzling Cro-Magnon didn't necessarily make for a complete idiot—Charles saw this was a no-win situation and chose to exit gracefully. "The hell with both of you!" The words rumbled around the bar long after he hit the street running.

Ike carefully stowed the shotgun under the bar. To no one in particularly, he muttered "Asshole, didn't even stay for his free beer." He smiled at Cap as Cap slid into his favorite stool. "Good. Sit down, Cap, and let me buy you another drink." Cap wasn't so certain now. Ike smiled even more broadly, "You can tell me another of your <u>true</u> life adventures."

ॐ FILLING SMALL SAILS WITH HOPE

Like many boys of his age, Jeffery had the ability to focus so acutely downward that his very narrow range of vision, like that of the world of a drop of water under a microscope, became the only world that existed. The fine white cotton thread that he maneuvered with tweezers into a drop of plastic cement carefully positioned at the end of the upper yardarm on the plastic foremast was more and less than a $15 plastic model kit of the racing clipper ship, the Cutty Sark. More because in Jeffery's peculiar vision the thread and cement were a lanyard and deadeyes with fine leather parceling and a good-looking Turk's head (not the sign of a barbaric mind, rather how the leather wrap on rigging was tied off). The plastic foremast was a beautifully turned hardwood carefully sanded and finished with a spar varnish. Less because historical accuracy played little part in Jeff's crafted vision of the world in a Monogram box—the Cutty Sark was a tea clipper taking all the advantages of the 1800's high technology with steel yards and masts and iron wire stays.

In this world, Jeff's room, squabbles over historical correctness were blown away by the sheer beauty of the multi-masted, fully rigged ships of old crashing through the waves bound for San Francisco harbor. Jeff's room was a tribute to those ships, and others more contemporary but less stately. The posters of baseball and football legends had never seen the light of day on his walls. The heroes of these walls were the Enterprise (long before "where no man has gone"), the Golden Hind and the Mary Rose. While he could not detail minutiae about any of these sailing eras he could wax eloquently about how it felt to be on any ship, a strong wind at his back and miles of open seas in front of him.

Tonight Jeffery had trouble seeing beyond the thread to the Turk's head, he had been energized by his confrontation with his father and saddened by his mother's defection to the enemy camp. As he replayed the dinner table argument, his normally steady hand missed the glue spot. He redoubled his focus, drawing his vision point down until he excluded everything but the tweezers' tip, the thread and the glue spot.

He set the thread down in the glue as his mother knocked softly on the door. Respectful of his privacy, Elise waited for a response and then knocked, a little louder. Jeff ignored the first knock and picked up his tube of glue. As much as he wanted to ignore the second knock, he could not. He sensed that his mother had come to mend fences. He answered the second knock with, "Yes?"

Elise stood outside the closed door straining to make the psychic connection to her only child, trying to pick up any receptiveness to her coming. There was too much interference from other Earthly spirits, like Ken, to make it happen. "Can I come in?" she asked.

Jeff played it cool, after all he was a teenager in the 1970's. "Door's open," he quietly responded and then quickly refocused on rigging the model with the white thread. His mother padded into the room, stopping for a moment to appreciate the sailing posters and the uniqueness of her son. She was certain that none of her women's magazine had articles about raising sons like Jeffery.

She moved closer to Jeffery's desk but not too close. She had to get a sense of who she was dealing with tonight; a rebellious teenager ready to strike again, or the frustrated boy with no Punch and Judy doll to hit. She figured the best approach took the middle road, disarming either persona with a little levity. "I'm glad to see you decided not to run away. Your models would have gotten dusty without you here." She paused for a laugh or some reaction. Jeff continued to rig rather than relate. Elise took a step closer. She whispered, "I would have missed you very much."

Jeff's shoulders dropped an infinitesimal amount, just enough to show that the tension had drained away, the wind had dropped from his sails. He turned and looked at his mother with a sweet grin, "I would have missed you, too."

Elise carefully plucked at her son's hair. "You better believe it, Buster." She grinned the same sweet grin back at him, a sign that they were indeed related by blood.

Having been totally disarmed by his mom, Jeff could only respond like the sensitive, caring young man his mother raised him to be, "I'm sorry I yelled at you, and Dad. I didn't mean it." At least the first part he didn't mean—his internal jury was still out on his father. But that was not something he needed to say to his mom.

Because his mom had the same sense as Jeff, she said, "I think we're all sorry that it happened. Your father..." She left it dangling because there was no end to the sentence. She tried again, "He really means well, he just..." She failed again and fell back into the silence that comforted her and Jeff. She and Jeff were not great speakers, nor were they good at baring their emotional souls. Like most common folks they struggled through the conversations that strike hard at raw nerves.

Jeff swiveled his chair so that they were face to face, eye to eye. "I think I understand why he said it." This was the salve meant to cover and soothe the exposed nerves on both of their psyches. More serious injuries would not be helped by this verbal potion.

Elise was comforted and tried to repay the favor. "He really loves you. I know it." This was a bit more like methiolate, the red stinging kind, and Jeff reacted to it.

"I know. Look, Mom, I'm kinda' tired. Can we talk about this in the morning?

"Sure," she replied. Almost perfunctorily, she bent forward and kissed him on the forehead. "Goodnight, Son." This brief venture into real exposed feelings had left them both a bit drained, as if the wounds opened in the argument had severely tapped their emotional resources.

"Goodnight, Mom." Jeff turned from his mom back to the ship model. He went through the motions of rigging the ship but his eyes had blurred from tears. He wouldn't dare let the flood go, at least until his mother left the room. He struggled until he heard the door latch click shut and then he sobbed.

℘ REACHING OCEAN BOTTOM

There wasn't a dry eye in the bar as Cap bid a hearty farewell to Ike and the few remaining denizens of Ike's bar. The smoke and foul odor of a partially comatose patron's cheap cigar were as much the cause as Cap's departure. Cap's ego and whiskey-blurred vision attributed the bar-wide melancholy to the imminent loss of his own story-telling virtuosity. As Ike escorted his friend to the door, as much to keep him from falling as to hasten his departure, he paused briefly to plunge the hand holding the offensive stogie into a convenient ashtray, namely the man's partially filled beer mug. All in a night's work for a Wendover bar owner.

Cap burst out of the bar. Well, burst was not quite appropriate. His foot caught on the doorsill sending him half-falling, half running into the night. Once he had regained his footing and the Earth had stopped rotating around his axis, Cap searched the horizon for signs of familiar life. It took a good five seconds for the empty highway and dark storefronts to register in his brain as being clues to the town of his residence. Once this was established he knew he needed a new direction for his life, like where was he going now. The brain cells budged a little but would budge no further. Cap drew several breaths of clean Wendover air and waited for the chemical reaction to take place on the cellular level enabling more cognitive action.

Salty rose to his feet and waited patiently for his master (using the term very loosely) to come and untie the rope that bound him to the side of the building. He had witnessed this drunken debacle many times before and he no longer had pity for Cap. He could appreciate the high quality of bingeing that Cap underwent but he could not understand why Cap must do it with such amazing regularity. It was bad enough that Cap destroyed his body with alcohol but why must he, a poor canine, have to sit in the cold and dark while the old man did it? He whined softly to let Cap know that he was still waiting. He whined louder to trigger the human guilt response, after all, it was a long cold night outside.

Unfortunately, the whine only triggered a few neurons in Cap's brain cavity. As if on a string, Cap staggered down the highway toward the Utah side of town. The motivation being to position himself directly above his cot before all of his systems shut down from hooch overload.

Salty strained at the rope as he watched Cap walk dangerously down the middle of the highway using the yellow line as his brick road to his home (and not to Oz). A thought crossed Salty's mind but he didn't quite say it out loud, something on the order of, 'that man couldn't find the ground if his shoes were glued to it.' More pressing was the need to get Cap back to release him from the building. He started barking in the voice he hated to use, the one that sounded like a dog overjoyed at the prospect of his owner coming home to feed him dinner.

It worked. Cap stopped in the middle of the highway and looked around. He said, to know one in particular, since there was no particular person nearby, "Ssh, stop your barking, Salty. You'll wake the dead." He continued to look around for his pooch, trying to whistle for him to come. After a minute of fruitless searching near his legs, Cap realized that Salty wasn't around. He hollered, "Salty, where are you boy?

Salty strained at his rope, barking furiously, and hoping that Cap had enough sense to get out of the middle of the Interstate to look for him. Cap weaved his way, like a man with a Geiger counter, back to the origin of the barking. He fumbled with the bowline knot that held Salty prisoner. After many unsuccessful efforts, he finally freed the rope. Salty leapt into his arms, a rather childish and emotional response coming from a reserved and self-style intellectual dog but he had become so impatient with his attachment to the building that his release felt glorious. The picture of the old man hugging his little dog while the little dog lapped at his face would have brought tears of joy to anyone wandering the streets of Wendover at this hour. With the possible exception of anyone and everyone who knew either Cap or Salty. Looks could be deceiving. And the streets were empty of life.

Through the licks, Cap apologized, "Sorry, pal. Didn't mean to leave ya behind. You're my best buddy." He set Salty on the ground and they headed toward Utah. Salty did his best to keep Cap on one side of the highway.

"If this is the way you treat your best buddy, no wonder you don't have any friends." Since this could also be said of Salty, he did his best to nudge Cap further away from the roadway.

Cap whistled a garbled sailor song as his mood brightened. It was a beautiful night out, the world was empty of his enemies, he was with his dog and he had a nice buzz on. He grabbed hold of a streetlight and did a very poor sailor's hornpipe around the base of the light. Salty did his best to stay out of his way and the inevitable—Cap spun too much, got too dizzy and fell on his fat butt. Cap sat there trying to catch his breath, smiling the smile of a happy drunk.

Since Salty had nothing to drink, alcoholic or otherwise, he was the first to see the sheriff's patrol car coming down the road, its' car-mounted spotlight hitting all the store fronts. "Oh, great, the perfect ending to a perfect day." Salty growled and tried to get Cap to notice the on-coming ticket to a night in jail. At the very last moment, Cap caught on and crawled behind the base of the streetlight. The patrol car passed harmlessly by, paying no attention to the mutt sleeping at the base of the light standard. Cap was sprawled on the ground, his grizzly face made that much more grizzly by its proximity to the salt and sand of Utah. He had, both physically and emotionally, reached rock bottom in this land of bottom-dwellers.

ಳ೮ NO GUTS NO GLORY

"I thought you told me he had calmed down last night? If he's run away, " Ken threw down the newspaper to accentuate his anger, "I'll paddle him." Elise stood next to him in a frumpy pink bathrobe, looking for all the world like she had just discovered a *Playboy* magazine under Jeff's bed. A sin tantamount to spitting on the flag and not returning library books on time. Social and sexual enlightenment had yet to infiltrate the simple homes of rural Utah.

"I didn't say he ran away. I said he isn't in his room. But his clothes are all there." The frumpiness of Elise's bathrobe nicely set off the color in her cheeks. A rose bush just starting to bud might be a little strong description-wise, perhaps, like a cactus just beginning to bear fruit.

"Then where is he?" Ken could see neither the bud nor the fruit, much less the bush and the cactus. He just saw his wife bringing him bad news at the beginning of a long day.

"I don't know, maybe he just decided to take an early morning walk. Will you go look for him?"

Ken groaned. His long, bad day was getting longer and badder. "I'd like to, but I have to pick up a part for one of the processors, in Salt Lake." This statement was true in a technical sense but Ken planned to take his time on the way into the city—the more time spent away from the office, the better.

"But he's your son."

Ken responded with just a tad too much anger, a trait he exercised with great regularity. "You just told me that he hasn't run away. I don't think I need to waste my time looking for him, if he's only off daydreaming somewheres."

Elise raised the emotional ante, "Don't you care about him?"

"Come on, Elise. I don't think there's anything to worry about. But if it will make you feel better, I'll drive through the towns a couple of times before I go in. When I see him, I'll send him home. Is that okay?"

If there was ever a nod of the head which meant 'yes but I know you don't want to and that makes you a real shit but I'm not strong enough to say it to your face' then this was the nod that Elise gave Ken. Ken missed everything but the nod itself, bussed his wife on the cheek and was out the door.

ᘓᘔ WALKING THE PLANK

While his father cruised through the towns looking for his wayward son, his wayward son was doing a high wire act on the northern rail of the Southern Pacific track. Jeff had elected to use his considerable powers of concentration to walk the "silver plank," tempting ghostly pirates waving cutlasses or scurvy sea dogs with knifes clutched in their yellowing teeth to knock him overboard. He replayed the highlights of the night wishing they could be washed out of his mind with the freshening wind. An unusual wind at that, since the sound of the wind was gathering in strength yet he could not feel its presence on his arm. The sand which normally lifted from the desert floor with anything stronger than a deep belch lay gently in its place, nary a grain moving from its appointed place.

Jeff took several more tentative steps down the rail and with each step the sound of the wind gathered strength. He looked up, puzzled by something that he could not explain, forgetting for the moment that he had been the one who had spent days trying to conjure up just such a mystery. He stopped, dead in his 'track,' feeling the sharp prod of the buccaneer's saber pushing him toward the deep six. The rush of the wind and the sound of rising water banished the vision of the plank and his visit to Davey Jones' Locker. He glanced behind him, barely able to keep his balance on the railroad track. Nothing behind him stirred. He turned back and watched in shock as a tidal wave, cresting pure white with gale strength winds behind it, towered over him threatening to inundate him and miles of desert around him. The curl of this wall of water rushed toward him. As the tons of water raced down toward his head, Jeff's eyes grew wide with shock. 'This is no dream, bozo, move or be mooshed.' As the first drops of salt water rained down on him, Jeff dove off of the rail and into the gravel embankment supporting the railbed. He hit headfirst and rolled down the embankment coming to a stop in a discarded pile of lumber. Impact with the ground knocked the sound of the wave and wind right out of his head. Jeff lay, covered in desert dust, on the ground staring up at the blazing ball of light. Waiting. Where was the water that would break every bone in his body and wash his lifeless form out of Wendover? Where were the floating wood frame houses blown high in the air by the typhoon winds? He rubbed his bruised head to make sure it was still connected to the rest of his body, pinching his ear just to make sure that he was still alive and not dreaming while he was on his way to heaven. The pain was enough to convince him that his corporeal address was still small-town USA. His bones were all properly connected, the houses still sat on their foundations and there wasn't a damp spot to be found in all of Wendover.

All Jeff was left with was one strange thought—if I had a boat this never would have happened. Although he was not particularly religious, he took the notion of his strange perceptions as a higher truth. He had seen the water, he had heard the wind and, remembering the day before, he had even seen the ship to carry him away. These were not comic book fantasies of his school almost-chums, they were the stuff of true vision. Something he must act upon now or be doomed to mediocrity and Wendover forever.

He gathered himself together and stood up, renewed with an inner strength and a positive direction to his life. He stepped toward his future and screamed in pain. A nail, attached to one of the pieces of wood, had pierced his tennis shoe. He bent down and gingerly pulled the nail back out through the sole of his Ked. He flung the dastardly board away and it landed on a woodpile, making a loud cracking sound. Used lumber was just trash to be discarded unless it was in the hands of a 13-year-old visionary, then it was like wet plaster to Michelangelo or soft clay to Rodin—strange sounding names that would mean nothing to this Utah-educated boy.

Jeff started tearing the pile of wood apart. Hurriedly flinging the 'good' wood into one pile and the bad wood out into the desert. Like a boy in the throes of Rapture, he was unaware of what a commotion he was making. The sound of wood-flinging could be heard for hundreds of yards, if there was someone who might have been listening.

୫ତ SHIPS PASSING IN THE NIGHT

Cap wasn't listening. He was doing his best to fight off his own booze-induced nightmares. He and Salty had not had enough strength (actually Salty could have made it to Salt Lake City and back) to make it back to their desert palace and had only managed to crawl into a shitty collapsing shack near the railroad tracks before consciousness had deserted them. The nightmare that was currently being interrupted by the workout at the woodpile had Cap facing off in a high-noon showdown with Amos. Amos had called him out and told him to draw first. Cap looked down to his holster and found it was filled with iron rivets. The townspeople started to taunt him but he was frightened of reaching for a rivet in the fear that Amos would kill him. Finally, he could stand the taunts no longer. He grabbed several rivets and threw them at Amos. Amos launched into hysterical laughter as the rivets turned into empty whiskey bottles and fly off toward the sun. Amos slowly reached down and pulled out his Colt and leveled it at Cap. Cap woke up screaming, 'No! No! No!' He scrambled to his feet, ignoring the feeling that his head had swelled to twice its normal size. Salty, wisely, stayed out of his way. The sound of another board landing on the woodpile drove though Cap's head in the same way the nail went through Jeff's Ked.

The old man staggered out of the shack into the bright sunlight. A lethal combination—harsh light and very red eyes—forced him back to the shadow of the shed. He waited for the solar flares in the back of his eyeballs to subside as the crash of another board echoed in the narrow cavity of his inner ear. Not waiting for his unencumbered vision to return, he lurched toward the sound and source of his audible misery. Salty, ever the faithful companion, followed at his master's heels, licking his chops in anticipation of a confrontation between Cap and the boy harmlessly playing in the woodpile.

Jeff looked up from his industry to see another vision; although not as frightening as the tidal wave it was nonetheless a strange sight. Definitely more real in its substance and intent. Cap and Salty came storming up to the woodpile as Jeff bent to pick up some weapon to defend himself.

Cap roared down at the boy, "What the hell do you think you're doing?" The dramatic effect was somewhat muted by a voice that quivered and cracked through parched lips and a sore throat. It worked just the same. Jeff scrambled up the pile and away from Cap. Salty barked at the boy just for the hell of it.

Jeff captured a board and gripped it like a baseball bat. Threatening to homer anyone who stepped near him. "None of your business," he bellowed to match the strength of Cap's first statement.

Cap liked this sign of bravado. He took a step back from the pile to appear less threatening. "Sure is. If'n you're going to keep banging them boards around, I ain't going to get my beauty sleep. And that's going to throw my whole day off. You wouldn't want to do that, now would you."

Jeff eased up on the board but he wasn't quite ready to put it down. "I didn't mean to bother you, Mister. But I'm building something."

Cap surveyed the woodpile trying to discern what Jeff could possibly be building. Salty sniffed at the base of the pile and lifted his leg to urinate. Jeff yelled at him and the dog backed off. Cap scratched his head and smiled, he had given up hope of figuring out the lumber puzzle. "More power to you, Boy. Couldn't you start a bit later in the day, say about noontime?"

"No, Sir."

Cap liked the politeness but not the impudence that went with this statement. He scratched the stubble of his beard hoping it appeared to the boy that he was in deep thought. Finally, "What could be so damned important that it can't wait until noon?"

This was the question. The question that visions do not prepare you for. It was one thing to know in your heart of hearts that what you seek to do was your salvation. It was quite another thing to have to tell it to a strange old man and a puny little dog. But there was no guile in youthful innocence and the issues of acceptance must be confronted head-on. Jeff whispered, just barely audible, "I'm building a...a boat." He then braced for a response.

Cap stood unmoved and stonefaced. Cap's hearing had never been good and advancing age had made it less so. "What's that?" He moved closer to the woodpile, Jeff involuntarily took a step backwards. Cap again, "Didn't hear ya'."

Jeff figured that Cap really did hear him but chose to ignore what he said. This pissed Jeff off so he said it a little louder, with a little more bravado, "I said that I'm building a boat, B-O-A-T." Spelling it out slowly and carefully so that even Salty could understand was wasted since Salty's hearing was excellent; his comprehension even better; and he had understood Jeff the first time he had whispered it. Cap laughed, further intensifying the hangover headache that he was trying hard to ignore.

"And they say I'm crazy. Boy, don't you realize you're out in the middle of the desert. There ain't even a pond to spit in much less float a boat." He gestured with his hands to the desert at their feet.

Jeff scrambled down from the pile to confront his first vision doubter. He looked at Cap and then at Salty. He turned back to Cap thinking that the dog didn't understand and further conversation with the dog was futile. "Who said I wanted to float it? And why don't you leave me alone?"

Cap shook his head, "Sorry, Boy." He turned to Salty and ignored Jeff. "This boy's been out in the sun too long. Let's git out of here before we catch it from him." Salty laughed, and it came out sounding like he got something stuck in his throat. He couldn't help but think this was an ironic situation, like the pot calling the kettle black. Humans are just so pitiful. Cap smiled at the friendliness of his dog.

Jeff watched coolly as Cap ambled off toward the town. He took one long look back at Jeff and the woodpile. "A boat? He said boat, I know it." He turned back to Salty, "We got to get to the market and buy you some food. Can't have you passin' out on me."

They continued to walk away from Jeff. He watched them leave, only slightly disappointed that he didn't make a convert to his vision. But then he didn't really have a chance to explain why he was building this boat. The more he thought about it, the less he could come up with that explained the 'why'. He shrugged and went back to work. After all, it only takes one to make a boat.

ᢙᢞ MOTHER'S GOOD INTENTIONS

To say that Elise was mad was an understatement. To say that Elise was concerned would make the previous understatement pale in comparison. Jeff, completely covered in sweat and dirt, stood in the doorway to the kitchen expecting a slightly different welcome.

"Where have you been?" We've been looking for you all morning. Your dad searched up and down the towns, several times."

Jeff's body slumped into the usual contrite and repentant boy shape, scrunched down and rounded at the shoulder to give the appearance of abject submission. No one could be upset with, nor punish, a child in this position. Jeff mumbled, "I'm sorry, Mom. I was working on..." He swallowed hard, using the time to come up with the satisfactory end to a potentially troublesome start. He continued, "On a secret project. Out by the railroad tracks. I didn't mean to worry you. I would have come home, right away, if I'd known you were upset."

The change in Jeff's shape and the shallow apology worked their magic on Elise. Her emotional pitch dropped an octave, "You could have left us a note or something. You had me going crazy, I thought you'd run away."

Although not consciously, Jeff instinctually knew, as 13-year-olds do, that he just needed to give a bit more sincerity and he had won his case. He tried a placating tone when he said, "Okay, Mom, I apologize. I really am sorry that I didn't tell you where I was going, or what I was doing. I didn't do it on purpose." He gave his mom a direct stare looking for that one sign that signals success.

Elise mulled it over for a minute and her shoulders dropped down a hitch, almost a shrug. Then she smiled a half-hearted grin. Victory was Jeffery's. He broke off his stare and scanned the kitchen looking for some grub. He spotted an apple, made a dash for it, chomped a bite and headed back for the door.

His mom was flabbergasted. She just got through wrenching an apology out of Jeff for going off without discussing it with her and he was back at it. "Now where are you going?" she asked.

Jeff, through apple-clogged mouth, "Back to work. I just came home for some tools and stuff." He finished the statement as the screen door slammed behind him. Elise stepped up and caught the door before it slammed back into the frame. "But we need to talk, Jeff. Tell me about your secret project." Too late. Jeff had passed out of the zone of parental interrogation and into the land of freedom and dreams.

Shouting back over his shoulder, "I'll tell you about it, tonight." He hurried back to the woodpile. Frustrated with this exchange, Elise shoved the screen door outward and let it slam back against the frame. Small, insignificant cracks began to appear her magazine-perfect facade.

๕๙ LEAVING THE EARTH BEHIND

The sun had begun to stretch out Jeff's shadow as he sat atop the woodpile. He was fiercely concentrating on prying large rusty nails out of a particularly long piece of wood. So intent on his task was he that he didn't realize he had company until they were standing next to him. He looked up to see the 'like' of his life, Mary, and the 'hate' of his life, Steve, watching him closely.

"Looks like fun," said Steve in a voice bereft of any feeling of brotherly love, "I'm afraid to ask what you're doing."

Jeff was embarrassed, his vision crumbling under the curious gaze of Mary. He hoped the warm feeling moving up and covering his cheeks and ears with a crimson blush would be viewed as the first stages of sunburn.

Whether Mary saw his discomfort or not she saved his butt and became more his icon of love and purity by saying, "Need some help? We don't have plans. For this afternoon."

With his blush now in check, Jeff looked to make this meeting into a social triumph. He said, with all the cool he could muster, "Yeah, that would be super. It's a pain working by yourself."

Mary answered, "I'm sure it is. Where do you want this? She pulled a broken two by four out of the pile and swung it around, narrowly missing Jeff's head and Steve's stomach. This small action was viewed by Jeff as great a feat as the building of the pyramids in Egypt. Steve viewed it more as wasted effort on a worthless project.

Jeff pointed to a small pile of usable wood to his right. "Just put it over there. Watch out for the nails, Mary."

Steve watched stoically as 'his girl' picked up another heavy board and staggered over to the new pile. She dropped it with a resounding crunch and turned to face Steve. With a move perfected by many hours of practice in front of the mirror, she raised her left eyebrow just enough to convey the message that Steve had better start helping or it would be the last time he would see her lovely lashes. Steve hesitated for only a moment as his poor-country-boy brain processed the sensory information obtained from his eyes and then he did the right thing. He followed Mary back to the big woodpile and helped her pick up the largest piece left there. Jeff watched carefully as they made several trips from the big pile to the new pile. He ducked his head to study the bent nails on the board beneath him primarily so Mary and Steve couldn't see him smiling.

"What are we making, Shorty?" Steve asked. He had stopped carrying and was now staring at Jeff. Jeff looked up from the nails, the smile had vanished from his face.

As casually as he could, Jeff answered, "A boat."

No statement could have solicited a stronger reaction unless it would have been uttered by Charlton Heston dressed in a toga hurling thunderbolts. Mary stopped in her tracks, her mouth frozen at half-mast. Steve dropped his end of the board, his mouth dropped open to no mast.

Steve, in disbelief, asked, " A boat! Like in water, splash, splash?"

Jeff, as a neophyte visionary did not see the warning signs that portend an attack on his sanity. He boldly went where no visionary wants to go but ends up going there anyway—straight ahead, full steam. To Steve he replied, "You got that right."

Now Steve wasn't any baby born yesterday, he's taken in a few movies that his folks might not have let him see if they had known he was going, and he's been to the big city, Salt Lake CITY, so he knows what's what and what ain't. But building a boat in the middle of the desert stretched his imagination far, far beyond the area visited in his sweaty dreams of Mary and several six packs of beer. Building a pretend race car, perhaps. Building a house away from the parents, slight possibility. Building a goddamned boat in the goddamned desert, no way! Steve yanked the board out of Mary's hands. He said, "No, you got it. You are off your rocker, Shorty. You high or what?"

"What's the big deal, Steve. I'm building a boat and your helping."

Steve ignored Jeff, "Let's go, Mary. Next he'll be asking us to get some garden hoses and shovels. Just so he can sail his boat right here in Wendover at Lake Shorty." He laughed at his own wry humor. No one joined him in the laugh since Mary didn't get the joke and Jeff was considering the possibility of building a lake as Steve had suggested.

This crush of two realities (or rather one reality and one dream) and the subsequent adventures might have ended right here but for one small coincidence. Steve and Mary might have picked up all the loose marbles that had rolled out of Jeff's head and gone off to do more mundane things with their lives except for the two witnesses to the crime (of building a boat in the desert). Cap and Salty have watched this tiny event take place and attached far greater significance to it than perhaps any other human/canine combination in the world would have done. Salty had just seen one more act of human unkindness to another human and it was the proverbial straw that broke the dog's back. He vowed right then and there to use his considerable canine powers to promote love and understanding between all animals, including humans, in the world. Cap's reaction to the tableau presented before him was considerably less altruistic. He saw Jeff being treated badly and, even worse, not being believed by some brain-locked flatlanders just like how Cap was treated on his regular visits to the Nevada Bar. And this made Cap mad, real mad.

But there was an infinite chasm between anger and action. And in Cap's case that chasm had been widened and deepened by a river of whiskey in bars with unreceptive audiences. It would take more than a few harsh words for Cap to become SuperCap - defender of the downtrodden. Something on the order of a box of dynamite?

Steve lit the fuse by saying to Mary, "Come on, we are wastin' our time here. Besides, I don't want to catch what Shorty's got."

Mary didn't want to leave. Caught on the horns of a dilemma: she could see the foolishness of what Jeff was doing but she didn't have anything better to do with her time. She looked between her 'men' hoping that the sight of one of them would persuade her to make the right choice. Jeff looked intent, pleading with his eyes. Steve looked like James Dean only cuter and younger. Mary's mind was made up. "I'd like to help. Jeff. But I think Steve's right. It seems kind of stupid. To build a boat. When there is no place. To use it. Why couldn't you build? Something more practical?" This lengthy combination of short sentences had so winded Mary that she was gasping for air.

Jeff looked like he had been sucker punched in the gut by his icon of love and purity. "Cuz I want to build a boat."

Mary shook her head sadly, whether this means she was saddened by what he had just said or she did a poor job of shaking her head was unclear. That lack of clarity not withstanding, she smiled at Jeff, much like the nurse at the oncology ward presenting the bad news to a terminal patient, "I wish you the best of luck with it." She stepped over the last board and walked up to Steve. To Jeff: "We'll see you later."

Steve, sensing the opportunity, put his arm around Mary's shoulder and guided her away from the woodpile. Also to Jeff: "Much later, Short Boy. Let us know when you recover your sanity." This comment coupled with the physical connection between Steve and Mary sucked all the wind out of Jeff's sails. He dropped his hammer onto the pile and his chin to his chest.

This scene of despair was the nitroglycerin to the fuse of Steve's critical comments. Cap's temper exploded, sending Cap flying over the chasm of inaction, smack into a commitment he might later regret. He strode toward Jeff with Salty right at his heels. Something close to purpose was flaming in his eyes; a warmth his face was so unfamiliar with that tears were forming in an effort to quench the fire. Cap began to speak loudly even before he reached the woodpile, "Ahoy, Matey! I'm back with the supplies you need for the boat. I'm rarin' to get to work." He passed by Steve and Mary, totally ignoring them. They couldn't have been more flabbergasted than if the boat up and built itself and floated down the highway to Salt Lake City.

Steve shook off his bewilderment and whispered to Mary, "Another loony. Let's get out of here before the funny farm people get here." They stumbled back toward Steve's truck. Mary took a backward glance to make sure that Cap was not a mirage. Yes, he remained a real object in the desert sun and no, she did not turn into a pillar of salt.

A spectral image formed above them in the shape of an ancient fish-lizard leaping out of the gravity-bound sand of the desert back toward the welcoming embrace of the inland sea. Alas no human lifted his head high enough to catch this sign and so, like the tree falling in the forest, it disappeared without leaving a sound or an impact below.

ඛ෴ TWO PEAS IN A POD

Cap reached the woodpile and extended his hand to a dazed Jeff. The emotional swings of the last few minutes have left him doubting his own sanity. First he had enlisted two allies to his cause in Mary and Steve. Then, moments later, he was betrayed and insulted by these very same allies when he revealed his vision. And finally, he was "saved" (hallelujah!) by an ugly old drunk who, just hours before, threatened him for making noise while creating that very same vision. Ain't life strange, even for a 13 year-old visionary in the middle of the Great Salt Desert.

Cap, with all the bravado he could muster, and he could muster a lot, asked Jeff, "Aren't you going to welcome your new partner in this project?" He gestured expansively, taking in all the grandeur of the woodpile and the sand around it.

Jeff looked up briefly, his eyes reddened by tears. "Go away, Mister."

Salty edged closer to Jeff, giving him an opportunity to pet his cute little snout. An opportunity, Salty knew, no right-minded American boy would pass up. Jeff pointedly ignored Salty's snout and the rest of his little body causing Salty to doubt his own omniscience.

Having leaped across the chasm, Cap was not about to be turned away by a little kid's poor manners. After all, this little kid's situation was what caused Cap to get involved in the first place. Cap responded to the initial rejection, "No, Sir. Me and my rattlesnake huntin' dog are here to sign on board your ship."

This line almost got to Jeff but having been so recently burned by his own honesty he was not ready to risk the pain again. "Go away, you're drunk."

"That is not so, I'm sober as a rock." He held out his arm, which only had a small tremor. Jeff was not impressed. Salty was very impressed. He had never seen Cap recover so quickly from his overnight alcoholic binges. "Salty and me were headin' back to our place out there, when we stumbled onto this sweet scene. We couldn't help but hear the trouble you was havin' roundin' up a good crew, so we come to volunteer.

The fish was nibbling at the worm. Jeff shaded his eyes to further study Cap. "You can't be serious, can you?"

Cap broke off a snappy salute. "Yes, Sir."

Jeff climbed out of the woodpile to face Cap, man to man. Salty might normally felt slighted but he was most interested in what Jeff was going to say. Jeff continued to size up Cap. Finally: "Why?

You saw how my so-called friends laughed when I told them what I was making. Why would you want to help?"

Cap didn't beat around the bush, "Nothing to it. Let's just say I got a point to prove to some folks in town. Mind if I sit down? These old bones need a rest." Not waiting for an answer, he sat down in the sand. Jeff hesitated and then did likewise. Salty, not wanting to stick out like a sore thumb plopped his chest onto the ground midway between the humans. Cap asked, "How much do you know about ship building?"

Jeff twisted a bent nail in his hands. "Not much." He tried to look Cap straight in the eye but couldn't. "Nothing."

Cap was feeling good now. With an uneducated audience, he had some broad latitude to work with. "That's what I figured. You need me, Boy. I worked in a shipyard during the war."

"No kidding. Which war?"

"The last one we won. I kin put a ship together, blindfolded."

Jeff was visibly impressed. "Fantastic." Salty was embarrassed. And if he felt he wouldn't get thumped for it, he would have covered his ears with his paws. He settled for a small whine of displeasure.

Cap was pleased that Jeff had simply accepted his story. He held out his hand to Jeff. "Then we got ourselves a deal? A partnership, just you and me?"

Jeff looked at Cap's hand and for a very brief moment he saw the hand of the devil holding a miniature clipper ship, perfect in every detail. The devil's hand faded leaving only the exquisite image of the sailing vessel. "Sure, why not." He shook the devil's hand expecting to hear an evil laugh issue forth at the consummation of their deal. Instead, he got a wink and a smile from Cap. So what else could he say but, "Okay, partner. My name's Jeff Cutter. What's yours?" He handed Cap the hammer.

Cap looked at the hammer as if it were an alien being, previously unseen in his long life. "Cap's the name, short for captain. And this is my first mate, name's Salty." He bowed a pirate's bow toward his supine dog. Salty one-upped his master by standing up, rolling over, and then standing up again.

"Were you in the navy?"

"How else do you think I got the name. But that's a whole 'nother story and we don't got the time right now." He checked the position of the afternoon sun. Looking for all the world like he could give the correct time down to the half-minute from his brief sighting. "We got to get to work." Cap struggled to his feet, his legs numbed from their short stay on the ground. Jeff leapt to his feet to help Cap up. After all, Utah boys were polite even if they've lost their brains to a vision. Cap leaned on Jeff more than necessary; old sea dogs were not inclined to pass up an opportunity to be treated with respect. "Thank you. Now the first order of business, Jeffey boy, is to find out what kind of boat you want to build. What'll it be, skiff or scow?"

Jeff visibly cringed at the 'Jeffey boy' but chose not to comment on it since good co-visionaries were hard to find. "I was thinking about a sailing ship." He wasn't thinking about any sailing ship but the one that had almost run him down on the highway.

Visions of Sabots and Lidos floated across Cap's mind—not having had the good fortune of encountering a three-masted black-hulled clipper ship either on the seven seas or the 80 Interstate. "Aye, that would be nice."

Encouraged by this slight affirmation, Jeff expounded, "A ship like the Cutty Sark."

"Heard of the whiskey but can't recall the ship," Cap chuckled his way through his response. "How many sails she got? One or two?"

Jeff had to hesitate and mentally count the sails he saw in his vision. But his recollection wasn't quite that detailed. He had to rely on the model he was working on in his room. "Maybe thirty or forty, an awful lot."

Cap was taken aback. The vision of Sabots and Lidos sank quickly amidst very rough seas. "How many did'ya say? Musta' got sand in my ear. Thought I heard you say forty sails." He rubbed his ears for the effect.

Jeff smiled and closed his eyes to better imagine the ship of his dreams. "I'm not sure it was forty but close. She was a clipper ship, fastest in the world. Oh, Mister, she was beautiful. Nothing could touch her."

Cap was suddenly quite worried. His small effort to befriend this strange kid had blossomed into a problem the size of the Titanic. He had a quick glimpse of himself hammering rivets on an immense ship—all alone. "How big did you say this ship was?"

"I don't know, maybe a hundred, maybe two hundred feet long. It might of been three hundred for all I know. I can find out exactly if its important." He was so eager to please if, in return, he could have assistance in creating this vision of his.

"Don't you think that's a mite big for the two of us to be building," Cap asked. "After all, it is just the two of us." He held up his middle and forefinger to emphasize the point. Salty, no slouch at math, elected to keep quiet and see how Cap extricated himself from this little jam.

Jeff was on this comment like a seagull on bait. His eyes narrowed in suspicion toward Cap. "You said you worked in a shipyard, didn't you? You had to build boats much bigger than that. Didn't you?" He looked Cap over and suddenly he didn't look quite like the hero he appeared ten minutes before.

"Hold on, hold on. We did build big ones, monster ships, but there was a whole gang of us, hundreds, thousands. Not just you and me. You expectin' more volunteers for the job?" This was a low blow but Cap felt backed into a corner and he was not above defending himself when verbally jabbed by a thirteen-year-old.

The the counter-jab scored a direct hit on Jeff's psyche. He looked around to make sure that there weren't any more volunteers, laughed at his own stupidity and returned his gaze to Cap, ready to make a few, minor concessions. "Well, we can make it a little smaller."

Cap, having been punched once, was not about to let down his guard again. "How much smaller?"

Jeff looked around and finally set his sights on the wood shack. "How about from here to there." He pointed to the shack. "That won't make it too big, will it?"

Cap, sounding dubious answered, "Looks to be about thirty feet. That's still a mighty big boat."

"Look, either you can help me build a ship or you can't. If you can't, leave me alone." Jeff was now clearly defiant, he had drawn his line in the sand.

"You have to understand, it's been a while since I worked on boats...in the shipyard." Cap was not used to this negotiative process. The only verbal interchange he had on a regular basis was with Salty and lately he had limited those encounters. Salty usually ended up getting his way.

Jeff went for the knockout punch since he felt he had nothing to lose at this point. His hero had feet, and a good part of his lower body, made of clay. "Just as I thought, you're nuthin' but an old drunk who talks too much. Get away from me." He moved toward Cap as if to physically move him away from the wood pile.

Cap grabbed Jeff's arm, his face was flushed with anger, "Don't ever say that again! We'll build your god-damned boat, and it'll be the prettiest thing this town will ever see. Although that won't be saying much." He let go of Jeff's arm and it slowly floated back down toward Jeff's side. "Now we best get started before the sun gets away."

The comments slipped, unnoticed, through the bliss caused by Cap's consummating the partnership but caused a few of Jeff's brain cells to note some concern about the lateness of the day, vis-à-vis getting yelled at by his folks for staying out too late after leaving home and not telling them where was was going. Double trouble. He checked his watch and gulped at the hour. "I can't stay too long, my folks will skin me."

Cap snatched his hat off his head and threw it down in the dust. "Can't stay?" Cap asked in a voice dripping with sarcasm that Salty didn't think his master was capable of, "You tell me that I'm all spit in the wind and when I'm ready to go to work, you're runnin' away. Some sissy thing about your mommy and daddy."

"I'm not running away. My folks are already pissed off at me. I can't be late for dinner, that's all. You'd understand if you had my parents. Please. We can start first thing tomorrow. I'll be here whenever you say. Please."

It was this last touch of pleading that Cap took for his TKO over Jeff. He used the opportunity to bend and pick up his hat and Jeff's hammer. "Okay, Jeffery, we'll call it a day. And we'll start from scratch in the morning." He handed the hammer back to Jeff. "I'll see you right here, come sun up."

Salty snapped his head to attention. 'Sun up?' This can't be his old Master talking. Strange (and wondrous) things were happening in the sands of Wendover.

Jeff examined the hammer as if it were a blood oath needing his signature in ink. "Can I trust you?"

"Trust me to do what, Boy?"

"Can I trust you to keep your word and be here tomorrow?" Jeff's eyes sought to make direct contact with Cap's soul through his bloodshot eyes.

Cap felt the probing of his soul and for the first time, in a long long time, he answered without hesitation, "We're partners on this thing. We shook on it, and that means I'll be here, come hell or high water. Now git on home to your folks before I paddle you myself."

Jeff broke into a smile that made the hot desert sun pale in comparison. "Yes, Sir, Captain."

He turned tail and started running toward home. Cap yelled after him. "It's just plain Cap," and softening his voice so that Jeff couldn't hear it he added, "partner." He watched his newfound friend race toward home and then surveyed the sandy plot he had christened the shipyard. Salty watched his every move, expecting at any moment for Cap to let loose with a string of vile epithets fit for neither man nor beast. Nothing happens. Not even one mild goddamn broke the plane of Cap's lips. He paced the distance from the woodpile to the shack, shaking his head as the numbers got larger. Salty rose from his spot and followed after Cap. They reached the shack together and Cap bent down and scratched Salty behind the ears—a surprisingly kind gesture. Salty was speechless. Cap smiled and said, "I'm countin' on you to help out. You know as much about building a friggin' clipper ship as I do."

ঙ⌀ SIDES ARE DRAWN UP - NO QUARTER TAKEN

Dinner at the Cutter house was the usual affair except for one uninvited guest—the specter of the clipper ship hovered just behind the perfectly cooked fried chicken. One of the anchor lines had snagged on a plate of Bisquick biscuits and the ship was listing to the starboard. Fortunately, the Lilliputian crew which manned this dream ship had opted to stay onboard rather than swim for their lives in Jeff's glass of milk. The heat of day seemed to have taken its toll on Ken and Elise, they were merely picking their way through the food on the table. Jeff, on the other hand, was shoveling food into his mouth in a manner previously unseen by his mother. Splotches of Wendover dust were now mixed with chicken grease, complemented by a milk mustache.

Elise was content to watch her child in amazement. Ken was not. "I'm really curious about today."

Jeff gulped down half his glass of milk. Leaving the crew of the clipper ship no choice but to weather this storm at their stations. Jeff answered his father reluctantly, "Couldn't we just leave it as my little secret?"

This was not the answer Ken wanted to hear. Perhaps he exploded because the upper fore yard of the illusory ship swung on the anchor line and pricked his ear. Perhaps it was a more frustrating than usual day. Or perhaps, Ken was just a wee bit on the quick-tempered side. No matter, he didn't like the answer. "No, we can't leave it as a secret. I want to know exactly what you were doing that made me waste the day searching for you. I almost didn't make it into Salt Lake in time to get the part I needed."

The crew of the ship reefed the sails in anticipation of the heavy weather coming in. Jeff chose to turn about and try to run away from the storm. He started to get up from the table. "Excuse me, I'm done with dinner."

Ken was as quick with his physical reflexes as he was with his temper. He was up with a hand on Jeff's arm before the air under Jeff's butt had a chance to cool. "Don't try and run away from the question. Your mother and I deserve an answer, and you'll sit here until we get it."

Jeff looked to his mother for support but she was just as curious as her husband over their son's mysterious activities of the day. She nodded for him to sit down. He looked back at his father, trying to stare him down. His father knew a weaker soul, having been on the other end of this kind of scrutiny. He finally forced Jeff to avert his eyes. "Answer the question, Jeff."

Jeff swallowed hard. Thinking the words before he said them. "I was building a boat." He waited for the immediate reaction and followed it up with: "Me and a friend are building a clipper ship."

Ken and Elise exchanged glances. That's it? He was worrying about telling us he's building another model? Ken, being more suspicious than his wife, wanted more clarification. "You mean, like your other models? Little plastic boats?" He held his hands a foot and a half apart—the exact space it would take for the ghost ship floating above the table cloth to fit, from bowsprit to the taffrail, a perfect fit in fact.

Jeff realized that avoidance and subterfuge would not work at this juncture. To steal a chestnut from the past, 'nothing ventured, nothing gained.' "No, Dad, not a model ship. This was a real ship. Thirty or forty feet long. We're building it out by the tracks."

His dad responded, "You aren't serious, are you? A 40 foot boat, by the railroad?"

Jeff answered forthrightly, "Yes, I am."

Ken was stunned by the answer. In order to regroup his mental troops he went for a delaying tactic. He asked his wife a question he already knew the answer to: "Elise, did you know anything about this?

"Of course not, Ken. This is all new to me."

"A clipper ship?" Ken asked of no one in particular. Elise's answer came too fast and he needed a little more time to put it all together. The puzzle pieces finally drop into place and he had an approach that he thought would work. To Jeff: "At least it is constructive. Not very practical since we don't have any oceans around, but at least it is constructive." Ken realized that he still had a scowl on his face and decided that his 'solution' required a little mood lightener so he turned the scowl into a tight grin.

Jeff was overjoyed. He really expected his father to blow up like a volcano or, at the very least, ridicule the idea entirely. He thought that he must have underestimated his father's sensitivity all of these years because it almost sounds like he supported the project.

Wanting to cement the good feelings, he asked, "Then I can keep building it?"

The grin almost slipped off Ken's face. "Hold on, I didn't say that." He made a deliberate turn of his head to face Elise. "What do you think? Do you mind having a ship-builder in the family?"

Unlikely as it was that Elise would initiate family policy, she had many years of practice getting the not-so-subtle hints from Ken and running with them. "At least it will keep him off the highway." She grinned and then laughed at her own joke. Any tension that remained from dinner dissipated quickly. The ghost ship lurched forward, breaking the snagged anchor line and sailing off toward the kitchen. The anchor remained embedded in one of the not-so-light biscuits.

"Good point, Elise." Ken smiled at his son. Jeff was too excited to sense that all was not right behind the smile. "Jeff, I mean Skipper, you've got the parents' seal of approval. Keep building your clipper ship."

Jeff almost exploded in gratitude. He gave his mother a big hug from behind. "Thank you."

Elise basked in the glow of this affection. "There is one condition, though..."

A wave of suspicion crashed across Jeff's face. How could his mother betray him after his father gave him the go ahead? "What's that, Mom?"

"You wash all the dishes tonight."

As quickly as the suspicion wave arrived it disappeard. Jeff smiled again. "No problem!" He started grabbing all the dirty dishes, piling them as high as possible. He then staggered into the kitchen, grunting from the exertion. The kitchen door swung shut behind him and, moments later, he turned on the water in the sink. He was, for the moment, content to float dirty plate-ships on Ivory oceans of suds.

ꝙꝡ PARENTS' TRUTH

Elise listened to the happy sounds coming through the closed door to the kitchen. She smiled at her husband, something that had become more and more difficult as of late. Then she reached across the table and gently took his hand. "Thank you, Ken," she whispered over the remains of dinner.

Ken played it cool, looking for a little larger thank you. "For what?"

Elise was a simple and direct person and Ken's attempt at subtlety escaped right over her head. "Thank you for not telling him he couldn't build his boat."

Ken let his wife's hand slide out of his own. Elise tried to regain her grip but Ken gently moved his hand out of reach. "To tell you the truth, I want to, wanted to."

This surprised Elise since she had never known Ken to do anything other than his first impulse. Not that his first impulse was always the right impulse. "Then why didn't you, what stopped you?"

Ken answered with all the weight of a Masters in Marriage and Family Counseling, a profession unknown to most families residing outside of Los Angeles and New York, "Because it would be a waste of time. He'd probably sneak out and build it on the sly, just to spite me. This way he'll spend a few days working on it, get tired or bored, maybe hurt himself with a hammer, and just give up on the whole thing."

Elise thought but did not speak the words, 'just like you would.' Instead, she offered, "And what if he doesn't?"

With a flip of his head, Ken tossed this comment aside like a piece of sea fluff on his ear. "Get a hold of yourself, Elise. You sound like you think he could actually build the boat. All right, I admit he's good at building little models, but not a real boat. Remember, he is talking thirty feet, not thirty inches." He chuckled at his clever wordplay. "Where do you think he came up with such a crazy idea? Must have come from your side of the family." He chuckled again.

Elise, always sensitive to slurs against her family, got pissed off. "That is not funny, Ken."

If Ken wasn't having so much fun at the expense of his wife's weird family, and Elise wasn't thinking so hard about defending her eccentric family, both of them would have noticed that the happy sounds of dishes being washed in the kitchen had disappeared. They might also have noticed that the kitchen door was just slightly ajar, the result of Jeff leaning his ear against it. But they did not, and so our story continues...

Ken wanted one final shot at the situation. "Come on, Elise. You have to admit the whole idea is ridiculous. This is Wendover, Utah not San Francisco, home of Rice-a-Roni and the Pacific Ocean."

Elise saw the "wisdom" of Ken but her mothering instincts kicked in ahead of practicality. "I agree, but that's no reason why he can't play at being a sailor. Remember, he is still a boy."

The kitchen doors swung back to level with the frame as Jeff removed his ear. Moments later, several dishes accidentally fell from the young boat builder's hands and crashed into a zillion pieces on the floor.

℧ THE CONVERSION

There is no exact point when visionaries become revolutionaries. Some fail to make the transition and are forever cast out from right thinking (most visionaries being left-handed) humans or they drift off to Northern California, hot tub for awhile, come up with very useful things that no one else thought of and become millionaire entrepreneurs. At that point their visions have succumbed to the greater glory of the business world and their eccentricities are looked upon as the necessary trappings of the wildly successful.

Jeff transited this visionary/revolutionary/evolutionary point while lying on his bed staring at the thousands of holes in the acoustical ceiling tile in his room. His negative mantra which took him over the threshold was not his father's statement of the ridiculousness of his ship-building venture but his mother's comment that he was just a boy and should be allowed to play at being a sailor. Even at this young age, Jeff had seen the foibles of his father and saw no reason to follow in his rather shallow footsteps. On the other hand, it was vitally important that he show his mother that he was becoming a man (with a capital M). If only to show her what a mistake it was to marry that schlub pretending to be his father.

The holes in the ceiling tiles blurred and focused and blurred again as Jeff's emotional range went from abject sadness to boiling ferocity to self-doubt about the honesty of his vision. With the automatic audio replay of his mother's statement reverberating through his head, the wheels of the revolutionary begin to grind forward. Jeff brushed away the tears and set a new course in life, 'damn the torpedoes, full speed ahead.' Notwithstanding that Jeff wouldn't have known David Glasgow Farragut even if he had swum down from heaven and presented Jeff with a solid gold cannonball.

Jeff cleared a spot on his desk with a sweep of his arm. Pulling paper and pencil from a discarded school notebook, he set about to sketch the almost-completed model of the Cutty Sark. Having more skill at conjuring up visions of clipper ships than draftsmanship, he struggled to capture the essence of the sleek racing hull on paper. Repeated attempts found themselves crumpled and haphazardly piled around his Yogi Bear wastebasket. Frustrated because the vision in his mind was so real and the paper image so shitty, Jeff resorted to the grade "D" art students ace in the hole—he traced the image of the clipper ship off of the model box top. He examined it carefully until he saw no flaws in his artwork.

And like a middle-aged man after an arduous lovemaking engagement, Jeff found that he was fatigued beyond description. He barely had the strength to turn off his desk light and crawl into his bed before his eyes fluttered shut to sleep the dreamless sleep of a tired and satiated man.

And as Jeff's lids traversed the vitreous sea, the image of the clipper ship gathered in strength upon the tracing paper. Not just the intensity of the carbon flecks from the Ticonderoga #2 but the vigor of the ship itself leapt off the crinkled onionskin. The lines forming the hull of the ship, earlier squiggly and sporadic from a hand unused to tracing, straightened themselves. The gentle curving ribs flowed from a deep dark line from stem to stern. The scraggly line piercing the sky at midpoint in the ship's deck took it upon itself to thicken, knowing the sense and shape of a steel mainmast that separated a tea clipper from that of ordinary mortal vessels. As Jeff slumbered, his vision put to paper became more real, taking on a life separate and apart of the likeness Jeff held in his noodle.   To complement the sails now hanging neatly from the freshly drawn metal yardarms, the Utah wind freshened in the desert night and blew in through Jeff's open window. The draft teased Jeff's nostrils with the (not Orange) tang of salty seas and then lifted the sketch off of the desk. For just a few moments, perhaps as long as it took for one ambitious Ichthysaurus to lift his body from the sea out into the air, the sketch sailed in the breeze. The sails filled with air, the flimsy paper moved forward and with this momentum a tiny rivulet of water vapor trailed behind its sternpost.   And then, just as suddenly, the breeze stopped, the sails luffed and the paper drifted back down onto Jeff's desk. This supervisionary effort so depleted the intrinsic energy of the sketch that upon settling on the desktop, the energy faded from the page. It returned to the less vivid and more subdued image that Jeff had put upon the paper. It would take more energy than that of the idea itself to keep this vision alive.

ᘓ𝄞 TESTING THE ALLIANCE

The folded sketch of the clipper ship flapped and danced in the breeze as it dangled from the back pocket of Jeff's faded but nicely ironed jeans. Jeff carried with him an air of great anticipation. Perhaps today was the day the eighth wonder of the world was going to be built. As he picked his way among the clumps of sage brush and highway jetsam he saw himself riding high up on the poop desk of His Ship crashing through deep troughs of roiled green sea, lifting and breaking through the foamy soup at the crest of each wave, only to slide back into another deep dark trough. His vision extended to the horizon where the Cimmerian-streaked clouds give way to more placid, sun-dappled waters. This tunnel vision was most effective for a young man's fantastical daydream since it overlooked a crew turned greener than the greenest wave. A crew that was scared shitless of the might of the ocean, taken to tying themselves to masts and railings to avoid the quick slide into the oblivion of the deep. Even the sound of the metal rivets popping free of the hull as the storm smashed into the timbers was mistaken by Jeff as the sound of a salt-encrusted sail snapping at the short leash of the sheeting. There was nothing more romantic than ocean travels to one who had never left the sanctity of terra firma.

The driving wind of his mental sea voyage came to a sudden stop and the ship began to take on water as Jeff arrived at the clearing near to the woodpile only to find that he was the one human occupant. Cap and Salty were nowheres to be found. Not wanting to jump to the rather obvious conclusions, Jeff wandered around, peeking into the old shack, lifting boards, kicking at tumbleweeds and softly calling Cap's name. Nothing. No one. Nada. Zippo. He checked the shack's interior 18 square feet thinking he might have missed a large human body and a small canine one in the first go 'round. Still nuthin.

He ambled over to the woodpile and began to sort through the wood. Several times he thought he heard the sound of footsteps, whirled around prepared to yell, only to find that his fertile imagination was capable of even mundane phantoms. The energy he originally brought to sorting the wood ebbed quickly as his mind began to take on the concept of abandonment. Jeff traced the outline of his shoes in the sand as his brain groped for a good reason why Cap would promise to be here and then deliberately not show. His knee-jerk response was that Cap was just like all the other residents of Wendover—too firmly rooted to the desert to let themselves be set free by a vision. But Cap had seemed different, even crazier than Jeff.

"Why aren't you workin'?" Cap asked as he and Salty made their way into the clearing. He staggered up to the woodpile and dropped several 4x4 beams and a bag of hardware on the ground. Salty was at his heels, concerned that his master would have a coronary before one nail was hammered on this human folly. In between deep, gasping breaths, "You hard a hearin', Jeffey boy? I asked you why you weren't workin'."

Cap dropped down on the ground next to Jeff. He sounded and looked like this amount of exertion had been the first and would be the last amount of work that Cap would do until his next life and new body come along. Jeff broke into a grin that could easily have swallowed a canary or five, "I thought you weren't coming back. You weren't here when I got here and I thought..."

Jeff didn't get a chance to finish his sentence. Cap leaned into him and said, "That so. I stopped to get us some good wood to build our ship with, and my partner kisses me off." To Salty: "Should we forgive the kid, or should we just build the dang thing ourselves?"

This cut it for Salty. He now knew that Cap was not getting enough oxygen to his already feeble brain. If Cap thought that he and some dog, some incredibly brilliant but nonetheless "dog" dog were going to build a silly boat, by themselves, just for the heck of it, his common sense had jumped overboard without a life preserver. Knowing that his dog biscuit was definitely buttered on the Jeff side, Salty went over and nuzzled Jeff's hip. Jeff responded favorable by scratching Salty behind the ear. Salty was willing to tolerate this demeaning behavior but only if the boy did a better job of providing for him than Cap had done lately.

"Traitor!" Cap yelled without a whole lot of conviction. After all, he didn't really mind sharing Salty. When it came right down to it, he wouldn't mind if Jeff kept him. On second thought, no way. It would get pretty lonely at night in the desert without this sorry excuse for a flea motel.

Jeff thought that Cap was yelling at him for doubting Cap's conviction to the boat. He apologized, "I'm sorry, Cap, it won't happen again."

"Oh, jeez, what a group we got here. I was talking to Salty not you. You," and he pointed at Jeff to make sure he got the point, "you just remember this. Come hell or high water, you and me and Salty are goin' to build this boat. And nothin', not anything is going to stop us. Right?"

Jeff stood up and snapped to attention. "Right!" He stared just over Cap's shoulder to where his dream ship was drifting aimlessly in the becalmed sea. But as he watched, the wind freshened and began to fill the sails. The first signs of a wake began to trail behind the stern of his ship. A pair of weathered and deeply tanned arms reached out and grabbed hold of the ship's wheel, holding the ship steady to a new course.

Although he could not see what Jeff was staring at, Cap responded to the positive attitude of his partner, "That's the spirit. Now let's get to work. We got a long way to go."

Jeff's vision faded and he found himself staring at the sketch of the 'Cutty Sark" he had drawn the night before. It didn't quite measure up to the scene that just dissipated in front of his eyes nor does it match up to the pile of lumber Cap was beginning to arrange in a line on the ground. Yet, it was the beginning of a stout and seaworthy keel if one put his mind and imagination to it. He asked a dumb question, shipbuilding-wise, but quite reasonable for a land-locked boy. "What's that?" he said, pointing at the line of wood and trying to line up his sketch so that some part of it matched up to what Cap was doing.

"Keel." said Cap. He cocked his head trying to figure out what Jeff was doing twisting a piece of paper, looking at the lumber and then scrunching his face like a monkey in the zoo. "What's that you're doing?" He stepped over and gently took the paper from Jeff's hand. He examined it carefully, recognizing the carefully drawn outline of a clipper ship. But he couldn't quite make the connection between this old ship and the boat that he was about to start building. "What is this?"

Jeff took the sketch back from Cap and proudly smoothed out the wrinkles. With an assurance fueled by youthful exuberance, he proudly stated, "This is the way our boat's going to look."

With a trembling hand, Cap took the paper back from Jeff and studied it carefully. "That is a mighty pretty picture, Jeffey, but it's a whole lot easier to draw it than to built it. We got to make some big changes if'n you really plan on building it."

Jeff's exuberance was dealt a crippling blow. Why can't Cap see the incredible beauty of this sketched ship and instantly want to turn it into the real thing, right here next to the railroad tracks? Anyone who looked at this ship must know that it had to be built just like it was. He gave the Cap the steely stare like he had faced down tougher men and never given it another thought. "Like what big changes?" he asked none too gently.

"Nothin you can't live with, I'm sure." He returned Jeff's stare knowing that they had entered into the negotiation stage and any sign of weakness would signal his own demise. After all, he was dealing with the most dangerous part of the species, a teenager. "My experience tells me that a ship this size sails best under one mast." This statement was voiced with all the confidence of one who had spent all his waking life working the shipyards—a statement that was as far from Cap's waking life as Bora Bora was from Wendover, Utah. And that ain't no hop, skip and jump.

"It has to have three masts, the Cutty Sark had three masts!" There was no give in Jeff's voice.

Salty chuckled a dog chuckle, which came out sounding like he was coughing to clear a hairball from his throat. He wished he had a bookie because he'd like to lay down a bet that this boat, if it ever got built, was going to be built with two masts. He could see it coming a mile away.

Cap got agitated, mainly because he had no idea of how to build a boat with three masts and he was too old to start learning now. "It don't have to have nothing! One mast will do just fine."

"Three." One word but it said so much. Loosely translated— You scummy lying old man. You're nothing but a big bag of wind and as soon as you have to show you're more than hot air you're going to shrivel up and blow away.

Cap's skin had gotten awfully thick from all the verbal abuse he had to take from Amos and the boys at Simon Locke's store so this one word cuts but it only cut the dead, unfeeling skin covering the fragile man inside. "One mast, no more. You are forgettin' something, remember, I'm the captain. What I says, goes."

Jeff replied, "So what? We're partners on this. You said so yourself and we shook on it." He mades it sound like shaking on it went far beyond the mundane boyish oaths administered by the like of Tom Sawyer and Huck Finn. You go back on your handshake and God would strike you dead unless, of course, he was too busy figuring out a way to sail a ship on the desert. After all, he had some experience with floating large boats where there was once land and doing some strange things to large bodies of salty water.

If Cap could have remembered how to grin he would have done so at this point. Here he was arguing with Jeff over the building of a boat, in the desert, with either one mast or three. And he didn't really have a clue how to build either one. Since it was never going to sail, he figured it didn't matter if he gave up a little. "Okay, okay, don't blow your spout. We'll compromise. You give a little, I'll give a little."

"Two masts?" asked Jeff with none of the force of his one-worded blade.

"Two masts, it is. Now if your royal partnership don't mind, I got me a boat to build." And Cap quickly took the sketch and folded it into his shirt pocket. "I'll be keeping this with me, just in case I forget what I'm building looks like."

Salty rolled on his side, seemingly unable to clear his throat of some obstruction. Both Cap and Jeff moved toward the small dog, concerned about his well being. Just as they reached him, he stopped laughing/choking, got to his feet and moved away from the very predictable humans. Cap watched him go, scratching his head. "I missed something here."

'As usual.' Salty said to himself.

"Grab them bolts, Jeffey, and let's get to work on this thing."

Jeff grabbed the bag containing the hardware and some tools and followed after Cap. For a split second, a mere speck on the cosmic time line, Cap and Jeff were unified in spirit and effort. And then Jeff said, "How soon do you think we'll finish her?"

Cap finally remembered how to grin and used it on his partner. "Oh, jeez. A lot sooner, if you'd stop yakking and start working."

Jeff grinned too. He handed Cap the bag of hardware and they began to work. Salty had to bite his tongue to keep from laughing at the folly of these two humans, supposedly far up the evolutionary ladder from this canine practicalis (a practical dog).

ꕤꙮ MAKING WAVES AT THE OFFICE

Time passed. Sometimes it ran off-tackle and sometimes it was forced into a fourth down situation. But it never loset yardage and it was never stopped by a good defense. And like the Crimson Tide it washed through a small town like Wendover carrying with it news of note and not so noteworthy. It even flushed into the backwaters of the Beehive Potash Works, a 1950s' homage to an industrial complex and second home to Ken Cutter. Situated in the potash-rich foothills halfway between Wendover and Salt Lake City, this thriving business employed a great many of Wendover's gainfully employed citizens. Which was not a lot but enough to carry some clout when someone was looking to maintain job security in a little town.

This explained why Ken was hunkered down at his desk with only a potash-dusted glass wall between him and the noisy machinery that processed the fertilizer-bound material. Over the years, Ken had developed the technique for turning the eardrum-shattering hullabaloo into just a little 'white noise.' Although there were days, just like today, when he heard the grinding of the machinery and thought that he heard the souls of his fellow employees being ground into oblivion. On his worst days, which were appearing with greater regularity, he could hear his own voice being sucked down the belt into the heart of the pulverizing machine. An involuntary shiver ran down his spine as he tried to suppress that image in his mind. He refocused his attention to the papers on his desk and took a pencil to them with a vengeance.

A big burly man dressed in coveralls and trailing potash dust walked past Ken's glass wall and opened Ken's door without knocking or waiting for permission to enter. He acted like he was everyone's boss even if he was just the plant foreman. But Karl, like his son, Steve, believed that if you act it you are it. He pulled up in front of Ken's desk with a big shit-eating grin on his face. Ken immediately visualized Karl, tied to the processing conveyor, being drawn in the malevolent heart of the equipment, never to be seen or heard from again. The thought brought a smile to Ken's face.

Karl dropped his meaty hands onto Ken's desk and said, "Sorry to bother, Ken. But I wanted to check on a rumor going round."

Oh, Jesus, thought Ken. A thousand bad thoughts ranging from rumors of the plant closing to promotions for everyone but himself zipped through his mind. Karl was a man not to be messed with even though he was in production and Ken was in management. "No sweat, Karl. What's the rumor?"

Karl answered slowly, and Ken had time to comment, to himself, that he never understood how a man with such little intelligence could flourish in the world. "Well, you know my boy, Steve?"

Of course Ken knew Steve. He was the biggest bully and largest loudmouth braggart this side of his father. This was what he thought and he said, "Of course I know Steve. Good kid." No use antagonizing the man especially when he could beat Ken to a bloody pulp if he had a mind to.

Karl was thinking that it must be difficult for Ken to sit up in his seat without a backbone. He despised everyone who didn't work (really WORK) for a living. Come to think about it, he hated even those who did work. He really didn't like people except to tease them unmercifully. "He told me the strangest thing. Told me that your son's building a big boat out near the railroad tracks." He paused, waiting for a reaction from Ken. Ken was stone-faced. Karl continued, "Now I told Steve to cut out the crap. Told him that I was going to belt him if he kept lying to me but he swore it was the truth. A boat in the desert, don't that sound crazy to you?"

Ken thought it sounded as crazy now as it did when he said it was okay for Jeff to build it. In fact, coming out of Karl's mouth it sounded a whole lot crazier. He replied as calmly as possible, "Maybe." Maybe he should get out and go home and put a stop to this crazy scheme right now. Maybe not. He couldn't see giving Karl the pleasure of scoring points on him.

"I just wanted to know if it was fact. Is your son really building a boat? Out in the desert?"

Ken straightened up his somewhat soft backbone and sat up in his chair. "Yes, he is." Calmly, like it was the most normal thing in the world for a thirteen-year-old boy to be building a boat in the middle of the goddamned desert. "I haven't seen it myself, but he tells me that it's coming along fine."

Karl's mouth dropped open just enough for Ken to catch a glimpse of a batch of tobacco-stained teeth and a whiff of stale breath. "And you're encouraging the boy? Don't it seem kind of a foolish way to spend his time?"

"I'm not encouraging him, but I'm not stopping him either. He's got to make his own decision on whether he wants to stop or not."

Unintentionally, Ken had just granted his son powers of adulthood. Something he had no intention of telling his son about.

Karl's mouth had dropped open just a little more and Ken couldn't help but see Karl's open orifice as a refining belt sucking up Ken's words and grinding them into squished syllables to be shit out in a pile. Karl's lips moved and he said, "Yeah, but a boat in Wendover? It don't make any sense. He should be out playing with the other boys. Like with Steve." He hesitated for a moment, then continued, "Not with Steve. Steve says he's a short strange duck."

Ken interrupted, "Hey, Karl, I appreciate your guidance on this, I really do, but I got a lot of work to do." He shuffled the papers in front of him. A gesture that worked on white-collar workers usually impressed with a pile of papers but to a grunt like Karl, it meant nothing.

But Karl knew he had gotten in his licks and tired of this game. "Oh sure, I understand. You can work it out with your boy. We can talk about it another time." He started to back out of the office, the grin returning to his face. "Maybe we can go deep sea fishing...in your boy's boat?" He laughed his way out of Ken's office, slamming the door behind him.

Ken felt the heat of a blush rising from his neck at this last jab. But he didn't want to give Karl the pleasure of a reaction in case he was watching through the glass wall. He counted slowly to ten and, feeling safe from observation, slammed his fist down on the desk. He looked up to see Karl wave through the glass and then stride off into the plant. Ken had the feeling that life for everyone involved in the boatbuilding project was about to get a lot more difficult.

ॐ BRINGING 'REALITY' TO THE FORE

If time had swept information and innuendo into the backwaters of the Beehive Potash Works, bringing a tidal wave of scorn upon Ken Cutter, then it had left the site of the boat becalmed. Three solitary figures toiled through the long shadows of sunset working to bring forth life where there was none. Cap and Jeff were struggling to brace the keel and sternpost upright. Salty was doing his best to bark instructions to these two misfits but they didn't understand or just weren't listening to his barkese. He did succeed in getting under Cap's feet, sending Cap into a stream of curses that were unrelenting until he realized that Jeff was listening carefully to them. He kicked at Salty and his curses slipped into a mumbled apology to both Jeff and Salty.

With the sternpost braced and a rough-hewn deadwood knee in place to support it, the ship was beginning to look like a ship. But only with those having a very active imagination (something not shown to be in great supply in this section of Utah). At just over twenty feet long, the boat looked more like a giant wooden framing square flipped over on its long edge. The keel and the sternpost were both constructed in a patchwork fashion of both new and recycled wood. Cap wiped his brow and, mostly for show, consulted the sketch Jeff had drawn of his clipper ship. He looked at the paper and then at the boat and then back at the paper. "Yup, looks like we are right on target, Jeffey." Jeff gave him the thumbs up sign and started dragging another 4 x 4 into place.

Ken stumbled across the sand that marked the dead zone between the back of the houses of Wendover and the railroad tracks. This could have been a more hospitable area except that the property owners adjacent to the tracks had long since given up the idea of forcing the desert to yield up flowers, much less a green lawn. Sweaty and tired, Ken had stripped of his jacket and loosened his tie. He was not a man looking forward to greeting his son and his first meeting with boat.

Concentrating on what his first words were going to be, he failed to realize he had walked into the Wendover shipyard. Jeff immediately spotted his dad and came racing toward him. "Dad!" He left Cap struggling under the weight of a precariously balanced piece of wood destined to become part of the keelson.

Jeff rushed up to his father and, in a moment of exuberance, hugged him. Jeff's short-term memory was stronger than his long term memory—he could only remember that his father was the one who gave him the okay to build the boat, even if it was for all the wrong reasons. "I'm glad you came." He grabbed his father's hand and pulled him closer to Cap and the giant framing square in the desert, nee boat. "Now you can meet my partner." He pulled him past Salty. Salty looked up at this human emanating bad vibrations and growled. Ken looked down at Salty and thought that Jeff could have found a better partner. Jeff continued to pull on his arm until they were both face to face to face with Cap. Cap turned and eyed Ken as suspiciously as Salty had just done. He set down the keelson piece.

Jeff missed the underlying tension and introduced Cap. "This is Cap. Cap, this is my dad."

Cap reached out and shook Ken's hand. "Nice to meet you." If this could have been said with any degree of warmth it would have surprised Salty, since he had heard Jeff talked about his father with Cap in less than glowing terms. "Jeffey told me a lot about you." Cap was thinking, 'nothing good, mind you.' And Salty was thinking, 'nothing good, you jackass.'

Ken responded, "Hopefully good, Mister?" He hesitated, waiting for Cap to fill in his last name.

Cap waited, just to make things a little more difficult on Ken. Then he answered, "Just Cap, like in CAPtain."

Ken looked around the building area. Taking in the size of the frame, the lack of materials and tools and the lack of any other humans helping. "Very impressive. You fellows have really made progress." And that was about as close to the truth as Ken was going to get tonight. He remembered his reason for being here and redirected his comments to Cap, "You're the friend that Jeff is talking about all the time?"

Cap smiled, pleased that he might be the focus of dinner table conversation at the Cutter house. "Must be, cuz we're the only two out here workin', less you count my dog, Salty."

Salty does not like the sound of that one bit since he had provided valuable expertise that had gotten the boat farther along than either of the humans could have taken it. He slumped down in the sand and decided to dogcott the project. Only by his absence would they see how valuable he was to the project.

Ken was momentarily distracted. He had prepared a speech to give to Jeff and whatever little playfriend he might have coerced into assisting him on the boat but the magnitude of the boat and the age of the little playfriend had thrown him for a loop. He went for the stalling tactic until he could rethink his approach. He said to Cap, "I see. Do you live around here? I don't think I've ever seen you before."

Cap was unused to participating in small talk but he was willing to give it shot. "Sure do. Me and Salty lives in the hills back there." He nodded vaguely to the north. "You probably never saw us before cuz' we don't come into town much. That was till we hooked up with Jeff." He smiled warmly at Jeff.

Jeff was standing between the two men he currently admired the most. A sign of how temporal and transient admiration was to a young boy. Until two weeks ago it was John Paul Jones, Admiral Farragut and Willie Mays—in no particular order. Ken looked down at his son and saw how content his son was to listen to these two 'great' men converse. This was not what Ken had in mind.

Ken knelt to face Jeff. "Jeff, do you mind if Cap and I talk alone for a couple of minutes? I'm sure you've got a bunch of things to do on the boat." He good-naturedly messed up his son's hair. A Rockwellian scene destined to warm everyone's heart if it wasn't so forced on Ken's part. He had gotten out of practice being affectionate with his son.

"Sure, Dad." He checked with Cap. Cap nodded back toward the boat and Jeff slowly walked away from them.

Salty was thinking to himself, 'Ha. I can hardly wait to see what he ends up doing. If he is very lucky he might keep from hurting himself.'

Ken laid his hand on Cap's shoulder and guided him further away from the boat and his son. What he was about to say he didn't want Jeff to catch even a few words. Cap was not comfortable with Ken's hand on his shoulder but he made no attempt to brush it off.

Ken stopped 30 yards from the boat. Cap stopped and waited patiently for Ken to make the next move. Ken didn't wait long, he started by saying, "Look, I don't know how to say this." He checked the distance between himself and his son. Decided that it wasn't quite far enough and took several more steps away from the boat. Cap followed him. When he did speak again, it was in a low voice, almost conspiratorial. "I thought when Jeff said he had a friend helping him, he meant another boy his age."

Cap waited patiently. He wasn't about to ruin a good thing. It had been a long time since another adult treated him with this much courtesy. This kind of thing would go to his head in the unlikely event that some other adult citizen of Wendover would take the time to converse with him. He pondered this thought while Ken searched for the right words.

Finally, Ken continued, "I mean, if it were someone his own age, they'd probably get tired of building this thing after awhile and go back to something normal." He gestured at the ship frame as if it constituted nothing more than a few scraps of wood and several bolts. Which was exactly what it was to Ken. An irrational thought borne in his son's mind now in the process of being miscarried on the desert floor—a visual oxymoron, desert ship.

Never one for the subtleties of civilized conversation, Cap was unsure of the direction Ken was headed. The only approach he could take was to respond directly and forthrightly. "I'm not stopping him."

"Yes, but you're here helping him. And he sees you, an adult, and he thinks that there really was a chance of building and finishing this thing. Your presence here is making everything so difficult."

Now this was something that Cap was used to hearing and he didn't like it. One of the many reasons why he moved into the desert was to lessen the chances of someone telling him that he wasn't wanted. It was bad enough when an idiot like Amos said it. He could take that since Amos probably said it of anyone who was in range of his spitballs. But to hear it from the father of someone who had begged him to stay just didn't sit well in Cap's craw. He answered with a bit of anger, "And you want me to leave?"

Ken responded as if it were the most perfectly logical thing ever asked. Completely reasonable by Wendoverian standards. Luckily, Cap lived just outside the town's border. Ken replied, "Well, you couldn't really have planned to stay and build it. I'm sure you have got better things to do with your time."

This line lit the fuse on Cap's very short temper. And it exploded at the same time as the words left his lips, "Mr. Cutter, I don't have one damn thing more important than building this boat. I got no job to do and I got no family to look after. I plan on being here till the last nails are hammered. If that don't suit you, tough. The only way you're going to stop Jeff and me is to keep him from coming here. Maybe you need to lock him in his room or something."

Ken protested, "I can't do that." He was shocked to be facing a man, albeit a scruffy one, who defended the boatbuilding as a serious and worthwhile endeavor. He was at a loss for words. This trip to the shipyard had turned into a total fiasco.

Cap continued with his speech. He really liked the rush of adrenaline he got from telling off this man in no uncertain terms. "That's your problem then. Now if you'll excuse me, my lips are kinda' dry from yakking and whiskey's the only cure. Tell Jeffey I'll be seeing him in the mornin', less you kin' find your way clear to locking him in your house." Cap turned on his heals, whistled for Salty and headed out of the area toward the drinking (Nevada) side of town. Salty ended his dogcott and headed after his master. He wondered what kind of mischief he would have to extricate Cap from this evening.

Ken walked over to his son. Jeff was staring after Cap and Salty, aware that something terrible had happened but unsure what to do about it. "Where's Cap going?"

As with any parent faced with explaining a difficult and complex situation to a too-young child, Ken could expend the time and energy necessary to allow his child to comprehend the predicament or he could lie. Ken chose the lesser approach because he saw it as a necessary evil in the short-run to be forgotten in the long run. "He said that he had some other parts to get for the boat. He'll meet you back here in the morning."

This was the wrong approach because Jeff had reached an age and he had long had the sensitivity to know when someone, particularly an adult, was lying to him. But with this maturity he also saw that confronting his father on this point would not serve his purpose. Building the boat was the only thing that matters right now and as long as his father wasn't saying no, Jeff was not asking why. Jeff elected to rise above the problem and asked, "What do you think of the boat, Dad?"

Ken stared up the sternpost and down the keel before answering, and this time he didn't lie when he spoke, "Its...its unbelievable."

⚬⚬ MAKING A SERIOUS COMMITMENT

Like any man with strong 'naval' antecedents, moments of high emotion drove Cap into the comforting arms of the Nevada Bar. He rumbled into the interior of the bar leaving Salty to fend for himself amongst the early evening prostitutes lounging in the dust of the entryway. It was truly a sorry sign of the state of social affairs that they had nothing better to do than to sexually torment a poor horny dog. Mind you, Salty wasn't complaining.

Cap hadn't wasted any time hunkering down on his usual bar stool. He had wasted even less time draining off the better portion of five shot glasses of well-drawn whiskey and was just getting comfortable. Ike had taken up a position nearby but not too close to draw attention to the fact that he was closely watching his friend. He was watching because Cap was not drinking like Cap usually drank. The drinking was the same but the attitude was different. Usually Cap came in and allowed the alcohol to loosen his tongue, although it didn't need a whole lot of loosening if someone was nearby willing to listen. Tonight, Cap was drinking like he had a bad grudge against each one of the shot glasses he slammed against his teeth in his haste to get the booze into his gullet. Now Ike didn't usually worry about his patrons' drinking attitudes, after all, the drinks are the same price with or without his concern. But Ike didn't like someone he knew wasting his time getting drunk if he wasn't going to get a good time out of it. So he asked Cap, "Something bothering you, Cap?" Subtlety not being something drunks picked up easily after their third stiff one.

Cap lifted his head from the last partially filled shot glass and glared at Ike through rose-veined eyeballs until the dark and the light versions of Ike melded into one almost real-looking man. "Nothing getting royally drunk won't fix up."

The night being slow and Ike bearing the mantle and responsibility of being the bartender then asked, "So you want to talk about it?" It was a question asked as a matter of form in every bar and boozing hole in the world but never with as much sincerity as Ike said it now.

"No that won't 'complish nothing." Cap dropped his head and refocused on the shot glasses on the bar top. Ike, quick as kangaroo rat moving away from an angry sidewinder, lifted the whiskey out of the well and filled the shot glass nearest Cap. He shoved it almost under Cap's nose but Cap ignored it, deep in thought. "How come nobody believes me when I say I done something? And when I git going on a new project, them same people laugh at me."

Ike eased in closer to his friend. "C'mon, Cap, they aren't laughing at you."

Cap looked up, mightily perturbed with his friend. "That is bullshit, Ike. I know when someone's laughing at me." He turned away from the bar counter to face the small crowd seated behind him. Fate or serendipity struck as a deep voice let out a bellow of a laugh just as Cap scanned the crowd. He turned back to Ike with a peculiar smile, perhaps more of a grimace, on his face, like his point had just been proven for him and he was not happy about it. "Everyone of them thinks I'm a no-good drunk. Spending my time wandering 'round the desert pissing into the wind. Screw 'em all." He fumbled in his pocket for some money, and found just a few loose coins. "I'm a little short tonight, friend. Can you loan me a few bucks?"

Ike quickly said, "For the drinks? Don't worry about it. You can pay me back next time your check comes in. Besides, we're friends and we're supposed to help each other out."

"That is real good of you, Ike. But I'd like to borrow a few dollars extra. Need to get a gift for another friend."

Ike was pleased to know that his pleasantly strange but not so pleasantly smelling friend had other people he could rely on. He reached toward his old wood cash register to get out the five or ten that he expected Cap would ask for. "How much extra?"

Cap hesitated in his request. He might not have asked but Ike had just offered up that 'friends need to share with friends.' "I need a hundred."

Ike's hand abruptly stopped inches above the "no sale" button on the register. He was more than a little surprised at the amount that Cap wanted. "A hundred! That must be some gift you're planning on getting." It was going to take a little more of an explanation to get Ike's hand to drop the last few inches to the button releasing the drawer which held his hard-earned moolah.

Cap pleaded, just a little, "Yeah, it's going to be the best present I ever got. A present no one else ever got or is ever going to get. Can I please borrow the money?"

It was not often that moral dilemmas popped up in the Nevada Bar but Ike's hand had been pierced by the horns of one right now. He wanted to help his friend out but he knew Cap too well to think that he would ever see a majority of the money come back to him. His palm, having been gouged and badly hurt by the horn of material self-protection, forced his mouth to establish the excuse for denying the request. "I'd like to, Cap, I really would, but business has been real slow..."

Cap didn't let him finish, he pleaded a little harder now, his not-quite-alert mind had fastened onto this idea is the only idea that would work. "I'll pay you back I swear."

The horn of me-firstness struck Ike again, drawing more blood. "I know you're good for it. Jeez, just take a look around, this place is dying. Maybe you could take a little less?" He screwed up his courage and looked Cap squarely in the eyes. He didn't like what he saw reflecting in Cap's penetrating stare. The horn of friendship looked for a soft spot under one of Ike's fingernails.

"Come on, Ike. I need the money, all of it. I'll...I'll trade you for it."

Ike saw an opening between the horns and dove through it. "What have you got that's worth a hundred bucks? And don't try offering Salty up as some pure-breed, rare dog because I know he's nothing but a fleahound who likes to bite me."

Cap searched his brain for something amongst all his possessions that had any monetary value at all. And he realized that he had nothing because he wanted nothing. Now he wanted to get something and couldn't unless he gave up something else. Or was there another way? Cap gave the option one more circuit through his brain path and decided that you always took the option particularly when you have only one. "I got something for you. I got a boat. She is really fine. I'll give you my share of her."

Ike was incredulous. He had known Cap for a long time and he couldn't ever recall him mentioning that he owned anything other than Salty and some worthless dinosaur fossils. "You got a boat? Where is it?"

Cap's brain was thinking fast, pushing all those alcohol-soaked blood cells coursing through his brain out of the way in favor of some oxygen-rich, MENSA-qualified fluid of life. And in the process got Cap thinking and talking a fine line between truth and fiction, now and the future. "It's near here. On the other side of town. It is a real beaut, worth a hell of lot more than a hundred bucks." He sat up and stared at Ike, his eyes clear and more focused. "You've got to make the trade."

While Ike was not necessarily the most sensitive man in the world, having suffered through enough bar insults to crush even the strongest ego, he recognized something in Cap at this moment that he had never seen before—a man truly in need. The wrong answer would, without any doubt, mash this human into a worthless lump. And when he saw Cap reach out to touch him, he knew that he could only give one answer. "Okay, okay, I'll give you the hundred bucks. Promise you won't beg for it." He brushed Cap's outstretched hand away with a casual flick and turned to the cash register. The "no sale" tab popped up with a half-hearted bell sound and the cash draws slide open as if to welcome the reduction in its cash deposits. Ike carefully withdrew five twenty dollar bills; torn crumpled and beer-soaked but still coin of the realm. He shoved the drawer shut quickly in the hopes that no more of the night's receipts would flutter away. A ten-spot made its move for freedom but was too late for a break-out and got squished when the drawer slammed back safely into the base of the register. Ike handed the bills over to Cap as a jaunty hornpipe played behind the transaction, although neither seemed to hear nor take note of the tune.

Cap stuffed the bills into his pocket fearing that Ike might have a change of heart. Ike's heart was still in the deal but his mind was really watching the bills flutter out of Cap's pocket, disappearing into thin air before they could hit the sawdust of the bar's floor. Cap gushed, "Thanks, Ike. You are the best friend I ever had. Give me a piece of paper and I'll deed the boat over to you."

"That's okay, I trust you." Its not that Ike trusted him to pay the money back but he just didn't feel that was necessary to go through with the hassle of filling out a 'deed' for a non-existent boat.

Cap looked up and down the counter and finally seized upon one of the bar napkins that Ike, in a moment of sheer stupidity, had sent away for. They had imprinted upon them an outline of the state of Nevada with the name 'Navada Bar' printed within the state. Ike had screamed and hollered about the misspelling but the printing company refused to take them back. Ike decided to use them anyway figuring that with the low lighting and the low intelligence of his clientele, no one would notice the problem. And to date, no one had. "Nope, a deal's a deal, Ike. I never go back on my word." Cap finished scribbling on the cocktail napkin with a stub of a pencil, signed it with a flourish, and handed it to Ike.

"All right, I'll take your note, but I'm still considering this a loan. You pay me back next month, and we'll tear this thing up." He took the napkin, folded it carefully and placed it in an empty beer mug. He then set the beer mug above the cash register. "This will be our special deal. And no one will be the wiser. Sound good to you?"

Cap, with the money firmly stashed in his pocket, would have agreed with anything Ike said at this point but Ike's proposition sounded just perfect to Cap. "Good to me, buddy."

Never had a soul or a dream been sold so cheaply.

❧ THE POLITICAL BACKWATER

Wendover, Nevada was not Washington, D.C. It wasn't even Carson City, Nevada. But it still required the trappings of American-style democracy. In plainer terms, a government of the people, by the people and for the people. As with many small towns, slight modifications needed to be made to this credo. In Wendover's case, by the people, for the people and of the person. The entire bureaucracy of this thriving community resided in the brain and the body of Dave Caster, mayor-at-large. This title was a not-so-subtle blending of his official title and his girth. No one said it to his face but Dave was a hugely overweight man with a kindly face. The problem was that upon viewing Dave one could rarely get beyond his size to look at his face.

Dave did not take his civic responsibilities lightly. He regarded the border between the two Wendovers and the two states to be meaningless except to mapmakers. He cruised through both towns in his Datsun B-210 well pleased that life went on as normal. Knowing that normal meant nothing happening and nothing happening meant no changes and no changes meant no work and no work meant Dave was a happy mayor.

He pulled his car off the highway and onto the dusty shoulder and then into the Chevron gas station on the Utah side of his fiefdom. He nudged the car up to the pumps and slowly extricated himself from behind the wheel. This was no simple chore, the car being small and the man being big. But Dave accomplished the task with a certain simple dignity. He looked down at his car and sighed deeply. He would not have chosen this car except for one small problem, the office of mayor carried no salary. The good citizens of Wendover had bestowed a position of honor on him, not a job. No matter, he had gotten used to the Japanese car and his visits to the gas pumps (at his own expense) were few and far between.

Today was one of those 'few' days. He pulled the pump nozzle off the catch on the pump and jabbed it into the thirsty car. The young attendant for the service station came running out of the small office, wiping his hands on his greasy coveralls. Mike was his name and pumping gas was his pain (as he was fond of saying). He took the pump handle away from Dave. "Howdy, Mayor Caster."

Dave glowed at this sign of respect. "Hi, Mike. How are things?"

Mike worked his way around the car washing the windows with a squeegee. What he lacked in good cleaning techniques he made up for with speed. Mike replied, "Just fine, thanks. What brings you to our side of the border?" He waited a beat, and then continued; the mark of a natural comedian. "Don't you have any good gas stations on the Nevada side?"

Dave smiled, this was an old joke. "Sure we do. I thought that since I was the mayor, I'd pay a goodwill visit to your side. You know, boost business a little, pick up some juicy gossip."

"You're out of luck today. The town is basically dead, as usual. How are things on your side?"

"Just as dead, thank goodness." Before Dave could respond further, the sound of a power tool cut through the desert air. "What's that, new house?" He turned slowly and tried to isolate the direction the sound was coming from.

Mike pointed to behind the gas station, toward the railroad tracks. "Nothing that exciting. Cutter kid is making himself a little boat."

Dave pondered the thought of a boat in his fair town and it just didn't add up. "A boat, you say? That is real strange."

Mike shrugged. "Beats being bored to death."

Dave shrugged in agreement. "You got a point there."

Mike topped off the tank and checked the gauge on the pump. "That'll be six bucks, Mayor."

Dave flashed his best politician's smile, which hadn't had much practice since there hadn't been an election in a long, long time. "What, no courtesy discount?"

Mike held out his hand. "Nice try." Dave fished out his wallet and gave the money to Mike.

Dave stuck his wallet back into his pants and began the process of climbing into the car. "Don't ever ask me to fix a speeding ticket for you." He winked at Mike and with a grunt achieved bottom contact with the seat. He pulled the door shut and drove out of the station. To himself, Dave said, "A boat in Wendover...damn."

⬥ CAPTAINS LOOKING FOR A CREW

While Dave Caster drove through his townships, Cap and Jeff sweated in the shipyard. Even Salty was affected by the heat. His tongue hung down, his mind forcing the water molecules to expirate as quickly as possible. Work had slowed on the boat as the temperature had risen.

Jeff was drilling holes into the four by fours forming the keel using a power drill newly purchased by Cap. The wood was hard, the drill bit dull and Jeff was becoming frustrated by the lack of progress on his dream. Cap was laying out the metal braces that would hold the four by fours together forming a continuous keel piece. He was more used to working in the sun than Jeff but it was still not a pleasant chore. As Jeff struggled with the drill, Cap spent more time observing his partner and less time lining up the brace plates. Finally Jeff hit a knot in the wood, pulled the drill bit out and dropped the drill motor on the ground in disgust.

Cap walked over to Jeff and looked down at the drill motor. "What's wrong, Jeffey?"

Jeff didn't want to look at Cap, he studied the whole in the beam where he encountered the knot. "Nuthin.'"

Cap picked up the drill motor and examined it. He knew that nothing was wrong but he wasn't one for psychological nonsense. If something was poisoning Jeff's gut then let him spill it.

Salty observed the dialogue and realized that Cap belonged to the Rogerian school of therapy. Although Cap would not know to admit it.

Cap asked, "Somethin' wrong with the new tools?"

With the least amount of effort possible, Jeff answered, "No, they're great." He continued to examine the keel boards.

Cap moved over and sat on the board that Jeff was so closely examining. He did it so that Jeff had no choice but to look at him. Cap abandoned the passive, Rogerian approach to problem solving and, literally, grabbed the bull by the horn. He took Jeff's T-shirt and gave it a yank. "Then what is it? Spit it out."

Jeff had to throw his hands down to keep from tumbling forward. He shouted at Cap, "Hey, stop it. Get your hands off me." He brushed Cap's hand away and stood up.

Cap stood up also. "I asked you a question. I need an answer."

"All right, I'll tell you." He licked his lips before continuing. "Its just that we'll never get this boat done without more money. We've barely enough wood to finish this part, whatever its called."

"Keel."

"Whatever. I know you don't have much money left, specially after buying me these things." He picked up the drill motor.

Cap grinned. "You're right about that." He indicated a spot next to him on the board. "Sit down, lets talk about it."

Jeff sat down close to but not next to Cap. Boys his age were just establishing their personal space and sitting too close to an old guy like Cap seemed like an infringement of that space.

Cap was embarrassed by what he was about to ask so he looked down at the ground, unsure of what to do with his hands. Fortunately, Salty took his cue from this moment of silence, came over and sat in the shade created by Cap's body. Gratefully, Cap scratched Salty's head. "You got any ideas on how to raise some loot? Legal, of course."

"I've been thinking about it. Maybe we could get some donations."

"Donations," Cap chewed on the word for awhile and then spat it out undigested and not understood.

"You know, like go to all the stores around here and ask 'em to give us some money to finish the boat." He reached over and petted Salty too. Salty appreciated all the attention but preferred the kind of attention that he had received from the ladies of the evening outside the Navada Bar. But like the old canine saying goes: 'beagles can't be choosers.'

Cap paused in his petting, "Now why would they want to do that? They'll want to see what they're giving us money for, and whatta' they get to see?" He gestured with his arm the whole of their construction. A grandiose gesture for such a pitiful thing.

Jeff took his hand away from Salty's back in order to create his new vision with his hands. As he talked, his hands seem to be building a structure. "Well... because we'll tell them we're building a monument to the town. Instead of a statue, we're giving them a ship, a great ship. We won't have to show it to them until we are finished and by then, by then it will be a great ship."

Cap laughed. "That has got to be the second craziest idea I've ever heard. And the first was building this thing in the first place."

Jeff was suddenly worried, "You aren't quitting, are you?"

"Of course not."

Jeff bore in on Cap. "Have you got any better ideas for gettin' the money?"

Cap scratched his grizzled chin for a good long time. "Can't say as I do."

Jeff answered quickly and got off the beam, "Then let's do it." He put his hand down for Cap to use to get up.

Cap looked up surprised, "Now?

"No better time, is there?" He struggled to get Cap off the beam. Cap swayed for a moment and then caught his balance. He squared up his shoulders and followed after the new leader of this nautical expedition. Salty breathed a sigh of relief. He was sure that Cap was going to have him do stupid dog tricks for spare change.

⬙⬙ WENDOVER, UTAH TAKES THE SHORT VIEW

The hustle and bustle of the booming and inflating 70's American economy had made a wide detour around Wendover leaving it unboomed and deflated. Much the way it was in the 60's and as it would be in the 80's, 90's and 00's. Daily commerce was defined on the Utah side by bathroom usage at the service stations and quantity of directions given to confused California travelers on the road to the Mormon Tabernacle. On the Nevada side, it was only slightly different; bathroom usage at the service stations and quantity of directions given to confused Utah travelers on the road to Las Vegas.

The Sand and Salt Market of Wendover, Utah had recently passed a milestone. Established in late fifties as interstate traffic was picking up, this market cum general store had recently added a second cash register to accommodate the overflow business. While no one from the major newspapers had come out for the affair, it was the number one topic of conversation on the Wendover grapevine for weeks. Mostly the talk went to how foolish the manager, Zack Mason, had been to spend good money on the second register. After all, he was the one and only employee of the Sand and Salt. Better he save his hard-earned money and lower his prices to make them competitive with the fancier market attached to Great Lake Casino on the Nevada side.

At the moment, Cap, Jeff and Salty were standing in front of the broad door leading into the Sand and Salt building their courage. Jeff was more relaxed than Cap but that meant he was just a bit more relaxed than a corpse in rigor mortis. "Now you sure you have everything straight?"

With his rising nervousness, Cap picked up a bit of testiness. "Of course I do, you told me to let you do all the talkin'."

"Exactily. Let's go." He took Cap's arm and literally pulled him toward the door. Salty, obediently followed behind. Jeff stopped and looked at Salty. "Not you. Mr. Mason doesn't allow pets in his store."

Salty stopped in his tracks and looked around for the pet that Jeff was talking about. When he saw that he was alone in the dust his ego was bruised. 'Since when did the general partner on this construction job get relegated to bone-carrier?' He plopped in the dust vowing never to speak to Cap or Jeff again.

Jeff, followed by Cap, entered the starkly lit interior of the market. Zack was dressed in what he imagined the big-time grocers in Salt Lake City were wearing; polyester slacks, yellow shirt and a wide, flowery tie. He was currently assisting an older woman at register number two. Register number one was not being used currently. Jeff and Cap waited as Zack rang up and then bagged each one of the woman's grocery items. Once this task was completed, the woman picked up her two bags of groceries and waddled past Jeff and Cap. But not before she shot a piercing glance at Cap. Cap returned the glance, caliber for caliber.

Jeff ignored the dueling match and marched up to Zack at his register (number two!). "Are you the manager?"

The penholder in Zack's shirt pocket proudly proclaimed 'Service with a smile' followed by the ubiquitous happy face. Zack did his best to remember that when answering Jeff. "Of course, Son. That and checker, bagger and everything else you can do in a market. What can I do for you?" He glanced quickly at Cap, ever alert for the potential shoplifter.

Jeff started his pitch formally, "My name is Jeff Cutter, and..."

Zack was in a hurry to restock his soup shelf and recognized a definite no-sale in this conversation. "Right. I've seen you in here with your mom a bunch of times."

Jeff didn't let this interruption slow him down. "That true. As I was saying, my friend and I are collecting donations for a worthy cause, and we thought you might like to contribute." He paused, swallowed hard and waited for a response from Zack. The manager continued to eye Cap like he wasAl Capone's wicked brother.

"I might be. What's the worthy cause?"

Jeff swallowed even harder. "We are building a...a..." He stuttered and looked to Cap for some support. Cap used his hands in the same way that Jeff did to describe the magnificent edifice that they were creating for greater glory of the good citizens of Wendover. Jeff picked up the thread of his speech from the pantomime, "a monument for Wendover. A beautiful ship to honor all of the people who live here."

Zachary Mason was a polite man, not prone to alienating potential customers, even 13 year-old crazy boys. But this was too much. The facade of proper store manager crumbled under this ludicrous sales pitch and he started to laugh before Jeff could finish. He had difficulty talking, he was laughing so hard. "I heard that you and that old man were building something, beautiful ship, hah, but I didn't believe it til' now. I ain't donating one thin dime to your very worthy cause."

Jeff's cool, calm and collected exterior was ripped apart by Zack's total lack of respect for Jeff's vision. If the boat ended up with as many holes as Jeff's psyche, at this moment, there would be no chance of it staying on top of the water. Maybe they should consider building a submarine?

Jeff rushed out of the market with Cap trailing behind him. He stopped in the sunlight of the parking lot and took great gulps of air. He thought it would be so easy to ask and receive. He had forgotten that nothing in his life seemed to work the way he wanted it to. Until he met Cap and Salty. Now boys of less backbone or dimmer visions or more saneness might have called it a day or a week or a lifetime after this humiliation but Jeff was already looking for the next store to hit.

Cap patted him on the back, "Sorry, Jeffey."

Jeff brushed his hand away. "Don't be. Let's go." He strode toward the next store on the thoroughfare, State Line Hardware.

Cap was slow to follow. Salty was content to lay-put in the dirt. Cap bent to talk with his dog. "That boy's not a quitter."

Salty whined. 'That makes one of us.' Not liking the implication of what he had just thought about himself, Salty got up and shook himself off. 'If I can't be leading the pack, I can at least give moral support.'

Cap, forgetting for the moment his own show of determination at the bar, saw the handwriting on the sail and fully expected more of a hostile reception ahead. Unlike his partner, Cap's life had shown a consistency that said never expect anything otherwise you were bound to be disappointed.

And by the time he arrived in the dusty and poorly-lit interior of the hardware store, Jeff was receiving another dash of disappointment at the hands of the store owner. The store owner, Ralph Mercer, was a kind soul but a man of undistinguished imagination. The thought of a boat in the desert serving as a monument to him and the other folks in town struck him as downright funny even if it hurt the boy's feelings.

Jeff was pleading with him. "You don't have to give us money, you could just lend us some tools to use."

The laughter died on Ralph's face. A small misplaced spark in Ralph's brain had been triggered by the suggestion that he was stupid enough to go along with the plan. The spark zapped the spot in his brain that responded with emotions first and common decency much later. "The only thing I'm going to give you is a swift kick with my boot. And you can be sure that I'm going to tell your parents that you're up to no good, hanging around with this one." He pointed, and he wasn't pointing at Salty. Cap remained stoic at the implied insult.

The spark that ignited the anger in Ralph had leapt across the counter and jumped through Jeff's left ear. The results were the same. He got angry. "You're wrong about my boat, Mister. And you're wrong about Cap. You'll be damn sorry that you didn't help out because my boat is going to get built, even if its without your support. You'll see." He backed out of the store.

Cap remained rooted in place. Ralph watched him closely, waiting for him to follow Jeff out the door.

Ralph said, "What are you waiting for, old man?"

Cap took his time answering, "Thought you might change your mind."

Ralph picked up a small box of nails from the counter and held them in a throwing position. "Get out of my store before I lose my temper."

Cap and Salty simultaneously thought the same thought, 'we could use those nails." Cap made no move to leave. "I'll leave when I want, asshole."

This was too much for a God-loving Mormon man to take. First, to be sworn at by a crazy boy and then to be profaned by a desert rat was just too much for him. He wound up and pitched the nails at Cap.

Cap allowed the box to carom off his well padded gut and deftly captured them between his two hands. He looked down at the box and smiled. "I knew you'd changed your mind about helpin' us." He turned, and with as much dignity as he could muster, he walked out.

Salty looked at Cap with a newly-found sense of respect. Taking a cue from him, Salty walked out the door with his nose held high.

As if abuse at the hands of two of the local merchants wasn't enough, Jeff had entered the I-80 Diner, Wendover's answer to Tavern on the Green. No, not really, since 101 out of every 100 restaurant-goers entering the I-80 would have no idea where or what the Tavern on the Green was. This was new territory for Jeff since the three squares a day he got were at the hand of his mother and Ladies' Home Journal's best recipes.

Only a few stools were occupied at the lunch counter and even fewer seats were filled at the chipped Formica tables. Those brave souls who had entered the diner were hunched over their plates, in no hurry to finish their meals, no rush to suffer the pangs of heartburn from gulping a barely edible meal and even in less of a rush to go back into the desert heat. Like all the other establishments in the town, there was a distinct absence of hope here. It hung in the air and refused to budge even as the overhead fan made a mighty and noisy effort to move the air.

Riding roughshod over this wild bunch was a waitress with a patina of toughness. Marjorie Gower arrived in Wendover with hope but hope moved on the next morning. She kept waiting for hope to come back through the door with a new customer but many years of disappointment had left her cynical and doubting. The rumor in town was that she wouldn't know hope if it came in through the door stark-naked and proposed to her kneeling on the lunch counter.

And when Jeff came over to her, followed moments later by Cap, she knew that hope was still several miles down the road...and out of gas. Jeff mustered up all of his damaged self-confidence and began to tell her of his need to build a monument to the people of Wendover and his need for her support, monetary support, for the project to ever get off the ground. Marge was too nice to burst out laughing like the other potential contributors, but her expression placed her a wee bit on the unbelievable side of incredulous. "My support?! Look, Kid, you seem pretty nice. At least you look like a normal kid. No drugs or anything. So it must be that gopher who came in with you who's putting this con on."

Jeff responded quickly, "It is not a con! We really are building a boat."

Marge ignored his earnest plea. "Why don't you lose this old guy. He's no good, I can smell it. Look, you get him out of the diner and I'll give you a piece of pie, no charge." She slipped a disgustingly red cherry pie out from under the cake glass and offered it up to Jeff. He shoved it away.

He backed away from Marge and screamed, "You're hopeless. You are all hopeless." He backed right into the arms of Cap and they both backed out of the diner. His declaration rang down on deaf ears. For it wasn't just Marge who couldn't see through hope's disguise, it was all of those who had come to call Wendover, Utah home.

Outside of the diner, Jeff broke from Cap's arms and raced across the highway, oblivious to whatever traffic was rolling through town. Jeff was crying and he wanted no one to see his loss of faith. The more he cried, the slower he went. And eventually Cap and Salty caught up to him. Cap put his hand on Jeff's shoulder but Jeff brushed it off and continued to walk.

Cap tried again. "Hold on a minute. Let's talk."

Jeff spun around and caught Cap by surprise. "No. We've got to keep trying. I'm going to build this boat." He was prepared for an argument with Cap.

Cap answered calmly, "I'm not telling you to stop. I'm just thinkin' you'd be better in the donation business if'n I wasn't looking over your shoulder."

"That won't help."

Cap continued, "It might. These folks seem to have a natural dislike for me. And they can't see you and your good cause with me standin' there." Salty agreed, in principle, but thought it might be the fact that Cap hadn't had a bath in several weeks that might be the real issue.

This suggestion struck Jeff in an unusual way. He felt that Cap might be right about doing better alone but it meant he had to do it ALONE. "But we're a team. I can't go into those places by myself. You and I have an agreement, we shook on it."

"We still got a deal, we're a shipbuildin' team, but that don't mean we got to do everything together. Just give it a try without me. Couldn't do any worse than we already done." To accentuate the point, he tossed up and caught the one positive contribution they'd gotten so far, the small box of nails.

Jeff was resigned to it. "All right, I'll do it, but it isn't going to help." Having made this decision, he looked around for another store to 'proposition.' The only one within spitting distance was the one Cap wished wasn't in spitting distance; Simon Locke's Dry Goods store. For Amos and his cronies were sitting up on the porch, looking like they had big chaws in the mouth and no place to go with them.

Reluctantly, the trio made their way across the spit-riddled dust. Salty was in the lead, feeling more secure since he made a much smaller target for the weapon in Amos' mouth. They stepped up onto the porch and got absolutely no reaction from the self-appointed guardians of the city. Bravery being a commodity in short supply when you could see the whites of your enemy's eyes.

Jeff turned to Cap. "Wish me luck."

Cap gave him the double thumbs up. "You got it partner."

Jeff disappeared into the cool darkness of the interior of the store. Leaving Cap and Salty feeling like tofu salad at a Cattlemen's picnic.

☯ CAP TRIES TURNING THE TIDE

Cap was not ready for a showdown with the group on the porch. As much as they had run him down from afar he really had no first hand knowledge of their animosity toward him. If it weren't for the bright sun and the need to squint through it, Cap might have even seen himself sitting where Amos was sitting. The big difference was that Amos had extracted all the bitterness out of life and let it build up inside himself. Cap didn't extract much, a few fossils and a middlin' amount of disappointment. Enough to make him expect more down the road.

Cap tried the friendly approach. Nothing ventured, nothing gained. "Howdy, Boys."

Absolutely no reaction from the 'boys' on the porch except that Amos launched a big wet lugie of tobacco juice out past the porch, missing Cap's belly by a foot. It unfortunately left a small wet mark on Salty's ear. He let out a yelp, more out of disgust than pain.

Cap let this spittlish comment slide by since he couldn't be certain that Amos' aim or eyesight were good enough to merit a counter-attack. "Nice weather we're havin'."

Silence. Could it be that these old men were collectively deaf? Or maybe, Cap thought to himself, they don't speak the same language that he did. To test his own sanity, Cap was about to converse with Salty (like talking with a dog was an accurate sanity test?), when Amos finally spoke, "Hear ya' buildin' a boat out by the tracks?" He posed it as a question without the need for a response.

It seemed to Cap like this was a straightforward enough question so he proceeded, cautiously, "Might be. What's it to you?"

Amos spat again. This time the spittle landed perilously close to Cap's foot. Amos leaned over toward the very old man to his right. The man continued to glare at Cap although it might not have been a reflection on his distaste for Cap. More like a stroke had left his facial features permanently mired in a grimace. Amos talked to him, loud enough for everyone on the porch, including Cap, to hear: "Told ya' he was loony. Buildin' a boat in the desert. Why he thinks he's Noah or somethin'." This thought caused him and his buddies to launch in a series of ear-splitting cackles. Enough to make a man go mad if Cap wasn't already furious.

He took a step toward Amos. "Why you old goat turd." He reached out to grab the shit brown suspenders lying across Amos' shirt. "You don't know nothin'."

Cap would have grabbed the suspenders and launched Amos into orbit except that his hand never reached Amos' chest. Jeff came racing out of the store and threw his arms around Cap. "It worked! Mr. Locke is giving us some old wood he's not using. Come on it's out in the back." He pulled Cap off the porch. Cap continued to eye Amos as he was pulled around the side of the store. Salty advanced, teeth bared, toward Amos. He made it halfway up the steps before he was hit smack in the face with a shot of tobacco juice. Discretion being the better valor, he retreated from the porch.

Amos cackled again. "Crazy, all of them. It will be a cold day in this town before the boat ever sails."

❧ FACING THE DREAM'S DEATH

As Cap, Jeff and Salty made their way around to the back of the store, Jeff could not contain his excitement. This was the first positive sign of support they had received and he saw it as an omen of better times. Cap was sullen, feeling his opportunity to bash an adversary was stolen from him.

Jeff pulled him around the corner. "Aren't you happy? At least we got some more wood for the boat."

Cap forced a ridiculous grin onto his face. "Right. That's dandy, Jeffey. More wood." The word 'wood' hung on his lips as he stared at the gift that Simon Locke had bestowed upon them.

Leaning against the back of the store were two partially damaged wood coffins. The lids of the coffins lay across the openings of the boxes but were not nailed shut. There were cardboard boxes nearby but nothing else was composed of wood—the essential boat-building material.

Cap and Jeff stopped several feet from the coffins and made no effort to move any closer. The grin had slipped from Cap's face, "This is got to be one bad joke. Locke wouldn't have given us..."

Jeff didn't let him finish. "He said it was a couple of old boxes. He couldn't have meant these." He gestured at the coffins as if the mere mention of the word 'coffin' would bring some kind of curse down upon them.

Cap advanced toward the larger of the two coffins. "Don't see that it could be anything else." He slowly ran his hand along the side board, feeling the texture of the lumber. "It seems in good shape, not been used." He hand slowly inched it way toward the cover. As his hand grasped the outside edge of the coffin cover, he and Jeff both held their breath. Cap gingerly lifted the cover off and he peeked into the interior of the coffin. He let out a long sigh and moved the cover aside. The coffin was empty. Jeff let out a long sigh, also. Not that he was frightened of the closed casket but the sight of large and small caskets as their 'reward' at the end of a long and trying day did not seem to portend good things. Cap put a foot inside the larger coffin and Jeff tried to pull him back. Cap turned back, surprised.

Jeff said, "It's kind of creepy."

"What's so creepy about it? Two empty boxes."

"You know what I mean. Maybe it's knowing that one day you and me are going to be buried in one of those."

Cap shook his head strongly, "Not me, no way, no sir."

"But you have to be, everyone gets buried in a coffin."

Cap laughed, or rather snorted in disgust. "That's only what city folks say. The Indians had a better way of doing it. After you die, they take your body and put it on a wood frame, with branches and stuff, and they light it on fire.

"Which Indians?"

"I don't know, the Indian Indians. What difference does it make?"

Jeff persisted, "Well, I just wanted to know if it was the Indians from India or the Indians from here.

Since Cap had no idea where this custom originated, he retreated to his usual, belligerent verbal stance. "Shush, Boy. I'm trying to teach you somethin' important and you're askin' for a geography lesson."

Salty was disappointed with this response because his own intellectual curiosity had been aroused. He couldn't decide whether Cap was referring to a Hindu sect's cremation ritual or an aberration of the American Indian's concept of the sacred burial ground.

Jeff backed off since he felt that Cap was trying to tell him something important. "I'm sorry, Cap. I'll shut up and listen."

"Good. Anyways, I was saying how the body gets burned completely. And when the fire burns down there ain't nothing left of you."

"Why is that better than burying?"

Cap shot him a 'I thought you said you were going to shut up' look. "First off, it doesn't leave any rotten bodies clogging up the ground. And secondly, it allows your soul, you know, like your spirit, to go up to heaven easier. Yep, that's the way to go if you have to go."

Jeff pondered the implication of this theosophical declaration with a great deal of thought and then he replied, "Sounds like it might hurt." This comment clearly showing that visionaries are specialists; they rarely hold unusual or unique views in anything other than the one field they hallucinate in.

"Ah, what do you know anyway? Lets git these boxes back to the boat. You haven't forgotten about the boat, have you?"

Jeff grabbed the smaller coffin and started wrestling it along the ground. "Hell, no. I'm ready to keep building, till we run out of wood. Between now and then, I'm sure we can come up with another idea to get us some boat money."

Salty laughed and it sounded, as usual, like a hairball lodged in his throat. 'You better put on your thinking caps, right now.'

Cap grabbed hold of the larger coffin and began pulling it through the dirt, making sure that he stayed out of sight of the porch boys at the front of the store. "I like you, Jeffey boy. You may be crazier than me and Salty combined, but I do like you."

That and a thousand dollars might help the prospects for the boat right now. A more impartial eye might observe that prospects for this vision look a little dimmer than bleak, a little lower than a deep hole, or on the way down Niagara Falls without the proverbial barrel for protection.

But for now, the dreamers were content to see the optimistic short side—they had wood for the hull and a will to hammer.

PART TWO

HOISTING SAIL

"If we were logical, the future would be bleak indeed. But we are more than logical. We are human beings, and we have faith, and we have hope."

Jacques Cousteau

ᘓᘍ SAVIOR ON THE TIDE

Phil Kurtzman had a whole carload of trouble. His engine temperature was rising and his fingers were aching from trying to tune in any radio station that played a close approximation of rock and roll. His last successful 'tune' was a Crosby, Stills, Nash and Young song from a pirate station out of Elko, Nevada. Why anyone would try and operate a radio station in this god-forsaken country was well beyond the grasp of Phil; he was just a hard-workin', almost-permanent staff journalist for the Salt Lake Tribune. He had earned his BMW 2002 the hard way—by stealing good stories from better journalists. And while the better journalists had griped about being ripped off by Phil, the local editor had seen fit to award his distinguished, almost thirty-year-old employee with a week's paid vacation.

Phil had wasted no time in gassing up his bad-ass 'B', as he was fond of calling her, and heading west. With no respect for Horace Greeley, Phil headed to San Francisco to find the last remaining members of the Love Generation. First, to bed down with them (in particular, the California goddesses he had dreamed of since Woodstock) and then to write the ultimate series of articles defining his generation and subsequently earning him a Pulitzer Prize and a permanent position with the New York Times.

Unfortunately, Phil's plans had not panned out in the new California Gold Rush. He was returning to Salt Lake City with his head down. Not in shame, but to focus on the intense itching he was undergoing as the recipient of better-left-unsaid social disease. The itching, the dry heat and the boring flatness of the countryside had put Phil in a bad mood. As he focused his attention on the wandering sounds of the radio dial, his bad-ass "B" moved through the suburbs of Wendover, Nevada, then the downtown area and finally the state line. By the time his fingers had tweaked the dial into holding a bubble gum rock station from Reno, he had missed all the highlights of Wendover, Utah. He didn't look up until the roughness of the noise coming from bad ass' engine and the steam whipping back over the hood caught his attention. His mood moved from bad to foul with the same speed that his radio dropped the Bubble Gum sounds for the dead air hiss of the hinterlands.

"God damn it!" Phil gave up on the radio dial and pulled the car over to the sandy shoulder. As the car rolled to a stop in the dust, a small geyser of steam erupted from under the hood. "No, not now." He slammed his hands against the steering wheel and stared out the windshield. He studied the eastern horizon and saw nothing but dust devils and a hot desert. Over his shoulder he could barely make out the smudge of a skyline created by the Wendover, Utah 'downtown.' He jammed his bad-ass and now badly dehydrated car into first gear and swung into a big U-turn. First crossing the asphalt of the two lanes of eastbound traffic, then spinning his wheels through the sand of the center divider and finally, back onto the tar of the westbound side.

With nary a look for oncoming traffic or ticket-hungry Utah troopers, Phil hurtled his car back toward Wendover, a gas station and his destiny.

His destiny was found in the one and only Chevron gas station in Wendover although Phil only saw it as a place to refill his radiator reservoir. He coaxed his steaming pile of German steel up to the water hose where it came to a wheezy but grateful stop. Phil hopped out, resplendent in a pair of perfectly faded jeans and a Grateful Dead T-shirt (courtesy of an unnamed but pretty Deadhead, carrier of the aforementioned social disease). He popped the hood on the Beemer and waved his way through a mushroom cloud of hot steam.

By the time the steam had cleared and Phil's cursing had subsided, Mike was leaning over his shoulder doing an in-depth analysis of the car's problems. Before giving his prognosis, he carefully wiped his grease-stained hands on the raggedy blue towel hanging from his ironed blue jeans. "Boil over," he stated uncategorically, as if he had just finished his umpteenth heart transplant and one more patient was guerneyed in.

Phil, no stranger to high school auto shop, accepted this statement with all the graciousness of a man on the receiving end of a bad fart in a small room. "How did you possibly figure that out?"

"The steam, it was a cinch." Having carefully cleaned his hands, he stuffed the blue towel back into his pocket. He removed one speck of grease from under a nail and looked up at Phil. "Want me to look her over?"

Phil realized that he was in enemy territory, or rather, car-repair-ripoff-land. He decided that tact might work better here than bullying his way through. "No, that's fine, thanks. If you don't mind my leaving her here, I'll just let her cool off, and then add some more water."

"It'll will take a little while." Mike, realizing that he would not be making any sales at this hippie's expense, eased back on his hard sell.

"I got time." He checked his watch as a matter of habit. "Shit. I'm already late for work."

"Where's work?" Mike asked.

"Salt Lake. Shit, I thought I left San Francisco in time to get there this morning. Guess I underestimated a little.

Mike broke out in a grin. "No more than half a day. You been on vacation?"

Phil nodded. "Damn good one. Shame to be going back to work." His radiator let out one last gasp of steam and then subsided into catatonia. Mike leaned in under the hood, whipping out his towel to wrest the radiator cap from its perch. Nothing happened when the radiator neck was exposed to air. He breathed in the radiator fumes, and a strange sense of whimsy overcame him.

Sounding more like Dave Caster than the hard-boil(over)ed car mechanic he was, Mike said, "Why don't you wander around our fair city for awhile. Take in the sights, enjoy yourself. When your engine's cooled down, I'll put some water in for you."

Phil was bewildered by this show of generosity and sheer idiocy on the part of this boy. After all, it was as plain as dandruff on a bald guy's head that there was nothing to be seen in this 'berg. As a

cynic of human nature, Phil couldn't believe that there wasn't an
ulterior motive behind this statement. Try as he might, he couldn't
quite figure out the angle so he resorted to his normal conversational
style; sarcasm with a heavy dose of patronizing thrown in. "Thanks,
that's real nice of you. Any highlights of the town that I shouldn't
miss?"

Mike couldn't believe he just said what he said and before he
could stop himself, he answered, "Nothing comes to mind but
maybe you'll find something."

"Fine. I'll just stagger off into the desert and watch the salt
crystals grow. Hope its not too exciting, I got a bad heart." He held
his hands up to the left side of his chest and feigned a seizure. Then
he chuckled and turned away from Mike. "God Almighty, why am I
stuck here? I should be someplace else, anywhere else!" He kicked
at a piece of tumbleweed as he headed out behind the gas station in
search of the unknown.

Mike watched the fine cloud of dirt following in the footsteps of
Phil's Adidas sneakers. The wind brushed past the gas pump island
blowing the dust up and around Phil's pant legs, creating the effect
of a man walking on top of two swirling waterspouts. To Mike,
landlocked since birth, this illusion had no oceanic reference but it
could only portend of more strange happenings to come in
Wendover. And that was the best news Mike could get since
excitement had never paid a visit to this section of the state.

While Phil chatted with Mike, Cap and Jeff had bolted in the last
beam in the "spine" of their ship. While they have made
considerable progress in their boat-building operation, to the
untrained eye their construction still fell far short of being a clipper
ship, much less an ocean going craft of any kind. Cap allowed Jeff
to take the final turns on the ratchet wrench setting the final nut into
the final bolt.

Phil's walkabout in the desert ended when he spotted a giant
lizard, or what Phil could best describe as a cross between an ugly
dolphin and a skink, splashing in the sand. He decided to tour the
desert in the opposite direction, putting as much distance between
himself and his 'acid flashback' as he could. This new path brought
him to the periphery of the construction site. Phil circled the

'shipyard' trying to get a perspective on what appeared to be a wood skeleton lying on the desert floor being attended to by a skinny little boy and an old man. Two strange sights in two minutes was enough to have Phil swearing off recreational drugs for the rest of his life. He observed, using his journalistic acumen, that the boy was of average boy appearance and the man looked like he was a casting reject from Gilligan's Island. They scurried about this wood edifice like two ants happening on the carcass of a dead, but delectable, rat. As his newsman's blood began to heat up and his major story nose began to twitch, he moved slowly toward the boy and old man. If his instincts were right, and his ego stepped in to say 'as usual', this was a story he didn't want running away. What he was having trouble figuring out was, what the hell could be interesting, story-wise, about two crazy carpenters in the desert.

Jeff saw Phil first and, like a frightened deer at sound of movement, he froze. He watched carefully as Phil moved toward him. Phil slowed his pace but continued coming, a frozen smile on his face.

Without turning his eyes from Phil, Jeff reached out to grab Cap's arm and his attention. He whispered, almost without moving his lips, "Cap. Cap, somebody's here."

Cap turned, caught sight of Phil, and turned back to Jeff. "So what. Just another non-believer. Ignore the bum, he'll go away. Help me straighten this beam, Jeffey." Jeff turned away from Phil to help Cap align a bracing piece in the frame but he couldn't help but sneak a peek at Phil. Phil had stopped a respectful 30 feet away from them and stood watching them. Jeff and Cap struggled to get the alignment just right consuming several minutes. Phil continued to watch and Jeff continued to surreptitiously glance at him.

Finally: "Excuse me." Phil took another step forward and then froze as Cap shot him a frigid glare. "Excuse me, can I ask you a question?"

With a shrug, Cap stopped working and turned to face Phil. "You jus' did. The answer is no, now go away."

Phil didn't like to be put off when he was in pursuit of a story but he could appreciate a good turn of the phrase, particularly if it helped to develop rapport with a hostile interviewee. So he smiled and forced a laugh. "No really, I just wanted to know what you're building? Some kind of free-form house?"

Jeff and Cap exchanged a quick glance. Salty lifted his head off the sand and got interested. It was boring watching two crazies work in the hot sun all day long but now he got to hear them converse with a complete blockhead. If things got any worse, he was thinking of finding a Joshua tree and opening a discussion on Hegel's view of the Universe. Jeff couldn't help but ask the obvious, "Are you new in town?"

"Right. I'm just passing through. My car's radiator boiled over, so I, well, anyway, the answer is yes."

"That's what I figured. Everyone in town knows."

Having shared some information with them, Phil felt the time was right to close the distance between him and the carpenters. "Knows what?" He glanced up at the ribs of the ship. "Is it some kind of sculpture?"

Jeff looked to Cap for a clue as to how to respond. Cap's face was inscrutable. He just stood there looking at Phil and noticing that dust devils were circling around Phil's legs, reminding him of two waterspouts pulling a sailor down into the cold, black ocean. Jeff to Cap, "Should we tell him?"

"Don't see why not. I'm real used to people laughing at us. Give him the big speech."

"The big one?" Jeff asked.

"No use saving it. Is there?"

Jeff shimmied up one of the hull spines so that he was above both Phil and Cap. He turned on his best tour guide voice, a la a Universal Studios' tour without the tram microphone. "What you see before you is the beginnings of a thirty-foot clipper ship. My friend, the noted shipbuilder, Cap, and I are building it because we are both escaped fruitcakes from the nuthouse, and we don't know any better. I know what you are thinking." He stopped his spiel momentarily and pointed directly at Phil. Phil pointed at himself as if to ask, 'are you talking to me?' Jeff continued: "Yes, we do know that we are in the middle of desert and there isn't an ocean for thousands of miles. But this is where we live. So it makes sense that we build it here. You may laugh now."

Phil didn't laugh, he continued to stare at the boat with an apparent new found respect for this 'wood sculpture.' "A thirty-foot clipper ship. I am impressed. Isn't that a pretty big job just for two of you?"

Jeff was visibly surprised by Phil's straightforward interest without the expected scorn. "Yep. No one in town thinks we're serious. They think we're crazy. But we aren't, really."

Phil's immediate internal response was to say 'the hell you're not' but his story antennae were quivering like the 'uncle' in "My Favorite Martian" and he knew that they, the antennae, were usually right on the money. "I gotta hand it to you, Kid, building a boat out here," and he pointed with a sweep of his hand to the seemingly endless desert, "takes a whole lot of something I don't have. What did you say about building it here?" He had a suspicion that the old man was trying to run some flimflam on the boy but Phil couldn't see the angle yet. He needed to hear the old man's story first, so he addressed himself to Cap. "I don't want you to think that I am not interested, I am. But I can't figure out why you're doing this." And suddenly, the picture and his story slant snapped into focus. "Know what I mean, it's like," he stumbled for the right visual metaphor, "like raising a whale in an aquarium." Visually this worked but Phil realized that the situation, beyond being ludicrous, was not really analogous. What the hell, he thought, these country bumpkins didn't know the difference between ludicrous and analogous.

A true statement for two thirds of the country bumpkins standing in the shipyard but Salty couldn't believe the mangled wordplay coming from this stranger. 'A whale in an aquarium.' That just didn't make sense. This man had obviously tasted the darker side of the 70's drug scene.

Cap had only heard the simple question being directed at him. The idea of a whale in an aquarium didn't seem that strange since he had been to Marineland in L.A. and they had a bunch of whales in a tank. "Look, we, Jeffey and me, mighta' started on it for different reasons, but I think we're both doing it now to show the pea-brains in this town that if you get a crazy idea, a dream or whatever, and you work hard enough at it, you kin make it happen."

The saliva nearly dripped out the corners of Phil's mouth as he listened to Cap speak. This was a story made in heaven and handed to him on a broken radiator hose. His eyes started darting around looking for just the right perspective for his photo. A boy, an old man, an impossible dream—life didn't get any better for a reporter. "That's fascinating. Look, I'd like to go back to my car and get my camera, so I can take some pictures of your...ship." He spoke gently, as if to an apparition that might blow away if his breath flew out too fast. "And if you don't mind, I'd like to find out more about your reasons for undertaking this project. How about that?"

Cap pushed the cap back on his head. The sweat and grime made finger tracks on his forehead. "Fine with me. We got to stop working anyway til' we can scrounge up some more timber. You want to jaw and take some photos, okay, it'll help to pass the time."

Phil broke into a genuine smile, as genuine as a reporter on the job could get, and winked at Salty. Salty was now sure this man had lost his mental faculties through the use of hallucinogenic drugs. 'Whale in an aquarium,' Salty just shook his head and dropped it back on top of his front paws.

"Thank you, very much. I'll be right back. Please don't go away. He spun around and left the boatyard, the dust typhoons still swirling around his legs. He stopped several times to look back, just to make sure that his story hadn't floated away on the heat waves.

Cap watched him leave and then broke out laughing. Jeff and Salty couldn't figure out what set him off. Finally Cap said, through his laughter, "Where's he think we'd go? For a sail?" Jeff joined him in laughter. Salty just burrowed his nose further into the sand.

ᘉᒯ SMALL CRAFT WARNINGS

As fast as the clouds could flee the sky and the sun dry the land that's how fast Jeff went from the ego-high of a journalist being interested in the boat to the balloon-bursting pragmatism of his father's dinner table pontificating. He hadn't really thought that Phil, the reporter, was serious about how great the boat was but at least he spent some time talking to them, taking a bunch of photos and he didn't laugh. Then again, he never thought that his dad would get uptight about him taking the initiative and doing something seriously. He was now realizing how wrong he could be.

Ken began the pontificating, "This whole thing has gotten out of hand. You've made me the laughingstock of the whole town. Who gave you permission to go around asking for DONATIONS?" He spat this word out like the act of soliciting funds for the boat had painted Ken, father of the beggar, as a pecunious leper drawn from the pages of Charles Dickens. "Anything my family needs, I will give them. They don't have to go around asking for hand-outs."

"You wouldn't have given me the money! I had to ask others for the money."

Ken verbally slapped his son with a "Shut up." Even Elise was startled by the ferocity of Ken's response. "I got talked into allowing you to waste your time building this thing, because I thought it would keep you busy and outta' trouble. I'm glad that your money ran out because now you are going to have to stop this fantasy and come back to the real world."

The atmosphere in the room had heated up to a level that the butter on the lukewarm petite pois peas was vaporizing. Jeff added one more log to the raging inferno. "We are not going to stop. We'll keep going."

Elise was searching in her memory banks for some article from the past that would have told her how to defuse this situation. All she could come up with was some psycho-mumbo jumbo from a *TV Guide* article on Mary Tyler Moore's problems with success. She settled for, "I think if we all just take a deep breath, we can calm down and talk about this reasonably."

She was ignored by both Jeff and his father. They were engaged in a battle of will in which the first to break the stare lost. Without blinking, Ken responded to Jeff's statement, "I don't see as you have any choice. No one in town is going to give you a plug nickel to build that thing. You'll have to stop, dammit!" The use of the 'D' word was intentional and effective. Elise's mouth dropped open and refused to close. Jeff took it as a sign of weakness and he stood up.

"No, I won't." He backed away from the table, fully intending to end the conversation by removing his presence from the dining room. His father jumped up from the table, almost knocking over his chair.

"Where are you going? You can't run away and cry this time. You aren't a baby anymore and I am not going to treat you like one."

Jeff heard the words but knew that they were not true. His father would always treat him like a baby because he knew no other way to treat him. Treating him like an adult would make his father's hold on the position of being the only adult male in the family even more tenuous. Even Jeff could see that the dominant male position was critical to his father's sense of value. But like the millions of American adolescents before him (and the billions that would follow), Jeff ignored his own good sense of intuition and launched into his own inflammatory statement. "I know that, Dad, but you seem to forget it everyday." That said, he turned on his heels and left the room.

Since his mother had yet to recover from her husband's swearing, she could only drop her jaw a few millimeters further. Ken slammed his fist against the table making the pretty but well-used Melmac jump off the table. The potential loss of the dishes snapped Elise back to reality. Her mouth clamped shut and she started reaching for those dishes closest to the edge of the table.

Ken rubbed his clenched hand, the impact the most violent physical confrontation he had had in recent memory. "I should take him over my knee for saying that."

Elise continued to calm down her agitated table. "What did you expect? You backed him into a corner so he had to fight back."

This sounded to Ken like a mother defending a son rather than the expected unified parental front against the child. And he didn't like the trend. "Now don't go and start defending him. It's time we brought him back down to Earth. If he thinks he's an adult, its time he faced the responsibilities of living in the real world."

A vision of her son burdened with all the troubles of adulthood pressing down on his shoulders immediately popped into her head. While she had no illusions about the perpetual joys of being an adolescent, she'd read enough articles to the contrary, she didn't want her son to launch into being a grown-up until he had the tools to succeed. Besides, the role model of a father who went to work every day hating his job but not willing to leave it didn't seem like a good way to start. "Why does he need to come back down? He seems to enjoy building the boat more than anything else he's done in a long time. What would he do, anyway? Go to work with you at the plant?"

In a night full of surprises, Elise's question cut through all the usual subterfuge of their dining experience and nailed her husband where it hurt the most. Ken, having fought the truth since he first took the potash job, was not ready to admit to it. "There's nothing wrong with him finding out what its like to have a job."

"Oh, come on, Ken. He's only thirteen. You can't expect him to go out and work with you?"

Ken flinched and Elise buried another barbed harpoon in his soul. Didn't every father wish for their son to grow up and work side by side with dear old dad? "And why not? I work there five days a week, fifty weeks a year."

Elise knew that she had drawn blood in their first-ever full contact exchange and strangely, she enjoyed the taste of it. "And you hate every minute of it. So does everyone who works there."

Ken, ever the man not willing to show that he had been hurt, lamely responded, "That's not true." His heart wasn't in it but he had no where else to go. Admission of the truth would invalidate what he had been doing for the last fifteen years.

Elise shortened her punches, knowing that she had already been declared the winner of a fight that no one should want to win. The champion having to live with the loser for the rest of their downtrodden lives. "Yes, it is. You know it, too."

He teetered on the ropes, knowing that one more punch, no matter how weak or poorly aimed would send him to the canvas. In a last ditch counter-attack, Ken flung himself off of the ropes, throwing his last ounce of energy into a punch that could only do damage but not win the fight for him. "So what if I do. Like your life is something so great. Gets you bouncing out of bed in the morning."

And as he hit the canvas for the count he caught a glimpse of Elise, the victor. Her face soured by his final sucker punch, a below-the-belt shot that made them both losers. Elise could only stare back at Ken. They had both spoken the truth, for the first time in a long time, and they were unsure of what came next.

⚘ THE LEVIATHAN IS SPOTTED

The wind had shifted almost imperceptibly in Wendover. In the past, it would blow straight through, never stopping for an extended visit. And now it seemed to blow and then swirl back, forming eddies and quiet pools of activities. And with the wind came new ideas and strange people. Brad Woodley had felt the electricity in the air, and like lightning to a lightning rod, he had thundered into Wendover looking to strike "the Whale."

To the townspeople of Wendover, Brad's arrival in town would not normally have been spoken of in meteorological terms, but the forces of change had found a chink in the armor of this dusty place and sprung the gate open. And Brad, in his faded and patched jeans, long tendrils of hair spilling over his shoulders, might as well have slipped in from another planet and announced the colonization of Earth, beginning with those people sitting on Simon's porch. But Brad had come on another mission, and the taunts and mumbled curses emanating from the porch did not deter him from his mission. His gaze crossed paths with Amos and then continued on, searching the town for what he had read of, what he now hungered for. The east bound train running on the Santa Fe tracks hooted its whistle to announce its daily departure from Wendover. This event drew Brad's attention and then his soul began to vibrate. That which he had come for was near. He ambled toward the train tracks and his small part in this nautical drama.

The children who were silently observing Cap and Jeff at work on the boat, uneasily made way for Brad. He was oblivious to these kids, he had eyes only for the monument in front of him. If he had given himself time to think about it, he would have said the sight of the boat was better than the best pot he had ever smoked. But he was too immersed in the contact high of the boat to waste time on unimportant memories of the past.

Circumstance, and lack of money and materials, had forced the boat builders to slow their construction to a sea snail's pace. Little had changed except the length of the futtocks and floor timbers, now the beast had a belly and the shape of a ship. Even the speed and attention that Jeff paid to the ship had changed. Where once he had leaped to assist Cap with every turn of the bolt and every draw on the saw, Jeff now took his time, measuring each move and expecting his father to arrive at any moment with shackles. The dinner fight of the century had left all contestants in the battle-royal bruised and fragile—no one willing to change what they were doing for fear of setting up another rematch. Cap didn't know all the details of the fight but he knew, or sensed, that Jeff's father had somehow managed to take the wind out of Jeffey's sails.

Brad knew nothing of the fight nor the change in Jeff's demeanor, and if he did, it would not have changed his commitment to this crusade. Jeff and Cap had paused in their efforts to watch the train rumbling through and with its passing looked back to their work at hand, and Brad. Cap, no stranger to negative snap judgments (both his and others], immediately didn't like what he saw in the package standing before him. Hippies are no stranger to Wendover. They usually pass through as quickly as anyone else who had the misfortune to be washed up on the shores of Wendover. Jeff wasn't quite so quick to make a judgment. He figured that this guy couldn't be any better or worse than the reporter who had passed through asking a zillion questions. And at least this guy wasn't getting in their way taking a whole bunch of pictures and getting their hopes all souped up.

"Is this the whale?" Brad humbly asked of Jeff. He would have dropped to his knees in supplication but Cap and Jeff didn't quite have the appearance of saints or other god-like creatures. Brad settled for a brief dip of his head to acknowledge these powerful beings.

Salty, who had tried to make himself as inconspicuous as possible since the project started heading downhill, chalked another notch on his mental scoreboard of flotsam who had wandered through the boatyard. Too many people with too much time on their hands and too little brain activity in their skulls had spent too much time telling Cap and Jeff why this venture was doomed.

Jeff's response to Brad was more direct. "The what?" As in, 'What are you talking about? Can't you see that this is a boat sitting in the middle of the desert. Even I know that whales live in the ocean and they don't make it a habit of beaching themselves in my backyard.'

Brad missed the cynical tone in Jeff's voice. As a prototypical hippie he was in the habit of accepting everyone and everything said on face value. "The Wendover Whale. You must be Jeff, and you must be Cap." He gave Cap a warm-hearted smile which Cap immediately took as a smirk.

"You got the names right but I don't remember ever meeting you before. Did I? And what's this poop about a whale?"

Now it was Brad's turn to be a bit confused. Like most readers of newspapers, he believed that the person or persons being written about generally have an idea that they are the subject of an article and thus subject to some public interest. "Sorry, it says that..."

Cap was frustrated with this conversation that made no sense and he interrupted, "What says? What the hell are you talking about?"

From his back pocket, Brad pulled out the front page of a deeply creased and many times read Salt Lake Tribune. Very carefully, and with a great deal of respect, he unfolded the page and gently handed it to Cap. "This paper says that your boat's name is the Wendover Whale."

Cap snatched the paper out of Brad's hand and carefully scrutinized the whole page. He finally rested his eyes on a small photo of Cap and Jeff in front of the skeleton of the boat. Just below the photo was a headline that read, "Whale Sighted in Desert," with a byline by Phillip Kurtzman. Cap slowly made his way though the story detailing their heroic struggle, against all odds, ridiculed by the townspeople, to build a clipper ship. It was a nicely written personal interest piece that might have embellished the facts but left the reader with the impression that Cap and Jeff were dedicated visionaries. "Holy shit," was all Cap could muster as he continued reading the piece. Jeff tried to read the paper over his shoulder and his eyes grew wide with amazement as he saw himself on the front page! Cap had unconsciously begun to shake his head back and forth. "This is god-damned amazin'. We never said half this stuff, and that's a lousy picture of me."

Jeff laughed, "Don't complain, at least we got our names in the paper."

"And you think thats a good thing? Before we just had these local folks laughin' at us. Now we get the whole state laughing. If you think thats a good thing, well then Jeffey, I might have to re-e-val-u-ate our friendship."

Brad cleared his throat. He didn't want to offend either of these people but he had come a long way to ask them a question and he couldn't be put off by their petty squabbling. He cleared his throat again, just a little louder this time.

This gesture was enough to get Cap looking at him. "Yah, whatta' you want?" He quickly realized that he had Brad's newspaper and shoved it back at Brad. Brad delicately took it, refolded it and slid it back into his pocket.

Then Brad asked, "I was hoping that you folks would let me help you build the Whale."

Jeff was flabbergasted and flippedygibeted. In all the many hours he had labored on the boat, no one, except Cap, had even come close to asking that question. "You're joking, aren't you?"

"No, really, I want to." Offered completely and sincerely without any guile. A simple offer that had repercussion beyond anything Brad could comprehend since he was not a visionary just one of the workers necessary to complete the vision.

Jeff was all over him. "That's great!"

Before he had a chance to add anything more, Cap stepped between Jeff and Brad. "Thanks, fella, but we don't need any help. Besides, we can't do no more building, cuz we don't have any money left." And that's that, and Cap turned away from Brad signaling the end of the conversation.

Brad reached out and pinched a small bit of Cap's shirt, enough to halt Cap's turn and return him to a position where he had to look Brad in the face. "Hey, I got a few bucks. If you and Jeff let me help you, they're yours." Another simple offer with no strings attached.

Cap none-too-gently removed Brad's thumb and forefinger from his shirt. "I don't think so." He started to turn away again but this time he was stopped by Jeff. Jeff yanked him several feet from Brad toward the boat, the 'Whale' as the story went.

Brad's offer had kicked Jeff's brain into high gear. He saw his vision going from vaporous to genuine, from nothing to something. And he thought that Cap was about to drive it back into the clouds. To Brad: "Excuse us for a second." He pulled Cap further away so that they could have a conversation in private, just the three of them; Cap, Jeff and the Whale. "Let's take him on. We can really use the money and the extra body."

Cap's vision of the two of them struggling against all odds vanished into an image of a cluster of army ants swarming over the boat paying no attention to a uniformed Cap bellowing out orders. "I thought it was just you and me. You know, partners?"

"I know I said that, but we'll never get the boat built if we don't get more money. And we really do need more people helping us. It'll still be you and me running the show." And for just a brief moment, the 13 year-old boy, and not the visionary, pleaded for something special from a grown-up.

"No," Cap answered without a moment's hesitation.

"Please," and this time the plea sounded a little more like a whine. And then Cap realized that he was dealing with a young boy with feelings right on the surface.

"Is this really what you want?" Jeff eagerly nodded 'yes.' "All right, its your decision to make. Remember that."

Jeff threw his arms around Cap's voluminous waist and gave him a hug. Neither of them were comfortable with this expression of affection but Jeff's joy overcame his normal reticence. "Thanks, Cap." He turned and walked back to Brad. He stuck out his hand and grinned, "Mister, you got yourself a deal."

Brad took his hand and shook it vigorously. His grin was as broad as Jeff's. "Where do I start?"

ঝ THE RISING TIDE

Phil Kurtzman was at home, the pile of crumpled copy, half-eaten granola muffins and scum-covered coffee all competed for space on his desk in the newsroom of the Tribune. He was feeling pretty smug, smugger than he usually was (which was a 9 plus on the smugness scale), all because of the old coot and the kid and their silly ideas about boat-building. Never one to let a big opportunity swim by, he picked up the phone, got directory information for Wendover, asked for the number for the Cutter family and then jotted it down on a piece of napkin ripped from the embrace of a jelly-filled doughnut. He dialed the number and waited, visions of giants snowballs rolling downhill danced in his head.

Elise Cutter was rummaging through her kitchen cabinets when the phone rang. She was trying to come up with a dinner which offended no one. A dinner that everyone would enjoy enough to only open their mouths to stuff food in and not allow any words (particularly angry and hurtful words) out. She waited several rings before picking the phone up. She led a solitary life when Jeff wasn't underfoot so she expected the phone to stop ringing on its own accord—as soon as the person calling realized that he or she had dialed incorrectly. When the ringing persisted, she answered it fully expecting that the person on the other end was calling to offer her a subscription to the newest magazine catering to housewives. Instead, she got Phil.

Phil couldn't help but smile before he launched into his pitch. "Is this Mrs. Cutter? Jeffery's mother?"

Elise was initially put off by this opening line, no one had ever tried to sell her anything because she was a mom, much less Jeff's mom. "Yes, I'm Elise Cutter, Jeff's mom. Who's this?"

"This is Phillip Kurtzman, I work for the Salt Lake Tribune as a..."

Before he could finish, Elise was ready with a response. After all, she had budgeted a certain amount each year to subscriptions and she was over, way over, for this year. And Ken had already given her a bad time about the 'lousy batch of woman's magazines' that were all over the house. "Thank you, anyway, Mr. Kurzom, but

I'm not much of a newspaper reader. Besides, we get the weekly Wendover paper and that has all the important news. If I think of anybody who needs a subscription to your paper I'll be sure to have them call." She started to put the phone down.

This was not how Phil had planned this phone conversation. Taken by surprise at her brush-off, his feet slipped off his desk, sending waterfalls of coffee and copy cascading onto the floor. He yelled into the phone hoping to get Elise's attention back before the phone dropped into the cradle. "Wait, Mrs. Cutter. Mrs. Cutter!" He held his breath until she came back on the line and then he let it out in a long sigh. "Mrs. Cutter, I'm not selling subscriptions to the paper. I'm a reporter. I wrote an article about your son and his friend building a boat."

Elise interrupted, not quite certain she had heard correctly. "Jeff and Cap? A story? Are you sure?"

Phil felt the 'nibble' of belief on the line and prepared to set the hook. "I'm not kidding you, Mrs. Cutter. The story ran about a week ago. It was very well received across the country. The wire services picked it up."

Elise emitted a nervous little laugh, she just wasn't sure whether her leg was being pulled. Why would anybody be interested in Jeff and his boat? In the county much less the country. "I sure would like to see a copy of that story, Mr. Kur, what did you say your name was?"

Now it was Phil's turn to laugh—it was all just too easy. "It's Kurtzman, Phil Kurtzman, Mrs. Cutter. I'll be glad to bring a copy of the article out to you tomorrow. If that is okay with you?"

"That's mighty nice of you Mr. Kurtzman. It really is a story about Jeff? I can't believe it."

"Believe it, Ma'am. And it gets better. The reason why I'm coming out is to deliver the checks and cash that have been sent for Jeff." He could visualize Elise's expression even if he couldn't really see her. He silently mouths the word 'money' as he waited for her response.

"Money? Why on Earth would anyone send Jeff money? I am totally confused by what you're saying. Are you sure you have the right number?" She looked as if she might set the phone down so she wouldn't have to deal with any more mind-boggling information.

"I know its hard to believe, Mrs. Cutter. If you'll make time for me tomorrow, I think I can explain everything to you. Let's just say, your son and his boat are the hottest story in Utah, no, make that the U.S., right now. Goodbye." He hung up the phone and speared the jelly doughnut. Like a tiger shark after a Hawaiian surfer, he stuffed the bloody red mess into his mouth and chewed contentedly, unaware that two red drips of goo escaped from the corners of his mouth.

Elise hung up the phone and immediately deposited her shaky body into the nearest chair. Forgetting for the moment that she should probably alert Jeff and Cap that the reporter was coming back to town tomorrow. With money! Elise's simple life of a month ago was getting crazier and crazier. She considered the unthinkable, a beer in the early afternoon, on a weekday. This moment of giddiness passed when she realized that for her family to survive tomorrow she would have to be thinking clearly.

ꍞꚉ THE SHARKS SMELL BLOOD IN THE WATER

The wind had freshened as it blew through town, bringing with it molecules of the country that had never before seen the desert. They drifted and floated, hovering above the ramshackle homes and businesses on the Utah side. They lingered on this side of the state line, not drawn to the gaudiness or the bright lights on the Nevada casinos and bars, rather, holding their position above the Chevron gas station. This collection of atoms co-mingled with the heady smelling ethylene molecules which had escaped from the slight leak in the premium pump handle. The gas group couldn't wait to head southwest into Texas to search for their ancestors amongst the wells of Galveston. The newcomers waited and watched as a station wagon filled with children pulled into the station and honked.

Mike came running out, wiping the ubiquitous grease on the ubiquitous blue rag in his back pocket. The driver rolled down the window as Mike lifted the leaky handle off the pump. "Fill it up?"

The driver tried to calm his excited brood, all of whom were chanting "we want the whale, we want the whale" ad nauseam. To Mike, "No thanks, it's almost full. Just want to know where the Whale is. Brought my wife and kids all the way up from Provo to see it."

Mike couldn't help but shake his head. All this fuss over Jeffery Cutter's crazy boat. Not that he had anything against Jeffery, smart little guy that he was. But, jeez, there had to be better things to do on a weekend than drive a hundred miles to look at someone pounding a nail. "Yes, Sir. Don't know if there's much worth seeing, but you can park your car at the back of the station. Its just a short walk." And then belatedly, "Oh, that'll be a buck to park." The driver reluctantly handed a crumpled bill over to Mike who pocketed it immediately. "Just park back there and walk south toward the railroad tracks. You can't miss it."

"Much obliged," the driver said before rolling up the window and pulling the car toward the back of the gas station.

Mike waited until the car was out of sight and then fetched the bill from his pocket. He stared at it and turned it over in his hands, not quite believing he had the balls to ask for it. Being no slouch in the mental molecules, he figured that where one dollar was found two dollars were soon to follow. He ambled out to the "I" to wait for his next whalewatchers. Good times and prosperity were about to surf into town on a wave of blubber.

While Mike waited at the station, harpoon in hand, Dave Caster sat in a nylon deck chair outside the office of the TUMBLING DICE MOTEL. While this establishment lacked most of the amenities of Caesar's Palace in Las Vegas, it had the cheapest room rates in Wendover, Nevada and instant access to the executive management, namely, Dave Caster. Since his duties as mayor were mostly symbolic, Dave supplemented his dollar-a-year salary as mayor fighting to maintain his motel's listing in the Auto Club's travel guide to Nevada. He had won the right to be listed in next year's guide and now he was waiting for the customers to roll in. As he waited, he pondered the little surprises that make his bachelor life in Wendover almost tolerable. The Wendover Whale was one of those surprises.

Dave had never thought of himself as a great thinker (and neither had the rest of his constituents) but he saw the little happening in the 'boatyard' as something that couldn't help but bring better times to the Wendovers. There was very little that made the towns attractive, any oddity could only make it better—Dave came from the Ripley's Believe It or Not! school of marketing. He was roused from his daydreams by the sound of a late model Chevy with Nevada plates pulling into the motel driveway. The car stopped and a man and a woman got out and walked toward the motel office. Both were dressed stylishly, which meant—in this part of the country—that the man was wearing a polyester leisure suit set off by a pair of silver trimmed Tony Lamas and the woman was wearing a dress one size too small with a hemline that ended closer to her hips than her kneecaps.

Dave stood, sucked in his prodigious gut and introduced himself as any proud proprietor would do. "Howdy folks. You be wanting a room for the night?" Upon quick re-evaluation of the cleavage exposed by the woman's dress, he asked, "Or perhaps for the afternoon?"

The subtlety was missed by the woman. With a voice used to calling out keno numbers 18 hours a day, six days a week, she asked, "Is this the closest motel to the Wendover whale?"

Dave was taken a little by surprise. He had thought the boat might attract travelers moving through Utah and Nevada on their way to somewhere else, who wouldn't mind a 30 minute detour to have their photo taken in front of a crummy boat sinking into the desert sand BUT real Nevadans driving up specifically to see the boat and spend the night. That was just too much for Dave's mind to process. Even if he couldn't figure it out, the least he could do would be to sell these folks a nice room for the night. "We'll no, Ma'am, but it's probably the nicest. We got a swimming pool, water beds, FM radios in each room." The phone rang in the motel office and distracted Dave from his spiel. "We got Magic Fingers if you don't like the water beds." The phone continued to ring and Dave leaned a little closer to the office door. Finally: "You'll just have to excuse me for a minute, folks. I'll be right back." He dashed into the office and picked up the phone. Just the few steps he ran was a major exertion for Dave. He tried to catch his breath and say, 'Tumbling Dice Motel', at the same time and he failed with the words coming out like 'rum ring ice or tell.' The reptilian voice on the other end of the line told him to cut out the crap and he immediately realized that it was a mistake to pick up the phone.

Evil was on the line. Not the Snidely Whiplash variety of evil where the audience knew his appearance on screen was their cue to boo but rather an evil that stemmed from doing business without regard for anyone's feelings. If this had been the eighties rather than the seventies, this evil would have been declared a national financial treasure (who would then have been imprisoned in the 90's). But this was the 70's and the evil known as Mr. Cinino was just a very mean man who happened to own the largest casino and motel in Wendover, Nevada. He also "owned" every other businessman on the Nevada side, not excluding the Honorable Mayor of the town, Dave Caster.

To Dave, being "owned" did not mean being totally obsequious. He prefered to think that he was just a friendly guy being just a little bit more friendly to someone special in his life. "Good afternoon, Mister Cinino. How is the casino business today?"

Cinino's long, narrow (and forked) tongue slithered along the telephones wires and poked Dave in his middle ear. "I don't need the chamber of commerce stuff from you, Caster. And lousy, that's why I'm calling. I want you to find out why my business has fallen in the toilet."

Dave looked out the office window to see the man check his flashy gold watch, bark something at his lady friend and clamber back into the car. His girlfriend pulled her short dress down a bit and then gracefully throw herself into the car. Dave considerd hanging up the phone to try and recover his potential motel guests but though better of it. To Cinino: "Maybe it's the Whale?"

"The whale?" Cinino asked with the tone of a man who had spent all his life dealing with incompetents and just now realized that his associates lacked even the brain power to remember that big fish needed big puddles of water to live in, "get a grip, Caster. I tell you my business is off and you tell me its because the fishing is good, right here in the desert? I think it might be time for a new election."

Dave tried to shift the friendly lever just a notch higher but the gearing was resistant. "I'm sorry, Mr. Cinino, you misunderstood me. I didn't say that everyone went fishing. I said that everyone went to see the whale, the Wendover Whale."

"And what, pray tell, is a Wendover Whale, Dave?" Cinino tried to sound sweet and nice, like adding a layer of jam on top of a batch of snake venom. The effort was wasted on Dave who was only trying to be helpful.

"Some kid's building a boat in his backyard or something. A big ugly thing from what other folks are saying." He chuckled at the thought that people were willing to drive hundreds of miles to see a pile of wood. Go figure.

The layer of jam disappeared as quickly as it arrived. Cinino switched back into his malevolent despot mode. "Don't be an idiot, Caster. Nobody was going to pass up a craps table to look at a snot-faced kid's row boat. Now listen, I want you to do some investigating, and find out the real reason. Or else." He slammed the phone down with such speed that his viper tongue barely had time to withdraw from Dave's ear before the connection was broken.

"Why me?" Dave asked into the silent phone. But he knew the answer was as plain as the nameplate on his desk; Dave Caster, Mayor of Wendover, Nevada. He put the phone down and walked back out of the motel office. He then watched as a steady stream of cars rolled by in the direction of the state line and figured that his first function as detective for Cinino would be to check out the hullabaloo known as the Wendover Whale. He reached back inside the door for a doorknob hanger that said 'Sorry we missed ya', Be back real soon!' He also hung a smile back on his face, the unpleasant business with Cinino behind him and a new responsibility to feel proud of. Dave didn't know it but he just might have been one of only two truly happy people in all of Wendover, both Utah and Nevada.

৩৫ A FEEDING FRENZY

Some time in the course of human events in the United States there comes a point at which small solitary happenings transmutate themselves into big deals. Neither the media nor the American public seems satisfied with something small and sweet remaining small and sweet (To EXPAND on the metaphor). If eating a chocolate kiss was good then eating a chocolate clipper ship has got to be better. What no one realizes until it is too late is that too much sugar corrodes the brain until all that remains is an ocean-size stomach ache and some faint notion of why the public started eating in the first place.

A mass of humanity had descended on the Wendover 'shipyard' intent on gorging themselves on the Whale. Tourists, townspeople and reporters were weaving ant-like patterns as they moved around the resuscitated ship looking for the opportunity to touch the magic or be interviewed by earnest young reporters looking for a new angle on the ship in the desert theme (already fully exploited by Phil Kurtzman).

The Whale had really begun to look like a ship. When Cap and Jeff had worked alone, progress could be imperceptibly measured in weeks. Now with the help of Brad and several other similarly aged, similarly attired 'sailors' drawn by the siren call of the Whale, the ship's headway toward seaworthiness could be seen to change hourly—not always in the right direction as evidenced by some unusual design flaws in the ribs of the hull.

Several reporters made a full frontal charge on Cap and Jeff, doing their best to avoid being 'boomed' by the 4x4 beams being swung around by the ship workers. Cap and Jeff ignored their questions in the hopes that they would be left alone. Salty barked for the reporters' attention, only too willing to grant an exclusive interview for the right price. Much to his chagrin, none of these reporters had taken the time to learn the proper way to interview intelligent canines.

Amos and his old men's group had somehow whined Simon Locke into bringing their rocking chairs over from his store so they could chaw and chat within sight of the 'goodfornuthin' boat being built by the 'goodfornuthin' nut from the desert. One or two brave journalists with no other juicy angles had made the mistake of entering into the free-fire zone around Amos. And if they were very lucky they only had a dry cleaning bill to show for it. The word was now out that Amos was a tougher interview than Howard Hughes (and there was a rumor that Amos was, in fact, Howard Hughes).

Mary and Steve stood near the couple who left Dave's motel. The woman was taking small hops trying to get a better view of the ship. Each time she jumped, her skirt rode higher up her legs. Each time she jumped, Steve's eyes got a little bigger and his lean (toward the woman) became a bit more acute. Finally the woman stopped jumping long enough to ask Mary which one of the men was Cap. Mary took the opportunity to step between Steve and the sexy woman and then pointed out Cap among the group of people near the Whale. The woman was disappointed that Cap was so old and ugly. Mary defended Cap but took pains to point out that the master mind behind the Whale was really her friend, Jeff. Steve's interest in the older woman dissipated when he heard the pride in his girlfriend's voice when she spoke about that dork, Jeff Cutter. He was about to comment when a splendid looking woman in her early twenties brushed by him intent on joining the knot of men hoisting a rib piece onto the ship's hull.

This strange woman, dressed in the uniform of the day; jeans, work boots and a carpenter's belt, had the aura of all-business. Which couldn't be further from the minds of the men her aura glanced off. She was the proto-typical California girl with blonde hair cascading in waves down her back, a light teak tan, ocean-blue eyes and a gorgeous figure barely submerged behind her grundgy clothes. She ignored the hungry stares of the male Whale spectators and pulled to a stop next to a scaffold attached to the Whale. Cap was directing his co-workers in adjusting a beam. He was unaware of the 'piece of work' below him since he had eyes for the 'piece of work' in front of him. It was only when the other shipbuilders stopped working and looked down at the sight below them that Cap did the same.

In a no-nonsense voice, the woman asked, "Are you in charge here?"

Cap didn't like the sound of her voice (that was self assurance talking, something Cap couldn't relate to) but he wasn't that old that he couldn't appreciate the look of her body. "Yes, Miss, I guess you could say that. What can I do for you?"

"My name is Nancy Morton. I want to help you build your ship." This was said like it was a normal request, something heard everyday. Except feminism had not hit the hinterlands yet. Bra burning and the like were bi-coastal phenomenons and only the most lurid aspects of this consciousness movement had reached this remote outpost of humanity in Utah. And even those aspects had not yet broken the virginity of Cap's ears.

And so Cap responded in a typical pre-raised consciousness mode, "That so? Don't you think that this work is a mite dirty for ya'?" He didn't mean to offend but in his mind women should be strolling the promenade deck of ocean liners and not torquing bolts on clipper ships. No argument. End of discussion.

And so it was except that Elise Cutter had not raised a 19th century boy. With the help of her magazines, her son knew a small injustice when he saw one. "Come on, Cap. We've let everyone else who wanted to work, do it. You can't say no just cause she's a girl."

Cap said, "Says who?"

Before Jeff could answer, Nancy answered for herself. In that same voice that might have made lesser men's sense of manhood shrink just a weenie bit, "Thanks anyway. You don't need to defend me. I've helped build some of the fastest yachts in Southern California, and if this old turkey doesn't want the best, I can find another job." What she didn't say was that these male yahoos standing and salivating right in front of her needed her badly. The ship, if it could be called that, looked like it was designed by an old man experienced in carving stick figures out of balsa wood. It was not even a case of seaworthiness, rather it was a question of whether these 'boys' could make both sides of the boat meet each other in the middle.

Having made her bluff, and since she had no other place to go, she turned away from the men and took a step toward rejection. It wasn't the first time she'd been booted from a job but it would be the first time it happened because she kept her sassy tongue in her mouth. Her sense of diplomacy and tact was minuscule compared to her ability to build sailing vessels.

Jeff didn't let her lead foot hit the ground before his mouth was open. "No, please don't go, wait." He scrambled up the scaffold to plead his case with Cap. "She has experience building boats. You've got to let her help." What he didn't say was that he had recently started to look at the progress on the Whale and it didn't quite fit with his image of a black and gold Cutty Sark blasting through the Pacific waves on its way to San Francisco. His visionary image of the Whale at times lost its clarity and sharpness and was replaced by a hodgepodge all-too-real collection of badly fitting lumber. While his confidence in Cap had not diminished, his pragmatic side said there were never too many good shipbuilders on the job.

Cap's immediate response was to say no but Jeff's eyes were begging for a different answer. Cap studied the crowd below him looking from something a little lower than divine inspiration. And it came to him in the form of Phil Kurtzman, weaving his way through the onlookers toward the Whale. "Hey, there's Kurtzman. I gotta' go talk to him." He slipped under one of the bars on the scaffold but was stopped by Jeff's arm on his shoulder.

"Can she stay and work? We need her."

Cap stopped climbing down and stared at Nancy. She didn't back down from his borderline glare. It wasn't anything she hadn't seen on countless other jobs and she fully expected she'd get on the next thousand she applied for. She wasn't that interested in changing society as long as she could work on building boats. Cap turned back to look at Jeff, "Shit, the more the merrier." He jumped to the ground, stumbled and Nancy grabbed for his arm to help steady him. He threw her arm off, and spat out, "I don't need your help," and rushed into the crowd to find Phil Kurtzman, the man who had destroyed Cap's life with one little newspaper story.

Phil Kurtzman surveyed the media circus swirling around him and envisioned himself as the top-hatted ringleader of the greatest show on Earth. That the lion tamers and the acrobats were unaware of his existence meant little. He knew that he built the very stage that they were performing on. Without the stroke of his pen (he was very pre-word processing), all of the people around him would be somewhere else. He had brought focus and meaning to their lives.

A tiny thrill ran down his spine and he savored the moment. This was what power was all about. To test this extraordinary feeling, he surveyed the crowd for an attractive girl. He walked up to her, waited until she noticed him and then smiled. "How do you like the Whale?"

She responded with an empty smile (matching her rather empty eyes and perhaps an empty skull cavity), "It's far out. Don't you think so?"

"Absolutely. Do you want to get closer?" The double meaning echoed through her brain without triggering any comprehensive response.

"Sure, can we?" Wasting not a moment, Phil took her arm and then slid his arm over her shoulders until they were real close, like two boards on a watertight hull. They started toward the Whale, the aura of power positively shooting off of Phil's body.

His Kirlian image ran smack into a decidedly un-Kirlian image of an raging Cap. Even before the corporeal matter of Cap laying a thick hand on Phil's chest, the negative energy of Cap's emotional being had enveloped the power vibes of Phil and dissipated them. As Cap's hand closed on and then crumpled Phil's shirt, the real and very frightened inner-Phil peeked out. "Hey, what the hell's going on. What are you doing?" Once he saw that his assailant was Cap, his bravado returned. Cap continued to pull and Phil reluctantly let go of the girl.

Cap pulled Phil through the crowd, ignoring the greetings and outstretched hands of the Whale-watchers. The crowd thinned as they got further away from the Whale and Cap's pace slowed down. Phil tried to free himself from Cap's grip. "Okay, okay, I'll go peacefully," and he flashed the peace sign to prove it. He finally broke free from Cap and stood his ground. "Now what is this all about?"

"This is all your fault." Cap pointed a lethal finger at the crowd surrounding the Whale.

Phil took in the whole scene and relished the breath-taking vista of his brethren drawn like moths to the bright flame of the Whale. "You don't mean all the tourists, the big crowd around your Whale, the money, the contributions pouring in? I know you don't mean that stuff."

"Yeah, that's exactly what I mean." If ever there were two men who saw the same scene in completely different terms, they were standing in the dusty dry sand of Wendover, Utah facing each other at this very moment.

"But its so beautiful," sighed Phil. The air of the Whale-yard was in some way so intoxicating that the longer Phil breathed it in, the less in touch he was with the feelings of those around him. "It's totally far out!"

Cap invaded Phil's personal space hoping to break through to Phil. "No, its not. It's a god-damned Coney Island. Before you came it was just Jeffey and me building our boat. Now you and your reporter friends have made it into a circus, and it stinks. This isn't what we wanted."

Cap's reference to Phil's 'reporter friends' had Phil worried that some other journalists or schlocking TV reporters had started to horn in on his special story because he had no friends, much less reporter friends. "Now, hold on, Cap. You seem to forget that when I first met you and Jeff, you were about to call it quits because you didn't have any money. Well, I got you money, a bunch of money, in fact, and I got the whole world rooting for you to build your boat. So don't start complaining. You got the money, you got the people to help, now go build the best damn boat you can."

"Don't tell me what to do, Sonny. I want you and your friends to stop the publicity and send all these people away. I want it to be just Jeffey and me again."

"And what about the donations that people are making?" Phil had to ask because he couldn't imagine anyone turning down free money to fulfill their dream.

"If it means the people will all go away, I'll give back all the money that I have left." Cap was just one of those people who never saw money, free or otherwise, as being the be-all and end-all of mankind's existence.

This response clearly made Phil re-evaluate whether Cap was a member of the same species as everyone else that Phil knew. Even so, Phil knew there was only one answer in this situation. "I'm sorry, Cap, but I can't do that."

"And why not," Cap asked angrily as if the implied threat of violence would stem the tide of progress in the shipyard, "you started it all."

"It's out of my hands," and he extended them, palm up, to Cap. "As they say in public relations, the snowball is rolling downhill, and there is nothing that you or me can do to stop it." He liked the turn of the phrase and he could actually see the Whale slipping its moorings at the top of a snow-capped mountain and sliding through snowdrifts toward the bottom, picking up speed as it went, sending waves of white over the tops of tall pine trees. It was a vision he might have shared with Jeff were Jeff not so busy turning his vision into a reality.

Visions and visionaries aside, the Whale had wind in her sails and was picking up speed—and not all the crew was happy about it.

ঞ JUMPING ONBOARD

If it could be said that the initial reaction of the townspeople of Wendover, Utah to the Whale was like that of an pimply-faced teenager faced with the prospect of being grounded for the weekend, the townspeople now had been brain-washed by over-use of Clearasil. They awoke to the new wind; clear of complexion and wholly supportive of 'their' Whale.

And like recent converts at a holy rollers' convention, no expense or activity was spared in the promulgation of their idol. The golden calf of the Sinai received a piker's welcome compared to the efforts made on behalf of the Whale. Banners were strung across the highway in both direction proclaiming, 'Welcome to Wendover, Home of the Whale!' And the passengers in the bumper to bumper traffic heading toward the shipyard had plenty more to gaze at as they impatiently waited for their chance to view the dream incarnate. At the Sand and Salt Market, Zack Mason had discovered deep pockets and produced an enormous hand-lettered sign, 'WWW— WHALE WATCHERS WELCOME'. Across the street at the I-80 diner, the dust-crusted window had a new sign taped up—

"Whaleburgers sold here." If these fine establishments had been somewhat restrained in their approach to merchandising, Simon Locke had no such compunction. He was perched on a shaky ladder draping a piece of cloth over his dry goods sign. As he spread out the cloth, the tourists could read about the metamorphosis of the store from simple dry goods into THE WENDOVER WHALE CURIO SHOP AND MUSEUM. Museum!? The Whale itself was little more than an embryonic vessel and it had been immortalized with its own museum.

All this commerce was a simple tribute to good ol' American work ethics. Where else could integrity and recent history (Cap and Jeff abuse) be cast aside in pursuit of an honest buck? Only Salty with his unbiased canine vision could spot the incongruities of life in the 'new' Wendover. And since he had already declared that humans were not very high up on the evolutionary scale, none of them, even the smarter ones, were going to listen to a mutt pontificate on the lack of exhibited virtues.

✂ PREPARING TO COME ABOUT

No crack, no crevice in all of Western Utah was safe from the bright lights of the Whale phenomenon. Even within the dusty environs of the Beehive Potash Works, reporters had burrowed in search of a new angle on the ship-in-the-desert story. This particular batch of journalists had latched on to the 'behind every great kid was a great set of parents' slant. Ken Cutter was holding an impromptu news conference at his desk. It might be the fluorescent lighting or the potash haze in the air but Ken was looking different these days. A little more alive, a little less the authoritarian dad with a power trip to inflict.

An unctuous young woman reporter from the Mormon weekly out of Provo had slid in close to ask the really probing questions of the father of the boy of the hour. "Did you have any idea that your son might turn out this way," she asked in a breathless fashion that endeared her to no one.

Ken hesitated before answering, more for drama than to mull over the finer points of his potential response. "I'm not sure what you mean. He's always been an industrious child, building models and things."

The Mormon wench immediately jumped on this tidbit like it was manna from heaven. "Ship models?" The other reporters couldn't hold back the guffaws at this fancy bit of detective work. How could this woman have made the big leap from the Whale to the father saying models to her figuring out he means models of ships. This woman was definitely in the wrong business.

Proving them all wrong, Ken responded, "Mostly, but a few car models, too."

This frank admission opened the door to all sorts of deeply probing questioning on the part of the other members of the press. One photographer saw fit to preserve the moment and fired off his strobe. The atmosphere in the small office reached a new level of intensity. An old and possibly feeble reporter for the Las Vegas throwaway, having learned his lesson from the Provo lady, flung another question at Ken. "Why do you think he switched from models to the real thing?"

"I guess he decided he was too old to play with models. He is very mature for his age." This remark, said with a straight face and an absolutely clear conscience merited a black mark for Ken in God's big book of honesty.

Not wanting to be outdone by the heathen from Sin City, Miss Provo struck back. Firing off another salvo at Ken and phrasing it so that no one else could follow up. "That's obvious, Mr. Cutter. One last question. How does it feel to be the father of the father of the Wendover Whale, the grandfather of the Wendover Whale?"

Ken chose his words carefully. Clear conscience aside, he knew that what he said would have a major impact on his family's future. Why worry about the truth at this point? He gushed, "I have to honestly say that it is the proudest moment in my life."

No one in the assemblage had the presence of mind to gag or hurl a razzberry at Ken. Both the Las Vegas heathen and the Mormon reporter started to applaud and thought better of it. Just barely.

CREATURES OF THE DEEP AWAKENING

As one interview ended, another one was just beginning. Only this one was not so pleasant, perhaps because the truth was being spoken here.

Dave Caster was led into the luxuriously appointed offices of Cinino. Led was the appropriate verb since all his movements indicated a reluctance to enter this hallowed ground. The presence of two, large heavily muscled (in brain and body) guards draped in the finest polyester double knit kept Dave from doing anything but entering the room. As his feet squished down in the deep plush of the royal purple carpet, the beefy bodyguards stepped back out of the room and closed the door. Leaving Dave to face his (political) maker.

"Come in and sit your butt down, Caster," Cinino barked at him. A surprisingly strong voice coming from a small balding man. The chair he was sitting in and the desk in front of him were both over-sized making him seem that much smaller by comparison. Even the lone bodyguard standing behind Cinino's chair appeared overly big. The entire room reminded Dave of a scene in "Alice in Wonderland" where Alice drinks from the bottle and she shrinks down while everything else remains normal size. The thought of Cinino as Alice might normally be enough to make Dave laugh except not now, in this room, with this person. Cinino waved at a chair across the desk from himself. Dave quickly sat down.

"Thanks, Mr. Cinino. It is a pleasure to see you again." The deference he showed the little man was thicker than the sap from a maple tree and like the sap way too saccharine-sweet. Thinking it proper manners, he waited for Cinino to speak. Cinino stared back at Dave, expecting Dave to answer the question that was asked in their phone conversation. A brief stare war ensued. It would have gone on forever since Dave couldn't recall exactly the question he was asked over the phone but Cinino's impatience ended the war.

"Well, what did you find out," Cinino asked. And then to make sure this question wasn't too vague, "about the boat business."

Dave breathed an almost inaudible sigh of relief. There had been many times in the past when Cinino had asked him to snoop around into things not totally savory. This boat business thing he was right on top of. "Oh, well, I think we can safely assume that the drop-off in your casino is due, in large part, to everyone going to see the boat." Having completed his report, he relaxed against the back of the chair. A job well done.

Cinino exploded out of his chair in anger. Although this explosion might be difficult to discern since he was almost the same height standing as he was when he was sitting in his chair. "Safely assume? I've been sitting here for the last few days watching bumper to bumper cars going into Utah to see that boat. I didn't need a bumble brain to tell me that. I want to know what you are going to do about it." He dropped back down on the chair, hands flat on his desk, waiting to devour Dave's next statement.

Dave was frozen in his chair. He thought he had done his job, isolating the problem of lost casino attendance. It seemed to him that it was up to the casino owner to solve the problem not the mayor. He was wrong.

"Do I have to spell it out for you. We're starving over here, while our lousy neighbors on the Ute side are getting filthy rich from the tourists." He swiveled his chair toward the window. His bodyguard had to leap out of the way to avoid being knocked over. "Makes me sick just watching those cars go by. Used to be they couldn't wait to get out of Utah to spend their money here." He spun his chair back towards Dave. The bodyguard, obviously hired for his nimbleness, leapt out of the path of the chair back. "You're the mayor here. It is your responsibility to see that the residents of this town don't go down the john. Now you best get to work on that, or you'll find yourself looking for a new job."

The force of Cinino's words had pushed Dave rigid against the back of his chair. If he could have co-mingled his molecules with the Naughahyde molecules of the chair and melted away, he would have done so. Unfortunately, his state of agitation did nothing but excite his sweat glands. "Yes, Sir. I'll do my best. You know you can count on me, Mr. Cinino." Well said for a man who had no clue as to what to do next about a problem he didn't see as a problem. After all, his motel had more guests everyday.

"Right, Dave. Let me know when you get it worked out." Cinino sat back in his chair and waited for Dave to disappear. The inquisition was over and he had other people to abuse. He picked up some papers and pretended to read them.

Taking the hint, Dave got up, a little shaky, and walked to the door. He opened the door and over his shoulder said, "have a nice day, Mr. Cinino." He didn't look back or wait for a response. He was out the door and closed it quickly.

৩৮ MOMS - STILL WATERS RUNNING DEEP

A reporter who intentionally got lost on his way to Ken Cutter's interview by taking a detour through several of the bars on the Nevada side of the state line decided to earn his pay by finding the ugly side of the Whale story. And what better place to do that than with the mother of all mothers, the mother of the Whale (by default], Jeff's mom, Elise. His reportorial skills, sharpened by several stiff drinks, straight up, were ready to attack Elise. His pencil would show no mercy.

Elise, on the other hand, was ready to counter attack with a cup of Folger's instant coffee and a batch of home-made Nestle's toll house cookies. The atmosphere in the Cutter dining was absent the potash haze, replaced by the coziness and charm of the heartland's wombiness which effectively disarmed the reporter.

"Can I get you another cup of coffee, Mr. Sawyer?" Elise reached for the reporter's cup but he waved her hand away.

Sawyer struggled to get back the merciless reporter's edge brought on by the afternoon's barhopping. "No, thank you, Mrs. Cutter. I'll just ask you a few questions, if you don't mind? Then I'll leave. I know how busy you must be."

Elise laughed an honest-to-goodness, you don't know the truth of it, buddy, laugh. "Busy? I'm not busy. If it wasn't for you TV and newspaper people interviewing me, I'd just be watchin' my soaps. I'm a big General Hospital fan."

This was not the candor he was expecting. Maybe there was more to the story and he need only ask the right questions. Frankly, this Whale story was just a little too mushy for him. Nothing like an unusual twist to a piece to make it front page material. "Aren't you involved in helping your son build the Wendover Whale?"

"No, not really. Not at all, come to think about it. Yeah, I've opened a few letters and answered the phone a lot, but that really isn't building the boat, is it?" She said this with a little shrug that said as much as the words. "Never gave it much thought before you asked the question."

Sawyer was beginning to like this woman a lot. "No, I guess it isn't. Would you like to be more involved? After all, the Whale is an important story for lots of people all over the world."

This wasn't exactly a revelation to Elise but she still hadn't been able to figure out what the big fuss was all about. When you think about it, aside from making her son happy, the whole thing was kind of silly. "No, I don't think so. Jeff started the thing on his own, well, with Cap, too. And I really shouldn't be trying to share the spotlight with him now that he's gotten some recognition. Fact is, my husband and I were pretty much dead set against it when Jeff first started."

"That so," Sawyer asked. Even though he missed Ken's proud father comments, the general feeling was that everyone in town fully supported Jeff's silly idea of building a boat. And no one, until now, was willing to admit that they numbered among the doubting Thomases in the beginning.

"The gospel truth, Mr. Sawyer. If Jeff hadn't stood firm to his dad he never would have hammered one nail on the boat." She seemed ready to expand on her husband's intractability on matters seaworthy when the phone rang in the kitchen. She excused herself and went through the swinging door into the kitchen. Sawyer waited for the door to swing closed and then snuck another cookie off the tray on the table. No sense taking notes because there was no story, or at least no story that anyone would want to read. Alas, poor Sawyer, for he did not read nor did he write for any of the magazines that Elise read. Knowing that Elise had survived the media blitz using the tried and true rules of engagement as dictated by Family Circle would have doubled the circulation of every homemaker-oriented periodical in the country. Yeah, right.

ꙩꙨ A CHANGE IN COMMAND?

Salty had commandeered a spot many yards from the milling crowd that still surrounded the Whale as the sun settled down for its short summer nap. His view, unobstructed by the careless and dog-crunching feet of the hayseed tourists, of the Whale was breath-taking. The mostly-completed ribbing of the ship silhouetted by the sun into an almost religious tableau—each rib held crucifitory potential for any ship-building carpenter who might run afoul of the current community 'leader', a.k.a. Cap. Neither the pretty scene nor the possibility of a new date for Easter in Utah was of interest to Salty. With all the commotion, and the influx of humans to the area, he was only too happy to sit back and pontificate on the greater virtues of dogdom when compared to the lemming-like behavior of those humans who gravitated to the shipyard. Salty's connection to Cap and Jeff was strained. They were too busy managing a cultural phenomenon to fool around with a dog who couldn't even hoist a hammer to help. It was only around meal time that Salty dashed through the throng, barking obscenities at those who dared block his path to gustatory salvation—a rusty metal bowl with Kibble and warm water.

But, right now, Salty wasn't smelling any Kibble, nor was it the unhealthy garbage that the schlock merchants were peddling to the Whale crowd. It smelled like chicken and it smelled like it should be in his mouth not some human's who couldn't appreciate it. He scanned the scaffolding surrounding the Whale using his special dog vision to see what his nose told him was there. When his sight and smell locked in on the potential target, his feet told him it was time to move in for the kill.

The object of Salty's desire was in the hands of Salty's master. Cap was munching on a chicken leg as he directed some of the workers above him. He answered a question or two from others working on the interior of the ship and kept Jeff company as he munched on an apple. Each held a paper napkin courtesy of Elise Cutter. The chicken leg recipe was courtesy of the *Ladies Home Companion* article on light and easy summer picnic fare. The apple was courtesy of the Salt and Sand Market, at a considerably marked-up (post Whale boom) price. In between bites of the apple, Jeff surveyed the progress on the ship with an expression just short of ecstatic. "This is unbelievable. We are really making progress." He couldn't keep the excitement out of his voice. Not surprising since, at that age, excitement was a normal kid's general state of being. He ripped off another hunk of apple to demonstrate just how excited he was.

One of the workers yelled down to Cap asking a simple question which would normally elicit a simple yes or, at the most, a suggestion of a more appropriate placement. Instead, Cap angrily yelled back, "No, dammit. Git that brace higher, much higher." He squinted through the glare, looking for Brad, who as the first volunteer, had become the whipping boy for all of the eager-beaver Whale volunteer builders. Cap spotted a silhouette that might be Brad. He yelled, "Brad, git over here and help this poor fool. He's threatening to scuttle us even before we get this tub to water." The silhouette moved toward the object of Cap's anger and Cap returned his stare/glare to Jeff. "Progress you say, hah. If it were just you and me, Jeffey, we'd a been done a long time ago."

Jeff chose to hear the surface joke and not the subtext of Cap's obvious mis-truth. He laughed. And then said, "But we wouldn't have had as much fun. And met all these people."

Cap almost flung the chicken leg at Jeff as he made his point. "Fun? You call this fun? You're changin' on me Jeffey boy. In ways I'm not sure I like."

Jeff laughed again. He had gotten so used to the way Cap talks that he was never quite certain if Cap was joshing him or was dead serious. His best response was to laugh knowing that Cap would stomp off if Jeff had misread Cap. And reconciling with Cap was pretty easy. "Aw, come on, Cap. I'm the same as ever."

The conversation came to a halt as a vendor wove his way through the crowd toward Cap and Jeff, hawking his wares to all around him. He was not intentionally working his way toward them since he had no idea who they were. The vendor had left his bootleg audio cassette business, mostly Mormon Tabernacle Choir ripoffs, in Salt Lake City to try and make a few extra bucks working the Whale crowd. He carried a crudely manufactured wood model of a sailing ship in each hand, swinging them back and forth to create a breeze that filled the bedsheet sails hanging from the popsicle stick masts. He repeated the pitch over and over as his voice carried over the muted conversations of the crowd. "Get your exact replicas of the famous Wendover Whale right here. Fully assembled and yours for only five dollars." He sailed one of his models through the air with a little too much gusto and the popsicle stick broke in half. The vendor ignored the damage and continued his pitch, "Here's your chance to get a perfect copy of the Whale. Hurry they are going fast. Step right up." He brushed past Jeff, oblivious to the hate daggers being shot at him by Cap.

Cap waited until the vendor began his pitch again, exposing his back to Cap, and then Cap flung his chicken bone at the vendor's head. The bone flew, end over end, and struck the vendor square between the shoulder blades. It dropped to the ground and milliseconds later Salty had it secured between his canines. The vendor whirled around to find his attacker but a family on holiday from Bellevue, Washington stepped between him and Cap. Finding no one to retaliate on, he returned to pitching his wares.

Cap was beyond disgusted, "Look at that. That cheap bastard was selling models of the Whale and I don't even know what the damn thing's going to look like when we're done. How's he know what it will look like?

"Relax, Cap." To Jeff, the vendor was just one more person pursuing his vision. As long as it didn't interfere with his own, Jeff didn't mind the crass commercialization.

"How can I relax? He's got the nerve to sell that shit for five bucks a shot. This whole thing is going to hell in a handbasket." He spat on the ground, missing Salty by inches. Salty didn't notice, his entire focus was on gnawing the chicken leg,

"I don't know what you just said but you should be happy if that man sells a lot of those models. We're getting fifty cents for each one he sells. Phil Kurtzman set the deal up for us. And he says that he has made a deal with everyone selling stuff around the boat."

Cap moved from being completely irked to totally exasperated. A shift unnoticeable to anyone but himself. He felt like he had now become a minor player in a very big drama and the only way to stay in the play was to grab on and hold tight. He said to Jeff, "I don't want to hear no more. Let's git back to work before I upchuck my dinner." He turned and started to climb the scaffold. The sooner he could lay his hands on the solid wood of the boat the sooner he was going to forget about the rest of the crap that was going on. "If you're smart, Jeffey, you'll keep your mind on the buildin' and ignore this bull."

"Anything you say, Cap. The boat and nothing else."

⚒ A "CALM" BEFORE THE STORM

Time passed. A fact of life everywhere in the world. It just passed a little more slowly in Wendover. If you put together enough hot, sunny, cloudless and slow-moving days, or slow-moving weeks, you could build a boat. Even a scaled down version of a clipper ship. And that was what had happened in Wendover. The Whale had progressed, the ribbing was complete and half the cross braces were in place.

And on this Sunday morning, with the sun still hanging low in the eastern sky, there was a stillness in the shipyard. Few tourists had left the comfort of their too-soft beds at over-priced motels to gather at the shipyard. Cap, Jeff, Brad, Nancy and a few of the other shipbuilders were dangling off the scaffolding trying to align and then finish the bracing. Progress was slow with most of the builders allowing their visions and work ethic to be replaced by religious imperatives or a few more hours of REM state sleep. As if to guiltify the remaining workers, the bells of the nearby churches pealed their way across the shipyard.

For Jeff, the bells had no significance. He had worshipped too long at the altar of the ship god, praying for the continued support of Cap and the other workers. Sundays spent with his mother and father in church were just a vague P.W. (pre Whale) memory. If he wasn't too tired to think about it, he'd have to say that a lot of his activities P.W. were now vague and hard to recall. The church bells continued to ring, almost in syncopation with his hammer as he pounded nails into the bracing.

As Jeff continued to strike the nail heads, with about a 90% success factor, Elise and Ken made their way across the shipyard toward the Whale. They were dressed in their Sunday finest and it wasn't too hard to guess that the shipyard was only a way station on their way to the ultimate destination; Wendover's Mormon church. The shipyard, bereft of most of the tourists, felt like the circus the day following its last grand performance. The vibrant life of the area had been sucked out even though the big top remained. Jeff remained oblivious to the progress of his parents until they were literally standing behind and below him.

To his mother's eyes, Jeff appeared small, dwarfed by the ever-increasing size of the Whale. To a mother's heart, Jeff too young to be involved in such a bit enterprise.

Elise spoke quietly, almost as if she was already in church. "Jeff? Son." Her voice contained a new amount of respect for her son not just that created by his physical position above her.

Jeff turned at the sound of her voice. The sight of his parents, dressed for church, triggered an instantaneous guilt response. And he did his best to sound penitent. "Hi, guys. Sorry I didn't make it home last night, but we had a lot of work to do. When we got done we just crashed next to the Whale. Right here. I hope you didn't worry too much."

Elise smiled the smile intended to warm every child's heart. "We knew you were safe."

"Sure was. I have all my friends right here." Feeling that he had confessed to his sin of not returning home and having been absolved by his mother, Jeff returned to his nailing project. His father and mother exchanged a surprised glance. They had discussed how they would approach Jeff this morning but neither had expected to be ignored.

Ken started to say something but Elise, anticipating a heavy-handed imperative, stepped in front of Ken. "Your father and I thought you might like to come with us to church. We haven't spent much time together lately and..."

Jeff cut his mother off with a strong and loud, "No." In the stillness of the morning, this single syllable word resounded through the shipyard. What little hammering and sawing that was being done by the others came to a quick stop. "I can't leave the Whale. If there is work to be done, I have to be here."

Ken responded quickly, too quickly, "We're not asking you to give the boat up, just come with us for a few hours. We aren't going to force you, Son, it's your decision." This was difficult for him to say because he still felt like he should be making all the decisions for the family, including when and where Jeff will spend his time.

Having heard that it was his decision to make, Jeff began to tell his parents that he was not going to come with them, "If it's really my decision..."

"Then he'll be goin' with you," Cap finished the statement for him. He climbed down from the scaffolding slowly. Extended periods of work had made him feel every bit his age and then some. He stopped next to Jeff and looked him up and down. "This would be a perfect time to be visitin' a holy place, specially with your folks."

"What about the Whale? You need me here." This was almost a plea from Jeff. Separation anxiety was running high on the tide this morning.

Cap wasn't really trying to make points with Jeff's parents but he was looking for help in trying to give Jeff a different perspective on the Whale. "We kin' spare you for a few hours. We got enough crew coming soon to cover for you. But we could use some extra help from our Friend up there." He nodded in the general direction of the sky. This might have been meant as an acknowledgment of an all-powerful God above them or just a studied glance at the small transparent clipper shipper hovering above his head. This ship was making more and more appearances in the skies above Wendover. Either way it made for a poignant moment, and Cap was kind of proud of himself.

Jeff brought him plummeting back to terra firma by saying, "Will you come with us?" Cap couldn't remember the last time he had been in a place of worship unless you counted the saloon in Nevada known as the 'Holy Grail of Whiskey.' And he had been to the altar there countless times to take the sacraments. Neat or on the rocks, it didn't matter to him.

"Me?" Cap coughed out. "Nah, I think one of us prayin' is enough. No sense in overdoing it." He took the hammer out of Jeff's hand. Jeff let go of it reluctantly. "I'll keep that safe until you get back."

"You better," he said dejectedly. He climbed down from the scaffold, looking very much the little boy he was before the visions began. His father put his hand out to help him down but Jeff pointedly ignored it. When he reached the ground his mother put her arm over his shoulders. This gesture he did not shrug off.

Cap and the rest of the crew watched as the threesome made their way out of the shipyard. Cap said a silent prayer to whomever would listen that he needed some help with Jeff. Not expecting an immediate response, he turned to face the rest of the crew. "Okay boys and girls, recess is over. Now let's get back to it."

As if commanded by the devil himself, the crew started hammering and sawing immediately, and with gusto.

⳯ HOLY INTERVENTION

The L.D.S. temple in Wendover (Utah of course) was a rather plain affair bearing little resemblance to its domineering father in Salt Lake City or its glamorous first cousins in Los Angeles and a dozen other cities in the world. The angel, Moroni, needing a new coat of high-gloss gold paint, beckoned all to its large wooden doors, and all entered willingly with the exception of one 13-year-old ceteceaous visionary. As his parents guided him down the aisle to the pew they had sat in since long before his arrival, Jeff glanced around the interior. He felt he was entering familiar but ancient territory. The faces and the places he could readily recognize but he had forgotten the reason for their being in this space at this time.

Elise gently pushed him down onto the polished wood of the pew and then sat down beside him. Although Jeff was not conscious of the rest of the congregation staring at him, his father felt every eyeball. Ken wasn't sure whether he was proud of the attention or embarrassed that it was directed not at him but at his son. The current priest of the congregation, the proud owner-operator of the Laundromat, cleared his throat to get everyone's attention. He was not unaware of Jeff's presence in the chapel, the buzz had gotten back to him moments after Jeff entered the doors. Being more a man of the clothes than of the cloth, this priest was going to stick to his pre-written sermon right down to the dotted "I" and crossed "T" even if it focused on the Words of Wisdom pertaining to abstinence from all alcoholic beverages and not on the 'visions' of the founder of Latter-day Saints, Joseph Smith.

Even if the priest had chosen to revel in the image of Joseph Smith, at fifteen, wandering down to a stand of trees on his parents' farm and conjuring up an image of God and Jesus speaking directly to him, Jeff would have missed the connection. Once seated, he had turned his mind inward toward more pressing secular issues. Namely, completion of the whale. Occasionally words drifted into his consciousness from the front of the room but ever so gradually they became a distant murmuring, like the sound of a calm ocean on a breathless day. When Jeff became aware of this sound simile, he smiled, and everyone, even the doddering matrons in the front in the temple turned into a half-human, half-whale. The starched priest became a barnacled humpback whale, breaching water everytime he pounded on the pulpit. The mini-choir, dressed all in white, turned into a pod of beluga whales, the white of their skin blending nicely with their choral robes. Jeff started to laugh aloud at this spectacle but an elbow nudge to the ribs by his mom chastened him. For the rest of the service he would keep his mind on the problems that besot other people, the Satan in the bottle. And for a moment, a very brief moment, he worried about Cap and his place in the hereafter. As quickly as it came into his mind, it left because he knew that Cap was a good and true friend who would end up in heaven after reaping great rewards on Earth. Such are the mental machinations of a boy who dreamed of ships and sails and not of deceit and the devil.

ᲛᲚ A SHIPBOARD ROMANCE

It was often said in places of unremitting sunshine or constant rain that the days have a tendency of running into each other. Long time denizens of these uni-seasonal spots say that life is just one long day since nothing ever changes. This adage might have held true for Wendover prior to the birth of the Whale but since its arrival full-borne from the noggin of Jeff Cutter, Wendover was running on a new calendar and a new clock. Even if the day dawned bright and sunny, and noon provided the same old 90 plus temperature, something was different—the whale was just a little bit closer to being a real live, honest-to-goodness, batten-down-the-hatches SHIP! The skeleton of a beached and dying animal was no more. In its place was an awkward looking hull with most of its external planking in place. Scaffolding completely surrounded it, giving it the appearance of a recently captured but still dangerous animal confined by, and watched over by, an army of zoo attendants. And these zoo attendants were frenzied in their activities as if this new animal exhibit had been hyped and promised to the public and the zookeeper was handing out bonuses if they could get the beast to perform today. The hyped public which surrounded the Whale did not seem put off by the fact that the exhibit wasn't finished, they were only disappointed that the scaffolding prevented them from touching the boat. Disappointed by the lack of contact, the way the moat separating the gorilla compound from the humans at the zoo was just wide enough to keep sapien hands from touching simian hands. No one ever complained about it but they go home wishing their arms were just a few inches longer.

Phil Kurtzman, wishing his head was a little larger so his ego could expand even further, had captured one of the workers on the scaffolding. He held out a microphone as if it were a banana snack. The worker, a child of the television generation, had never seen a microphone that wasn't connected to TV film crew. He looked at the mike and then beyond it, unsure why there was only one man in front of him and that man wasn't holding a camera. Phil noticed the young man's anxiety but ignored it. He asked, "What's it like to work on the Wendover Whale?" Not exactly the depthy questions of an Edward R. Murrow or a Walter Cronkite. Phil was not standing on the shoulders of the great investigative journalists who had gone before him, rather he was laying the foundation for the great ones to come, like Geraldo Rivera and Oprah Winfrey.

Since his interviewee was only eighteen and yet to sip too deeply from the well of life's knowledge, Phil's question was perfectly appropriate. The young man said, "I don't know, pretty good, I guess. Hey, am I going to be on TV? Where's the camera?"

Phil winced. His Achilles' heel had always been that he was jealous of those TV pretty boys who got all the glory while he had to scrounge around in the backwaters of America. He took little comfort from the fact that the television crews had all come to do stories about his creation, not His Creation. Maybe if he put together a promo reel of gut-wrenching, tear-stained stories 'from the Whale' he'd have a shot at a network job. With that in mind, he pursued his quarry with a vengeance. "Sorry, no TV. Maybe you'll get your name in the newspaper."

The worker broke out his best Pepsodent smile. Although he didn't read newspapers, he knew his folks wouldn't come down so hard on him if they saw his name in a newspaper story. "That's okay, too. Go ahead and ask me some questions."

"All right, that's the spirit. You aren't getting paid for working, are you?"

"Nope, I'm doing it for the good vibes." He wasn't sure whether to explain further. He couldn't quite figure if Phil was part of the establishment. You know, the kind of dude who buys an ounce of pot, rolls it all up on a cigarette roller and then doesn't smoke it for months at a time. He just keeps the joints around for show. The young man really wanted his name in the article so he didn't explain the marijuana analogy to Phil. No use antagonizing the man.

Phil thought that the worker had used up his entire vocabulary so he figured the multiple choice of questions approach might work better. "So how come you're doing this, I mean, what do you get out of working on someone else's boat? There can't be much glory or satisfaction in that?"

The young man spent a little time thinking about the questions, then he dropped to his knees so he could look square in Phil's sunglassed eyes. "It's not for the glory, man. I'm not sure why I'm doing it, you know? It just makes me feel good to be helping out. Comprende, amigo?" He used up all of the 10th grade Spanish he could recall.

Phil, no jerk when it came to ditching foreign language classes in high school, replied, "Si, amigo. Do you think that's true for other people working on the boat?"

Before he could answer, Nancy dropped down from a higher level of scaffold to confront Phil. The little bit of exertion brought a nice touch of red to her cheeks or maybe she was just pissed off at this cocky reporter. "Why don't you give it a rest. You're keeping this man from his work." She shot a righteous, get-your-butt-in-gear glance at the worker and he had no trouble translating that into action. He grabbed his tools and headed for higher ground. Nancy re-focused on Phil.

Phil looked amused but inside he was ticked off at this bitch who had decided who it was appropriate for him to interview. He didn't know why but there was something about Nancy's self confidence he didn't like. "Really? I guess you don't think it's worthwhile to get a little publicity for the Whale?"

Nancy had the same level of dislike for Phil, although they had never said more than a hello or good morning since Nancy started working on the Whale. Never one to pull any punches, she answered his question without any guile, "Since you asked me, no, I don't think so. This whole thing is getting out of hand. I'm surprised that you guys don't have anything better to do."

Phil's look of amusement disappeared and was replaced with a look just short of outright hostility. "I'd watch what you're saying about the media. If it weren't for GUYS like me, you wouldn't be working on the Whale. You wouldn't even know it existed." This was said with a great deal of pride and no small amount of arrogance.

Nancy only heard the arrogance and it reminded her of all the schoolyard bravado she had to endure while growing up. And she replied in the manner of all school kids not willing to back down. "Oh, really?"

"Really. If it weren't for me, you would probably be sitting on your sweet little ass on some beach, watching some boys try to impress you by flexing their overdeveloped muscles."

Phil had stepped over the schoolyard line, and she wasn't going to take it. With a firm hand to the midsection, she pushed Phil toward the edge of the scaffold. "Why don't you take that microphone and shove it up your sweet little ass!" She stalked off, unconcerned about the precarious position she was leaving Phil in. He struggled for his balance, catching a glimpse of the crowd below him. Finally, he grabbed hold of a galvanized pipe supporting the scaffold and breathed a sigh of relief. Secure that he wasn't about to swan dive, he looked for his assailant and saw that she was safely out of fighting distance. "Bitch," he yelled after her. But his heart wasn't in it. His massive ego, the only organ of love that he was aware of, had been pierced by Cupid's arrow.

☭⚥ THE COMMANDER IN CHIEF IS PIPED ONBOARD

Not all personal interaction around the Whale was of the romantic kind. Elise had found that more and more of her time was spent being secretary to an unfinished boat. Piles of letters, both opened and unopened, were stacked in every flat nook and cranny of the Cutter home.

While Elise was flexible enough to handle this disruption in her daily routine, after all, this mail was supporting her son's efforts, she was having trouble keeping the house as clean as her very high standards required. At the moment she was moving piles around in the kitchen looking for the breakfast dishes. Frustrated by her inability to find her husband's favorite coffee mug, she called a ten minute recess and retired to the small table in the corner of the kitchen. She pulled a chair out only to find that it, too, was covered with a pile of mail. In a gesture symbolic of her mood, she swept all of the letters onto the floor and flopped herself down on the chair.

Massaging her temples, she tried to imagine a time and place of peace and quiet. Her mind started to drift and she was lying on a beautiful palm fringed beach in the South Pacific. At her back was a tropical rainforest, alive with the bird calls and animal sounds of the last Tarzan movie she saw. Her toes wiggled luxuriously in the black sand beach as the clear, warm water washed up around her. Elvis Presley, from his Blue Hawaii days, wandered down the beach strumming his guitar. He was vibrantly alive right down to the Hawaiian shirt with the repeated image of the clipper ship and palm trees. He stopped by her side, slung the guitar over his shoulder and dropped into the sand next to her. He picked up her hand and started to stroke it. Elise was terribly excited, this was by far the best dream she had ever had. Elvis began singing "Love Me Tender" and Elise closed her eyes. As every muscle in her body unknotted and stretched out, Elvis stops in mid-verse. Elise murmured, "Don't stop, King. Please." But he was shaking his head and beginning to fade. "You've got to answer the phone, Babe. I'm outta' here." He disappeared in a puff of smoke taking with him the rain forest and the ocean, leaving Elise with a kitchen full of somebody else's mail and a phone ringing off the hook.

Fortunately the phone was a wall unit otherwise she never would have found it. Even with the image of the king of rock and roll quickly fading from her memory, she answered the phone professionally. "Wendover Whale central. I'm sorry but Jeff and Cap are in the shipyard and they have asked not be disturbed for phone interviews." She started to put the phone down, expecting that the caller would quickly launch into a story about why it was imperative that he or she speak to Cap or Jeff. Even Salty, the filthy dog of Cap's, had gotten several calls. But this call was different, there was silence on the other end. A first. Elise didn't know what to do. "Did you hear what I just said. No one is available to speak with you right now. I'm sorry."

A male voice on the other end of the line, trying to sound as official as he possibly could, ignored what he heard. He was working for a higher authority and didn't believe that this brush-off was intended for himself. "Is this the Jeff Cutter residence, in Wendover Utah?" The voice waited patiently knowing, having made these kinds of calls before, that the woman on the phone was now a little worried. He liked that. Working in politics, he had found small thrills in exercising power over the little people, the voting public.

And Elise was worried. She didn't like this person's tone, after all, she was the mother of the Whale. "Yes, it is."

If a tone of voice could sound like "Hail to the Chief" that was what the man's voice sounded like when he said, "Please hold for the White House. The President of the United States will be with you in a moment." There was a sharp click and Elise Cutter, mother of the Whale, was put on hold by the personal secretary of the President of the United States.

Elise wasn't buying it. She had heard enough wacky phone sales pitches in her life to recognize a poor attempt. She was almost certain. "Sure...the President." Before she could hang up, although she would have done it slowly because of the small gnawing doubt that the call was on the up and up, there was another click and she was reconnected.

A man with a deep Southern voice, sounding a great deal like Jimmy Carter, too much like Jimmy Carter to really be the President said, "Hello? Is this Jeff Cutter?"

The doubt stopped gnawing and Elise stopped believing. "No, this isn't. Like I told the other fella', Jeff is at the shipyard and isn't to be disturbed. Reporters have been bugging the hell out of him. So, if you'll excuse me, I'm hanging up now."

She started to take the phone away from her ear. The President, because he really was the President, shouted (in a Presidential fashion, of course], "Wait a peanut-pickin' minute. Don't you know who this is?"

Elise was firmly in control now, "Well, the other fellow said you were the President."

"It is not <u>were</u>, I <u>am</u> the President, Mrs. Cutter." He was striving to sound convincing since many people, even his close friends, didn't really believe that he was President. A nuclear physicist yes, but President, of the U S of A, no way.

"Sure, just like the reporter who came last week and said he was the Governor." She wasn't trying very hard to hide her skepticism. "You and everyone else is just trying to get an interview with my son. Phil Kurtzman told me this would happen." She had decided that the sooner she got off the line the sooner she could get back to being loved tenderly by Elvis on the sand. In this day and age, that would certainly be worth hanging up on the President, even if he was the President.

Trying to sound supreme-commander confident, the President asked, "Mrs. Cutter, can I call you Elise? What would it take to convince you that I really am the President?"

An image of Elvis unbuttoning his shirt leapt into her mind. She tried hard to shake it out and the image was replaced with a clearer picture of Jimmy Carter unbuttoning his Hawaiian shirt—a striking combination of tropical fish and flying peanuts. She tried even harder to shake this out of her mind. "I don't know."

"If you gave me a couple minutes, I could tell you how much your family paid in income taxes last year. Or maybe how much you spent on toll calls to your sister last month?"

It dawned on Elise that bad Hawaiian shirt or not, she was talking with the President of the United States. This made her more than a little nervous. "That's not necessary. I'll take your word for it."

"Thank you, Elise. Now if you'll convey to your son and the Captain, my hope that the construction of the Whale is a speedy and successful one. I think I express the feelings of the whole country when I say that."

Elise relaxed. The Prez was just another fan, albeit an important one, of the Whale. In her best motherly voice she replied, "Thank you, Jimmy, I mean, Mr. President. That's very nice of you."

"And you tell your son to stop on by the White House next time he's in Washington. Amy's real eager to meet him." He chuckled at his own wry sense of humor.

"I'll do that, Mr. President."

The President wrapped it up, "Fine. Nice talking to you, Elise."

Elise was feeling pretty good now. She might have missed with Elvis but she had a new buddy in the President. "Nice talking to you, Sir." She hung up the phone, not altogether 100% positive that she was just speaking to the President. But close enough to be thrilled that the next garden club meeting was just a week away.

ஐ STORM CLOUDS

Salty had tired of the humans' folly. The building of the boat had seemed an overwhelming challenge to his master and the boy but with the addition of all these other bipeds, the strange wooden structure had become nothing more than a large source of shade in an otherwise very hot spot. As he made his way through the onlookers, he alternately cursed and praised their presence. With their focus lifted upwardly toward the Whale they were oblivious to smaller creatures cruising underfoot. Salty's paws had taken the brunt of their selective focus and he cursed aloud at their unkindness. A small, fat boy next to him tried to swallow an enormous bit of his Whale Dog (a reference to its size and not its meat content) and only succeeded in pushing the frankfurter out of its bun resting spot onto the ground next to Salty. Without hesitating a moment and certainly without remorse, Salty swallowed the hot dog in a flash. While the name of this food was odious to him, the subtle blending of nitrates, nitrites and assorted pork parts was like manna from heaven to Salty. As he raced away from the crying boy and potential action on the part of the boy's father, Salty reconsidered the notion that the Whale was not valuable, after all, he had never eaten as well before the arrival of the Whale and its fans.

Although there was a substantial difference in brain power between Salty and Dave Caster, Dave was thinking pretty much the same thing. His motel business was doing well, thanks to the Whale, and his civic pride covered a larger physical area than Cinino's. Which meant that he was proud of Wendover and its Whale even if the Wendover in question was in Utah. But Cinino's business was his business and if Cinino wanted him to talk to the boat builders, so be it.

This was Dave's first chance to really study the Whale. He was no architect, nor was he an engineer but he could detect a certain 'homemade' quality to it. Like the sign crafted by 8-year-olds to sell lemonade on a hot day. Not stylish nor slick but it got the job done. He watched as Cap held an animated discussion with several crew members on the appropriate placement and securing technique for the outside planking. The crew members listened intently and Dave had no trouble seeing who was in charge of this operation. Even without knowing Cap, seeing Cap in action had given Dave a certain level of respect for the old man. Dave had always harbored a secret desire to be a leader among men, to be strong enough to order and not to be second-guessed. He had hoped that the conferring of the title of mayor would magically give him that strength but it had only given him more people to be responsible to.

As the meeting between Cap and the crew broke up, Dave saw his opportunity. Before Cap could climb the scaffolding, Dave tapped him on the shoulder. "Excuse me."

Cap was too busy to even turn and acknowledge Dave's presence. His eyes remained on the Whale even as he replied to Dave, "Not now. I am very busy."

Dave was insistent. He had been given an order and if he couldn't be a good leader then he was going to be a damn good soldier. "It's kina' important, otherwise I wouldn't be bothering you."

This plea at least got Cap to turn around. He eyeballed Dave up and down but he couldn't place him. He didn't look like a tourist and he didn't look like a potential crew member which meant he was a Wendoverian but Cap still couldn't place him. Allowing that he, Cap, was not the most sociable resident of Wendover, it was no surprise that he didn't know the mayor. "Do I know you?"

"I don't think so, Mr. Cap, Cap." Dave stumbled for the right amount of respect. He opted for the more friendly approach. "I'm Dave Caster, mayor of Wendover...the Nevada side." He extended his hand and Cap reluctantly shook it. Up until now, no official personage of the town had even acknowledged his existence much less wanted to talk with him about something important. Dave continued, "Very nice to meet you."

Cap answered with both a distinct lack of enthusiasm and a strong note of distrust, "Same here." He turned to look at the construction as if his lack of direct supervision of the work for one minute would inevitably lead to the destruction of the boat. What he was really worried about was the idea that he was totally useless and the boat would be built with him or without him. The more time away from building, the more likely he would be found out. "I'm really busy right now, Mr. Caster. What is so important that you need to talk with me right now?"

Cap's gruff style of talking had a way of attracting attention. Several people standing near Cap and Dave had shifted their attention away from the boat toward them. Dave noticed the interested bystanders and it made him less sure of himself. "Couldn't we talk somewhere a little more private?"

Cap was definitely intrigued. First, the mayor wanted to talk about something important and now he wanted to talk about something important in private. Cap couldn't remember the last time someone wanted to have an important <u>and</u> private conversation with him. He was more than a little pleased but he wanted this drama played out in front of an audience. "Right here's fine, Mister."

"If you say so, Cap." He took a moment to compose himself, and then continued; "I've come on behalf of some interests on the Nevada side, who want to know if you'd be willing to move the Whale, your ship here, a little closer to the state line? In that way, both towns could benefit from its being built."

Cap could not believe his ears. First an important conversation, then an important, private conversation and now a formal request for Cap's help. This was all too much to believe, In fact, Cap didn't believe it. "What did you just say, in plain English?"

"We want you to move the Whale a little closer to the other side of town, you know, 'bout a half mile that way." He pointed toward the state line.

Cap didn't let him get anymore specific. He had heard, or misheard, Dave's request as more of a demand. And Cap didn't take kindly to anyone demanding anything from him. He verbally jumped all over Dave. "That's what I thought you said. Let me tell you something." He stepped in closer to Dave. Dave stepped back in self-defense. "I'm not building this god-damned boat for the good people of Wendover, and I mean both towns." He tried to make it more private by stepping in closer and lowering his voice. "I don't know who put you up to this, but you can go back and tell them that the Whale will remain here til she's ready to sail, and that the next time she sets her belly down, it'll be in water, not in some shit-ass place closer to the good-for-nothing state line."

Dave was not good at defusing emotional situations. Like a bulldog, he plunges straight ahead, ignoring the brick wall dead-ahead. "I think you should reconsider," a trait that Cap might have related to under different circumstances. "Powerful people in both towns..."

Cap didn't let him finish. Statements like Dave's only add fuel to the emotional fire. "Reconsider, shit. I hope both these towns rot. Now get the hell outta' here before I stop being friendly."

Dave started to speak again, fearing Cinino's reaction more than Cap's but Cap balled up both his fists and assumed the classic fighting stance. Dave recognized the hopeless situation and turned tail. He disappeared into the crowd without a backward glance. Leaving Cap to duke it out with an invisible opponent.

Cap held this position until the snap of splitting wood returned his attention to the Whale. The crew members he had just spoken to had started planking the hull of the Whale. The first board placed for securing snapped into two pieces as the crew screwed it in place. It was an accident pure and simple, one that happened through no fault or incompetentcy of the crew. However, the short fuse attached to Cap, ignited by his conversation with Dave Caster, now hit the powder keg inside Cap. In a loud voice, loud enough to carry throughout the shipyard, Cap yelled, "You stupid idiots. I told you to be careful with that wood. Now you gone and ruined it."

Everyone was embarrassed into silence, both crew and onlookers alike. Anyone who had spent time around Cap (but there weren't many in attendance this day) was aware of his mood swings and his basic intolerance of other humans. Nancy, although she hadn't spent much time around Cap, had pegged him as a grouchy old cuss from the moment he growled at her. Since she represented the only female on the crew, her first instinct was to try and placate Cap and defuse the bad scene. But in her role as the only Woman on the crew, she felt the need to tell him what an asshole he was and to shut his squawk box. Her female side won out, and she said, "Mellow out, Cap. It's only one piece of wood, for god's sake, we can replace it in no time."

Who knows whether the other approach would have worked better? What was clear was this one didn't. To silly-putty the metaphor, the short fuse that led to the explosion of tempers burned on and broke the straw that broke the camel's back. In other words, Cap bailed out. The last few minutes had given him an excuse and he took it. To Nancy, "Oh, really? Well, while you're at it, why don't you find a god-damned replacement for me. Cuz that's what you're going to have to do." And then, mocking her, he added, "It's only one man for god's sake, we can replace him in no time." He turned away from the boat, and his crew, to a man, were left with their jaws hanging wide open at this outburst. He whistled for Salty who reluctantly left the shade of the hull. "C'mon on Salty, let's get out of this place. He brusquely pushed through the crowd, and disappeared in the direction of the highway.

Nancy was the first to react after Cap's departure. She quickly moved to Jeff's side worried that Cap's departure would have the most impact on his partner. Jeff was standing stock still watching Cap storm down the highway. Nancy gently put her hand on Jeff's arm. "I'm sorry, Jeff. I didn't think it would work out this way. I was just trying to calm him down."

Brad joined her at Jeff's side and added, "Don't sweat it, Nancy. He just had to blow off a little steam. The pressure was getting to him. He'll be back, better than before." Like a tough piece of beef allowed to stew in its own juices.

Jeff took a moment to respond. He was trying hard to hold onto the image of his clipper ship under full sail but the image of Cap and Salty sailing down the highway kept trying to push the image under the waves. The ship struggled to stay above the water but it's continued existence depended entirely on Cap and Salty. Jeff blinked away the image and looked at Brad. "You sure?"

Brad's mistake was in trying to answer honestly. The situation, given years of parental experience, called for reassurance at the expense of truth but Brad had only been a child and never a parent. He hesitated to evaluate the situation. Finally, after too long a wait, he told Jeff, "Well, I don't see why he wouldn't."

The words were barely out of his mouth when Jeff started running through the crowd in the direction that Cap and Salty took. He yelled above the crowd, "Cap! Wait up, Cap." Like the angled prow of his beloved dream ship, Jeff cut through the waves of tourists. They parted for him, creating a path without be forced to. As quickly as they stepped aside for the young boy, they closed ranks behind him.

Nancy, still feeling responsible for this disaster, ordered the crew back to work. In tones, not dis-similar to Cap's, she strongly cautioned them about breaking any more of the hull planking. The crew responded immediately but Nancy couldn't help but feel the ship's future was in jeopardy with the departure of Cap and Jeff. The crowd around the ship appeared physically the same but the emotional connection seems strained as if the absence of the dreamer (Jeff) and the dream fulfiller (Cap) have turned the ship into just another tacky tourist attraction. There was nothing Nancy could do about that. Her commitment was to building the best boat she possibly could and let other's work on the ego and psyche repairs.

ℰ℘ THE CAPTAIN STEPS DOWN

It didn't take Jeff long to catch up with Cap and Salty. He found them working their way up the hill near Cap's shack. As he neared them he called out, hoping they would stop and wait for him. "Cap, please wait. I have to talk to you." Salty heard the pleading in Jeff's voice and stopped to wait for him but Cap kept on trucking up the hill. "C'mon, Cap, you have to stop. Remember we're partners." Cap slowed at the mention of the word 'partners', and Jeff caught up to him.

Cap turned as Jeff reached him. Both were out of breath. In between gasps for air, Cap said, "We were partners, not any more. That's it. Now leave me alone." He turned away from Jeff. But Jeff grabbed him and spun him around.

"I'm not going to let you go. I need you. We have to finish the Whale."

"You don't need me, Boy. You've got a whole crew workin' for you. Look down there." He pointed down the hill back toward the shipyard. From their vantage point on the hill, the Whale looked like a queen bee with hundreds of worker bees swarming around her. "You've got more than enough folks to finish her."

Jeff drew himself up to his full five-foot, two-inch height and spoke firmly, imagining that this was the way adults talked to each other, "Maybe so, but you and me are partners. You and me were the ones that thought up the Whale, so we're the ones that have to finish her. She's ours, Cap, just yours and mine."

Cap's face softened at these words. He had waited to hear that the relationship that was crucial was his and Jeff's, not Jeff and a completed Whale. If they needed a common goal to keep their relationship strong, so be it, as long as it really was just Cap and Jeff (and Salty]. Cap's ego had softened in the process of building the Whale and he needed to be sure. "What about them?" He nodded down toward the Whale. "What about Kurtzman and Nancy? And Phil? What about those guys?"

"They're helpin' us, Cap, but its ours. Will ya' please come back?"

The plea touched the right nerves but Cap was still teetering on the brink of decision-making. He was trying to think only about his relationship to the boy in front of him but the aggravations of the boat-building process kept rearing their ugly heads.

Jeff sensed that precarious situation in Cap's mind and begged, "I need you. I can't do this without you, Cap."

This was exactly what Cap needed to hear. Although he made a show of thinking about it, scratching the stubble on his chin, his mind was already made up. Suddenly he broke into a big fat grin, "Hell, yes, we're partners, aren't we? We gotta' do it together." Jeff jumped into his arms for a big hug.

Elated, Jeff shouted, "All right, let's do it!" The vaporous image of the clipper ship which had luffed its way up the hill trailing Jeff immediately brightened in its vibrancy to the point where Cap, the non-visionary, could have seen it sailing by if he had only looked up from Jeffey's beaming face.

✂ A PIRATE'S PLAN

While the partnership of Jeff and Cap was reaffirmed on the hill, down in the flats of Wendover, Nevada, the sinister association between Dave Caster and Mr. Cinino was having its rockier moments. Dave, while always nervous in the presence of Cinino, was even more fidgety because he knew that he had failed in his mission. Cinino gave Dave the voodoo stare treatment before he began his verbal beating. "That was a very poor first effort. You will most certainly have to come up with a better plan for your next meeting."

This comment caught Dave square in the chest. He had expected to take some heat for failing to talk with Cap about moving the boat but he figured Cinino would pick someone with a little more clout (not confusing clout with mass) to follow up, if he was going to pursue the boat. Dave hoped that he would be allowed to fail, get his tongue lashing and be allowed to quietly go back to his motel. No such luck. "My next meeting, Sir?"

Cinino had no pity for Dave, actually he had no pity for anyone. Actually he pitied everyone, they were all worthless creatures. But he needed Dave because he recognized that his usual heavy-handed approach to life would not work when it came to civic responsibility, clipper ships, little boys and old men. "Yes, fool, your next meeting with the coot and the kid. You don't think I'd give up on the Whale after just one little try, do you?"

Dave was struggling. He wanted to find an answer that would allow him to bow out gracefully without invoking Cinino's ire. "No, of course not, Mr. Cinino. But Cap, the old man, he was pretty stubborn about moving the boat. Besides, I don't think it is necessary to do anything about the Whale."

Cinino did his best to control his temper, a temper as short-fused as Cap's but with a lot more firepower to back it up. He had always liked Dave Caster because he didn't get a lot of guff from him. Just a 'hello sir, yes sir, when do you want it sir' attitude. But this reply sounded a lot like disrespect. Just the same, he needed to find out what Dave knew that he didn't know. "And why, pray tell, is that?" He leaned forward, appearing to be very interested in Dave's answer but really getting into a position to leap from his desk and wring Dave's neck if the answer didn't suit him.

Dave saw the superficial gesture and took it for honest interest. "Well, there seems to be enough tourists to go around. I mean my motel is almost full just from the overflow that can't get places on the Utah side." What he didn't say was, 'Wendover, Utah, normally without any attractions, is pretty short on hotel space.'

Cinino barely kept his butt on the chair but he was unsuccessful in keeping the anger and sarcasm out of his voice. "That so, Dave?

Tell me, did you happen to notice many cars parked outside when you came in?"

A simple enough question. Dave knitted his brow trying hard to visualize the parking lot when he arrived to give his report. "Let see, there is your limo, and a couple of your employees' cars." It slowly dawned on him that the question was rhetorical, Cinino already knew the answer to the question he asked. "Oh, I see what you mean. But I'm sure it'll pick up this evening." And to show that he was no meathead he decided to go for some humor. "Hey, when the sun goes down it'll probably be too cold to stand and watch 'em building the Whale." He smiled, waiting for at least a chuckle from Cinino. Or at least the beginning of a smile.

The thought of Dave staked out in the middle of the salt flats, the sun beating down on him and Cinino standing nearby holding a pitcher of ice water brought a smile to Cinino's face. When this hauntingly beautiful vision faded from Cinino's mind, he stood up. "No, Dave, it won't pick up tonight. And not because its going to be cool. No, its for the simple reason that men and women who bring their families into town to see the Whale, rarely slip out at night to gamble away their hard-earned dollars. Do you get that, Dave?"

The warm feeling Dave got from seeing a smile on his boss' face vanished as quickly as the smile did. "Yes, Sir."

Cinino sat back down. His emotions firmly in check, he got back to the important issue. "Good, now you understand why it is necessary for me and you to get possession of the Whale."

Dave jumped to an obvious but incorrect conclusion based on who he was dealing with. "You mean steal it? It's thirty five feet long. They'll know it's missing right away!" The thought of this heinous crime—grand theft/whale—with ten years behind bars eating nothing but krill was enough to unsettle him.

"Dave," Cinino said soothingly, adopting the tone of a kind father dandling his son on his knee before telling him a bed time story. "Dave, you will soon find out there are many ways to get something without stealing it, in the strictest sense of the word." He smiled a smile that could sink a thousand ships, or Whales for that matter. Helen of Troy and Cinino of Wendover—great names in history, second edition.

♌ THE WHALE GOES POLITICAL

It was inevitable that a promotion/cultural phenomenon the size of the Whale would soon garner the attention of Hollywood. Not Hollywood the town, since the town had enough urban problems to keep busy it for decades, rather Hollywood the entertainment machine. The instrument of celebrity that was always lusting after more people and events to consume, sensationalize and spit out as yesterday's news. Phil Kurtzman didn't see it that way. He saw the Whale as an enormous fish in a very small pond. Hollywood, through its minion, television, could make the Whale a whale in the largest ocean on Earth—even if it was for only a few weeks, maybe even days, depending on which fish was next hooked by daytime talk shows.

And that was why there was a limousine parked at the outside edge of the shipyard, well away from the Whale and the WWhalists (a term Phil had recently coined to describe the people interested in the construction of the ship]. A honest-to-goodness chauffeur held the door open into the back of the limo. A sight previously unseen within the confines of Wendover, either Utah or Nevada. Due to recent slack times in the casino business, Cinino had to go without a chauffeur. This chauffeur, with the real name of Neil, but a name tag reading Niles (a case of mis-spelling creating increased respectability), was dying of the heat. Standing at attention under the shady trees of Salt Lake City was one thing, but doing it under the brutal desert sun of Wendover while waiting for some pipsqueak kid was a whole 'nother thing.

Jeff was the problem. Dressed in a wool suit, two years too small, he stubbornly refused to get into the back of the limousine. No matter how much coaxing Phil used on Jeff, he would not budge. Neil/Niles was starting to waver, without the support of the car door he would soon pitch forward, a victim of heat prostration. Jeff had no sympathy for his plight. Talking to Phil, "I'm not going without Cap. You can't make me."

Phil had lost his cool (but nothing compared to Neil/Niles) but this foray away from Wendover was critical to his plans for the Whale. "He's coming, Jeff. Your mom was just going over his outfit to make sure he looked good. We want you, both of you, to make a good impression on the boob tube. The better you come off, the more money will come in for the Whale."

Jeff threw a zinger look at Phil. "Is that all you're interested in? The money?"

The question caught Phil by surprise. He expected that kind of question from Cap or Nancy but not from the kid. "It's not the money, Jeff. Its what the money can do for you and Cap and the Whale. Without the money, your dream boat won't get finished."

Before Jeff could ask what Phil was getting out of it and if all the money was going to the ship building, Cap and Elise came into the clearing. Cap was literally being chased by Elise who was trying to pull a brush through Cap's hair. Cap kept pushing Elise's hand away but the damage had already been done—Cap was almost unrecognizable—his face was freshly shaved, he was dressed in a semi-respectable corduroy jacket and almost matching pants and a freshly laundered yacht club cap. "Git your hands off me, woman." He caught sight of Jeff, the limo and finally the beet-red chauffeur. "I don't even want to be on television."

Elise took one more stab at getting the brush through his hair. "Stop fussing. I have to finish making you beautiful."

Cap growled, "impossible," at exactly the same time as Phil and Jeff did under their breath. He reached Phil. "Kurtzman, I don't know how you talked me into this mess."

Phil laughed, "It wasn't easy." He sized up both Cap and Jeff and, surprisingly, he liked what he saw. They were neither too slick nor too cornpone to be believed. In fact, he believed that the American TV watching public, which was as good as saying all of America, was going to take the two of them to their bosom, like a mama to a nursing baby. "Okay, you'll pass. Now get in the car."

Jeff and Cap started to climb in the back much to the sheer joy of Neil/Niles. Anymore time in the sun and he felt certain he was going to explode or melt. He swore silently to himself that he was going to quit the limo trade and move somewhere far away, a land devoid of motor vehicles and starched uniforms.

Phil poked his head into the interior of the limo for some final words of advice. "Remember, when they ask you about the Whale sound humble and tell them you aren't sure you can finish building her. They'll ask you why, and try to casually, very casually, mention that you are running short of funds."

Cap was uncomfortable with the 'business' of building the ship, the subject lacked the purity of Jeff's dream, so he tried to cut Phil's spiel short. "Sure, sure, you already told us all this stuff. Hey, where's Salty?"

Phil's head snapped around, immediately looking for signs of the dog. "You can't take that ugly mutt on television."

Cap began to get out of the limo. Neil/Niles let out an audible groan. He saw himself standing in the sun while his feet melted into the sand. It was not a pretty picture, no-sir-ee. Phil saw that Cap was determined not to go if he couldn't take Salty along. He put his hand over the top of the door, blocking Cap's exit. "Okay, okay, I'll make a deal with you. You can take the dog with you but he has to stay in the car while you're in the studio."

"No deal." He ducked underneath Phil's arm and out of the car.

Jeff got into it by adding, "Come on, Cap. It's better than not having Salty with us at all."

"Take it. It's my final offer." Phil pushed Cap back into the seat and Neil/Niles quickly slammed the door and threw his weight against it. No way was anyone getting out of this car until they were back in the city. Cap rolled down the window and whistled for Salty. Neil/Niles went around to the driver's side and got in. He started the car and began to pull away. Salty came racing out of the crowd where he had been scrounging a last-minute snack for the ride and launched himself at the open window. Cap caught him before he smash into the door panel and hauled the little dog into the car.

Phil remembered something at the last minute and jogged alongside the limo. Neil/Niles refused to stop the vehicle for fear that he would be forced out into the sun again. "One more thing. Who did you leave in charge of the Whale?"

"I didn't think we'd be gone that long. Don't worry about it, Kurtzman."

Neil/Niles tapped the gas pedal and the limo picked up speed. He figured it was payback time since Phil was the man who hired the limo. Phil struggled to keep pace, shooting a glare at Neil/Niles. "You should have someone, just in case. You know, emergencies."

Cap enjoyed seeing Phil huff and puff alongside the car. "Okay, Kurtzman, you can be in charge. Just don't let it go to your head." Which was like warning a heroin addict to go cold turkey for the fun of it. The limo pulled away from Phil as Cap said, "I hope the crew decides to mutiny."

Phil staggered to a stop on the sandy shoulder of the highway. He was grinning between gasps for air. "Mutiny, never! I am the captain now."

∾ CAP "DISCOVERS" AN OCEAN

The drive in to Salt Lake City was a strained one for Jeff and Cap. Given that they didn't have the Whale to plan for or work on, they really didn't have a lot in common. Much to the dismay of Neil/Niles, Cap kept the window rolled down so that Salty could keep his nose in the breeze. Salty was ecstatic as the scents and smells of the ages blew under his nostrils.

Although it was common knowledge in the animal kingdom that dogs have a highly developed olfactory sense, no one, except dogs of course, know why. Those intelligent enough to make guesses, namely man, have guessed, wrongly, that the canine sense of smell was used to sniff out other dogs. But Salty had more on his nose, and mind, than transcontinental travels and pissing spots of other dogs. He was smelling the ages. In a dog's universe, all things are lost through time except the essential scent of a creature. As time progressed and dogs evolved, those with the ability to scent or sense what creatures and events had come before them ended up with an intrinsic advantage over their canine brethren in the survival game. Those enlightened dogs, among which Salty was considered a 'primeur dogeur', knocked their rivals scentless and won the evolutionary game.

Right now, Salty's nose was diving back through the ages. As Jeff, Cap and Neil/Niles suffered through the dry heat of the Salt Desert, Salty was surfing the smells all the way back to a wetter time. A time when creatures swam and frolicked in the waters that covered the desert. While the three humans felt the heat-generated sweat run down their sides, Salty was nasally inhaling the long desiccated guano of the bird-like beasts that glided through the air currents above the inland ocean.

Both Cap and Jeff took surreptitious glances at each other, trying to make any kind of connection that could begin a conversation. Jeff, less used to the silence, having his mom to bounce ideas off broke it first. "You okay, Cap?"

Cap leapt at the chance to converse but he had nothing to say. "Sure, Jeffey, Boy, just a little nervous. Never been on TV before. Never wanted to." He lapsed back into silence.

The limo made its way east along the highway. Neil/Niles drove a steady 70 miles per hour. The seemingly endless and monotonous flatness of the desert gave way to occasional glimpses of the Great Salt Lake several hundred yards north of the highway.

Something about the way the light bounced of this overgrown salt pond caught Cap's attention. He slid across the seat so that he could watch the lake edge roll by over Jeff's shoulder. Jeff was daydreaming and didn't notice Cap scrutinizing the view to the north. The lake seemed to go on for miles and miles since there were no high points on the far end to delineate an end to the water.

Cap leaned forward and tapped on the glass. Reluctantly Neil/Niles rolled down the window separating the limo front seat from the expanded rear compartment. He had nothing against the Wendover trio but he had his air conditioning going full blast and he just gotten the temperature to a tolerable level. The hot air from the back was an unpleasant slap in his face. "Yes, Sir?"

Cap pointed to the lake. "You ever been swimming in the lake? I hear that it's just like swimming in a real ocean, 'ceptin there ain't no waves."

"I wouldn't know about that, Sir. I've never been out of the state in my life. No that is not true. I did go to Colorado with my family when I was twelve." Cap slumped back against the seat, his attempt to engage in social intercourse over. Neil/Niles continued anyway, "But I do have some friends who told me that the lake is even saltier than the real thing. By the real thing, I mean the ocean. That is what they tell me."

Cap had lost interest and tried to express it, "That so?"

Where Cap had lost enthusiasm, Neil/Niles had gained. "Definitely. I have a friend who's got a little boat, he takes it out on nice weekends, he swears it's so."

Cap's mind had drifted off toward the water. If he were prone to visions on the Jeff scale, he would have seen a giant salt shaker drifting over the lake spreading its content. He didn't see that vision and even if he had, he wouldn't have been equipped to decipher its meaning. His mind, like an aquifer, took a lot of time to filter out the extraneous or unimportant, and allow the important things to trickle down—distilled and pure. Perhaps Cap would have appreciated the analogy if it had been couched in terms of a still since he had always preferred whiskey to water. "That's nice," he said to the driver and that was the end of that conversation.

THE WHALE GOES HOLLYWOOD

Although the soul of the Wendover Whale remained firmly anchored to the sand and salt of the Great Salt Desert, its ego, if it had one, was now planted in front of three video cameras and a small studio audience in a Salt Lake City television studio. Mike Douglas had made a special trip from his slicker production facilities in Los Angeles to broadcast this program and he was running through an intro for the two guests who would fill the chairs next to him. "Let me tell you a little about my first guests." He carefully read from the TelePrompTer since he didn't have time to meet his guests before going on. He glanced off-camera to acknowledge Cap and Jeff standing in the wings but more to make sure that his researchers were nearby in case he needed help with more Wendover filler.

He had liked the idea of the Wendover piece when it was first brought to him but he was concerned that it was just a little too sweet. He chatted it up with his producer to see if his key demographics would buy into the story or would they prefer something more provocative. The producer, a man who was bicoastal but totally unfamiliar with the three thousand miles in between, felt that they should do the 'heartland' piece and, to protect themselves, run the lesbian mothers of Mormon missionaries section at the end of the show. Mike deferred to the wisdom of his producer.

"In the small town of Wendover, they had a dream, an impossible dream. But with courage and tenacity, not to mention help from the good citizens of America, they are making their dream come true."

The only thing that bothered Mike once he got the sense that his audience would buy into this taste of Americana was the continual intrusions by the hick reporter from the Salt Lake paper. He had enough people in Hollywood and New York telling him what to do and say that he didn't need some beehive-headed Mormon sending him lists of questions to ask the geezer and the kid. His associate producer had complained about the constant phone calls from Kurtzman suggesting everything from set design to lighting and background murals. Lucky he was a patient man or he would have called off the whole thing. After all media manipulation was just okay when it was done with taste and style as only he, Mike Douglas, could do.

He broadened his smile and emoted for his studio audience. "Without further ado, will you please welcome our first guests, Jeff Cutter and the Captain." The audience, well prompted, broke out into thunderous, spontaneous applause as Cap and Jeff walked onto the stage to shake hands with Mike Douglas. Salty slipped between the legs of the stage manager and sauntered onto the stage. He was not as stunned by the boisterous nature of the audience as Jeff and Cap although he felt slighted when Mike didn't offer either his hand or a special seat for the dog. Mike, Jeff and Cap all took their seats as the applause died down. Salty jumped into Mike's lap provoking real, spontaneous laughter. Ever the consummate entertainer, Mike reached back into his memory of the researcher's notes for some help. He petted Salty and laughed along with his audience waiting for an opportunity to throw the punch line and regain control of the show. Sensing the time was right, he got up and set Salty in his seat and then turned to the audience. "I apologize, what I should have said was, welcome to the Salty show." The audience laughed, Mike's entourage was mortified and Salty failed to see the humor in the line. After all, he was no bitch like that Lassie dog. He really deserved his own bark show.

⚭ EGOS IN THE RIGGING...

While the show "Salty Knows Best" was being played out in front of the cameras in Salty Lake City (renamed for the occasion to honor one of Utah's best known canines), a melodrama rivaling Mutiny on the Bounty was taking place in the Wendover shipyard. While the Whale seemed to be intact, its exterior was completed, the hull and cross bracings for the masts were in place, the action in this theater of the egos was taking place on a higher plane—the partially completed deck. Phil was pacing the deck strip from bow to stern, examining each joint like his life depended on it.   After each inspection, he straightened up, clasped his hands behind his back and marched forward. Marlon Brando, as Fletcher Christian, would have hated him on first sight, Humphrey Bogart, as Captain Queeg, would have recognized a kindred soul. Brad, Nancy and some other members of the crew had stopped working to watch the charade. Nancy was tempted to whistle a sailor's jig to see if Phil would break out in an impromptu hornpipe.

Before she had a chance to test Phil's dancing ability, a big truck pulling a flat bed trailer roared into the shipyard. The flatbed carried the thick wooden sections that would make up the masts of the Whale. The driver honked his way through the crowd toward the Whale. The crowd reluctantly, but intelligently, parted to let the truck through. Nancy let out a whoop of joy and then led Brad on a charge to the truck. They reached the driver as he nudged his rig up as close to the scaffold as he could humanly make it. Unfortunately for Nancy, Phil saw how quickly she was moving toward the truck and moved to intercept her.   As acting captain, it was his responsibility (as he saw it) to stick his nose into every piece of business concerning the Whale.

Nancy, Phil and Brad all reached the truck at exactly the same moment. The truck driver, a bearded, burly mother-trucker named Terry who hadn't heard about the Whale and if he had he wouldn't have cared a whit, worked his large gut from around the steering wheel and rolled out of the cab, clipboard in hand.

Terry looked from one huffing and puffing face to another to another. Phil, Nancy and Brad were all gasping for air and waiting to regain enough strength to speak. Terry beat them to the punch. "I got a delivery of wood here. Why, I don't know. Do I care, no. If you want to use 'em for telephone poles or the world's tallest stilts, its no skin off my ass. I just need someone to sign for 'em."

Nancy finally said, "I will," and she reached out to take the clipboard.

Phil, none too politely, snatched it out of her hand. "No way. Cap left me in charge, so I'll sign for it." He took the offered pen, a leaky model that had seen better days, signed the bill of lading and then handed it back to Terry. "There you go. Anything else?" He didn't wait for an answer. The man-in-charge who knew the answer even before he was asked the question. Except he was wrong.

Terry stripped off the shippee's copy and jabbed it back at Phil. Then he pulled another sheaf of papers from the bottom of the clipboard and placed them on top. "As a matter of fact, Mr. Grabby, I do. I got some, sorta' special, fittings. They were ordered separate." He squinted and carefully consulted with the top sheet on the pile. "Nancy Morton ordered them."

Phil turned on Nancy. He didn't like her attempt at usurping his 'earned' position at the top, however temporary it might be, and he let her know it. "Since when did you start special ordering materials?" Then his devious mind clicked in and he started to think that maybe Nancy wasn't such a straight shooter and maybe, just maybe, she could stoop as low as Phil to get what she wanted. "I don't know anything about these fittings?" And then the important question. "Does Cap know about this?"

Phil had pegged her correctly. She could be as pigheaded as any man to get what she wanted but she wasn't going to give Phil the pleasure of catching her with her pants down. She figured an indirect response was better than a lie. "Simmer down, Mister Kurtzman. The parts that I ordered were necessary to make the ship more functional. Let me translate for lubbers like you, that means sail better."

"Really," Phil responded. He had been lied to and misled by far better liars and misleaders. Her response wouldn't even pass muster coming from a freshman state senator in a politically naive state like Utah. "You and who else made this big decision? I know if you had talked with Cap about it, he would have told me." Not true but it was very easy to lie to a neophyte liar.

Nancy decided this tack wouldn't work and came about onto a different course, one that she knew Phil was weak on. "You're right, Phil, Cap doesn't know. But the rest of the crew knew, and they all agreed that it was a worthwhile investment." She punctuated her comments with an icy glare.

Phil returned her glare, negative degree for negative degree. "Worthwhile investment, my ass. You just want to be in charge."

One more word from Phil or any step in her direction would have seen Nancy throw a punch. Terry stepped between them, a big shit-eating grin on his face. "Listen you two little love birds. You settle your problems on your own time. Right now you're on my time and I got a tight schedule that don't allow for you kissy-facing. The parts are paid for, so they're yours. You can decide to use them or not some other time. Right now, you all are going to help me get the wood and fittings down so I can be on my way." He started moving back toward the flatbed. "Now. Not tomorrow."

Nancy and Brad move to follow Terry. Phil grabbed Nancy's shoulder. "You aren't going to get away with this."

Nancy shoved his hand away. "With what? All I did was order a few parts. Come down off that high horse, already. I mean, shit, I paid for the goddamn things myself."

"I'm going to tell Cap as soon as he gets back." he sounded like a petulant little boy. Even he found it hard to believe that this came out of his mouth.

Nancy laughed at him, "Get a grip, man."

"I'll do it." Implying that he would tattle, and not get a grip on himself.

Nancy heard the threat and ignored it. "You don't have to because I'll do it myself. Now if you'll excuse me, the driver said he needed some help. I have some masts to unload and put in." She was by him in a flash heading for the flatbed.

He started after her. "I'll help. I'm still in charge here."

⊗𝜎...WISDOM ON DECK

Several physicists have declared that time is not linear nor is it cyclical rather it moves in waves. Whether they mean that measurement of time speeds up and down, ebbs and flows, or it is the human perception that a constant passage of time has the feel, at times, of racing along under a strong headwind and at other times, coming to a screeching halt, as if caught in some backwater eddy, is unclear.

Time at the shipyard had elements of both positions. Time must have sped up in this portion of Western Utah because for Cap, Jeff and the crew of the Whale there never seemed to be enough of it to finish the work they needed to do on the ship. To individual members of crew, depending on their specific responsibilities in the construction process, days went by dazzlingly fast or stretched out toward infinity.

For Nancy, who had assumed responsibility for the installation of the masts, time was something she milked for all it was worth. She worked from dawn to well after dusk, driven to complete the task better than anyone else could. A positive byproduct of this intensive, time-consuming effort, was her ability to completely avoid Phil Kurtzman. Avoiding Phil did not stop her from thinking about the promise she made to him—telling Cap about her unauthorized purchase for the Whale. Now it was time to put up or shut up. The two masts were in place and the crew was finishing the decking around the foremast.

Nancy carefully led Jeff and Cap along the scaffolding until they reached a point just aft of the mainmast where they could walk on the completed deck. Nancy was moving them along slowly, stalling for time, while she contemplated her approach to disclosing what she had bought. This alone was going to be difficult but she also knew that Cap didn't know diddly about ship-building. Nancy was brought up to be honest but she didn't want to screw up what looked like a good relationship between Cap and Jeff. Jeez, why couldn't she have left well enough alone. It was so obvious that this ship wasn't going anywhere. It wasn't a real ship. She just thought that it might as well be as close as possible to real.

Cap picked up on her inner turmoil but not having spent much time around bright young women, his question came out wrong, "What's so important that you have to drag us up here? I can see you got the masts in fine. Now let's get out of the way so they can finish up here." He, too, was fearing this conversation. He knew that Nancy was the most experienced shipbuilder/sailor and didn't want her asking him any questions that might show his lack of depth in this area.

Nancy continued along until she reached the base of the mainmast, drew a deep cleansing breath and turned to face Cap and Jeff. "No, Cap, this is something I promised that jerk, Kurtzman, I would show you. So I have to do it."

Cap's nervousness came out in the form of impatience, "Show us what?"

"This." Nancy placed her hand on an enormous stainless steel coupling that appeared to join two pieces of the mast, four feet above the deck line. A series of holes in the coupling formed of semi-circle with a bolt going through one hole into the mast timber and out into the coupling on the other side.

Neither Cap nor Jeff had any clue as to what 'this' was, and even less of an idea of what could be so important about 'this' that Nancy would promise Phil that she would show it to Cap. Having broached the subject, Nancy was now stuck in the position of explaining what it was and revealing Cap's lack of knowledge. Cap was equally stuck since he had no idea what it was but couldn't be placed in the position of asking a mere girl what he should have known. The guardian angel of the Whale intervened and allowed the impetuosity of youth, in the form of Jeff, to ask the right question at the right time. "What is it?"

Nancy didn't wait for Cap to answer (or she would have been waiting a long time), "It's called a rake adjuster. They use it in racing sailboats to change the angle of the mast so the sails become more efficient. You know, catch more air. More air and the boat can go faster. Simple." And because she was relieved to be out of the dilemma she threw Cap a morsel, "Right, Cap?"

"Right." Cap only nibbled with the answer. It still wasn't clear where the conversation was going and he didn't want to fall into any traps. He stared at the rake adjuster rather than looking at Nancy or Jeff.

Jeff, guided by the benevolent spirit of the Whale, again asked the right question. "Why do we need it? The Whale isn't going to do any racing."

An obvious question but one Nancy didn't have a good answer for. Cap noticed her reticence to respond and felt that putting her on the defensive would keep him from losing any face. "Good question, Jeffey. I was thinking the same thing, myself."

"Look, I know it seems ridiculous now, but it will make the Whale a better boat once she's afloat. You have to trust me on this one." She left the statement dangling, waiting for either Jeff or Cap to support her decision with a little trust. Neither responded. So she went on, "If it matters, I paid for them myself. It didn't come out of the donations for the Whale." The males were still silent. This was turning out far worse than she had imagined. To keep it from becoming a disaster on the level of the Titanic, she resorted to begging. Not a pretty sight in someone so young. "Okay, so it doesn't mean anything to you. But to me it is a matter of face. Please don't make me take them off."

If Cap was uncomfortable with having to work with a young, dynamic and aggressive woman he was stricken by the thought that if he turned her down, she would become a sniveling, red-eyed girl. "I don't give two hoot about no rake adjusters." Nancy heard the words and teetered on the precipice of a breakdown but Cap went on, "but the masts seem strong enough with them things on there, so there's no sense in taking 'em off. Right, partner?" He looked down to Jeff.

Jeff didn't disappoint. "Yes Sir, as long as she holds the sails, we don't care."

Both Cap and Nancy breathed very deep internal sighs of relief. A catastrophe had been averted, for now.

ᘉᘍ NEW LANDS ON THE HORIZON

Before Cap could beat a hasty retreat from the menace of the rake adjusters, Brad joined the group around the mainmast. He had grown in self-confidence as the Whale itself had grown and he stood before Cap as a new man. Still a hippie but one with a purpose other than to get stoned and groove on the vibrations. While Cap started out resenting Brad's intrusion into the boat-building partnership, he had grown to respect Brad for his commitment to the boat and his lack of need for ego-stroking. Brad asked Cap, "Am I interrupting something?"

Cap resigned himself to the fact that he was going to be on top of the boat for some time. "No it's all taken care of, Brad. Now what can we do for you?"

"I don't know how to put this, Cap, it might be kind of a downer."

"Spit it out." Cap was not interested in pulling this conversation out of Brad.

"Cool. I just wanted to let you know that I'll be leaving at the end of the week."

Jeff and Nancy couldn't believe it. Brad was the most dedicated worker on the Whale this side of Nancy and Jeff. Everyone liked him, and even Kurtzman didn't give him too bad a time. If Brad was leaving the crew there must be an important, or terrible, reason for his action. Nancy asked first, "Why are you leaving? We aren't done building it yet." She shot the words fast.

"Whoa, slow down man. You're acting like I was the only one building the boat. I'm not even that good. Cap said so himself, many times."

Cap started to protest but Jeff cut him off. "But why are you leaving? We want you to stay and finish the Whale with us."

Brad pulled a sweat-stained and crumpled letter out of his pocket as if this was the conclusive reason for his early departure from the crew. "Look, folks, nothing personal, I just got this letter from my folks. They told me some kids in my hometown are building their own Whale. I'm going to help them out."

In spite of herself, Nancy said, "A whale in Nebraska? I can't believe it. Why there's no place to.."

Brad interrupted with a chuckle. "Yeah, in Nebraska. Sounds crazy, doesn't it. Weird even. But no weirder than building one in Utah."

"I couldn't agree with you more," Cap answered for all of them. And then the bunch of them stand around in silence, waiting for each other to say what was on their minds. Finally, Cap said, "We'll miss you." He stuck out his paw for Brad to shake. Brad gave him 'five', saw how uncomfortable Cap was with this move and shook his hand normally. "You'll let us know how it turns out with your Nebrasky whale?"

"Totally. You guys keep on truckin' on this one. Maybe one day, we'll have a big meeting of all the Whales, somewhere out in the Pacific. Far out."

"That'll be a real nice, er, cool," Cap searched for just the right word to show how 'with it' he was, "scene, Brad. I'll look forward to that day. Given that we ever finish this one."

⅋ FILM HISTORY

Numerous documentaries were shot around the shipyard as the Whale was being built. Almost all of them were done by budding young film-makers on summer breaks from their studies. By the time Brad resigned his post, a whole commune of film-makers had taken up residence in the Utah desert. They competed for the best camera angles and the most probing interviews.

But Wendover, Utah in the summer time was not the most hospitable of places for either neo-Spielbergs or any other life form. The bright light and deep shadows made framing a scene tough, the blowing dust and lack of electrical outlets made filming even tougher. Even the subject matter tested the patience of all but the most persistent and inventive. Building a clipper ship in the desert using an inexperienced crew and primitive tools forced the pace of progress to almost a standstill. Waiting for a new part to be added to the Whale was the pits.

With the development of other Whales in other towns, the allure of this Whale lessened for crew and cinema auteurs alike. When a crewman left to work on a Whale closer to home, in more temperate climate or closer to sailable bodies of water, and many a crew member did so, the urge for the rest to stay until the cinematic denouement fell as quickly as the thermometer rose in the desert sun.

If Cap or Jeff noticed the gradual decimation of their crew due to Whale clones, they did not discuss it with each other. Salty was more aware of it since he had carefully cultivated relationships with most of the kind-hearted crew members in order to garner extra snacks at crew meals. He was seeing a major decline in the calorie flow and he wasn't happy about it. Although he understood the human desire to leave and be close to home and family, he couldn't fathom how they could leave behind a poor, sweet and starving dog—this was Salty's blind spot, his Achilles' stomach.

⌘ PURISTS CONFESS

With the end of another shipbuilding day, prompted by the sun sinking below the western horizon, a tired crew and a sated bunch of sightseers stumbled out of the shipyard. Most of the crew had been adopted by families nearby and their only dream was that there would be a hot meal on the table, a hot shower waiting in the bathroom and some cool sheets nearby. The sightseers had similar aspirations but had to settle for over-cooked and greasy Whaleburgers, warm water in tiny shower stalls at the Tumbling Dice Motel and a fitful sleep on some threadbare sheets listening to the 15 year-old air conditioners huff and puff through sorry attempts to cool the rooms. Such was the stuff that never made it into the home movies, slide shows and scrapbooks of tourists returning from their summertime travels to the Mecca of maritime marvels— Wendover, Utah.

Jeff bid a good evening to Cap and Salty. Even his 13 year-old's energy level, amplified from the Whale vision, had hit the red line on his internal tachometer. This was definitely a night to be swept into the energy-restoring bosom of his mom. Only the thought of a bath slowed his steps as he moved toward his house.

Cap and Salty had no such warm embrace (aqueous, maternal or otherwise) to return home to. But the shack was home. And so they retreated into the desert's growing darkness. Salty to dream the dream of Kafkan metamorphosis with the usual canine twist. He awoke (or so he dreamed) to find himself still a dog but the Wendover Whale had become the world's largest bone. Cap retired to his cot where he had hidden away some damming literature, literature so offensive to the Wendover community that Cap would not, could not, show it in public; a book on sailing for the beginner and (horror of horrors) a primer on building wood boats. Although he had gotten this far on bluster and hot air, Cap wanted to protect himself against the very remote possibility that the Whale would ever make it to water. No sense building a boat that wouldn't sail, or, even worse, sink like the proverbial stone.

A different spirit descended on the shipyard with the absence of human beings. The spirit of the Whale remained as vigilant as ever, hovering over the near-completed ship, but it now time-shared the property with a far stronger but less flashy presence. The air, so recently surfing the endless tube rides created by the heat waves, got a chance to cool its jets(tream) and reflect back on a good day keeping the sky separated from the ground. It received a celestial pat on the back from the goddess of the desert as she evaporated upward from the desert sand (thus becoming an ev-apparition), transpiring from the cells of the desert's flora and sweating from the pores of the desert fauna as they rousted themselves from their daytime stupor.

If the building of the Whale was a carnival sideshow, nighttime in the desert was, as Phineas Taylor Barnum might have put it if he had made a foray through the Great Salt Desert, the Biggest Show on Earth. Unfortunately the only two humans in attendance in the shipyard were more interested in the freaks than in the headliners. As the secrets of dessert goddess were thrown over the desert like a quilt made of stars and angels' wings, Nancy was busy caressing the outside planking of the Whale checking for loose boards and warps that would have to be caulked. The gossamer quilt had brought a complete silence to the area, an utter abject silence that would frighten a noisy ocean girl like Nancy if she weren't totally focused on her job (literally) at hand. Her dedication to the Whale was on level with zealotry. If Jeff was the "nut" because he was the committed visionary then Nancy was the "bolt" that held the practical aspects of building the Whale together.

A footstep sounded behind her but not loud enough to break her reverie. A hand reached out and touched, almost caressing, her shoulder. Nancy let out a yelp that rent a hole in the heavenly quilt, letting some of the magic of the night escape to the heavens. She whirled around to face her adversary and found herself looking into the handsome but still arrogant face of Phil. "Oh, shit, you had me scared." She took a deep breath and waited for her heart to get back under 200 beats a minute.

Phil, not usually at a loss for words, stumbled through his apology. "I'm sorry. I really didn't mean to scare you. You all right? You look pretty white."

Nancy did look white although in the pitch darkness it was anybody's guess how Phil could see her complexion. She inhaled several more goddess-laced lungs full of air and in so doing, opened herself up to the magic infused in every molecule that moved past her trachea. "Yeah, I'm okay. What the hell are you doing out here? I thought I had the place to myself." She was not yet enlightened enough to realize that she would never have the desert 'to herself.'

"Believe it or not, I like to come out here when there is no one else around." He only knew the magic of the Whale, and the desert did not hold him, yet. "I think she looks better without the people climbing all over her? I mean, not that the people, like you, don't look good, you do, but she looks better alone."

Nancy was incredulous, "You, the publicity hound? I thought you'd feel terrible when there wasn't anyone around to see your creation. No people, no money, no ego strokes."

"Can't you get off it awhile, Nancy? I'm just doing my job. I want to see the Whale finished as much as you do. Maybe more."

Nancy jumped on this line like it was a life ring and she was drowning. "So you can get on to another overhyped story?"

Her coldness and anger hit him in the kidneys and he counterpunched, "No! That's not it at all. You don't know shit about me. From the moment you met me, you've been making snap judgments. And most of them are wrong. I'm not saying all of the things you think are wrong, just most of them."

The desert's magic had drifted far down Nancy's windpipe and lodged near the largest cardiac muscle, allowing her to believe what Phil was saying. The psycho-pharmacological response continued and she felt compelled to respond in a way not totally under her control, she apologized by simply saying, "I'm sorry. Perhaps that was uncalled for. Maybe I don't know anything about you."

The lessening of hostilities was contagious and the "love-germ" leapt the space between them, instantly infecting Phil (which was where the expression 'smitten by love' comes from). "Thank you. I guess I owe you one also."

"For what."

Try as he might to stop it, he couldn't resist the temptation to be honest. Could this disease have no cure? "For being such an ass about those special mast fittings. I got a little power-crazed."

"Don't sweat it. You were right to hassle me for it. I should have cleared it with Cap before I ordered them."

The goddess of the desert smiled down on Phil and Nancy. She thought to herself that more people should come to the desert to take the air. At the next convention of goddesses and gods she would make just that proposal. And with it would come the birth of the human potential movement. But for now it would allow two people to be with each other for some purpose other than killing each other. 'Nice concept,' the goddess thought to herself. And the stars twinkled in affirmation.

Phil, never one to let someone else be more contrite than he, answered, "But I didn't need to come down so hard."

"Forget it. It's over." Nancy figured the conversation had run its course. Time for Phil to pull up anchor and head home, wherever that was.

Phil was not so sure. "Good." He smiled at her. A genuine smile without the normal weight of insincerity behind it. The smile came out lightly and sat nicely on his face. "Can we be friends now?"

Nancy liked the adjustment to his face but had not yet succumbed to the magic molecules laying siege to her heart. "Sure. Why not?" She reached out to shake his hand. Phil took it between his two hands and held on. It was a tender, touching gesture which he was willing to continue into eternity (must be the goddess talking for him).

Phil's smile grew even more beatific. "I like this better."

Nancy got uncomfortable with the emotions being funneled through Phil's fingertips into her own body. There were just too many weird things happening internally. She freaked and pulled her hand out of Phil's. "I've got to get back to work."

Phil answered, with a new human-ness to his voice, "I'll help you." His internal apparatus doing 'jibe ho's' while his head was spinning from a Cupidian boom bang laid on by the she-god of sand (a kissing cousin of the desert goddess).

It was an offer Nancy could not refuse. "Thank you." The two stumbled off in search of work to do. Oblivious to the fact that the desert night was darker than the inside of a Mississippi mud pie with the kitchen lights turned off. The goddess above reached into her hip pocket, withdrew a gargantuan Swiss army knife and made another notch in the nearest Joshua tree—mark another one up to the magic of the air around Wendover.

ೞ THE PIRATES ATTACK!

With the arrival of the sun to the flatlands of Utah, the goddess and all her playmates beat a hasty retreat into the interior coolness of the cacti and substrata of desert terra firma (not so firma that the goddess couldn't wiggle her way through the terra). The full glory of old Sol caught everyone else asleep. This lack of discernible activity in the two towns created its own sort of miracle; without human life to observe, the differences between the two burgs slipped away, leaving just one unified blemish on the desert floor. The tranquillity of small town living could be seen only when small town life can't be seen.

As the first inhabitants, not Neanderthal, just early risers, made their way out from their homes and into their daily lives, the unification of the towns began to crumble. The first movers and shakers on the Nevada side were the early shift at Cinino's casino. They walked or drove into the parking lot in time to wave artificially cheery greetings to the insomnial gamblers blinking their way out into the sunlight. On the Utah side, mothers and fathers staggered out of their small houses, wrapped their bathrobes more firmly around themselves and blinked their way toward the crumpled form that denoted their early editions of the Salt Lake Tribune. If their early morning staggers coincided with their neighbors' totters, they waved artificially cheery greetings to each other as they were drawing their bathrobes even tighter around their bodies.

While this behavior on both sides of the border appeared to be identical and detestably shallow, it was the crux of the difference between the two towns. The Utes characterized the Nevadans' behavior as crude and mercenary, all done in pursuit of ill-gotten lucre in a Satan-worshipping environment. Pretty harsh words for someone just trying to 'make a buck' and keep up with the house payments. Having trashed their almost-fellow Wendoverians, the Utes saw their own behavior as wholesome and neighborhood-centered. Smacking of the family values that the 90's generation would wish for and attempt to legislate into national law. The Nevada folks spent little time analyzing the morning habits of their dreary neighbors. The thing that really put a hitch in their giddyup was the sanctimonious nose-in-the-air behavior of these people who had nothing to be happy about—they led the same shitty lives as the rest of the folks in a thirty mile radius—they were just too dumb or God-smitten to realize it. The only people who remained aloof from this societal snobbery were the pragmatists who lived in Utah where the neighborhood was nicer and who worked in Nevada where there were jobs that didn't require you to have a strong fondness for potash dust.

Dave Caster didn't care one whit about who lived where and who did what for a living. He might be more interested in what was under certain Wendover ladies' bathrobes except he was asleep in his favorite deck chair at the Tumbling Dice dreaming of ladies without bathrobes. The truly illuminated souls of our times are not those who are aware and recognize the importance of everything in the world, it is those nincompoops who are aware of nothing. Without the constraints of 'universal responsibility' these unthinking masters have the freedom to operate in an unweighted and un-'n'ed state, and thus the name 'n'lightened fit them perfectly.

It might be a stretch to put Dave into a category containing Zen masters but in his slothfulness he was working his way toward that goal. In the same way the destination was to be totally oblivious, it seemed appropriate that the path was to do nothing to get there. His morning nap was nothing more than a major step toward Grace which was why he slept so peacefully.

The arrival of Cinino and his two bodyguards in a large black Chrysler did nothing to alter Dave's sleeping pattern. He knew (diurnally) that this path to nirvana required diligence in pursuit of nothing. Cinino, unaware of his nearness to greatness, made a grand show to his bodyguards of slamming the car door to awaken his sleeping sycophant (not an alliterative pachyderm just a drowsy brown-noser). The sound snapped Dave out of his bliss into a reality not of his choosing. Not to get metaphysical, since in the early 70's this meant going to see your family doctor once a year for a large check-up. If he had a choice he would have chosen the unreality of his dream world.

"What a nice surprise, Mr. Cinino," Dave chirped at the little man. He would have greeted the bodyguards, too, except no one had ever introduced them by name.

Cinino had not come for small talk, surprising considering his own diminutive stature. "This isn't a social call, Caster. I'm here because I figured out a way to get the Whale." He then watched as Caster tried to extricate himself from the deck chair on sleep-numbed limbs. If there was one ounce of compassion in his body, Cinino could have lent a hand to Caster. But Cinino had reached his own kind of perfection—he saw the universal connection in everything and just didn't give a shit about it. He was only motivated by one thing, achieving his personal goals in whatever odious and unsavory method he decided upon.

Dave finally managed to come to a standing position, no thanks to Cinino. "You didn't decide to steal it, did you?" He winked at his de-facto boss. An in-joke among equals.

It was not a joke to Cinino. He and Caster were not equals. He was great and Caster was less than scum. Even worse, Caster was tall. "No, Caster, I'm not going to steal it. It will all be perfectly legal."

Having seen no reason to dislike Cap and Jeff for building a boat that brought paying customers to his motel, Caster was pleased that nothing bad was going to happen to them or the boat. It was a measure of his Eisenhower-era morality that he equated 'legal' with 'good.' "That's grrreatt, Mr. Cinino. How you gonna' do it?"

"I just paid a little visit to the Wendover Bank, where a teller not adverse to making a few extra bucks this week, told me some interesting facts. One, the Whale Fund is almost non-existent. She says that the kind-hearted saps of America have stopped sending money to build the boat. Fact number two, the builders have some big bills for sails and other equipment which are about to come due."

Dave, bless his little pea-pickin' heart was confused and wasn't afraid to show it. "So?" he said.

"Do I have to add two and two for you, you whatever? That simply means that they will not have enough money to pay their bills. They will go belly up, K-A-P-U-T, without someone helping them out, money-wise."

"And that's where you come in." Dave didn't need for Cinino to spell E-V-E-R-Y-T-H-I-N-G out for him.

"You're catching on. I'm going to offer them enough money to finish the Whale if they will give me possession of it for a year."

This concept was too strange for Caster to get a handle on. Why was this midget so hot to get his hands on the boat and then turn around and keep it for a year. Dave always thought that very short people were a little hinky. "Why a year?"

Although Cinino wouldn't admit it, this kind of response was exactly why he kept Caster around. The more stupid, the more questions he asked, the more Cinino could show how brilliant he was. Too bad his audience was limited to Cinino and two goons who had even tinier IQs. "We can't appear too greedy, can we, Dave? Besides, I think the public will lose interest in viewing the boat in about a year."

"That's very good thinking, Mr. Cinino." This was spoken with true admiration and Cinino recognized it. He put his hand on Dave's shoulder. He could only accomplish this on his tippy toes but the gesture of camaraderie was important.

Cinino turned on his charming voice. "Thank you, Dave. Now all you have to do was go and convince the old man and the boy that it's a good idea. That won't be too hard, will it?"

It sounded so simple to Dave when it sounded like Cinino was going to do the talking. When it came to Dave being the mouthpiece, the concept got a little tougher to chew on. He whispered back at Cinino, "Why can't you do it yourself?"

"Oh, come on, Dave. It would look so much better if the mayor presented the plan to them. Like the whole community supported the idea. You know, Dave, like a helping hand being extended from one Wendover to the other."

"I don't know, Mr. C., Cap almost beat me up the last time I went to visit him."

Cinino stretched on his toes so he could extend his arm around Dave's broad shoulders, in a gesture of real friendship. "It'll be different this time. I guarantee it. Now be a good friend and run along. Time is a wasting." He guided Dave to the door of the motel office.

Dave opened the screen and ducked his head inside. He caught the attention of his assistant, a teen-aged girl more interested in the soaps on the TV than handling the front desk. "Amy? I'm going out to do some city business. Please watch the office till I get back." He didn't wait for her acknowledgment since it wouldn't be forthcoming unless he was lucky enough to catch her during a commercial break from "The Young and the Restless." He shut the door and headed toward his car, Cinino in close pursuit.

"Thataway, Dave. I'll be in my office when you get an answer to my proposal. I mean, to the city's proposal." He chuckled. Dave didn't.

They separated as Dave went toward the back of the motel where his car was parked and Cinino headed back to the shiny black Chrysler. Cinino watched Dave amble back while speaking out of the corner of his mouth to one of his bodyguards. "Follow him to the boat. Now that it's going to be ours, I want to make sure that nothing happens to it. Understand?"

Like all good bodyguards, properly trained bodyguards that is, this one answered without missing a beat, "Gotcha', boss." This answer while stunning in its simplicity gave rise to that age-old question; was it genetics, environment or the resurgence of old "B" movies that shaped our character (actors)?

ꝏ CAP TURNS BUSINESSMAN

The positive energy generated by Cinino in Dave to consummate the Whale 'deal' was dissipated almost instantaneously by the meeting he had with the brick wall known affectionately as Cap. The constant hub-bub of noise and activity in the shipyard did nothing to dampen the vocal strength of Cap as his vowels arched over crowd and crew alike. "I told you not to come back here," he yelled at Dave even though Dave was within spittle range. Lately Cap had developed a fondness for the theatrical since his fondness for imbibation of alcohol had not been granted many opportunities to get satisfied. In the more simplified terms of a habitual abuser of whiskey, 'the public's eyeball don't allow for elbow bending.' A phrase that only another elbow bender could understand.

With no backbone to speak of, Dave was in no position to back down from his commitment to Cinino even if it meant catching the salivary spray being jettisoned from Cap's mouth. "I'm sorry, Cap, but it's important I talk to you." As an outsider; an interloper in the complex triad formed between Cap, Jeff and the Whale, Dave could only see that what he was offering was ideal for everyone.

Physically Cap was no match for Dave although in a gut bumping contest it might go down to the wire. Cap offered no challenge to fight, just a final, "Go away."

"I know the Whale Fund is going bankrupt," Dave blurted out. These words had a way of hanging in the air. Where Cap's words shot out and up reaching their apex quickly, exploding in a brilliant flash and bang and then disappearing, these words seem to detonate in a muted first blast and then shock everyone watching with a multitude of powerful, secondary blasts which were watched until they finally drifted down to Earth. As if he, too, had felt the impact of these words, Dave talked a little more quietly, "You don't have any money, Cap."

"And how, the goddamned hell, do you know that, you big baboon?"

The insult didn't really hurt Dave but he reminded himself to start doing more sit-ups and less soda popping. "It doesn't really matter. I just do. And I have a way of helping you to finish the Whale before your money runs out." He sucked in his gut hoping that the combination of his physically imposing stature and his calm utterance of these words would convince Cap that he, Dave Caster, was a man to be reckoned with.

Cap eyeballed him and then turned away. "You're full of shit, Caster. And I'll prove it." He looked for some crew member not doing anything important which was all of them since they had stopped to listen to the conversation between Dave and Cap. He pointed a crooked finger at one of the younger members and spewed out. "Get me Kurtzman, now!" He turned back to Caster with the knowledge that very shortly this damaging conversation would come to an end with Caster, once again, beating a hasty retreat.

Phil didn't take long to join the twosome. He had never had the pleasure of making the acquaintance of the mayor of Wendover, Nevada but immediately pegged him as a nobody who knew nothing. A serious under-estimation since a nobody who knows someone or something suddenly becomes a somebody of his own. Cap didn't give Phil any more time to size up Dave. "This bozo says we're close to the bottom of our money barrel. You been keeping track of the money coming in and out, is it true?"

Phil felt the klieg lights suddenly shift away from the Whale and onto his own face. Not the kind of attention he wanted at this point in time. He talked in a tone of voice that answered the question long before he finished the first sentence. "I've been meaning to talk to you about that. You guys are racking up some pretty big bills."

Cap heard what he didn't want to hear but he confirmed it with a question. One that needed to be answered quickly. "Do we have enough to finish the boat?"

"I don't know. Maybe yes, maybe no." Which in every language known to man and guardian angels meant, 'you don't have a pot to piss in' unless you have a very small bladder.

If Cap had learned anything in this long process to build the boat with Jeffery, it was that no solution was thrown out. You stopped considering it only after it had been tried and failed. And suddenly, Dave Caster was looking like a solution waiting to happen. And Phil Kurtzman looked like the man who could get you a view through the fence but not a seat in the stands. He was no longer important to Cap. But Dave was. "Okay, Mr. Mayor, you got my ear and I hope you got a big fat wallet. What's this plan of yours?"

Never one to exploit his position, Dave didn't even smile. "If I could just have a little of your time? Alone?"

Phil started to protest but Cap stopped him with a simple wave of the hand. He took Dave by the arm and led him away from the boat. "You got a car? I know a good place to talk, and drink."

While Dave led Cap through the shipyard toward his car, passing the few hardy souls who remained to view the construction, Phil had to be content to stew in his own juices—his devious mind worried that other more devious minds were at work corrupting his 'plan.' Phil was not alone in his mental gastronomics.

The Cinino bodyguard who had been left to watch over the ship, was diligently making sure no harm would come to his boss' future possession. Finding no other goons to fend off, the bodyguard was content to muse (although muse might be too subtle a word) over his chances for having dinner this evening.

ꙮ SO DOES JEFF

An ill wind blew across the Wendover desert flaring Salty's nostrils as he rested in the shade of the Whale. It was a strange scent carried along with the wind; a mixture of familiarity and larceny. He lifted his head off his paws and scaned the almost deserted shipyard in search of the source of this strange brew. The closest being to him was Jeff, methodically hammering some deck pieces down. His (Jeff's) scent was of innocence, blended with purity and persistence, unblemished (but for the three zits caressing his cheek) by the astringency of misdeed. Several other crew members were finishing a section of the Whale near the stern post. And while their smells were an unpleasant mixture of human b.o. and Whaleburger flatulence, they were not tainted by the perfume of perfidy (Salty's own choice of words).

As Salty was garnering the strength to rise and investigate this unique stereochemical phenomenom, Cap slowly lifted himself over the edge of the scaffolding and down onto the deck of the Whale. Rather than have the unusual smell disappear to be overpowered by Cap's usual high-proof alcohol and canned vegetable breath, the malodor grew stronger. Salty gave his snout a whack with his paw to make sure that his smell detector was not on the fritz. It didn't help. Cap strolled over to Salty and stroked his head. The smell of betrayal overpowered the boozy smell emanating from his fingers. Salty backed away.

Cap didn't seem to notice. His eyes were watching Jeff pounding nails. "You got a second, Jeffey boy?"

Jeff glanced up long enough to smile and drop the last remaining nail in his hand. He swept the planking with his hand looking for the rogue nail. "Sure, Cap, just let me get this last piece down." He finally corraled the nail and slammed it into the board with the hammer. Practice had made him a better nailer not a good nailer. The hammer head marks in the wood were a visible reminder of this fact. "It's really coming along, don't you think?"

"Sure is." Cap struggled, on stiff knees, to get down to Jeff's level. Jeff noticed, for the first time since he was first startled by Cap on the day of the Whale's birth, that Cap was an old man. Not a middle-ager like his dad or the principal at school but a real, honest-to-goodness old guy. By the time Cap managed to get his butt onto the deck, Jeff had decided not to drive his partner so hard. The Whale vision time-line would just have to be stretched out a little. "Finishing it's real important to you, ain't it," Cap asked.

Jeff lay his hammer down. "You're kidding? I know you're just joking."

"I'm not kidding, partner. I just need to know how you'd feel if you couldn't finish her."

Jeff looked around the Whale, puzzled by Cap's question. After all, the ship was almost completely finished. A few more weeks would turn his crazy vision into a solid-as-stone (a poor phrase in light of the buoyancy issue) boat. He couldn't figure what Cap was getting at. "That's crazy. We're almost done."

Cap's breathing was becoming a bit labored. And his stench, as sniffed by Salty, had taken a turn for the worse. "I know we're almost done. But let's just say something happened where we just had to stop workin' on her. You know a hyperthetical situation."

"What are you getting at, Cap?"

"It's simple, Jeffey. I want to know what's important to you. Finishing the Whale or owning her?"

Cap was taking the conversation in a direction totally unknown to Jeff. Salty had put one bad scent together with another and come up with the answer; too much deception going on.

Jeff said, "But we own her and we're going to finish her. I don't understand."

Cap's breathing had turned shallow and his pallor had reached the grayer side of dead. "Let's just say you had to choose between finishing the Whale and having someone else own it, or not finishing the Whale but still owning it. Damn, this is hard to say."

Hard to say but even harder to understand. Jeff's single-minded determination about building the boat had not allowed him to see the complexities of life. Like the free market stresses placed on a single-function economy when competition arose in distant, more hospitable geographic areas. Roughly translated as 'not enough gamblers in the Wendover Nevada casinos'. Or the insatiable desires of a mini-megalomaniac in search of new toys to own. Mr. Cinino wanted it all. While Jeff had not seen the intricate nature of his dream, he had seen the obvious; the dwindling crowds in the shipyards, the media exodus, etc. "Does this have to do with the Whale donations slowing down?"

Cap was relieved that Jeff had caught a small piece, a hook to hang the rest of the conversation on. He knew that Jeff was a bright kid and if you gave him enough time that he'd work out the missing parts. "Kinda'," he ventured, hoping to draw Jeff out.

To give himself time to think, Jeff slid the head of the hammer across the decking. Unconsciously looking for the nail heads that rose above the level of the wood. "Well," he started slowly, "I think more than anything else, I want to finish the Whale. It doesn't matter whether someone else owns it as long as I can say that I built her. Does that answer your question?"

Cap breathed a sigh of relief that blew more of his personal aroma under the schnozzola of Salty Durante. Jeff's response had somehow rearranged the smell molecules to lessen the betrayal component. It wasn't so bad but it wasn't exactly sweet-smelling. "I'm glad to hear you say that, Jeffey boy. Cuz' I kinda' feel the same way you do..."

Jeff shrugged. "Whatever you say, Cap."

Cap was pleased. "Then it's settled, let's do whatever the heck needs to be done to get her finished." His mood and physical demeanor had brightened knowing that he had avoided the tough questions. What remained was the doubt whether he chose the right course. He knew he had taken the easier one, the path of lesser resistance. If Salty had known the deal struck by his master he might have characterized it as 'going with the flow' as in 'current flowing into a giant whirlpool.' A path once started, was near impossible to resist.

Fortunately, for Cap, Salty was not aware of the duplicity of his master. His keen sense of nostril value detection had been diverted away from the crime scene to the remains of a partially eaten double Whaleburger casually set down by a crew member. Where once the atoms of betrayal frolicked, now played molecular matter of recently deceased bovine (with a healthy dose of decayed tomato and a smattering of oatmeal flakes thrown in]. What great moments in history were delayed, even aborted, for the love of two all-beef patties slathered with secret sauce?

⚘ THE DEED IS DONE IN BLOOD

The business world had yet to see the diabolical leveraged buy-outs of the 1980's and the more treacherous derivative trading of the 1990's when Cap and Jeff sat down in Cinino's office to do the 'dirty' deal. A deal so significant that it made all past Wendover business transactions pale in comparison.

Cinino recognized the importance and dressed accordingly. He had special-ordered a nattily cut double knit polyester from his tailor (reputed to be in tight with Sinatra and the Rat Pack) in Las Vegas. The fashion statement was all but lost on Cap and Jeff. Salty, who had very reluctantly been allowed to attend the meeting, under threat of non-attendance by Cap, recognized the nice lines of the suit but felt the color was all wrong for a man of Cinino's size. If Cinino had asked, Salty would have recommended an Edwardian double-breasted sports coat with a silk four-in-hand.

Cinino didn't like the way the stupid dog was looking at him so he cleared his throat to bring the meeting to order. He had an impressive stack of papers in front of him to add more credibility to his running this meeting. "I think you'll find these pretty easy to understand. Basically they say that I will supply you with all the funds necessary to complete the Wendover Whale. In exchange, I will take possession of the Whale for one year following its completion. And then, after that, the boat will be yours again." He pushed the sheaf of papers across the desk toward Jeff and Cap. He then selected a pen from an odd collection inside his coat pocket and handed it to Jeff.

Jeff took the pen and beamed back at Cinino. Whether it was his general good nature or the selective focus of a dreamer, Jeff saw Cinino as a giant life preserver for a floundering Whale. He had no reason to look beyond the obvious; a worthwhile project was being allowed to continue because it was the right thing to do. "This is real nice of you, Mr. Cinino. I mean giving us the money and giving us the Whale back after a year."

Cinino just ate up this mini-adulation. Respect given you by an employee was one thing but when a little boy looked UP to you—it didn't get any better than that. "Well, Jeff, it would be unfair of me to keep it longer than that. You and Cap have worked so hard on it. I couldn't see taking it away entirely." It was a true measure of this man's evilness that he could say this with a straight face knowing he did not plan to honor one iota of the contract. He smiled at Jeff. "You just need to sign at the bottom of the last page." He pointed to a spot marked with a red 'X'.

Jeff took the pen and leaned toward the page. Cap reached across and covered the signature line with his callused and dirty hand. He fixed Cinino with cold stare and then tried to make it a bit more friendly. "S'cuse me, Mister Cinino. I was just wondering how soon after completin' her, we had to turn her over to you?"

Cinino forced a smile to his face. It works about as well as Cap's smile. "Why do you ask, Cap? You got something special planned?"

Jeff looked at Cap with a wrinkled brow. He had no clue what Cap was up to. Cap tried to reassure him with a wink. Then turned his attention back to the short man. "Well, if me and Jeffey could scrape together the money, we was hopin' to truck the Whale out to the Coast fer a quick sail. Nothing too long mind you." Jeff was as surprised by this as Cinino. Cap continued, "Then we'd be bringin' her right back."

"Hmmm," Cinino rubbed his chin as if seriously contemplating Cap's plan. No sense springing the trap too soon. String them along. Play them for the mindless marionettes they were. "Interesting thought. Now how long would that take, Cap?"

'This was too easy,' Cap thought to himself. But what the hey, maybe this midget had a brain to match his height. "If'n all went well, and I'm sure it would, a week, ten days at the most."

Cinino continued his serious contemplation/chin rubbing act, noting to himself that he should considering shaving twice a day. The stubble was sharp enough to scratch his palm. "A week? I don't see why we can't give you that extra week."

"Fantastic!" Jeff almost leapt out of his seat to hug Cinino. He restrained himself, quickly signing the contract instead. He checked to make sure that he spelled his name right and then pushed it toward Cap. Cap hesitated, looking at Cinino rather than the contract.

Cinino provided the push to send Cap over the edge of reluctance. "I mean, what's a week, between friends?"

Cap took the pen from Jeff and with a shaky hand signed his name to the demon document. A millisecond after Cap finished signing, Cinino snatched it back. He stuffed it into his desk drawer and then rose. "Thank you, gentlemen, it was a pleasure doing business with you." He reached out and shook Jeff's hand first. And then, perfunctorily, shook Cap's grimy hand. "It's smooth sailing from here."

ঞ AND DOUBLED IN RUM

While the Last Chance Bar was never known for the quality of its clientele, this quiet afternoon its reputation dropped several notches. Even having the reputation of having served Cap, the-builder-of-the-very-famous-Wendover-Whale, would not save the bar's esteem once Cinino and his bodyguard entourage stepped through the door. With only a few Wendover 'high' society patrons frequenting the interior, enjoying the companionship of a tall cold one and nodding off to the country music wafting out of the jukebox, Cinino's grand entrance was wasted. Still wearing his double-k suit, he smartly strode up to the bar. Ike was carefully studying his own reflection in each of the glasses he was so attentively polishing. The one beer mug he didn't take down to inspect sat on a glass shelf above the liquor bottles. He had no need to clean it since it contained a folded cocktail napkin with some smeared writing barely discernible through the thick glass.

Cinino tapped a gleaming silver dollar on the bar to gain Ike's attention as if Ike wasn't aware of his presence from the moment he opened the front door. "Ike, my good man."

Ike polished off one last smudge and set the glass on the bar. He looked at Cinino with a curious mixture of contempt and respect. He didn't like the man but he liked the size of the wallet he carried. He responded this time like he was talking to the man not the wallet. "Cinino. What brings you to my place of business. Run out of the rotgut at the casino bar?"

The short guy forced a chuckle out of his mouth which sounded so stale that it might as well have been a dry heave. "No such thing, Ike. I've had a run of good luck and I'm here to share the wealth."

· "That so? You roll a drunk gambler, or what?" Ike casually looked around the bar to make sure no one was paying too much attention to his repartee with Cinino. He would have preferred to conduct business with this man away from the Navada Bar. Fortunately not a single customer of his had so much as lifted a head from their drink. Ike's hope was that he could conclude whatever business Cinino had in mind before any barfly needed a refill.

"Be nice, Ike. I have just concluded a deal to bring the famous Wendover Whale into my possession. My sole possession. Now if that doesn't call for a double scotch I can't think of what would. And don't give me the shit you serve your regulars, break out the good stuff."

Ike was suitably impressed. He had heard that Cap and Jeff were pretty stuck on the funny boat. Well, stranger things have happened (like the boat being built in the first place]. He reached under the bar, forgoing the shotgun for the bottle of J&B. He poured a very generous portion into the newly cleaned glass and slid it over to Cinino. "You bought the thing from Cap and the boy?"

Cinino took a self-congratulatory sip before answering: "Sure did."

Ike did a slow whistle. "I knew that Cap did some stupid things, but selling the boat to you, now that takes the cake." He refilled Cinino's glass as a gesture of new-found respect for the little tyrant. He couldn't help but think that Cap was getting drunk at someone else's bar and in a moment of total inebriation signed away the boat (again).

Cinino chuckled, and this time, because of all his practice, it almost sounded like a chuckle. "Like I always said, every man's got his price...and I'm willing to pay it."

All of a sudden, the beer mug with the cocktail napkin needed to be cleaned. Ike took it down from the shelf and put it on the bar in front of Cinino. "That so?" He was about to break a promise to a friend but the promise of financial reward sent him to the brink. The fact that his friend had already 'done the deed' himself sent him plummeting over the precipice and into the treasonous act. "I have something you'd might like to buy. Kind of an insurance policy. It'll cost you though."

"These guys are my insurance policy," he nodded at his bodyguards, "but I'm willing to listen." He pulled up a bar stool and sat down like he had all the time in the world.

Ike took the napkin out the glass and unfolded it. "It is kind of a long story."

ॐ LOOSE LIPS SINK SHIPS

As slow as it was at the Navada Bar, it was far slower at the shipyard. Cinino's bodyguard, having survived a night without a proper dinner, had nothing to do but watch two young man do finish work on the stern decking. He glanced around to make sure no one was watching, stepped into the shadow of the Whale and lit up a cigarette. He drew a deep breath full of tobacco smoke, leaned against the hull and exhaled a lung-full of pre-carcinogenic smudge. It drifted upward, passing the two workers and triggering a complex chemical reaction in one of them which would eventually bring on the onset of emphysema in 1997.

This worker, dubbed 'Doom' by the rest of the workers for his pessimistic view of the world, dropped his hammer, sat back on his heels and started to laugh uncontrollably. His partner, used to Doom's dour look, looked at him like he was crazy. "What is so god-damned funny?"

Doom struggled to control his laughter. Little bits of mirth still leaked out of his mouth like champagne bubbles around a lose cork. He started to laugh again, clamped his hand over his mouth and then let it slowly drop away when he thought his giggles were under control. "Nothing...I was just thinking." Thinking was too much for him and he guffawed again.

"Thinking isn't that funny. Come on, what's the joke," his partner asked, upset that he wasn't included before the laughter started.

Doom bit his lip to suppress the laugh mechanism. "I was just thinking about how much time we put in on this sucker." He tapped the deck with his hand. "Wouldn't it be a kick in the ass if they took her out on her maiden voyage and the damn thing just sank? Just flat sank. Like a stone." His hand impersonated a submarine on a crash dive.

His buddy, less pessimistic and more idealistic, didn't like the sound of that. Doom spoko of something worse than mutiny—the bad end of a good dream. "You know that's not going to happen. This baby is solid." He slapped the deck hard and there was a resoundingly solid thud.

Doom tittered like a man on the second joint of some Maui Wowie. "Get real, man. Look at the people who designed this thing. And old dude who might, I repeat, might have spent some time in a shipyard, and a little kid who doesn't know shit. Especially about boats. Great pair."

"You don't know what you're talking about, Doom. You never think anything is going to work out. Besides, if you feel that way, why are you working on the Whale?"

Doom gestured for his friend to calm down. "Cool out. I didn't say it was going to sink. I just thought it was an interesting possibility." He punctuated this last statement with another loud guffaw. If Doom's workmate was less than thrilled by Doom's gloomy prognosis on the seaworthiness of the Whale, the bodyguard below was frozen by the possibility. Only the cigarette burning down to the first knuckle of his middle finger jolted him into action. He ground the cigarette out with his heel and then headed for his boss. Pronto.

DOUBLE CROSS

Cinino had a positively warm glow about him. Things seemed to be working out better than he had even planned. Perhaps the effects of one third of a bottle of J & B had taken away his critical edge and replaced it with warm fluffy dollar signs floating in the sky. The beer mug, without the cocktail napkin, sat alone on the bar top. Ike was hovering nearby looking more than a little pleased with himself. The thought of buying this nice warm cozy bar drifted fuzzily through Cinino's head. He was just about to mention the idea to Ike when his bodyguard from the shipyard bursted through the door and yelled his name. Everyone in the bar, including Ike and Cinino swiveled toward the sun-lit door frame. The bodyguard, his eyes adjusting to the dimness of the interior, saw his boss and barreled toward him.

Something in the way the man moved triggered the fans in Cinino's head, sweeping the wooly cotton candy out of his neural pathways. He felt a brief jolt of panic like his lucky streak might be about to end.

"What is it," he asked as he slid off the bar stool.

Never one for subtlety, the bodyguard answered directly, "It's going to sink. I heard two workers say the boat would sink as soon as they put it in the ocean."

"Calm down, Felix. You sure?"

"I swear to God, Mr. Cinino. I heard it with my own two eyes. They said the boat will sink."

In a rare show of compassion, Cinino handed the overwrought bodyguard the remainder of his scotch. Felix was stunned by this unexpected generosity but gratefully downed the entire glass. Cinino thought to himself and then spoke to no one in particular, "This is an unfortunate situation. I believe it's time to call a meeting of the town's elders." He took the glass out of Felix's hand and set it back down on the bar. He took out his wallet. "Thanks for your help, Ike. You know, for my new insurance policy." He patted the breast pocket of his coat. Then he carefully fanned out a row of hundred dollar bills on the bar. "I hope this will ease your guilty conscience, at least a little bit." He turned and exited the bar with his hulks trailing in his wake.

Ike gathered up the bills and stuffed them into his pants pocket. Smiling to himself, he picked up the empty beer mug and began to polish it.

ᕯᔗ ALL QUIET ON THE HOME FRONT

The Cutter family had expanded by two. More often than not, two additional places were set in the family's dining room; one at the table and one on the floor. Miraculously, Cap and Salty chose the appropriate places to sit. Although there were times when Salty was certain that Cap should be the one lying on the floor lapping food out of a doggie dish.

Elise had warmed to the idea of an extended nuclear family. She had sent away to the Good Housekeeping Institute, the research arm of the magazine, for helpful tips on stretching recipes from four to five and a half. She had learned that Cap had a preference for canned green beans while Salty preferred his steak on the raw side. The joy she heard in her son's voice when he talked about progress on the Whale was enough for her to overlook the small quirks presented by this strange, big family.

Ken had adopted a slightly different philosophy to his new circumstances. He still didn't trust Cap but nothing that took place at the shipyard had given him grounds for kicking the old man out. Besides, his son had grown into a young man since the first nail was hammered on the Whale. Better to wait and see, wait and keep quiet. As long as the Whale was the biggest thing in town, some of the admiration seemed to rub off onto Ken. And he was a big enough man to admit that he liked the feeling.

To Salty and Jeff, the new arrangement was nice but not worth commenting upon. After all, it made sense from a convenience point of view that they all eat together at the Cutter house. It was so close the shipyard, and Elise was a great cook. If Jeff had been more reflective, he would have thanked his lucky stars (and apparitions) for his loving family. He wasn't quite able to see how much he loved his friend Cap because the massive image of the Whale kept floating between them. Salty definitely liked the new arrangement. Regular and large meals filled his stomach and made a soft spot in his heart for Elise. The ship be damned as long as the soup bones kept coming.

Cap sat at the table and saw the mixed blessings before him. A family to call his own. One that treated him with some respect and shared with him. A family that trusted that he knew what he was doing when it came to building a sailing ship. A family that entrusted the hopes and dreams of their only son to his (supposedly) capable hands. The black cloud that went with this silver lining was that it was all bluff, a sham, a grandiose scheme that had gotten totally out of hand. He had not been privy to Doom's insight but he would have not disagreed with the sentiment expressed. What was he going to do when he arrived with the Whale at the Pacific Ocean, the very big and very deep Pacific Ocean? Would he allow Jeff to step onboard, unfurl the sails and steer toward open water? Only to stand beside him as the waves started rolling up over the bow. If he had half a backbone, he would tell them all the truth, that he was a complete and total fake. He saw himself rising from his chair, clearing his throat and telling them all the plain unvarnished truth. He actually saw himself doing this until the sound of a spoon banging on a glass broke his reverie.

Ken had risen from the table, water glass in hand, and proposed a toast. "A toast. To the two best sailors in Wendover, Utah. May they have a wonderful voyage and prove all of the naysayers, including myself, wrong." He clinked glasses with Elise, then Jeff, tipped his glass toward Salty and then tried to clink Cap's glass. Cap was a little slow on the uptake and it required several attempts to make the glasses touch. Finally they did, and water sloshed out of both glasses. Hopefully not an omen of the future.

Cap quickly put his glass down before any more damage could be done. "From your lips to God's ears." And swore to himself that he would reveal all to the Cutters tomorrow night. For sure. Absolutely.

☙❦ A TURNCOAT SPILLS HIS GUTS

It was a cruel twist of fate and time that every afternoon must come before every evening, that lunch must always precede dinner. If it were otherwise, Cap would have bared his soul to his family-by-construction and the world would be set right. The sun would rise in the East and the Whale would not sink in the West. But fate and time being what they were, Cinino had gathered people in his office for a special meeting long before Elise had set the crock pot to crocking (or potting?) for tonight's meal.

The fine folks that had gathered, or been summoned, to Cinino's office all hailed from west of the state line. They represented the power elite of Wendover, Nevada and it was a measure of the business dynamism of the town that they could all fit in Cinino's office without the need for extra folding chairs. Dave Caster had been included, although his lack of prosperity or business acumen had him sitting far away from Cinino and nearest the door. He didn't mind since the loudness of Cinino's tie today hurt his eyes and the perfume worn by the woman manager (Madam to her friends) of the massage parlor created a tightening band of pain around his head. Cinino looked around the room, ready to launch his new plan. Felix stood behind him. By sounding the trumpet of alarm, 'the sinking ship alert,' he had been promoted to chief bodyguard. To drive home this point, he had carefully selected a tie that was almost, but not quite, as loud as his boss' tie. Cinino tapped his silver dollar on the desk to call the meeting to order. "I've called you all here because you are the ones that stand to gain the most from the moving of the Whale to our side of the town. I have purchased the rights to the boat for a rather hefty sum of money." This revelation was met with murmurs of surprise and admiration from the group. Cinino smiled at this. "And I expect each of you to help defray that cost to me." The good murmurs were replaced with soft groans. He expected this and continued, "It will be worth it to you, since all of your businesses will do better having the Whale near them."

The man who ran the town's sport book from the back of his drug store had the temerity to ask, "How much will it cost us?" A conservative man, by nature, he wasn't looking to cause trouble, he just wanted to start decreasing the pay-offs to his betting customers if he owed Cinino a lot.

Cinino waved aside the question, mentally noting that it was time his own casino had a sports book. "No need to worry, Gil. That'll all be worked out, later. Your fair share."

The massage parlor queen waved her bejeweled hand to get Cinino's attention. "When do we get the boat? I can't wait much longer, the girls are starting to leave."

"The arrangements I have made call for us to take possession when construction has been completed. That should be fairly soon, if things continue at their current pace."

Dave Caster was feeling pretty smug. Not only did he know all the details of the agreement, he felt like the mediator who put the deal together. It was a good feeling knowing that both parties got what they wanted. A win/win situation before the term was even coined.

Cinino continued to lecture the crowd. "I had planned to allow Cap and Jeff, the soon-to-be former owners, a week to take the Whale to the West Coast and sail her. Considering how much we all have at stake here, and considering new information that has come to my attention about the seaworthiness of the vessel, I have decided to withdraw my permission to sail the boat."

Dave's smugness was drowned under a powerful wave of betrayal. This was not the plan he helped put together. The wave rolled through him leaving behind a different vision of the mini power-monger in front of him. He could barely keep his seat as Cinino calmly told the others, "And since there was nothing in our written agreement forcing me to give them that week, we will, most assuredly take possession of the boat immediately upon completion. That is my plan and it will happen."

Dave tried his best to slip out of the room un-noticed as the rest of the crowd stood and gave Cinino an ovation.

Cinino basked in the glory until Felix tapped him on the shoulder and whispered that Dave had left the room. Felix was pumped and ready for action. "Do you want me to go after him? Rough him up a little?"

Cinino smiled broadly at both his audience and Felix. To Felix: "No, that's not necessary. Even if he tells them our change of plans, I have something that will insure Cap's compliance and our success." He rose from his desk. To the group, he said, "Lady and Gentlemen, if you'll follow me over to the bar, I'd like to propose a toast to the completion of the Wendover Whale." This was met with more cheers and applause from the Nevadans. Not a bad bunch, mind you, but plain folks who had cast their lot with the Wendover version of Beelzebub. There was no alternative in this lose/lose situation. No one, other than Cinino, stood up to offer a way for them to keep their businesses afloat in the wake of the poor location of the Whale.

ᏬᏇ SWORDS ARE DRAWN & OUR HERO BACKS DOWN

Destiny had placed Dave Caster in the middle of the Whale war and he was an unlikely combatant and an even more unlikely hero. If Sergeant York had sized up the forces massed behind Cinino and those allied with Cap and Jeff (i.e., nobody but Salty) he, too, might have considered turning tail and running. Dave had no place to run to, so he found himself in the middle of shipyard trying to convince Cap that the deal he, Dave, had made with Cap was about to be betrayed. As Dave ratted on his boss, the Whale sat glumly in the background; appearing to strain at its support bracing. Just waiting for the wind to freshen and its sails to be unfurled. It was quite simply an illusion since the Whale was without sails, rigging and ballast. Cinino's worst nightmare would take place were the Whale to be dropped into water at this point. She would calmly keel over, fill with water and vanish—without a puff of smoke to complete the disappearing act.

Dave had a tough time convincing Cap. "But I'm telling you, he's not going to let you sail the Whale. I heard him say so. In front of witnesses."

Cap didn't want to believe Dave. His plan for finishing the boat and sailing it worked too well for it to be ruined by Dave or anyone else. "Why should I believe you? You're one of his boys."

In a case of self-denial, Dave was not willing to admit his duplicity in the sordid events now taking place. "That's not true. I didn't want to help him, but I had to. He controls the town and everyone in it." His voice took on a pleading tone, hoping that Cap would forgive him and believe that he had turned over a new leaf.

Cap wasn't buying the redemptive act. "Sure, Caster. Why you telling me his plan? If he's got your balls in vice, why you spillin' the beans? He could make a whole lotta' trouble for you."

"I don't care what happens to me. You and the boy worked too hard not to get a chance to sail her. Besides, Cinino's going to eventually wind up with it, so you might as well have your shot." The pleading tone was gradually replaced with a spot of altruism with a touch of self-righteousness thrown in. "I want to help you and Jeff sail the Whale. I'll do whatever you want me to do, anything at all."

Cap was naturally suspicious of people, even more so when they were offering to help him. This protective reaction came from years and years of people saying one thing and doing another. He worked this problem over in his mind, hoping that the gray matter stuck between his ears could figure the angle that Dave was working from. He shook his head hoping to open a few more neural passage ways but it didn't give him anymore insight. He just might have to believe the big guy. Take everything he said with a grain of salt but at least listen to him. "Okay, Caster, I'll bite. The little punk is going to keep me from sailing my boat. I got it now, what's to keep me from taking her down to the shore for a quick spin. He gonna' traipse over here when it's real dark, slip it into his coat pocket and casually walk out of here?"

Good question. Two-masted sailing vessels are not the easiest thing to move. Nor could they be placed in a safe deposit box in the Second Nevada Bank of Wendover. Although the Second Nevada Bank's offices might be squeezed into the hold of the Whale.

Dave shrugged his shoulders, "I'm sorry, I don't know. I left before he finished talking."

"That is convenient, Caster. You come here telling me about some wild scheme but when I ask for the details, you can't tell me squat. I don't know about you." He left this line dangling like a juicy lure on the end of trolling line.

Caster bit hard. "I can find out. Cinino trusts me. I'll find out and then I'll come back and tell you, okay?"

"Sure, you do that, Caster. I'll wait here to make sure no funny stuff happens to the Whale while you're gone." He considered the level of sarcasm in his voice and decided that it couldn't hurt to be a little nicer. Maybe, just maybe, Caster was on the level. A spy in Cinino's court couldn't hurt. "I appreciate you helpin' us out. Really."

Dave was embarrassed which only strengthened his resolve to help Cap maintain his hold on the ship. "Sure...sure." He turned to leave. "I'll be back as soon as I find out something. Trust me." And he was gone.

The word trust lingered in Cap's mind like the heat hanging onto the desert floor. There were just too damn many ways of looking at such a short word. Salty trusted Cap to come up with grub each day. Jeffey trusted that Cap knew enough to build a cockamamie ship. The short guy, Cinino, trusted that Cap would build the Whale and then turn it over to the short guy and his friends. Whole lotta' people trustin' Cap to do what was right. Who did Cap get to trust? Dave Caster? Not any farther than he can throw 'em. Phil Kurtzman? Ditto. When he got right down to thinkin' about, the only warm body he could trust was his own. And he knew that wasn't going to make it any easier to fall asleep at night.

Since he was now the head of the trust department, his first order of business was to make sure that the Whale was sittin' pretty. If he could follow through on all of his promises to various folks about building the boat then he just might not disappoint too many people. He strolled along the port side of the ship, gently running his hand along the hull planks. Trying to sense if there were gaps to be pitched or boards to be tightened down. He made it to the forefoot, the leading edge of the ship that would normally be below the water line, without detecting any irregularities, other than the major one of his not knowing how to build a boat and building it anyways.

He walked under the bowsprit and almost strode right into Cinino's face. He clumsily jumped back. Cinino was grinning from ear to ear, not unlike that of the skull's grin on the skull and crossbones. Two of Cinino's ubiquitous bodyguards flanked him. "It's a real pleasure to see you again, Cap," oozed out from between Cinino's lips.

"I can't say the same fer you, you little weasel." Cap spat back.

Cinino ate it up. Life did not get any better than when you hold all the cards and the other guy dumped all his money into the pot. "Temper, temper. We wouldn't want any violence with people getting hurt." He glanced at both of his guards if only to make sure that if the old man was crazy enough to attack Cinino they would be there to protect him. "Especially with the Whale so close to being finished. Our Whale." His grin returned.

Cap would have preferred to turn and retreat but that damn 'trust' word kept poking him in the spine. He couldn't go backward so he might as well find out what the little fart had on his mind. "Yeh, our Whale. So whatta' you want, Cinino?"

Why was it when you need someone to witness a dastardly deed there's a two-for-one sale on Whale souvenirs on the other side of the boat? Even the crew doing some last minute construction on the foremast rigging seemed to have spotted a mermaid hawking maps to the lost city of Atlantis on the port side. Cap was all alone with the evil trio.

Cinino carefully folded up his shit-eating grin and replaced it with his neutral business expression. No sense using it up on someone who didn't appreciate it. "I'll get right to the point. I am aware that our mutual friend, and until very recently, a business associate of mine, Mr. Caster, has told you of my change in plans concerning our Whale. I know how that must have upset you. Which is why I am here to make sure you appreciate your precarious position and don't try and cause any problems."

"Now how you gonna' do that? Have those baboons break my neck? You are smart enough to know the Whale won't get finished. No Cap, no Whale. No Whale, no cash for you, you little pissant." At this verbal threat, one of the simian-sidekicks started moving toward Cap. Cap threw up his fists in a parody of Popeye the sailor. Cinino placed on hand on his bodyguard's groin, and pushed him back, hard. The B.G. (big guy/body guard) winced and froze in place.

The skeleton grin tried to unfold itself and creep back on Cinino's face but he was having none of that. This was business and business required brain not brawn. "I'm not going to lay a hand on you, El Capitan." He pulled the deed/napkin out of his pocket with a flourish. Cap didn't recognize it and he didn't see much reason to flourish a wrinkled cocktail napkin at this point in the conversation. Cinino continued, "I purchased this little item from a poor, now not so poor, bartender, who said he was a friend of yours. Isn't it amazing how weak friendships are these days, society has really gone to pot?"

None of this was making sense to Cap. He shook his head to clear whatever cobwebs were keeping him from making the Whale to Cinino to cocktail napkin connection. "What is that? A little surrender flag? I think you lost what little you had, Cinino."

"Don't be so coy, Cap. I'm sure you recognize it. This is a little note signing away your half of the Whale. You gave it to Ike at the Navada Bar when you came up short on your bar tab. An experience, Ike tells me, happened with great regularity." Cap made a grab for the note. Cinino stepped back as his bodyguards shielded him. He stuffed the increasingly more wrinkled paper back into his pocket. "Tut, tut. It's mine now."

With the deed well out of his reach, Cap tried a different approach. "Don't matter," he said just a little too casually, "just a piece of paper. You already got the Whale for a year, you don't need that."

Cinino felt that this card game was coming to a close. The sucker had bet his last dime and now it was time for Cinino to call the bet and lay out his straight flush. "Ah, but I do. It's my insurance policy. This paper says that you'll deliver the Whale to me without complications." To emphasize the point, he stepped between his bodyguards to be close to Cap. "If you don't cooperate. I'll show the whole world, starting with a little boy named Jeff Cutter, that you're nothing but a worthless drunk who sold away his share of the Wendover Whale for a few lousy drinks."

The sucker, after seeing the unbeatable hand, crumpled. "That's not true. I haven't been drunk since then. I swear on my mother's grave."

Cinino started raking in the imaginary pile of poker chips. "Who is going to believe that sob story when they see this note? This whole town's been waiting for you to show your true colors." He snorted. "Trying to pretend that you're a hardworking old sailor. Helping a little boy make his dream come true. That is pure bullshit, excuse my French. Once I show them this note you might as well crawl back into your bottle because no one is even going to take the time to shit on you." Cap's life felt like it was being sucked out of his body. Swept out with it was the word 'trust' and most of his spinal fortitude.

With as much deference as he could muster, Cap asked, "All right, what do you want me to do?" Cap acting meek and compliant was a pitiful sight. One that Cinino seemed to relish.

"Buck up, old timer. I'm not asking much. Just get the boat done...fast." The word 'fast' seems to have been honed on a carving stone. It flew through the air, perfectly balanced by the crossed 'f' at one end and the crossed 't' at the other, and pierced Cap in his heart. "The faster the better." And he tapped the wooden hull for good luck.

As he turned to leave, he acted as if he just remembered a small bit of verbal fluff, nothing too important but since he was here, he might as well say it. "Not that I have any doubts, but in case I haven't quite made my point, I'm leaving my associates here to make sure things go smoothly. To keep others from obstructing your accelerated efforts, so to speak." He patted both of the bodyguards on the shoulders, slid past Cap and disappeared on the other side of the Whale. Cap was left with the two smiling thugs, the sound of Cinino whistling the theme to "Popeye the Sailorman" and a tarnished image of Jeff's once-glorious vision, now heavily shadowed by storm clouds.

ଦ୨ଟ RED SKY AT MORNING

While the storm clouds rolled across Cap's brow, the weather pattern around Jeff was sunny and bright. Call it youthful selective focus or a visionary's tunnel vision but Jeff was oblivious to anything but the Whale. He strutted the deck enjoying the sound of his feet on the wood. He could look up to see the crew attaching yards (cross arms) to the masts. If he were only to gaze beyond the midships' fence, he might see the Whale rushing toward the edge of the Earth. Even Columbus might have ordered his three small ships to come about when faced with the certainty of this oblivion. But Jeff's internal weatherman was as upbeat as your typical TV forecaster—no one got raises by predicting bad weather.

"Ahoy there, Captain Jeff," the lilting almost teasing voice of Mary drifted up the gangway from the small crowd below. Her voice was one of those pre-Whale memories that struck a responsive chord in Jeff's heart. He took a casual captain-of-this-ship poise and waited for the cute body that usually came attached to that staccato-paced voice. She made her way up the steep pitch of the plank. Unfortunately, for Jeff, her bobbing head rose above the deck level in close proximity to another bobbing head, Steve Bergstrom's. The bobbing heads were connected to two non-bobbing bodies which, unluckily, were joined at the hands. Making for a nice looking couple and a red cape to Jeff's bull.

Time and zealous attention to the building of one's dream boat had a way of erasing all wounds except those suffered to the heart. A case of one dream boat not quite able to replace another dreamboat. As the red cape (Mary and Steve) reached the top of the gangway, Jeff, seeing red, charged across the deck, steam trailing out from his ears, to block access to the Whale. Steve waved at the oncharging Jeff-bull, and in a saccharine sweet voice, meant to enrage even the most mild-mannered steer, said, "Thought we'd come onboard and see how your little boat's coming along."

Jeff screeched to a halt at the gangway entrance, physically blocking further encroachment on his little boat. The steam blowing off his head would have taken the slack out of the Whale's sails if any had been hoisted. Jeff's voice was angry and loud, carrying from stem to stern, "Who gave you permission to come on my ship? You'd better get off. Now."

Mary almost jumped backward off the plank. The dynamism of Jeff's outburst might have been attractive to her except her initial reaction was of outright fear. Steve didn't budge. He recognized the blustering of someone who wouldn't, couldn't physically back up his threats. This behavior was perfectly consistent with his own 'bully' behavior. "Aw, come on, Jeff. We won't bother anything. We just want to see what it's like up here."

Mary had regained her composure at the same time she remembered how effective feminine guile could be. "Please, Jeff. Just for a minute. We'll stay out of your way." She batted her eyes with the awkwardness of someone still practicing the dating rituals in front of a mirror.

In the bull ring of romance, the Jeff-bull charged blindly. He saw neither the roses of the crowd nor the blade of the matador. In the

Wendover shipyard that translated into spite over reason. Jeff
bellowed, "No! You wouldn't help me when I was getting started.
When I really needed help, you laughed at me. Well, it's my turn to
laugh at you. Now get off my boat!"

Before Steve and Mary could react, the man who wrote the book
on bullheadedness, Cap, rumbled up the gangplank and bellowed
back toward Jeff, "No." Then to Steve and Mary: "You stay."
Mary and Steve were caught between the two raging bulls, looking
at the possibility of leaping from the gangplank onto the ground.
Cap continued, "Let them on the Whale, Jeff."

Jeff looked pained, as if gored from behind by another bull.
"What? They're the enemy. They didn't help."

Cap interrupted, "I don't matter what they did or didn't do. Shit,
if we kept everyone off who laughed at us, we'd be a pretty lonely
pair. What's come over you, Boy? Next thing, you'll be chargin'
admission." He turned away in disgust.

Jeff had a staring contest with the back of Cap's head. A contest
he couldn't win unless the back of Cap's head blinked. He felt
betrayed and at a loss for why Cap was acting the way he was.
These same people laughed at Cap, laughed even harder at Cap.
Finally, he stepped aside. Head down, he allowed Steve and Mary
go by without acknowledging their quietly spoken "thank yous."
He looked up and saw Cap was still standing on the plank, midway
between the Whale and the ground. Jeff went up to him and tapped
him on the shoulder. "Why'd you do that?"

Cap continued to stare out at the desert. The hot desert breeze
blew below him, below Jeff and below the scaffold, causing swirls
of dust to lift off the shipyard. The breeze strengthened and lifted
more particles into the air. And for a moment an ocean of fine sand
drifted below Jeff and Cap. The dirt-brown sea covered the bottom
third of the boards causing Jeff and Cap to be caught walking the
proverbial gangplank; the safety of the Wendover Whale to one side
and the unknown dangers of the milky soup on the other. Cap
continued to watch the breeze form eddies and backwaters in the
dust as he answered, "You was losin' sight of why we were building
this thing. You once told me that all that mattered was building a
ship, a god-damned clipper ship, if I remember. You didn't care

who helped, or didn't. You just wanted your boat." He paused. The waves of dirt seem to invite him to come down for a swim. "We'll you got the boat now. Take a look at it. It's a beaut." He turned and with a dramatic gesture swept his arm from the bowsprit to the sternpost. "Give yourself a pat on the back cuz' you made this all happen. Now don't be a damn fool, enjoy it while you got it." And with that he marched down the gangplank into the swirling sand. The wind pushed the sand into waves which lapped at Cap's knees, grasping and pulling him further away from the Whale and Jeff.

Jeff watched him leave, instinctually knowing that a grown-up had just kissed-him-off. He yelled after Cap, "You built it, too! It's yours as much as mine." Cap continued away from the shipyard never turning around to acknowledge Jeff. His mind was working at 868.975825 knots an hour on a problem that has no apparent solution. How do you get back something you gave away when you never really owned it in the first place?

PART THREE

MAKING HEADWAY

"Now then, Pooh," said Christopher Robin, *"Where's your boat?"*

"I ought to say," explained Pooh as they walked down to the shore of the island, *"that it isn't just an ordinary sort of boat. Sometimes it's a Boat, and sometimes it's more of an Accident. It all depends."*

"Depends on what?"

"On whether I'm on the top of it or underneath it."

Winnie-The-Pooh by A.A. Milne

ᘛᘚ A COUNTER ATTACK

For the next few days, even the hot sun could not overcome the coolness of relationships in the shipyard. Cap spent a good deal of time avoiding Jeff and the other crew members, seemingly lost in deep thoughts. Jeff didn't avoid Cap but he didn't know how to approach him, either. He felt like he and Cap were no longer sympatico—running on the same wavelength. Salty had made the acquaintance of a fairly intelligent basset hound, named Mel, whose views on animal hierarchies made for many a good discussion. Given a fellow intellectual to deal with, Salty felt no need to resolve small human problems however pressing they might be to the ship building community.

Progress on the Whale ground to a halt, as much out of lack of work as dissension in the ranks. For all practical purposes the Whale was finished. Seaworthiness was a whole 'nother matter. While Nancy had grave doubts about the Whale's ability to float, much less sail (after all, no one had consulted her on the initial design of the boat], her more immediate concern was teaching a bunch of landlubbers their rights from their ports, their asses from their afts. The most attentive, though not the most apt of her students was Phil Kurtzman. While Phil had not entirely turned over a new leaf, social intercourse with him was now more like touching a stinging nettle than a brush with poison oak. This mini-transformation allowed Nancy to re-examine her relationship to him. She thought with a little more work on his bowline and a little less machismo, she would enjoy spending time on a sailboat with the reporter. A large sailboat in case the 'old' Phil resurfaced.

It was one of those basic sailing lessons taught by Nancy and attended by Phil and several other crew members on the edge of the shipyard that Cap chose to interrupt. His interruption was by chance and not because he objected to this class on seamanship. A dim bulb had gone on over his head. He needed to speak with Phil before the thin filament broke and he lost the small glimmer of hope he had seen in its illumination. He put a hand on Phil's shoulder and in a normal voice asked, "Kin' I talk to you for a second?"

Not wishing to interrupt Nancy's discussion on the finer points of tacking against the wind, Phil whispered back, "Sure, Cap, what is it?" Nancy continued her lesson but those around Phil turned to listen in on a more interesting (or so they hoped) conversation between the two men.

Cap flashed his 'if looks could kill, you'd be dead' stare at all the potential eavesdroppers and said to Phil, "Not here. Come with me." He gently pulled Phil away from the other novice seamen to the privacy of the railroad tracks. He didn't say another word until he was sure that no one was close enough to hear them. He kicked at the gravel between the railroad ties.

Phil, whose disposition around Nancy may have improved but his patience level was still next to zero, couldn't wait for Cap to initiate the conversation. "All right, why the secrecy bit?"

Cap ignored the question and started walking down the tracks toward Wendover, Nevada. He got several yards ahead of Phil before Phil caught on that he was to follow. He took giant strides until he was shoulder to shoulder with the old man. Cap didn't look up from the crossties, he merely asked the question gently, "How good are your connections in Salt Lake City?"

"What kind of connections? With the newspaper? What?"

Cap continued the walk toward Nevada. "Don't bull shit me now, Kurtzman. If I need some strings pulled can you pull them?" He suddenly looks up and stared into Phil's eyes, looking for a sign of candor.

Phil didn't back down. Well, maybe a little. "I can still pull a few. I think. It has been awhile what with the Whale story taking up all my time."

"Good. I might be need them, real soon. I got us a plan that has no chance of working. But least its a plan." With that he dropped his gaze back down to the ground and walked away from Phil, leaving the reporter with far too many questions left unanswered.

◯❦ BAITING THE TRAP

Although Nancy remembered taking several drama classes in high school back in Manhattan Beach, Cap could not recall any thespian experience that he had ever been associated with. In a cosmopolitan community like Orem or St. George this lack of experience might have been a dramatic problem but in a backwater town like Wendover if you could string five multi-syllabic words together you were considered a prime candidate for the Royal Shakespeare Company. Why the anxiety over play-acting? The plot thickened without the benefit of a roux or cornstarch.

Our two histrionic artists had chosen the taffrail near the rudder as their stage and they dangled their feet high above their target audience. There was no stage manager to cue them their opening lines so they said nothing until the Westbound train rumbled by. Once the noise of the locomotive faded into the desert air, Cap opened the scene. In a voice that could carry way past the mainmast, much less Nancy's ear just to his port side, Cap said, "You know, Nanc, it wouldn't be hard t' steal this thing." While this use of the diminutive name was a nice affectation it was lost on the intended audience below and downright shocking to Nancy.

She regained her stride and responded in a voice loud enough to shiver a forest full of timbers and cause at least temporary damage to Cap's middle ear. "What are you talking about, Cap?"

Cap peeked over the rail before answering in an even louder voice, the result of the deafness brought on by Nancy's vocalization. "The Whale, silly. We wait until its nice and dark. Arrange for a train with one of them flat cars to pull up alongside the Whale. Keepin' real quiet, we pull in one of them giant crane-thingeys. Swing her over onto the train flat car, and away we go. Next stop, Frisco and the Golden Gate." To this point, what was lacking in dramatic finesse had been more than made up for, even obliterated, by the decibel level of the dialogue.

Nancy, unsure that this verbal pas-de-deux had touched the hearts of their intended audience, increased the timbre in her voice, stretching for just the right touch of incredulity, and said, "You think that would really work?"

Cap tried to smother a grin behind his hands. "No sweat. And the best part of it was that Cinino would never be the wiser." He slowly counted to ten on his fingers. And then he and Nancy carefully leaned out and over the railing of the Whale. Their audience had fled the scene. No doubt horrified by the performance. The guards which Cinino had left to watch over the Whale were now making a hasty retreat through the crowd. Rather than being distraught at this apparent rejection of their carefully enacted mellow-drama, both of the sailors were quite pleased with themselves. Cap flashed Nancy with a big 'thumbs up' salute.

ᘛᘖ THE TOO HUNGRY PIRATE

The stage reviews were in and they weren't pretty. Both of the guards stood huffing and puffing in front of Cinino's desk, stepping on each other's lines in order to tell their boss of the chicanery afoot in the shipyard. If Cinino's angry face was a critical lightning rod then "The Whale Theft" by Cap and Nancy would close long before it made it to the great White Way in Manhattan. Cinino jumped out of his chair, bracing his arms against the desktop. "That old fool! He'll never get away with it. Does he think he could just pull a train up to the Whale without my knowing about it?" He purposely slowed his breathing, calming himself and allowing his brain to function without the heat of anger driving it. Angry, but less so, he said to the guards, "I want you to go back to the shipyard and stick with Cap like a fly on shit. If he even thinks about moving the Whale, I want to know about it."

The guards started to leave. The deep breathing finally took effect on Cinino. He released the strain on his elbows and slid back into his chair. "Wait." The guards froze in their tracks and then slowly turned back toward their leader. Oh yes, those wheels were slow to turn in Mr. Cinino's head. But when they started grinding, they ground exceedingly fine. "Maybe Cap has provided me with the answer to my own little problem." The gears moved a couple notches more. "How close do the railroad tracks run behind the casino?"

The more intelligent of the two guards, meaning the one with his shoes on the correct feet, replied, "Runs right next to the back parking lot, Mr. Cinino."

Mr. C let out a long breath and plopped his size 6 shoes on top of the desk. Life was good here in Wendover. "Excellent... excellent. I think we can use Cap's little plan to move the boat ourselves. For now, Boys, let's keep this scheme to ourselves."

The less intelligent guard, looking to one-up his companion, was quick to reply, "Right, Mr. C., you can trust us."

Cinino smiled beatifically, "Like my own two sons. Now get the hell out of here. Cap still needs watching."

His two sons, thinking raises and possible inheritance, left Cinino to his musings.

౪ళ CUTTING TIES

A mile down the tracks toward Salt Lake sat the remains of a deteriorating railroad line shack. Outside the remains of the line shack sat the remains of a deteriorating Cap. Whether it was his foray into thespianism or carrying the responsibility for the future of the Whale around on his shoulders, Cap looked like a man needing a long vacation. He had to settle for the shade of the shack and teasing Salty with a bit of old rope. Salty appeared to be enjoying the tease but he, too, was play acting. He figured if he looked like he was having fun then Cap might lighten up a little bit. Lately, Salty had been wondering how to add lithium into Cap's diet, the mood swings were almost too much for the dog to bear. Maybe even too much for a bear to bear, but that was neither hare nor lair.

What Salty might have appreciated if he could mind-read his partner was the gnawing uncertainty of setting a trap and then walking away from it. Cap could only guess if Cinino had taken the bait. Was he really hooked with the barb set or was he just holding it in his mouth feeling for the telltale metal taste, ready to spit it out at any moment?

Jeff felt like enough time had passed since the plank incident that he could try and regain his earlier high-quality relationship with Cap. In order to re-connect with the old man, he had searched high and low through the shipyard and the better portion (perhaps a geographic oxymoron?) of Wendover looking for Cap. He ambled toward the line shack knowing that this had been a place of refuge for Cap when things didn't go his way in the shipyard. He peeked around the corner of the shack and, to his relief, found the object of his search. He teasingly asked if there were too many autograph hounds bothering Cap back at the shipyard. Cap didn't rise to the tease. Salty didn't understand the question. Was that like a pointer with a penmanship problem? Jeff switched tone, "What's wrong with you? You've been floating in outer space for the last couple of days. If it's because I acted badly, I'm sorry. If it's because you're worried about getting the money together to get the Whale out West, relax."

Before Jeff had finished his thought, Cinino's recently adopted sons/bodyguards strolled by. As if strolling down the railroad tracks in the middle of the desert was something they did everyday, and twice on Sundays. Just to let Cap know that they weren't going to let him escape again, they found an interesting piece of rock to examine in the railroad bed, not more than 15 feet from where Cap sat. Jeff eyed them curiously but didn't see them as a threat. He continued, "With all the people coming back to see us finish the Whale, we'll get plenty of donations. Plenty to get us there and back. So stop worrying."

Cap glared at the C-boys and then up at Jeff. He knew that with an audience watching he couldn't really explain what his long-term plan was for the Whale. Better to confuse the eavesdroppers now and explain to Jeff later. He said to Jeff in a harsher than necessary tone, "Aren't you suppose to be painting right now?"

"Sure, but I thought you needed someone to talk to. We are still partners, aren't we? You can talk to me."

Cap gritted his teeth in anticipation of what he had to say next. "Well this partner needs a little break. Some time alone. So, if you don't mind, why don't you skedaddle back and do your job?"

Jeff squinted at Cap like an old man trying to recognize a stranger through a myopic fog. He gave him the once over, making sure that this wasn't the evil twin of the man he had spent the summer with. He looked like Cap, he smelled like Cap, he even snarled like Cap. But Cap usually did his snarling at other people, not his partner, Jeff. "Right. I know when I'm not wanted. But I'll tell you something, you better get that bug outta' your butt before the big party." This was a pretty daring statement for a young Utah boy and he ducked back around the shed before Cap could respond.

Cap was stung by the remark but he knew he could do nothing to straighten Jeff out until he wasn't being spied on. He continued to wiggle the tattered rope through the sand but Salty had lost interest in the game.

After several hours, even Cinino's boys figured no new conspiracy was going to be hatched by the old coot and his mutt sitting in the heat. They retreated back the relative coolness of the shipyard where a Coke vendor was always within hailing distance. Cap and Salty watched them leave and then Cap threw the rope on the ground. He stood up and dusted his pants off. "You know, Salty, I think I coulda' handled that better."

Salty had no clue as to what the Man was saying. He still couldn't quite get a grip on what an autograph hound was. A coon dog who collects pawprints? He followed after Cap, both of them shaking their heads, looking for clarity.

ᘉᙡ A BAPTISM WITHOUT WATER

It was a little known physical property of visions that the longer they exist in the consciousness of humans the more they weigh. At birth, no amount of pulling and hanging could bring them down from the atmosphere. They seem to float above everyone's reach, tantalizingly close but unattainable. Then one person defies gravity to grab hold; a Michael Jordan-like jump where the spectators are left wondering if he or she will ever come down. This is the beginning of the end of the vision, it begins to drift, inexorably, downward.   Other humans, sensing that the gap between their outstretched arms and the amorphous vision's mass had closed, made the leap and grabbed on.   The weight of these hanger-on-ers accelerates the gravitation of the vision. Suddenly it is within reach of anyone willing to lift their arm even the tiniest bit. But when they, too, grab, they touch something of substance, a solidness that did not exist for the first leaper. The vision has metamorphisized, it has now become real, and by definition, it is no longer a vision.

The vision known originally as the Whale in the Great Salt Desert had been hog-tied and devisionized.   Cap and Jeff's grandiose, impossible-to-build project had been dragged down to the Earth and brought within the reach of even the most frail.   The shipyard was now awash with those 'real' people who were good at celebrating the success that others had brought to fruition.

To accommodate these party animals, a wood stage had been set up in front of the Whale.   A country western band with the improbable name, "Go East," was cranking out a countrified version of the "Orange Blossom Special."

The crowd was as large as could uncomfortably fit within the confines of the shipyard.   Everyone was having a good time or pretending to—'real' people were good at faking happiness. All of the characters in the saga of the Whale had found their way into this giant party. Phil was showing Nancy why he had a better chance of winning a Pulitzer Prize for his journalistic skills than he did for making it at Grand Ole' Opry as a back-up dancer. Nancy didn't seem to mind since he was keeping his mouth shut, concentrating on not stepping on her toes. Several crew members were competing with each other to see how quickly they could devour a quarter of a watermelon without using their hands.   Amos had cornered the 'rocking chair club' and was allowing them all sips from his secret stash of demon alcohol, so long as no one put their dirty lips on his hip flask.

In a surprising show of maturity, Jeff had swallowed his pride and was pointing out the important features of the Whale to Steve and Mary. The good feelings of the occasion had even softened the hardest of the hard-asses, Steve was actually listening to what Jeff had to say. "Go East" finished their song in a crescendo of almost-right chords and backed away from the microphones. There was thunderous applause, most of which was certainly undeserved. The townspeople seem to have learned to acknowledge the effort, with much less concern for the outcome.

Simon Locke climbed up onto the stage and took hold of one of the mikes. He tapped it to make sure that it was on, sending a 'thump' through the speakers and out into the crowd. Only the slightest bit nervous, having rehearsed in front of a tough audience in Amos and his cronies, Simon launched into his master-of-ceremonies spiel. He said to the band, "You were great, fellas, thanks a lot." He hesitated on the fellas since several of the band members' hair far exceeded the length Simon allocated to women of the species. To the crowd he said, "I hope you all are enjoying yourselfs." The crowd responded with cheers, applause, hoots and hollers and cowboy 'yee-haws'. "Glad to hear it. Now if you folks are gettin' thirsty or hungry, why don't you step on over to the refreshment table?" He pointed to a table heavily laden with cold cuts, bowls of punch and a rapidly melting ice sculpture of the Wendover Whale. The craftsmanship exhibited in the sculpting of the ice surpassed any artistry shown in building in the actual boat. It was a better than even money bet among the wise asses in the crowd that the ice would sail better in the ocean than the Whale, and probably stay on the surface longer too. Simon continued, "It's all free. Generously donated by the merchants of Wendover, Utah. Just our way of saying thanks to the builders of the Whale." What was thought but not said by Simon and the other merchants was that they had made a hunk of money on the tale of this Whale and in an effort not to appear to avaricious they were giving a little, very little, back to the people.

The crowd stirred and then parted enough to let Jeff make his way toward the stage. Everyone was patting him on the back or shaking his hand or thrusting their baby into his arms for a quick snapshot. He couldn't have been any happier. Simon spotted him in the crowd and pointed a digit at him, "And speaking of the builders, here's the young man that started the whole thing off, Mr. Jeffery

Cutter! I believe he's got a few things he wants to say to us. Come on up, Jeff."

The crowd elevated its applause level as Jeff climbed up onto the stage. A small shudder of jealousy went through the lead singer of "Go East." He just couldn't see the point of building a big ugly boat in the middle of the desert. Call him a pragmatist, or call him a cynic, but he just didn't see what the big deal was. Then again, Jeff probably didn't see much value in spending every night on the road playing bad music in sleazy dives. Simon adjusted the microphone downward on the stand for Jeff and then stepped aside.

Jeff unfolded a piece of paper and read from it. He was far more nervous then anyone else on the stage and it showed. He motioned for the crowd to quiet down and then said, "Thank you, very much. I won't keep you away from the partying for too long, but there are a few people I'd like to thank." He checked his notes on the paper and then looked up and smiled. A smile that could soften even the hardest of hearts, except for Amos, who had no heart. "I never thought we'd make it this far." The crowd cheered as if on cue. "Anyway, I'd like to thank my parents, for giving me the time and support I needed to get this done." As he looked past Simon to his parents standing at the side of the stage, Jeff couldn't help but feel a twinge, an involuntary shiver, at this small white lie. While his parents seemed to back him 110% right now, there was more than a little time when he was closer to a spanking from his dad over "the stupid boat idea" than he was to the beaming approval he was getting at this moment. Time seemed to heal old wounds, or at least scab them over so they weren't so sensitive to the touch. Not wanting to get bogged down in the reverie of past crimes, real and imagined, Jeff consulted his notes. "I'd also like to thank all of you who contributed money, or time, or both, to see that the Whale became more than just a dream of mine. I'd mention all your names, but we would never get back to partying." This elicited some chuckles from the crowd. A few more edge their way toward the freebie food on the tables. "So know that I mean it when I say that without each of you, this wouldn't be possible." He gestured toward the Whale and with a simple wave of his hand, the boat took on a 'solidability' that was lacking even after the last nail was hammered. Jeff's personal vision (the Whale) through the collective efforts of the 'perspirers' jumped from the apparitional stage into mass.   Was it a jumbled mass of scrap wood, odds and ends hardware and the dorkiness of mis-engineering or the finely honed mass belonging to the only hand-built clipper to reside in the state of Utah? Beauty was truly in the eye of the beholder but MASS could not even be disputed by the blind. It was.

Whether it was the angels above or the ship's spirit within or the desert sprite, the Whale stood before the crowd changed.   And almost all saw the change but could not place their metaphysical finger on exactly what the change was. Jeff continued, "Last, but certainly not least, I'd like to thank the man who really made the Whale." Having waited for this verbal cue, members of the crew began to assemble behind Jeff on the stage. "Without this man, there would be nothing except dirt, and maybe a little kid, me, with a crazy idea about building a boat." He pointed to himself as if there was still someone who hadn't heard the story. Jeff need not have bothered, since the story of the boat in the desert and the boy who had dreamed it up had already entered the beginning stages of mythdom. But this neo-myth had yet to have an ending. He looked around to capture Cap in his adoring stare but couldn't find him in the crowd. "I can't see him out there, but I know he's around. Cap, wherever you are, I want you to know that I owe you everything, and I love you."

The crowd applauded this obviously heart-felt statement. Phil stepped up to the mike. He handled it like he was born to it, a huckster with easy access to a bunch of huckees. "Before Jeff slips away, the crew members of the Wendover Whale have a special presentation to make. But we also need Cap up here. Come on up here, Cap."

Cap had tried to drift away from the stage, away from the limelight, away from having to show his treachery. But the crowd had been moved by the moment and they would not let him escape. Gentle hands clasped his shoulders turning him around until he was facing the stage. Other hands, attached to insistent voices, guided him toward the stage. He was almost lifted off his feet and carried by the positive energy and 'respect', a word he was totally unfamiliar with, of the crowd. New hands, both small and large, helped him up onto the stage where he was hugged by Jeff and warmly greeted by Phil. Phil looked back at the crew while leaning into the microphone, "Nancy, if you'll do the honors?"

Nancy came forward, carrying a small bundle. She looked very good, particularly to Phil. He couldn't help but appreciate how much the Whale had changed his life, and in ways that he could never have envisioned. Nancy smoothly moved a compliant Phil out of the way so that she could stand next to Jeff and Cap. She spoke, haltingly, "Speeches are not my thing, so I'll just present this banner." And with that, she unfurled the small bundle which became a spectacular banner. On a cerulean blue background was a white silk whale, spouting water. Underneath the whale was hand-stitched, 'Cap & Jeff' in shiny black thread. Nancy took a deep breath before continuing with her mini-speech. "In appreciation for letting us have the chance to work with the two of you on this Whale, we want you to have this whale. To fly high over your ship, letting everyone who sees it know that this is one very special sailing vessel. We love both of you. You are the greatest!" She handed the banner to Jeff, hugging him in the process. She turned to Cap and gave him the most effusive bear hug he ever had the pleasure/misfortune to receive. Those close to the front of the crowd swore on the Book of Mormon (a very serious oath) that they saw Cap blush crimson. The crew and crowd let out a thunderous ovation, several of them calling for Cap to speak.

Jeff whispered to Cap, "Go ahead, Cap. I've got something to do." He took the banner and hopped from the stage up onto the deck of the Whale. As everyone watched, he began to climb the rigging of the foremast. Cap started talking into the microphone. He had truly been touched but was trying hard not to lose his rotten-egg persona. "Thank you. Thank you very much. I wasn't going to say nothing but this present is the best I've ever gotten. It's a real change for me to be gettin' somethin' from other people, 'specially for doing somethin' right." A few in the crowd laughed. A few others thought back to the hard times they gave Cap when he stepped foot in town. He continued, "Thank you for that. And while I got the chance, I'd like to apologize to the town people here. I cussed you out more times than I care to remember, Jeezus some of you were so mean-spirited, but I got to take my hat off to you this time. You really came through when we needed you."

Jeff had successfully climbed the rigging to the top of the foremast and was struggling to tie the banner while listening to his partner speak. No easy task but one within the capabilities of a visionary turned reality-maker. Cap continued, "If it wasn't for you, well, I don't know. I wish there was someways to show my appreciation."

Jeff shouted down from the foremast, "How about giving them all free rides when she's afloat?" The crowd loved the idea, cheering and laughing and clapping. Phil, Nancy and Cap were the only ones who didn't seem to respond well to the suggestion.

Cap waited for the crowd noise to die down before he went on, "Unfortunately, I don't think that's going to be possible. I wish to God it were. Oh well, no use cryin' over spilt milk. You just give Jeffey and me a chance; we'll come up with some way of saying thank you. That's all I got to say for now. Thanks again." His speech ended, coincidentally, with Jeff unfurling the banner. There was enough of a breeze at on top of the mast to extend the light material so that all could see it from below. The crowd cheered as everyone began to leave the stage.

✺ BEFORE THE BATTLE BREAKS

The breeze stiffened enough to keep the banner aloft. Unfortunately, it was the proverbial ill wind that swept across the shipyard and carried the great diminutive one (a unique Wendover oxymoron), Cinino, onto the stage just as it had been cleared by the good guys. With all the grace of young Mickey Rooney (an obvious physical match), Cinino hotfooted it across the stage and grabbed the mike before he lost his audience to the morsels still remaining on the free food tables. "Excuse me. I hate to interrupt this wonderful celebration but I have an important announcement to make." He gave the crowd time to swivel back toward him and quiet. "There will be a special town meeting tonight of the citizens of both Wendovers. I strongly suggest," dramatically pausing before continuing, "that all town residents attend tonight since the topic of the meeting will be the future of the Wendover Whale." He almost bit his tongue suppressing the 'my' that his subconscious wanted to throw in before Wendover Whale. His words barely have time to drift down to the masses below the stage when the buzz of surprise worked its way back to Cinino.

All of the Whale crew members were stunned with the exception of Cap and Phil. Even amongst these two, their expressions were not those of people expecting something this strange to happen. Cap was the most effected by the mini-speech. He looked like a man forced to chart a course through a mine field rather than take the super-highway that AAA recommended. Cinino was not done with the crowd, he continued, "The meeting will be at seven-thirty in the school gymnasium. Please don't miss it." Many people called out from the crowd with questions that Cinino couldn't hear or understand nor would he answer even if he could hear or understand. "All of your questions will be answered then." He tried to calm everyone down with a smile and a reassuring gesture with his hands. It didn't work but he had gotten his message across. And that was all his script, the one he mentally rehearsed for an hour prior to the coming-out party, called for. "Now let's get back to having a good time. Yee-ha. Have a wonderful day, folks!" He quickly moved off the stage and into the crowd. For all the Wendoverians, the party had ceased to be a party, as they huddled together and speculated on what Cinino meant. The tourists tried to regain the high spirits of earlier moments but without the cooperation of the townspeople the party quickly sank into the social quagmire of disasterville.

Jeff had listened to Cinino from the top of the mast and, having absorbed the few words spoken, quickly worked his way down the rigging. He jumped down the last few feet and landed heavily on the deck. He got to his feet, scrambled off the Whale and down into the crowd. He caught up with Nancy and some other crew members who were yelling at each other about what it all meant or didn't mean. Cap and Phil had fled the scene so Jeff had to make do with Nancy. "What did he mean about deciding the future of the Whale? I thought the future of the Whale was already decided between Cap and me."

Nancy was as clueless as the rest. She shrugged. "Shit, if I know. Caught us all with our pants down."

A completely unsatisfying answer for Jeff to hear. He looked around for another credible source to ask. He couldn't see the one person who would have the answer. "Where's Cap? I gotta' talk to Cap?"

Nancy shrugged again. "I don't know, Jeff. I turned to listen to that stumpy bad dude and when I turned around, he and Phil had flaked out. You know, took a powder."

Jeff's brain translated the SoCal speak into something more closely resembling English. "I gotta' find him." He pushed past Nancy and into the crowd. He stumbled, looking for his friend. Everyone was trying to grab him, stop him, question him but he kept on going. He pushed away friendly arms and smiling faces.

One face and arm were a little more insistent than the rest, they belonged to his father. Ken asked his son, "Jeff. Jeff, what did Mr. Cinino mean?"

Jeff started to panic. He felt comfortable in the role of visionary and town hero but having the town count on him to come up with answers made him sick to his stomach. Maybe it was too much free food or maybe it was because he didn't have any of the answers. Even his father had to be put off. "I don't know, Dad. I'll talk to you later." He ducked under his father's arm and squirmed his way through the crowd in the direction of the highway and, hopefully, freedom from questions. As he broke free of the crowd, he spotted Cap and Salty making a hasty, and obvious, retreat from the catastrophe, down the road and away from Wendover. A wise move if you didn't want the spotlight of public inquiry to shine down upon you.

⠶ PLAYING DUMB

Jeff, adrenaline-driven, with younger leg muscles, quickly closed the distance between himself and Cap. Cap heard him coming but he wasn't looking to stop for the confrontation. Perhaps he felt that if he made it to the city line he'd have hit an olly-olly-oxen-free-free-free-zone where no one could ask him anything. Regretfully, for Cap, he didn't quite make it. Jeff caught him with yards to spare. He closed the final few feet with a scream, "Cap!" Cap (almost imperceptibly) slowed. Salty, not quite sure what had transpired but smelling something very fishy, moved off the side of the road and feigned death. A good move on his part. Jeff was on Cap with a vengeance, "What did he mean? I thought we had a deal with him?"

Cap, never the diplomat, tried his best to downplay the situation. "We do, Jeffey. That was nothin'. Just Cinino trying to make himself important in front of a crowd."

If Jeff were six and not thirteen this placation would have still sounded suspicious. "No, that can't be it, it's something else." And in a daring leap into adult-hood, Jeff expanded his vocabulary, "He's trying to screw us. I know it. That asshole."

Cap ignored the vulgarities, or maybe he just didn't recognize them as such. He couldn't remember a time or a conversation that he had been part of where language like that (and much worse) wasn't used. "Now take it easy, Kid. You don't know the man. He was like a little fish trying to make a big splash. Nothing to it."

"You sound like you're defending him." And since his verbal virginity had been breached, he continued to expand his lexicon, "Cinino's a son-of-a-bitch. You know it."

Before Cap could attempt to defend himself, or attempt again to explain Cinino's behavior, Nancy came jogging into the conversation. Cinino's impromptu speech seemed to have shaken everyone's peace of mind enough that they had forgotten their manners, and their rhetorical restraints. She interrupted, and asked of Cap, "Where's Phil? I saw him leave with you." She waited none too patiently for an answer.

Cap was initially relieved that he didn't have to answer Jeff's questions because of Nancy's interruption, but now finds that he had jumped from the frying pan directly into the fire. His plan, shaky to begin with, now began to resemble the proverbial house of cards with Jeff tugging on a bottom card and Nancy blowing on the top card. Best to answer directly but vaguely, "He had to go into Salt Lake City. On business. Didn't tell me what kind. Said he'd be back in time for Cinino's meeting."

In a brief span of time, Nancy felt like she had come to know the way Phil's devious mind worked. This sudden visit to the city didn't sound like that Phil. Or Cap wasn't telling her what really was going on. "Sure," she said, her voice hovering between sarcasm and sheer disbelief. "What is he really doing there?"

Cap elevated his own voice to the exasperation level. It grabbed the lip of exasperation but barely hung on, threatening to fall back down into the valley of guilt and suspicion. "How should I know? He doesn't work for me." He tried to back away from Nancy. She two-stepped with him.

In something less than a cotillion voice, "Cough it up, old man, something's fishy and it isn't the Whale."

The 'old man' comment never ceased to rub Cap the wrong way. It made it worse that Nancy's feminine intuition had it's antennae up and zeroing in on the truth. "Listen, little girlie, there is nothing going on, nuthin' at all."

Salty, with his own brand of intuition—canine clairvoyance— also knew that Cap was lying through his dog-teeth. Jeff was totally lost but looking for map. He wanted to get a word in edgewise but there were no cracks in the Cap/Nancy dialogue.

Nancy knew she was onto something and with a bulldog's tenacity, of which Salty was quite jealous, she charged ahead, ignoring or unseeing the risks. "Another secret, old man? You never did tell me why we played that little escape scene with Cinino's hulks. What gives?"

There were no escape scenes on the map Jeff was looking at. He interjected, "What scene? What are you talking about?" He aimed his questions at both of them.

Nancy looked at Jeff with surprise and figured that the kid was as much in the dark as she was. Which was strange since she thought he really ran the boat show. She then looked at Cap hoping that he could enlightened both of them. Cap didn't want to look at either one of them. Instead, he was checking around his feet making sure that there were no 'ears' in the desert. "Calm down, both of you." He surveyed the scene one more time before continuing: "Look, you are both going to have to trust me." Nancy was already starting to shake her head at that prospect. "Don't worry 'bout what's going on now. Take my word for it, everythin's going to be all right."

Jeff and Nancy, in unison, said, "But..."

Cap pushed away from them with his hands. "No buts. You got to trust me. Now I got things to do." He turned away from them and quickly made his exit into the hills. The calvary was in full retreat. Nancy and Jeff each took a step to follow. Cap, using his own brand of extrasensory perception, sensed their movements and said over his shoulder, "Don't you follow me." There was enough of an implied threat in his voice that Jeff and Nancy stopped dead in their tracks. Salty, knowing better, followed after Cap.

Яℬ A DEAL IS A DEAL IS A DEAL

If ever a war had started in which the two sides were as confused as the warriors that crowded into the Craig Breedlove Junior High School on this night, it took place long before the written word was invented. Members of the Cinino casino public relations staff were manhandling the crowd, separating Wendover residents from the outsiders like wheat from the chaff. The chaff, including all of the Whale's crew members, and bunches of tourists and media types, were rising to the occasion and becoming as surly as the P.R. staff. The Wendover 'insiders' were directed into the bowels of the gym where they were forced to stand and sweat, thereby increasing the ambient temperature beyond overheated and stuffy.

In direct contrast to the heat and stuffiness of the gym, the atmosphere surrounding the shipyard was cool and serene. The lone Cinino bodyguard on site was drifting in and out of a light sleep. The flapping of the Whale pennant on the mast and the distant murmuring of angry people were swept together into a sound not unlike gentle waves lapping at the shore. This, too, added to the guard's sleepiness.

Back at the school, the outlander chaff were milling around (wasn't the wheat supposed to be milled?) waiting for something to happen. Phil arrived back, parking his trusty Beemer headfirst between two school busses. With just barely enough room to open his door, Phil twisted and shimmied his way out of the car and onto its roof. He then did an awkward roll and slid down the windshield and hood, landing on his butt in the dirt and weed-infested parkway. He hopped to his feet, dusted himself off and made a beeline for the gym door. He dodged, feinted and ducked his way past friend and foe alike. He took aim on a potential crack between two no-nonsense P.R. flaks guarding the entrance, readied himself for the lunge and tensed his leg muscles to leap. His take-off was terminated as an interceptor missile of an arm shot out, deploying a grappling hook of a hand on his shoulder and aborting his launch into outer gymnasium.

"Where the hell have you been?" the voice attached to the launch aborter asked with obvious relief. Nancy released his shoulder and gently brushed off the wrinkles caused by her strong grip. "Cap, laid some bogus line on about you having business in Salt Lake City."

Phil was relieved that he had been intercepted by friendly forces. He wasn't looking forward to fisticuffs to gain entry into the meeting. Seeing Nancy was a pleasant shock but one that had to be minimized. Phil was a man on a mission. "I can't explain now, Babe. I have to get inside for the meeting."

Nancy let the 'babe' remark go by, passing it off to the high emotions running around the meeting. "Forget it. That Cinino character has ordered that only town residents be allowed in. Rest of us out. He makes Tricky Dick look good."

"Let's just tell those Bozos who's responsible for actually building the boat. If it weren't for us, " he didn't get a chance to finish. Nancy put her hand over his mouth.

"I tried that, but the pigs didn't buy it. Seems they barely have enough room in there for the Wendover people."

"Come on." Phil took her hand away from his mouth, after discretely kissing it, and pulled her away from the crowd and around the back of the building. "We have to at least hear what's going on in there." They disappeared into the shadow of the wall, as a gavel pounded inside.

The small gymnasium, a Quonset hut built like thousands throughout the U.S. after World War Two, was stuffed with people. Chairs had been set up but the crowd was so large, after all this was both Wendover communities, that most of the people were sitting on the floor or leaning against the walls. Several clever, and energetic, kids had jumped up and were sitting on the basketball backboards. Small clusters had formed amongst various like-minded thinkers. The Cutters were at the opposite end of the floor from Cinino and the merchants of Wendover. Amos and his cronies had found themselves isolated from the rest of the citizens by a distance equal to Amos' spitting range plus one foot. Cap, shielding Salty with his body (bi-pedal citizens welcomed, four-legged ones prohibited), had given new meaning to the word 'wallflower'. Phil and Nancy finally managed to find a small window at the back of the gym. A small enough window that they had to take turns peering through the dust-encrusted pane to glimpse the proceedings inside.

Dave Caster realized that it was time to begin the meeting when he succeeded in chewing through his lip. A nervous, and dangerous, habit for a public speaker. One he would have to learn to live without if he wanted to live. He banged his honorary gavel down on a small table drug in from Jeff's homeroom. The crowd quieted at the sharp sound of the gavel, then, realizing that it was only Dave, resumed their conversations. Dave banged the gavel down again. Three times, each louder than the previous one. "Please be quiet. The sooner you get quiet, the sooner we can get started." The crowd's anticipation of events-to-come quieted them more than Dave's quavering voice. "That's better. Now the reason this special town meeting has been called is so Mr. Cinino, the owner of the casino on the Nevada side, can discuss with you the future plans for the Wendover Whale."

A middle-aged man rose off one of the rickety chairs and waved to be recognized. He was primly dressed, as befit one of the more conservative Mormons living in Wendover. Dave didn't see the hand waving in the crowd or chose to ignore it. The unrecognized Mormon threw his caution to the wind and barked out, "What's that man got to do with our Whale?" Several other voices, seated around the conservative one shouted out in agreement. Dave, under strict instructions from Cinino, tried to regain order with more gavel pounding.

"I think if you'll let Mr. Cinino speak, he'll explain everything. Isn't that right, Mr. Cinino?"

The Diminutive One walked through the crowd to the table in front. With obvious relief, Dave set the gavel down and retreated to a seat under one of the basketball backboards. In deference to those in the audience, like the conservative Mormon, Cinino had picked more conservative threads. He had foregone his 100% polyester for a cotton/poly blend. This move, while a daring fashion statement, still kept him miles apart from this audience which was dressed for the most part in well-used denim and well-cared-for cotton dresses. He cleared his throat, smiled his best ingratiating smile, and stepped up to the microphone. Without any hesitation, he readjusted the microphone stand downward before beginning. "Good evening, ladies and gentlemen. I'm very sorry to have taken you away from your familial obligations this evening but this was a matter I felt necessary to talk to you about."

"Get on with it, Cinino!" a not-so-gentleman shouted from a crowd in the back. Anonymity making the voice sound more hostile and impatient than the conservative Mormon's voice was to Caster. Cinino was flustered by this heckler since it disrupted the timing of his patter.

"All right, my friends, I'll come right to the point. I have made arrangements to have the Whale moved to a more desirable spot." He paused to squeeze the most drama out of the moment. "It will be moved to the parking lot of my casino." The gym floor erupted with more protests then the varsity basketball team ever made in twenty seasons of bad officiating. Not so remarkably, the protests came almost exclusively from the Utah citizenry. The Nevadans, particularly those engaged in tourism-related business, tried their best not to break out in unrestrained adulation. Dave launched himself out of his chair and flung himself at the gavel. Failing to secure a strong grip on his first attempt, he tried again. With more success, he hammered the table to regain order. The only calm among the storm was Cinino. He patiently waited for the hue and cry to drop down below hue level, "It is all perfectly legal. When you, the good people of Utah failed to give enough support to Cap and Jeff and the construction of the Whale, I offered them a deal."

His steady voice, unfazed by their demonstrations, forced the crowd to quiet and listen. "In return for enough money to finish the Whale, they, Cap and Jeff, the legal owners of the Whale, gave me complete possession of the boat for one year following completion. Since we celebrated its completion this morning, and it was a glorious celebration, wasn't it, I plan to move it tomorrow morning."

Jeff was in complete shock. Just when his vision had taken on substance and was his to physically possess, he was to be dispossessed of it. Tears welled up in his eyes and he turned to those people trained to deal with these kind of emergencies; his parents. "He lied to us. He said he was giving us a week after it was finished." His mother wrapped her arms around him. His father lay a comforting arm over his shoulder and then showed he missed more than a few parenting classes by asking, "Why didn't you tell us? We could have helped out."

Cap maintained his wall-flower pose but more than a few of the crowd had turned to see what his response would be. Cap managed to maintain a stoic exterior even while his mind raced for the appropriate reply.

Cinino was loving every minute. His pre-speech run-through anticipated everyone's response. To a megalomaniac, there was nothing like the feeling of anticipating and controlling all the people you come into contact with. Cinino's brand of megalomania had a mean streak of sadism attached to it. "I'm sorry if this will inconvenience the merchants on the Utah side, but fair is fair. You've reaped the benefits of the Whale for three months. Now it's the Nevada side's turn." What he left out but everyone knew was that a completed Whale, one that people could touch, or photograph or even stand on, was far more valuable commercially than one that resembled a pile of mismatched lumber. The groans of the soon-to-be poorer Utah businessmen succumbed to strong cheers and applause from their counterparts over the state border.

Zack Mason, owner of the Sand and Salt Market, and Simon Locke looked like they were sharing a heart attack. Forgetting for the moment that they had survived, if not prospered, pre-Whale, they had visions of little Wendover Whales, dollar signs emblazoned on each unfurled sail, sailing over the edge of a flat earth into the bleak nothingness of space. Zack defribulated long enough to shout, "You can't do that!" A weak response at best but heartfelt nonetheless.

Simon Locke, having a moment to get more blood and oxygen into the thinking portion of his anatomy, chimed in. He asked, "What's Cap and the boy get out of this so-called deal? They do all the work and get nothing. It's a rip-off." A very funny statement if one looked at the person making it. Simon, along with many others, had leeched on the Whale, sucking much out of it and returning nothing to its builders. But like any good sound bite, the cry of 'rip off' created resonance with the crowd and they began to chant it. The gym rocked with the chant but no one enjoyed it except Cinino. Beneath his cool cotton/poly blend he was so gleeful that he wasn't certain he could keep from peeing in his pants.

Squeezing his legs together to suppress the urge, he verbally played his trump card. He had to shout into the microphone to be heard over the chanting. "You're forgetting what I just said. I only get the Whale for one year, after that it goes back to Cap and Jeff. It will be theirs forever."

Amos made his way toward the microphone and Cinino. As if an invisible force (or just his reputation as a nasty spitter) moved in front of him, people cleared out of his way. Even Dave Caster, seeing the charge, elected to sit this one out. Amos stopped about ten feet in front of the little table and clamped his hands on his hips. He gave his meanest stare to Cinino. Cinino returned it without even a blink of an eye. The crowd quieted as this staring contest took on the trappings of a western shoot out. Finally, Amos said, "That is bull crap if I ever heard it. They're getting screwed." In lieu of an exclamation point, he hocked a lugey at Cinino's feet. The splatter of the spit created a measles-pattern on the Short One's Hush Puppie casuals. Cinino glanced from his shoes back up to Amos. Amos didn't back down, and his cronies stood behind him, backing up their 'leader'.

A little bead of sweat stood out on Cinino's upper lip, not unlike his idol, Richard Milhous Nixon, during the Kennedy/Nixon debates. This kind of confrontation was something he thought might happen but when faced with the reality of it, Cinino was more than a little nervous. His bladder problem was now forgotten. "I know it sounds like a tough deal, but they agreed to it. They didn't have to. I didn't twist their arms. Ask them."

The crowd, having seen the first gunfighter take his best spit and only wing his opponent, fully expected that Cinino would aim to kill. When he chose to turn and walk away from the fight, they were disappointed. In their disappointment, they booed the coward. Or they booed Amos' bad aim. Or maybe they were booing the deal. But a boo was a boo was a boo-boo to Cinino. Now was the time to throw crumbs to the angry mob. "I'm glad to see such an outpouring of sympathy for Cap and Jeff from their own community." This really confused the boo-ers so they stopped booing. "Listening to you, I am troubled." He paused as if wracking his brain for a better solution, and then continued, "Yes, it will please you to know that I have reconsidered my agreement with them." The crowd quieted. The Nevadans got a little nervous, moving back and forth on their feet. "How does this sound? So that they won't have to be without a boat for an entire year, I have purchased them a substitute. Please open the side doors." Like the impresario at a small circus, Cinino waved his arm toward the doors on the side of the gym. This was the cue for several of his public relations employees to fling the door open. Although the drum roll and trumpet fanfare were missing, the staging was quite impressive.

On the shoulders of his biggest guards, came a 13-foot Laser sailboat. The bow of the boat made it into the gym but its progress was abruptly halted as the aluminum mast smacked into the door lintel. The door height was eight feet, the height of the mast was 16 feet. Cinino missed the structural impasse as he directed his next comment to Cap and Jeff. "At this time, I would like to present to the builders of the Wendover Whale, Jeff and Cap, the Wendover Whale Two. One of the Laser-carriers had enough good sense to have the boat backed up. The mast was pulled up and out of the mast hole and laid on top of the deck then the small boat was brought into the gym in pieces. Not quite the same grand entrance but an entrance just the same. The crowd stared at the boat, not sure as to how to react. Several Benedict Arnolds, having been prepped and bribed earlier in the day, began cheering and clapping loudly. A few Nevadans added more applause, and then, lemming-like, several Utes did the same. Only slightly put-off by the mast snafu, Cinino picked up his patter, "I know it's not quite the same as the other Whale, not by a long shot, but then it only has to last a year." He got a little laughter, a little more applause. "Why don't you come up here and accept your new boat? Jeff? Cap?" He searched the crowd for Jeff, knowing that he was the key to pulling off this mock drama. It was a tribute to Cinino's staging of this event that no one had questioned his having purchased the Laser prior to changing his mind about the deal he struck with Cap and Jeff.

Jeff was frozen in his spot between his parents, like a deer caught in the headlights of oncoming car. He knew that he had been betrayed. He felt like everything had turned against him. With his whole world crashing down even the little sailboat was better than nothing. And it only needed to last for one year.

His mom read his jumbled thoughts and tried to make it easier. "You don't have to accept it."

Jeff responded indirectly, "He's a liar and he cheated us. I can't take it."

His father, in a fabulous display of new-age parenting, said, "It's up to you, Jeff. I'll support whatever you decide."

Jeff shook his head, hoping the action would force the bad thoughts out of his head exiting through his ears, leaving him with the one appropriate action. "I don't know." This turn of events had blown the 'vision' right out of his body, leaving a desperately insecure 13 year-old in its wake. If either his mother or father had, at this moment, told him to do something, even something crazy, he would have done it. But they weren't offering him even directions, so he turned to the only other authority figure in his life; Cap.

He yelled over the voices of the crowd urging him to go and accept the gift, "Cap!" He yelled again as he moved around the crowd looking for his main man. It was a plaintive cry, plaintive enough to move Cap's heart. He stepped away from the wall and into the light so that Jeff could see him. Jeff ran to him. "He lied to us. What do we do, Cap? We can't let him get away with it."

Cap looked at Jeff and saw a boy willing to fight for what was his. But over Jeff's shoulder he could see Cinino watching the two of them. Cap looked back at Jeff and Jeff's eyes were begging. Jeff pleaded, "We can't let him take the Whale...he promised."

Cap started to speak and caught sight of Cinino out of the corner of his eye. Cinino had casually drawn from his pocket the cocktail napkin 'deed' that had become the bane of Cap's life. Cinino, never one for subtlety, pantomimed the question, 'should I ask this crowd if they are interested in this little cocktail napkin?'

Something inside of Cap appeared to crumble. He grabbed Jeff by the shoulders and yelled in his face, loud enough for everyone around to hear, "Take his stinkin' little gift. The Whale is cursed and good riddance to it!" He pushed Jeff away so strongly that the boy had to be caught by some of the people around him. Cap jostled his way through the crowd and fled through the side door. The same door that WW2 (the boat not the war) had made its arrival through.

The people that caught Jeff helped him to regain his feet but he had been (spiritually) crushed. Not by the heavier bodies around him but by the psychic betrayal of his best friend. He had lost the two most important things in his life; his vision and his only true friend. He began to cry and his mother raced to comfort him by wrapping her little boy in her arms.

Cinino was unmoved by this last string of events. Everything had gone swimmingly. He never liked Cap and now the old man had been showed to be spineless and heartless in front of both towns. Yes, indeed, life could be good for the power-hungry and ruthless. He would have liked to walk out the door now but there wre a few loose ends to tie up. "Well, I guess it's all settled, folks." He waited to have everyone's attention before speaking again. "Isn't it nice to see this story end with everyone happy? And now I'd like to take this opportunity to invite you all to my casino tomorrow. The fabulous Wendover Whale, the original that is," with a gratuitous nod toward the Laser, "will be transferred by train to its new resting place in my parking lot at nine o'clock in the morning. I know thats early for some of you but please come, there will be refreshments, and plenty of free parking." This final comment elicited a good laugh from the crowd since there were hundreds of square miles of 'free' desert parking surrounding Cinino's casino. Cinino stepped back from the microphone signaling the end of the evening's fun and games. The crowd, as if on cue, struggled to its collective feet and moved toward the exits. There was a murmur emanating from some of them that hung like a collective bad feeling just inches from the arched ceiling of the gym. If the crowd stayed any longer and the bad feeling got any heavier it might rain down and ruin Cinino's parade.

Remembering his role too late, Dave Caster returned to the mike to say, "Thank you for your generosity, Mr. Cinino." He stumbled over the word generosity, sarcasm wasn't a normal part of his lexicon. Cinino shot him a 'shut up and get the hell away from me' stare. Caster interpreted the meaning correctly and quickly backed away. Cinino seized the moment, not willing to give up the last word, and leaned back into the mike, "Don't forget, that's nine o'clock, at my casino." He chuckled to himself. He was on a hot streak with no end in sight.

❦ KEEPING SECRETS

Not too far away from the gloating Cinino, but far enough away that wandering ears could not inadvertently listen in, Phil Kurtzman dialed a number at a phone booth. Outside the glass-walled booth, Nancy was pacing back and forth. A car drove by the booth and both Nancy and Phil stared at it until it disappeared into the darkness. Someone answered on the other end of the phone line and quickly Phil turned back to the receiver. "Hi, this is Kurtzman. Yes. Run the story, page one if you can get it. Yes, yes. The Whale is on the move." He listened for a moment. "Yah, thanks, we'll need lots of it." He hung up and turned to Nancy. She had been eavesdropping on his side of the phone conversation, hanging on every word like the secrets of long life were going to be revealed.

She didn't wait for Phil to engage her after he hung up the phone. Her SoCal cool had been blown away by the day's happenings. "What the hell is going on? First, you run away to Salt Lake City at the first sign of trouble. And now you don't even seem concerned that Cap and Jeff just lost the Whale. Are you the real Phil Kurtzman or are you one of the bodysnatchers?"

Phil flashed a weary smile at her. She deserved more than that from Phil. He added a gentle hand to her cheek but that wasn't going to satisfy Nancy on this night. "It's a long and very complicated story."

"Well, I've got lots of time." She blocked Phil's exit from the booth. "And I mean to hear the whole thing."

This bravado brought a real smile to the reporter's face. He was smitten with this lady in front of him and he didn't have a problem admitting it to himself. "All right, I guess it won't hurt to tell you the plan."

Nancy's jaw dropped the proverbial mile. "This is all a 'plan'? You knew this shit was going to happen? The whole thing?"

Phil took her arm and led her away from the phone booth. "Let's take a walk."

She put her right arm around his shoulder and pulled him close. And then she shoved her left fist up close to his nose. "You knew the whole time and you didn't tell me sooner? You are a real jerk."

꧁꧂ BEING PARENTS—FOR ONCE

Ken and Elise opened the back door of their house and called out to their son. Ken closed the door without thinking about locking it. This lack of concern indicated that the threatening evils of the big city had yet to make their leap across the desert in small towns like Wendover. Or, perhaps, the lack of materialism exhibited in the meager furnishings of the Cutter's house meant they had nothing to lose to any itinerant burglar working the neighborhood. Or maybe he was just more worried about his son than anything else.

The kitchen and the rest of the house were dead silent. Ken, followed by Elise, moved from the kitchen into the dining room. "I'm sure he came home. I saw him running this way."

For the first time in his life, Ken realized how small and confining his home was. Not uncomfortable but restrictive, like a favorite old shirt that repeated washings had made just a little too small. He imagined now what his son must feel when he sees the possibilities that exist beyond these four walls and the outer limits of Wendover. A boy eager to burst out and taste the strange new fruits of the world being held back by a father who was always too scared to sample the same delicacies. They reached the end of the hall that led to Jeff's room and were faced with a closed and locked door. Locked doors to the outside world said that the family had issues with its neighbors, while locked doors on the inside of the house said that the family had issues with its members. Ken knocked on his son's door. "Jeff, Son, can we talk with you?" There was no response except that of crying being muffled by a pillow. Their was a gentleness in Ken's voice that surprised Elise.

This summer had been a season of surprises for her. The newly discovered strength of her son. The dream-to-reality journey of the Whale. And now her husband showing sensitivity where none existed before. Amazement wasn't a strong enough word, miraculous might fit better.

Even though his approach this evening was good, Elise felt that Ken brought too much baggage to the relationship with their son. In times of trouble, it must be the mom, with a capital M, who nurtures the injured soul. She put her lips close to the door and whispered, "Honey, we know how you feel. It was terrible that Mr. Cinino lied to you about the Whale." Jeff's crying slowed and then sputtered to a stop. He was listening because he couldn't hear a soft voice over his crying. A clever tactic on the part of his mom. She continued, "Unfortunately, there's nothing we can do about it. Bad people do bad things and in the process they hurt good people. Won't you please open the door so we can talk about it?"

There was no answer from Jeff. He wasn't crying behind the closed door but he wasn't making any move to unlock it either. Elise couldn't think of a *GH* magazine article that prepared her for dealing with shattered dreams. Ken put a hand on his wife's shoulder to comfort her. Could it be that his new-found sensitivity extended to his wife as well as his son? Miracles really did happen in Wendover. Ken took over the dialogue. "Look, Son, your mom and I are both sorry about what happened. If it is any consolation to you, what happened tonight helped me to make up my mind. I've decided that our family needs a change of climate. If I can find a job, I was thinking, we could move to California, or somewheres near the ocean." Elise began to cry. The tears that ran down her cheeks contained molecules of pure joy, making each drop a jewel more precious than the finest diamond. "How does that sound, Son? I just want to do what's right for you."

It sounded real good to the squished pillow and rumpled bedsheets on Jeff's bed. It sounded like a dream come true to Jeff's desk and the clutter of model-making paraphernalia scattered on top of it. It sounded perfect to the flimsy curtains that blew in the breeze from the open window. It probably was the perfect response from his parents to his problem, but Jeff wasn't in the room to hear it. Ken's voice filtered under the door jamb "You hear me, Jeff? I said your mom and I are committed to making it work. Whatever you want..."

☜☞ DEATH TO THE WHALE

The same breeze that Jeff escaped into from his house, snapped the Whale banner on the foremast of the Whale. With a billion stars zapping their illumination down out of a clear black and blue sky, the ship stood out from the desert floor better than a scantily-clad starlet at a klieg-lit movie premiere. The same clean, clear air that allowed some pinpoints of light a million miles away to shine brightly, amplified any small sound in the desert. If a lizard brushed past a precariously balanced pebble causing it to roll a foot down a gradually sloping bank it sounded like part of an Antarctic glacier cracking and cascading into the ocean. So the noise created by Jeff as he piled up hot dog wrappers, cotton candy cones and anything else he thought flammable against the hull of the Whale sounded like a poorly-tuned Zamboni cleaning the ice at a hockey game. When a Whale burned in the desert did it make a sound if no one was there to hear it? The collecting of combustibles sounded loud to Jeff but he just didn't give a damn. When he struck the match that lit the fire, he did not hesitate one iota. When the fire caught in the trash and licked around the edges of scrap wood that he piled on, Jeff did not falter. When the flames leapt up and blackened the shellac on the hull, his only response was to blink away the tears caused by the acrid smoke. The same dark smoke carried up into the sky, lifting the spirit of the ship high into the night, separating the spirit from its Earth-bound charge. Its commitment to Jeff and his vision went up in smoke without a second-thought.

If the non-corporeal observers seemed nonchalant to the destruction below, the very corpo-real, in the form of Phil Kurtzman, blew a gasket when he saw the fire. "Jeff! Stop it," he yelled as he and Nancy came charging toward the fire. Their romantic stroll in the starlight instantaneously forgotten as the image of a small boy dancing in front of a fire appeared before them. The fact that the boy seemed to be celebrating the cremation of his own dreams made this vision a tragedy written in hell. Phil grabbed at the flames and then snatched his hands back from the searing heat. He kicked at the burning wood and succeeded in spreading the fire out and away from the edge of the hull. A shower of sparks and embers shot skyward, a belated fireworks display for the Whale christening. The spirit, peacefully floating on the heated currents of smoke, was jolted awake by the embers burning his butt or whatever spiritual beings sit on. Nancy scooped up desert sand and flung it onto the still-flaming wood. Within a minute, the combined efforts of Nancy and Phil prevailed against the fire demons. Although much of the fire was still smoldering, the Whale had been saved from all but superficial damage. Jeff had stood by numb as these heroics had taken place. The matches used to start the mini-inferno still gripped in his left hand.

Nancy patted down Phil's pant legs, momentarily examining the new hem line created by an ember which had taken up temporary residence in Phil's cuff. In a gentle reciprocity, Phil tried gamely to wipe the soot off of Nancy's cheeks. Once reassured that they were both unharmed they turned, in unison, and spoke, in unison, to Jeff. "You're crazy!" Phil added, "What did you think that would accomplish?"

Jeff was staring through Phil and Nancy at the Whale. He had the look of a boy who had survived a terrible catastrophe while all who were dear to him had perished. It was a look of longing, a wistfulness that suggested he should have gone up in flames too. The catastrophe was not that all others were lost but that he survived. He finally answered Phil in a voice as insubstantial as the weight of the Whale spirit above him, "I didn't want Cinino to have it. Cap didn't care. So I burned it up." Whether his vision had been impaired by the smoke or he was in an emotional cocoon, he acted like the Whale didn't exist anymore.

Phil snatched the matchbook away from Jeff. Like this would snap the boy out of the spell. It did not. Phil grabbed him by the shoulders and shook him, the boy's body was limp and moved effortlessly whenever Phil shook it. "Burning the Whale won't do anything for anyone. That was a very silly, stupid thing for you to do." He wanted to slap the boy across the face but didn't. It finally, slowly, painstakingly entered his thick skull that Jeff did what he needed to do based on what he knew—he had been betrayed by friends and his most precious treasure had been stolen from him. Under the circumstances, Phil might have considered the same course, if he had the guts that Jeff had. He hugged the boy with a show of affection that was beyond his capabilities only weeks before. Nancy observed this small act and knew that her wild bachelorette days in Southern California would soon be coming to an end.

This Rockwellian scene—a man, a woman, a boy, a burned boat—is intruded on by the sound of a heavy beast hurtling itself toward them. Moments later, sound traveling much, much, much faster than a big overweight oaf could run, one of Cinino's men huffed and puffed his way into this heart-warming milieu. He managed to spit a word out after every gasp for oxygen, "What-the-hell's-going-on-here?" He saw that the fire, deprived of its fuel source, was merely glowing and smoking embers. Phil let go of Jeff and comically attempted to shield the evidence of the fire from the eyes of the Cininoite. Nancy lunged against Phil in an awkward embrace, trying to further protect their hot secret from this thug. Even the two of them, working together, were inadequate for the job. The thug continued, "What is that?" He waved his hand at all the smoldering wood.

Phil, the fastest thinker on his feet, if not the most clever, stepped forward to intercept this threat. He tried the simplest approach, a bald-faced lie, "Nothing. My friends and I were having a marshmallow roast to celebrate Jeff's new gift and Mr. Cinino's good fortune. As you can see, things got a little out of hand." He eloquently gestured to the remains of the fire. The thug struggled with the vision of a fire this size and could only imagine the proverbial 800 pound marshmallow being spit-roasted like a side of beef. He thought to himself (it was a slow and painful process) that anybody who was stupid enough to eat marshmallows without Hershey's chocolate and graham crackers deserved the benefit of the doubt. Phil continued, "Don't you worry, we don't want anything to happen to Mr. Cinino's Whale, either." He made no apologies for not offering any s'mores to the thug.

The thug said, "Okay, but you gotta' be more careful with your fires. 'Sides, my boss don't want anybody near the Whale until it gets moved. You understand?" The bodyguard stomped out the remains of the fire, relishing the scrunching sound his boot made on each of the coals that he extinguished. Phil and Nancy leapt to assist him.

Phil said to the thug, "We'll just help you with this mess, and then we'll be out of here in a flash. Less than a flash." Jeff hovered at the periphery, a half-boy/half-apparition, as if the stuff of dreams had been removed, leaving him an empty vessel. With the process of fire-fighting completed, Phil pulled Nancy and Jeff away from the Whale and the thug. The thug watched them suspiciously. He had done a complete search of the area and could find no sticks suitable for marshmallow roasting. No marshmallows, no sticks, no chocolate and no graham crackers added up to a not-quite-believable story.

Making sure that the guard remained out of ear-shot, Phil urgently whispered to Jeff. "Look, Jeff, I know it's been tough on you, but I'm warning you, stop messing around with the Whale. For your own good." His voice rose a little at the end, and he checked to make sure the thug wasn't listening.

Jeff was confused. And he was angry at Phil for telling him what to do and what not to do. If it wasn't for Phil, the Whale would be a pile of charred wood and Jeff would be a happy camper. The more he thought about, the angrier he got. He shouted, since he didn't give a shit whether the thug heard him, "Why should I listen to you? You're as bad as Cap. When I need you, you aren't even around.

And then when I don't need you, you pop up, like, like, Smokey the Big Bad Bear."

Phil pulled Jeff further from the thug and motioned for him to keep his voice down. "I need you to trust me. You need to give me," he lowered his voice even lower, "one more day. Stay away from the Whale."

"Give me one good reason and I will," Jeff answered. He wanted to believe in Phil. He needed someone, anyone, to believe in at this point. Nancy was biting her lip, waiting for Phil to give Jeff the answer he needed but Phil was too aware of the thug drifting toward their conversation.

Phil answered lamely, "I can't explain it now, you'll just have to trust me. One lousy day, Jeff, please." He knew that was not enough but, under the circumstances, he couldn't say anymore.

"Hah! That's exactly what Cap said to me. And then he went out and screwed me." He picked up a rock and flung it at the Whale. The rock bounced off the hull with a dull thump and nearly whalloped the thug in the back of the head. He yelled at the boy but Jeff had raced out of the shipyard. The thug gave up the chase almost before he started. His job was to protect the boat, not to chase scrawny rock-throwing kids.

Nancy grabbed Phil by the back of the belt and yanked him in the opposite direction from the one taken by Jeff and the thug.

Ⳬ KEEPING A SECRET

"You stupid son of a bitch," Nancy spat at Phil when they were a good distance out into the desert. She was pissed-in-her-pants angry, and the angry radiated out of her like a red-hot sun. Whether it was her breath or this radiant heat, Phil felt it on his cheeks. If she were any angrier, his face would have looked like the toasted marshmallow the thug was still looking for. "You had your chance. Why didn't you just tell him the truth?" She didn't wait for an answer. "That boy is totally bummed out and you just sent him on another bad trip."

"I'm sorry, Nancy. Cap gave me explicit instructions not to tell anyone. If it leaked out, we'd never get away with the whole thing."

"So, why'd you tell me, bozo. I don't count? Women aren't people?" She was getting wound up, like the rubber band on a model airplane and Phil was afraid of jumping in and getting his hand chopped by the propeller blade. "I got a mouth. I could spill it, too."

She paused for a breath and Phil hopped in. Damn the propeller, full speed ahead. "No, you wouldn't." He gently stroked her arm. Almost the same as unwinding the rubber band. "Besides, I don't want to have any secrets between me and my future wife." This statement hit her like a neophyte boxer's combination; a weak jab of pleasure followed by a right hook of disbelief.

Nancy being in the heavyweight class of social pugilists countered with a straight shot to the midsection. "Oh, really? At any other time I might consider that a serious proposal, but not right now. I am too angry and too disappointed with you." Fortunately the blow landed to the right and below his heart, allowing Phil a chance to recover for the next round. He lifted his hands in resignation, hoping to lull his opponent-in-love with pacifying words, "What can I do? I made a promise to Cap." Nancy saw a wide-open target and moved in for the kill. "You can go find Cap and tell him how bad Jeff feels. Convince him to tell Jeff about the plan for tomorrow. He can't let Jeff spend the rest of the night feeling betrayed by his best friend."

Phil fended the blow off as best he could. He pleaded for mercy, "But Cap gave me specific instructions."

Nancy sensed the white towel being picked up in the corner and wanted to get in one final blow, "That man that I would consider as my future husband would do it. In a flash." The white towel, a sign of total surrender sailed in and hit Phil squarely between the shoulder blades. Deceptively powerful, the towel knocked the air out of his lungs and Phil collapsed into absolute submission. "I'll go talk to Cap."

The victor smiled and, in a gesture of compassion to her fallen foe, bestowed a kiss upon his lips. "I knew you would."

⚡ RED SKY AT NIGHT

From a distance the spotlight which bathed the Whale in dingy
yellow light created the illusion that an alien spacecraft from a
watery planet had crash-landed in the middle of the desert. The
picture was incomplete since there was an absence of life, both alien
and terrestrial, surrounding the craft. Whoever plunked the Whale
down on this tiny dot in the desert seemed to have walked away
from the smash-up and headed for the nearest phone booth to call
the Auto Club of the Milky Way. Not knowing the neighborhood
and being prudent, the alien commander probably took the keys out
of the Whale's ignition.

Salty didn't care one whit about whales, aliens or Auto Club
spaceship tow services. He had reached his limit in the frustration
department and was giving serious thought to finding a new master
and a new domicile. Cap had dragged himself and Salty up the
small hill outside of town to contemplate who knew what and to
stare down at an ugly boat. 'Life just doesn't get any worse than
this,' Salty was thinking to himself. Cap might have been thinking
great thoughts but he wasn't sharing them with his dog. A cooling
breeze snaked its way through the sand and up the hillside. It
brought with it the scent of fish to Salty's flaring nostrils. The tiny
hairs lining his nose quivered from the distinctive fetidness canned
tuna long since gone bad. The freshness date had expired well over
a million years ago. The stench excited a long-forgotten gland (and
organ), the primordial-beast gland, in this dog. Salty looked
longingly at Cap's leg while his modern brain did battle with his
raging pre-historical hormones. If not for the arrival of Phil, the
hormones would have routed the brain and taken Cap's leg for the
post-battle orgy. Phil's scent was the olfactory equivalent of
saltpeter and Salty's libido dropped lower than his belly in the sand.

Cap looked up as Phil reached the top of the hill. Phil was
respectful of the peacefulness of the hilltop and spoke softly. He
wasn't worried about being overheard but his own voice had begun
to grate on his nerves. The softer he spoke the better he liked it.
"Cap?"

Cap answered, "How'd you know I was here? No one knows I come up here."

Phil laughed softly and said, "I didn't know you were here. I already looked everywheres else." He waited for this mini-joke to get a response. None arrived. "I need to talk to you, Cap."

Cap ignored the statement. "I got a pretty good view from up here. Thought I might have seen some sort of commotion down by the Whale?" It was a question but it carried with it the sense that Cap knew something bad happened, all he needed was the details. Phil handed him the book of matches that Jeff used to start his raging unferno. "What's this? You know I don't smoke."

"Jeff tried to set the Whale on fire." What else needs to be said?

"Yep, that's what it looked like from up here. Saw the flames, heard some shouting." He was silent for a few moments, digesting the idea that Jeff had the guts to burn the Whale. "How much damage did he do?"

Phil exhaled a large breath before answering. The reaction, unknown to his conscious mind, was his body's attempt to remove the fish stink (that Salty had found so attractive) from his lungs. "Not really any, but that's not the point." He exhaled again, the smell was stuck and tickling his throat. "Jeff's hurting real bad right now. I want to tell him about tomorrow."

This got Cap's attention in a hurry. He had no trouble breathing, age and whiskey having deadened the appropriate sense organs. "No! We have to keep it a secret."

"What's the point? He is dying tonight. What good is your plan for tomorrow if he needs some good news tonight." He coughed hard and the last lingering molecules of prehistoric sea life drifted down into the sand. And with them went Phil's determination.

Cap said, "Look, Phil, he's a strong kid, he can survive it." He waited to see if this was enough of a reason for Phil to back down. Phil waited for more. "Right now Cinino, the little prick, thinks everything is going his way. He's relaxed and not looking around. If one word, even a hint of what we got planned, gits back to him, we'd be done for. He'd be on guard for something. And then we'd never pull it off."

"I still don't see what harm there'd be," Phil replied but he was cut off by Cap.

"It's got to look like Jeff and me lost the war. Like we turned tail and ran. Do you understand that?" He got up off his rocky perch to stared down Phil.

"Maybe I could sneak over to Jeff's house?" Phil said this without a lot of conviction. He knew Cap had made up his mind, right or wrong, and he wasn't going to change it. Phil only continued the conversation because he needed to tell Nancy that he put up the good fight.

"Why risk it? Jeff will make it through the night all right. And if we pull this off, he'll forget all about the last coupla' a days. If we told him now and we screwed up, he'd feel like we messed him over twice." He extended his hand to Phil in a gesture of friendship that had been lacking since the day Phil's car overheated. Phil shook his hand. "Why don't you go back down and keep Nancy warm for the night. Maybe even get a little shuteye. We're going to have a very busy morning."

Phil released Cap's hand. "Okay, you're the captain. Good night. Good night, Salty." He shuffled back down the hill, pulling with him the primordial-beast fragrance. It was unlikely that he or Nancy would get much sleep, thanks to urges Phil hadn't felt since he his wild times in San Francisco.

Cap looked back out at monster he had created. The yellow light cast upon the hull of the Whale did nothing to loosen the tightness in Cap's gut. The snowball had started to roll down the hill and he didn't want to get caught on the wrong (down hill) side of it. He absent-mindedly tossed the matchbook up and down.

Salty, now that Phil and his post-mordial scent have left, moved in on Cap's leg. Cap misread the affection as support for his efforts. "You think I'm doing the right thing, don't ya'?" Salty growled his most macho growl, hoping to get Cap's leg to submit. Cap bent to pet his loyal buddy and put the matches into his shirt pocket. "I'm sorry, if you don't agree. I'm doing it for Jeff, really." Salty jumped up, hoping to wrap his forepaws around Cap's leg. Cap chose that moment to start down the hill. "Come on, dawg, we got to get some sleep, too." He kept on walking, unaware that Salty was groveling in the sand, fighting the itch that he just couldn't scratch. He let out a mournful wail, bringing tears to the spirits floating overhead. They, too, were excited, knowing that tomorrow would be a fateful day in the desert.

ൠ THE WIND FRESHENS

The sun must have been tipped off that something big was going down. It exploded into the sky before most residents of Wendover had a chance to blink the sleep out of their eyes. Using the Great Salt Lake as a giant tanning reflector, the sun's rays streaked across the flat desert sand, raced up the tarmac of I-80 and radiated right through the grimy window panes of the Cutter household. If Jeff wasn't sprawled face down in his bed with a pillow keeping the cruel world out, he might have been caressed awake by the solar energy bouncing off his neck. But the pillow did its job and Jeff remained asleep even as Cap and a noticeably shaky Salty (not a salt shaker) crept across the patchy grass of the backyard. A good-looking cat, roused from its slumbers, zipped past Salt on its way to the wide open space. Salty, the primordial-beast still attached, got off a snappy come-on to the cat. In his state of mind and sexual deprivation, Salty saw the feline as a major step up from the human leg he was trying to 'date' during the night. Cap shushed him to silence. Together, quietly, they crossed the last few feet to Jeff's window, undetected by friend and foe alike.

Cap tapped on the glass of Jeff's window and waited. Nothing happened. Jeff's pillow continued to act as an effective barrier. Cap tapped again, a little louder this time. Silence from within. The best laid plans could be doomed by the smallest of consequences; a kid that slept heavy. Cap muttered a curse, followed quickly by a mumbled prayer, before he slid the window up and threw himself into Jeff's bedroom. He landed with absolutely no grace on the floor but with a minimal amount of noise. He crawled on all fours to Jeff's bed. The un-Santa-like entrance had not disrupted the visions of sugar plums dancing in the boy's head. Cap gently pulled the pillow away from Jeff's head. Jeff stirred and grabbed to hold onto the pillow. Cap said, "Jeffey, Boy."

He pulled the pillow out of Jeff's hands and Jeff cried out, half asleep, "No, no, it's mine. You can't have it."

Cap bent down so that his head loomed over Jeff as Jeff opened his eyes. "Jeffey, Boy, time to wake up."

Jeff opened his eyes, saw an enormous, scruffy face just inches from his own, and jerked up. Cap had to snap backwards to avoid a 'heads'-on collision with his partner. Jeff blinked several times to make sure that the reality was not the tail end of a bad dream and said, "What are you doing here?" And then he remembered the sordid details of the last twenty-four hours, and added, "Get out of my room." He pushes at Cap. Cap leaned back just far enough to give Jeff a little breathing room and then held fast.

"No, Sir. You and me have some business to take care of."

Jeff grabbed the pillow and hugged it to his stomach. This armor gave him a little more strength to respond to Cap. "I'm not doing anything with you. You stink. You gave away our ship and you didn't even fight for it."

Cap smiled broadly, displaying the decay caused by 40 years of not having a toothbrush. "Maybe I did, maybe I didn't." He winked at Jeff in a fashion that might have changed some people's opinion about Cap's ability to be Santa Claus. "And if I did, I'm changing my mind. This morning we're going to take it back. And then you and I are going to go on a nice little sail." Jeff was trying to match this statement to Cap's action of the last few days and it just didn't add up. Multiple acts of treachery and betrayal did not total out at heroic gestures. But this was the new arithmetic of the 70's and Cap was standing in front of him not only promising to get the Whale back but to also sail it. This was the kind of problem Jeff was willing to deal with.

Jeff could hardly get the words out of his mouth in his excitement, "Getting it back? You mean we're STEALING the Whale? We're taking her away? San Francisco?"

Cap laughed infectiously, perhaps insanely was a better term, knowing what they were about to attempt. "Close enough, partner. Now get your sailing clothes on." Jeff, performing at the level of a whirling dervish, managed to put on his clothes in less time than it would take the Mormon Tabernacle Choir to say 'Hallelujah!' three times. At he peeled pajamas off and threw clothes on, with his mouth moving as fast as his body, "I knew you wouldn't let 'em take it without a fight. I just knew it." He paused, his head not entirely through the neck hole of his shirt, "This is a plan, right? You worked it all out?"

Cap pulled the shirt down and Jeff's head popped up. Cap said, "We don't have time for big explanations. Wind's coming up and my nautical nose is getting itchy." He climbed back out the window with Jeff close behind.

⏃⏃ SMALL CRAFT WARNING

This glorious new day was starting well for almost everyone who was up to greet the sun. The most obvious exception to this statement was the Cinino goon assigned to guard the Whale in the shipyard. While the night was uneventful enough for him to sleep through it, he awoke suddenly to find himself bound and gagged, courtesy of Nancy and Phil. They then dragged him into the makeshift guard booth. As Cap, Jeff and Salty arrived, they were complementing each other on their knots.

Cap viewed this tableau with a mixture of hope and dismay. His plan called for the resistance (the guard) to be eliminated but the presence of Nancy was not anticipated. "Well, well. I wasn't expectin' any female company for this trip."

Nancy grinned and bore it. "I just happen to be in the neighborhood. Being a former girl scout, and all, I thought you might need some help."

Cap looked to Phil for a better explanation. Phil shrugged, "I had to tell her. She threatened to hurt me in places I don't want to talk about." Cap checked his watch, already moving past this small glitch in his plan. "It don't matter now, we've got to get going." Cap, followed by Salty, followed by Jeff, followed by Phil, exited the shack. Nancy followed behind collecting the goon's pistol as she went. "You won't be needing this. Besides, guns are bad, bad, bad." She quickly followed after the rest of the crew.

Even though country folks like those who livd around Wendover were early risers, they didn't rise early and head down to the railroad tracks to watch boats sit in the sand. Which meant the rescue crew had the shipyard to itself. A giant trailer crane had arrived in the middle of the night and parked itself between the Whale and the railroad tracks. On the tracks sat a short haul train; engine, two specially-braced flatcars and a caboose. Cinino had done an excellent job of getting the correct technology to make the Whale-move to Nevada as quick and painless as possible. He had even been so kind as to set the time of the move late enough to allow the crane operator to sleep in. And by sleep in, he meant sleep in the cab of the crane, heavily bundled against the cool night air.

Nancy volunteered to provide a wake up call to the operator while the rest of the crew prepared the Whale for its maiden voyage—a voyage rolling on tracks, not rolling in waves.

Nancy's bright and cheery voice calling hello as she stepped up and into the cab made the operator feel like he was getting an early bonus in the form of a Nevada call-girl. An 'advance' on the job to be well-done in an hour. Nancy chirpped, "Morning, sweetheart."

The crane operator was not a morning person but in light of the pleasant female company he croaked out, "What time is it, Honey?" He had entertained ladies of ill repute in his cab before, but he usually had time to spruce the place up, making sure the plastic slipcovers were in place and the like.

The rankness didn't seem to bother Nancy. She didn't check her watch before answering, "I don't know. Let's just say about seven. Beautiful morning, don't you think?"

The operator made a clumsy move to grab Nancy. She moved just out of reach of his arms. "We got plenty of time to get to know each other."

"Come on back in. I don't have to load this poor excuse for a boat for another hour." He grabbed again. He missed again.

Nancy purred her response, "My friends and I were hoping, if you don't mind of course, loading it now." She gave him a big whorey wink.

The operator licked his lips. Nancy displayed enough of her feminine charms to seriously excite this old boy. "You're crazy, Sugar. I got much better things to do with my time. If you know what I mean? Come here, dammit." He reached for her and Nancy pulled the goon's pistol out and stuck it against the operator's forehead. He froze. Imitating, badly, the operator's accent, Nancy answered, "Oh, Sugar, you're just the nicest, sweetest man. I know you'll do your best to load that little ol' boat on that little ol' train right now. Right, Sugar?"

The operator licked his lips again. Only this time they were really dry. The spit in his mouth just up and disappeared. Right about the time the big gun appeared in the pretty lady's hand. "Whatever you say, lady. If you want it picked up and dropped now, you got it."

Nancy smiled. "I knew we'd get along. I just knew it."

⚸⚸ MAN OVERBOARD

Nothing provides motivation like a gun to the head. The crane operator, perhaps unused to threats upon his person by beautiful young women, set a record in directing the crew in placing the crane's cable system around the Whale. The thick corded steel cables formed a nest in which the ship gently rested. Cap was standing amidships on the deck making sure that as the cables lifted and tightened, they didn't stove in the hull planking. Although nominally in command, Cap had no clue about the transshipment of a boat. His efforts at supervision amounted to little more than kicking the tires of a used car before its purchase—much ado about nothing. Phil and Jeff walked around the perimeter of the Whale performing the same non-function as Cap above them. Nancy had the only real job as she watched the crane operator jig the shift knobs. She had no need to give orders, the gun in her hand spoke for her. The crane operator gave her a nod and said, "I'm ready." Nancy pointed the gun barrel up. The operator gunned the engine and shifted the lifting mechanism into gear.

As the master cable lifted, the supporting cables tightened and groaned. Cap leaned over the railing, yelling at Jeff. "Why don't you go and have a chat with the train engineer?" He had to raise his voice as the pitch of the cables rose under the weight of the Whale. "We wouldn't want him movin' the train at the wrong time." The

Whale shifted slightly and Cap grabbed for the railing. Jeff gave him the high sign and ran off toward the train engine.

The crane continued to lift. The Whale stabilized enough for Cap to release the railing. The Whale lifted from its scaffolding 'home' and was air-borne. The crane continued lifting and now swung in a gentle arc toward the train. Once free of its Earth-bound encumbrances, the Whale began a swing not unlike the gentle rocking of a pleasure boat buoy-moored in a calm harbor. Cap spread his legs and adopted an exaggerated bow-legged stance that Popeye would have been proud of.

The train engineer, a Southern Pacific lifer by the name of Fred, leaned his substantial bulk out the window of his engine to watch the flight of the Whale. He wished he had a camera, any kind of camera, because what he was saw he just didn't believe. A strange looking boat, named for a big fish, built in the middle of the desert was being moved by a special train to a spot less than a mile from where it was built. Fred had seen a lot of strange things from the cab of his train but this beat all, by a country mile. What was even stranger was a weird bunch of people seem to be coordinating the move, including the young boy who was running toward him waving his hands. As long as he got his paycheck, Fred wasn't going to waste too much time trying to put the puzzle pieces together. Jeff ground to halt on the sloping area just outside the tracks and parallel to the cab window.

Fred asked, "I thought they weren't loading her til' later?"

Jeff instantly sized up Fred as a man who had traveled through a million small towns like Wendover but he had never really been in one. "Well, Sir, we in Wendover like to get things done as early as possible. You know what they say, the early bird gets the worm."

"They didn't change the time for me to move it over to the other town, did they?"

Jeff gave him his most ingratiating country bumpkin smile and answered, "Oh, no, Sir, you still have plenty of time. You just relax and enjoy the sight." He turned to watch the progress of the Whale as it moved toward the waiting flat cars.

Cap was enjoying his commanding view from the deck. The 'plan' seemed to be working flawlessly. No one had come into the shipyard screaming that the Whale was being stolen. Although more relaxed, he was not totally relaxed. His left hand was twisted in a rigging line to help him stay upright. His eyes were focused on the intended path of the Whale onto the flat cars and he didn't like what he saw. The Whale's flight was flat and would have it running into the outward bracing on the railcar if adjustments weren't made. He yelled to Nancy and the crane operator, both isolated from the noise by the Plexiglas window of the cab. "Higher! Get her up!" He waved with his free right arm trying to get one of them to respond. Neither of them was looking, both concentrating on the distance between the cradle on top of the train and the leading edge of the Whale. That edge was dangerously close to the support. Cap released the rigging, jumping up and down to attract their attention. "Dammit, the get boat higher!"

Boats were meant to sail on water. They were designed to keep water out. They did poorly when they ran into big objects, like icebergs, even though icebergs are just clumps of frozen water. Just ask the Titanic or what's left of the Titanic. Fortunately, the bracings on the flat car had nowhere near the mass of a iceberg. Unfortunately, the Wendover Whale was not even one five hundredth the size of Titanic. And when the hull of the Whale met the steel and wood support on the train something had to give. The wood in the brace cracked as the forward momentum of the Whale came to a dead stop. Without anything to hang onto, Cap was sent sprawling backwards into the open hatchway between the two masts. He had the presence of mind to grab for the edge of the hatch but his reactions were slow and his hands grabbed nothing but air. His body dropped into the hold of the ship and landed with a sickening thud in the dark interior. A sack of potatoes would have made a similar sound if dropped any distance onto an asphalt street.

Nancy had caught sight of the flailing arms as Cap descended into the hatchway. She yelled for the crane operator to stop the crane. The crane ground to a halt as the gears shifted into neutral. Nancy was out of the cab and yelling for Phil long before the boat came to a complete stop. Phil tried to climb up the side of the Whale but there were few handholds on the bottom of a hull, hanging five feet above his head. After unsuccessful leaps, he managed to find a rope hanging down and shimmied up it until he reached the railing. He swung himself over and onto the deck and raced for the hatchway. He yelled down at Cap, "Cap? Are you all right?" He saw Cap's body draped over the ribs of the hull and it didn't appear to be moving. "Cap, Cap, talk to me. Oh, Jesus, I think he's dead."

Jeff couldn't see or hear anything from his position below the Whale. He was worried and scared. "Is he all right, Phil? Can you see him?" He tried to get up the rope that Phil used but it was just beyond his reach. Frustrated, he banged his hands against the side of the Whale. "Please say he's okay, please say it."

Phil lay down on the deck and bent the upper half of his body down into the hold. Phil lied loudly, "Of course he is. He just needs some help getting out." Then softly to the blackness of the hold, "Don't screw it up now, Cap. I can not pull this thing off without you."

If this was a plea from Phil to the gods, one of the deities was having a slow day and responded by throwing a jolt of life force at the old man in the hold. Cap groaned and slowly moved his body around in the hold. "Don't I know it." His voice was strained and forced but was definitely Cap's voice. "A little tumble isn't going to sink old Cap. Maybe you could just give me a hand outta' here, Phil?"

When Phil reached down to grab Cap's arm, a thousand tiny but sharp daggers pierced Cap's ribcage. The three broken ribs, two in the front and one in the back, hurt him so bad that he couldn't feel the massive internal hemorrhaging occurring at the same time. He finally managed to get a leg up on the hatchway and roll himself up and onto the deck, Cap was sweating like sauna-ite and was white as Casper the friendly ghost. Phil noticed the change but was so relieved that Cap was alive and talking that he wrote off the body changes to the terror Cap must of had in the fall. "You sure had us scared." He tried to help Cap to his feet but Cap pushed his hands away.

His voice strained, Cap said, "It was nuthin'. Let's get this thing loaded and outta' here." He drew a deep breath and felt the daggers bite into his side. Beyond that he felt a rising fatigue that was non-existent before the fall. He needed another jolt of the life force pronto but the god had found other mortals to trifle with. So Cap was left with the feeling that his clock was ticking fast with no watch repair in sight. Putting his best face on, he walked to the boat railing and gave the thumbs up to Nancy and Jeff. "Everything's hunky dory. We've got some time to make up so let's get a move on." If smiles could heal internal injuries (excluding broken hearts, of course), the smile on Jeff's face would have mended ribs and sealed arteries. Alas, it did nothing for the pain and only strengthened Cap's determination to get the Whale to water. Phil climbed down off the Whale. He and Jeff took up positions between the rail car and the Whale. This time there would be no collision.

Nancy jogged back to the cab of the crane. The malevolent look on her face at twenty feet was enough to get the operator sweating bullets. By the time Nancy stepped up into the cab, the operator was feeling worse than Cap. Nancy made him feel even worse. She pointed the gun at his groin and said, "I'm thinking that was just a very unfortunate accident. You are very, very sorry that it happened, and this time you will do it right." She pulled the hammer back on the pistol and slid the muzzle of the gun between the zipper flap and zipper of his pants. "I would hate to mess up your equipment, if you know what I mean?"

Human beings, given the right motivation, could achieve anything. Jeff only needed a dream to create a ship where no ship existed before. Cap, needing the love of Jeff and the respect of others, was driven to put the ship into water even at great personal risk to himself. The crane operator, hoping to succeed Elvis Presley as America's Heartthrob, a task impossible without proper functioning 'equipment', placed the Whale onto the wood cradle on the flat cars as softly as a Pamper hugs a baby's butt. His attention was so concentrated on the task at hand that he didn't feel the gun removed from the folds of his clothing. Nancy slipped away to help the others release the cabling from around the Whale. The operator breathed a mammoth sigh of relief and collapsed in his seat. While his vision of heart-throbbin' was still intact, he was giving more serious thought to the dangers of crane operation.

The four members of the rescue crew were quick to release the cable hooks and begin the tie-down process. More accurately, Phil, Nancy and Jeff were quick to the task. Cap labored over every step he took and every knot he tied. Jeff stopped working and watched Cap struggle through a bowline. Several times he dropped the rope and then painstakingly reached down to pick up the end. Jeff couldn't bear it and zipped over to pick the rope up. When he handed the rope to Cap, he noticed how pale and sweaty his friend was. "Are you sure you're all right? You don't look so good." This was quite a statement since Cap, even on his best days, would never be mistaken for Steve McQueen or even Butterfly McQueen. And this was definitely not one of Cap's best days.

Cap said, "I'm peachy, Boy, just peachy." He managed to tie off the last support rope without showing too much pain. And since he was sure that the last answer hadn't satisfied Jeff, he added, "You know me. I just don't work too well when I got to get up early."

The crane operator didn't wait for them to signal him that his services were no longer needed. He reeled the master cable back up moments after the last hook had cleared the rigging. Like a man on a mission, he leapt from the crane cab and into the truck cab as soon as the crane structure had nested. Forgoing the paycheck that awaited him in Cinino's office, he roared out of Wendover, making a bee-line for Memphis, Tennessee, 1,350 miles away. Wresting the crown from the king of rock and roll would be easier than another morning like this one.

ର୍ଗ A NEW TACK

Oh, what a beautiful sight. The Whale sitting pretty on the flat cars, its twin masts towering over the top of the caboose and the engine, just waiting for the train engineer to blow his whistle and highball it to the big "O"—the ocean of peace—and the completion of a dream. The worst was over. All that stood in the way of this dream team was 1,000 miles of railroad track, the entire population of Wendover (Nevada), a demented short person who would stop at nothing to get his boat back and whatever law enforcement agencies Cinino could muster out between here and San Francisco. A piece of cake. A cream puff trip. A stroll in the park. Right. And Elvis was going to meet the crane operator at the Memphis city limits and hand over the keys to Graceland.

First things first. Cap, Jeff and Salty hunkered down in the caboose while Phil and Nancy made their way up to Fred in the engine. Phil wanted the gun back from Nancy but she wasn't letting loose of it. She liked the way men seemed to listen to her when she walked softly but carried a big piece. Fred watched them come, thinking to himself what a sweet couple they made and how boring life must be for them in this po-dunk town. He figured they were going to ask if they could have the thrill of their life, God bless them, and ride in the engine with him all the way over to Nevada.

Sure enough, Phil helped Nancy up the steps and into the cab. Fred grinned at both of them and they grinned back. Fred spoke first, "Name's Fred." He made a great show of shaking both of their hands. "I hope that old man didn't get hurt too bad?"

Phil replied, "He took a bad spill but he says he's okay Thanks for asking, Fred. I do know something that would make him feel much better."

'Oh, jeez,' Fred was thinking, 'things are going to be mighty crowded in here when they ask if the old guy and boy can also ride up front. But what the hey, you got to show these folks that city people aren't all bad.' Aloud, he said, "I'll be glad to help out."

Phil couldn't believe their good fortune. "That is very neighborly of you, Fred."

Nancy was looking around at the interior of the engine. Like all good Southern Californians, Nancy thought that private cars were the only form of transportation outside of jets, surfboards and sailboats. She had never been on a train, much less in a train engine. She touched everything with a light touch, not so much frightened that she would break something, rather fearing that the engine would roar to life. Her fingers lingered over the massive shift rod. Fred watched her, taking obvious pride in his powerful machine. Nancy, asked demurely, "Can this train go in reverse?"

"Of course, young lady. But we prefer moving forward." He chuckled at the simple-minded question.

Phil was less amused. "Fred, I would like you to put the train in reverse and bring it up to speed as quickly as possible."

"I can't do that, young man. I'm sorry but I have to take your boat that way." He pointed straight down the tracks toward Nevada and the Pacific Ocean beyond the horizon.

Nancy withdrew her new-found high-caliber friend, and in deference to Fred's politeness, let it dangle down next to her pant leg rather than rudely point it at his chest. "Mr. Fred, you misunderstood. We are not asking you if you'll do it, we are telling you to do it. Now."

"But I was told to go west. That way." He just couldn't believe that someone would be crazy enough to hijack a train. A plane definitely, a bus possibly but a train which was tied to two rails of steel? Never.

Phil said, "Think of it as a slight change of plans. You were going to go that way and now you are going to go this way. It's that simple. Put the train in reverse and we'll tell you when to stop." With great reluctance, Fred put the train in reverse and slid the accelerator up a notch, just enough for the wheels on the track to engage. The first surge was felt all the way through the train. Fred leaned out the window and, by force of habit, looked ahead to make sure the track was clear. He quickly realized his mistake and looked to the back of the train. "What if there's a train coming behind us?"

Phil answered, "There won't be. It's been taken care." Nancy added, "Stop wasting time, Freddy. Let's jam." Fred moved the accelerator up another notch and then pushed it forward a big jump.

The whole train lurched backward. In the caboose, Jeff had his head stuck out the window looking expectantly westward. Cap was trying to find a comfortable position on the bench seat. He was looking like death warmed over and then left out overnight. His rib problems had been reduced to a dull ache but the heaviness in his chest had grown worse. He couldn't get rid of the feeling of an ever expanding water-filled balloon lodged halfway between his heart and his lungs. Salty was watching his master like a hawk (making him a 'bird dog') and all of his extra-sensory dog perceptions told him that something was dying nearby and it was not the usual road kill on I-80. The train took another pitch backward and then started moving steadily to the east. Jeff couldn't believe it. He pulled his head inside the caboose and then, just to be sure, he stuck it outside again. "We're moving backwards!"

Cap, even in great pain, found sarcasm was the best answer, "You know, you're pretty sharp for a young cuss, Jeffey boy."

Jeff's eyes were as big as Quarter Pounders when he brought his head back in and stared at Cap. "But San Francisco is the other way. The Pacific Ocean is getting away." He was trembling with apprehension and lack of comprehension. Understandable since he had been buoyed by Cap to build the Whale, betrayed by Cap into giving up the Whale and convinced by Cap that there was a master plan for stealing and sailing the Whale. All of this in a few short months.

"That so?" Cap skimmed across the seat so that he could see that the train was indeed moving eastward. It didn't come as a surprise that the train was moving in that direction, but it was a complete surprise that they have gotten this far without anyone catching on. "I never exactly said we was going to the Pacific Ocean, did I?"

Jeff pondered that for a moment and then grabbed both of Cap's shoulders. Cap had to bite his lip to keep from passing out from the pain. Jeff thought he had the plan figured out. "You mean we're going all the way to the Atlantic? That'll take forever."

"If we were goin' all the way it might. But I know of this great big 'ol lake, this way," he noded to the east, "just waiting for a couple of fellows to sail their ship on it. God willin', we should be there in less than an hour." Now Jeff was totally confused.

Jeff's mind was spinning. He couldn't think of anything within an hour of Wendover until he got 'it.' And then he slapped his forehead in disbelief. "The Salt Lake? We're going to sail the Whale on the Salt Lake?"

Cap was tickled bloody red, "You're a little slow but you're finally catchin' on."

♋ THE PIRATE TRAP IS SPRUNG

The Dishonorable Rudolpho Cinino was giving a tour of Wendover, Nevada's answer to Disneyland, namely the back parking lot of his casino. But it was a parking lot no more. Sparing no expense, he had constructed a wooden edifice to the Wendover Whale, replete with special family viewing stations, photo opportunity sites and multiple concessionaire stands. Nothing was missing from this pantheon to the odd—clipper ship in the desert—except the ship itself. As Cinino glanced at his watch, he thought this special problem would be remedied in less than an hour.

The sycophants and other, less harmonious hanger-ons were following Cinino through the amusement park, oohing and aahing over every detail. The only discordant character to the place, aside from the neon colors of Cinino's latest suit, was the diagonal stripping on the asphalt, a reminder of the park's earlier incarnation.

One of the folks in the tour, overcome by the wave scrollwork on the corn dog stand gushed, "It's so beautiful, Mr. Cinino."

Cinino, never one to miss an opportunity for self-glorification, responded, "It will be even more beautiful, in an hour, when the Whale, MY Whale, is sitting here. The jewel in my crown, so to speak." This act of self-coronation, perhaps self-deification, was interrupted by the arrival of Dave Caster in his Datsun. Dave weaved his way through the parking lot cum Whale-land, honking his horn and scattering the early arrivals for the Whale's grand entrance. His approach was both maniacal and joyful, the car attacked the people, veering off at the last possible moment and then leaping ahead to find another target. Dave finally spoted Cinino, difficult in a crowd of normally-heighted people, and then pointed his under-powered, gas miser at the neon double-knit target and put the pedal to the metal. Everyone scattered as the car made a bee-line toward Cinino.

The last to bail out were Cinino's bodyguards. They had the misfortune of leaping out of way and landing on each other inside the (rigged) knock-down-the-milk-bottle carnival booth. Misfortune was heaped upon misfortune when the bottom-weighted milk bottles crashed down upon their heads, rendering them both unconscious.

Cinino held his ground, staring directly through the windshield at Caster. At the last possible second, Dave slammed on the brakes. The car fish-tailed and then brodied, the tires laid thick patches of rubber on the asphalt. Finally, the car came to a stop several feet from Cinino. Dave cursed himself for having the brakes redone at the end of winter and thus avoiding a possible fatality. He rolled down the window and smiled at his former boss. A genuine smile backed up by an aura of freedom from stress and responsibility. Something had happened to this man to make him believe in the basic goodness of life on planet Earth. "Good morning, Mr. Cinino."

Cinino was thinking that it was until Caster's arrival. "What do you want, Caster? You've caused me enough trouble already."

Dave couldn't keep the glee out of his voice. "I have an interesting story to tell you."

"I really don't have the time."

"You really should make the time for this one. It could be important to your plans."

"Okay, Dave, make it short."

Dave had no intention of making short. He was going to savor every word of his story. "Well, Mr. Cinino, I was just cruisin' through town, the Utah side of town, that is, when I thought I'd pay one last visit to the Whale. You know, before she was moved over here, and I had to pay admission to see something I kinda' feel like I helped to build." Cinino was getting angry and impatient. Dave continued, "And when I got there, the ship yard I mean, Mr. Cinino, she was gone. The boat just up and disappeared." He closed his story with another beatific smile.

Cinino didn't believe the story or maybe he misunderstood what Dave was saying. "Gone? Whatya' mean the Whale was gone?" And for a brief moment the superficial polish that Cinino had carefully applied to himself, slipped off to reveal the petty hood underneath. "I'll break your face, you fat slob. I know you're lying."

The fat slob remark hurt enough to make Dave suck in his stomach but not enough to make him stop smiling. "I'm not lying, Mighty Mouse. The boat was gone and so was the train."

Cinino leapt at the open window. "Now I know you're lying, fatso." Dave rolled up his window crank as fast he could work his left hand. "I've been here all morning. The train never came by."

Cinino hooked his fingers over the top of the window glass to keep the window from shutting completely.

Dave could have continued to crank and ruin two sets of perfectly good (albeit dinky) fingers but his revenge came when he said through the crack in the window, "And you called me dumb."

The 'rescue plan' exploded out of Cinino's brain like a vinegar and baking soda mixture in a clay volcano. "They're heading east." He yanked his hands back from the window and the safety glass shattered into a thousand small cubes of crystal, spraying Dave in the car and Cinino outside the car. "What an id..." He can't quite bring himself to say the i-word. "They set me up. Shit." He ran around to the other side of the car as Dave struggled to get his mouth to function and protest the demolition of his window. Cinino opened the passenger door and jumped in before the last of the broken glass tinkled to the ground.

Dave pivoted in his seat, difficult because his stomach and the steering wheel were two immovable objects. Something had to give, his stomach flinched first, and Dave found he had an unwanted passenger. "What are you doing?"

"We're going after them. Get a move on. Go." Cinino leaned forward and literally willed the car to move ahead. Unfortunately, the car only recognized Japanese 'ki' power and refused to budge without an engaged clutch and a spinning drive shaft.

Dave protested, "You can't catch the train in my car." This was not meant to demean his car which he dearly loved, rather to indicate his unwillingness to help Cinino.

Cinino just heard the no. He produced a stiletto from a holster hidden underneath his executive-length 100% polyester sox and began exploratory surgery on the subcutaneous layers of flab Dave had protecting his internal organs. This was done on an ouch-patient basis, more for effect than arterial bleeding. "We're going to try. Move it." Dave reluctantly put the car into gear.

ৡ৵ BASS ACKWARD BOAT

Rockwell couldn't have painted it. Disney couldn't have animated it. Freud wouldn't have analyzed it. A simple scene. The perfect flatness of the desert. The azure blue sky with the yellow fireball of a sun blasting downward. The railroad tracks glistening in the sunlight paralleled by the gleaming blacktop of I-80. The little choo-choo train chugging along with its precious cargo held tightly between its engine and the caboose. The engineer in his blue denim cap peering forward toward the caboose with the wind blowing in his face. Picture Gary Cooper in overalls. Whoops. Something was definitely wrong here. God had played a practical joke on Southern Pacific by flipping the train around ass backward.

Phil and Nancy, peering out the other side of the engine compartment were the only ones who enjoyed the joke. The train was moving at a pretty good clip and they had to yell their conversation over the wind and noise. Nancy had never looked more radiant with the wind whipping her blonde hair around, framing her face into a 3-D Rembrandt. A worry creased her face as a bad thought ran through her mind. "How much of a head start do you think we have?"

Phil was totally smitten and he didn't care two hoots about who might be chasing them. "I don't know." He shrugged, "Not much probably."

"How long will it take us to get to the lake?"

"If nothing goes wrong, which is unlikely, another hour and a half, maybe less."

Stealing a boat by train robbery was good but getting away with it would make Nancy a whole lot happier. She looked over at the engineer to make sure he wasn't fudging on the accelerator. "Can't we go any faster?" Fred just glared at her.

Phil laughed loud enough to be heard high above the drone of the train's engine. "Trains weren't meant to run backwards, remember?"

♋ RULER OF THE ROADS

Not withstanding all of the Datsun advertising to the contrary, Datsun B-210's were never considered muscle cars. Dave Caster knew it and the steady 65 miles per hour he was driving on I-80 East was keeping all four cylinders happy. Cinino watched the tracks that ran in a straight line next to the highway. With no sign of the train or the Whale, he constantly checked the speedometer. There wasn't even a wobble to the needle, stuck on 65. He looked back to the tracks, then down at his watch and then back at the speedometer. Suddenly he jabbed Caster with the stiletto. Dave reacted by throwing the wheel over and the little car swerved before righting itself. Cinino barked at Caster, "Stop the car!"

Caster responded, "Why? What's wrong?" He looked around for the cause of Cinino's outburst. Nothing there, just Cinino, Caster and the B-210.

"You're driving too slow. We'll never catch them."

"I'm going the speed limit. I don't want to push it around here."

"That's not fast enough." He brandished the stiletto but Caster didn't need any reminders of the pain. "Stop the god-damned car, now." Dave veered the car off the highway onto the shoulder and skidded to a stop. A cloud of fine dust and sand drifted over the car as Cinino scurried from his side of the car to Dave's. Dave reluctantly climbed out, watched as the last few shards of glass fell out of his window when he opened the door and stepped aside to let Cinino get by. Cinino slid behind the wheel with plenty of room to spare. He pulled the seat as far forward as he could and still the foot pedals were a stretch for his feet to reach. Fearing that he would be left behind, Dave bounded around the car and got into the passenger seat. Cinino shifted through the gear box until he found a gear willing to be entered without benefit of a disengaged clutch. The gears crunched and the car lurched forward. A vivid reminder to both Dave and Cinino that Cinino had missed Driver Training in high school in favor of rolling drunks in alleys. Something he regretted until he found the fourth gear in the Datsun.

Dave watched the speedometer needle climb steadily out of the 50's, making a brief stop in the 60's before pushing onward and upward into the 70's. "I wouldn't do that if I were you." Whether he was concerned about his car's capacity to speed, Cinino ability to drive or the propensity of the Highway Patrol to use this particular section of the highway as a heavy-footer's speed trap was unclear.

The accuracy of the warning was overlooked by Cinino who seemed driven to find out just how fast a rice-eating Japanese auto could go with only two tires making contact with the road. "They've got my boat, I own that sucker and I intend to get it back." And to accentuate his remarks he drove the car into a small dip where it bottomed out, and then over a small rise with all four wheels leaving asphalt firma.

The Highway Patrol officer stationed in his car in the median strip between the two sides of the highway was impressed with the stability of the car while airborne. With a little less weight in the car, he felt certain it could have stayed up for at least another 10 feet. He flipped on his lights and slipped his good-ol' American eight cylinder gas guzzlin' muther into drive and took off after the 'suspected speeder.' It was his intention to reward this daring young man in his flying car with a certificate of the highest order (a.k.a. a ticket) and, if necessary, a couple of free nights of accommodations at the U-HiP motel (d.b.a. the jail).

Dave sensed something was wrong and the patrol car siren confirms it. Looking over his shoulder at the flashing lights approaching fast, he was more than certain. "I told you so." To his credit, this was said with only a wee bit of gloating.

Cinino glanced back and swore, "Oh, shit." Throwing caution to the wind, where it was quickly blown backward, sticking to the windshield of the patrol car, Cinino pushed the accelerator pedal all the way to the floor. The cylinders start screaming in Japanese at the spark plugs who were already red hot under the collar. They fired off their own salvo and succeeded in blowing a gasket.

Dave saw that his speedometer was topped out at a piddling 84 miles per hour and looked back to see the patrol car licking the sweat off the Datsun's tailpipe. The peace officer, behind his mirrored shades, was smiling, just waiting for an invitation to play a little highway billiards, bumper car deluxe. Dave said to Cinino, "Don't do it. This is only going to get us in more trouble." Cinino didn't back off, not even one little muscle twitch in his foot. Not even when the patrol car pulled alongside and then in front of the Datsun. Not even when the highway patrolman eased off his accelerator and allowed his back bumper to kiss the B-210's flimsy front. Dave groaned. Car smooching had always gotten him hot around the collar.

ॐ BROKEN HEARTED

The original threesome had the caboose to themselves. Salty, in a manner of all dogs since moving vehicles immemorial, had his head out the window smelling and tasting the myriad of events, past and present, that were windblown along the tracks. Cap was staring out the window trying to will the pain and lethargy away. Although he had not reached the delusional stage, he was dreaming of a sea voyage on which the wind and the water washed through his body, sweeping out the pain and replacing it with peace. The poor suspension in the train car constantly interrupted the dream with public service agony announcements. Jeff was watching Cap's every move. Every facial quiver and awkward body movement. Finally Jeff said, "Thank you, Cap."

Cap didn't even open his eyes to respond. "For what, Jeffey?"

"For having this plan, and not letting me down. I thought you were going to give Cinino the Whale without a fight. And when you walked out of that meeting, well, I thought you didn't care about me anymore." A small sniffle and perhaps a tear or two accentuated this statement.

Cap opened his eyes and turned to Jeff. "Jeffey, I care a hell of lot more about you than I do about anyone or anything else, and that includes the Whale. And don't ever forget that, Boy."

"I just wanted to apologize for thinking what I was thinking about you."

Cap shook his head angrily. "Don't do it. Let's just see if we can get the Whale in the water, first. And if that miracle should ever happen, well, then, you can start all that apologizin' garbage." The train went over a washed out portion of the track and jounced violently. Cap winced in pain. What little color was left in his face drained away. He staggered to his feet. "Scuse me for a second. Got to catch a breath of air. Bad case of train-sick. Keep an eye on Salty, there." Cap stumbled out of the front of the caboose onto the small platform over the coupling to the back flat car. He hung on tight to the iron railing as his body was wracked with a coughing spasm. He released the railing and grabbed his chest in pain. The coughing lessened and he hacked into a dirty handkerchief pulled from his back pocket. Bright red splotches of blood were mixed with the phlegm. Cap examined the hankie, hoping that the pattern was in the cloth and not the insides of his lungs. "Damn." He coughed again, and then gulped for fresh air. He stuffed the soiled handkerchief back in his pocket and mumbled a thank you for at least being alone and unobserved.

Nancy spotted Cap on the platform as she hopped from the engine to the first flat car. She was as agile as a cat from many years of boom-ducking and sheet-clearing on the ocean waves. She worked her way along the keel of the Whale, hopped to the second flat car, checked the tie-downs on the Whale and made a final leap onto the little platform. All of this before Cap could duck back into the caboose. "Greetings, Chief, how you feeling?"

As nonchalantly as he could, Cap covered the hanging-out portion of his bloody handkerchief with his hand. The fresh air had revived him enough that his complexion was on the healthier side of Morticia Addams. "Fit as a fiddle, little lady. Why you askin'?"

"Because you look like shit and I care. And Phil thinks you're walking kinda' funny. Whatever that means."

"I think Phil is ugly as sin but that don't give me a right to complain about him." He cranked his face up into the best smile he could offer at the moment. Which was pretty good when you think that his blood pressure was dropping faster than stock in Cinino's casino without the Whale.

"Hey, lighten up, willya'? You pulled it off, big time."

Cap was contrite, after all, without Nancy, the Whale would probably be a pile of lumber in the desert. Then again, it still might sink like a stone when they get it onto the water. "Sorry. Still wound up from the kidnapping. How are things with our train engineer?"

"He actin' so cool but we got him scared stiff. Thinks we're hijacking this thing and taking it all the way to Kuba." She gives her best Fidel-impersonation which got Cap laughing. The pain daggers dug in deeper and cut off another piece of Cap's intestinal fortitude. Nancy grabbed him to keep him from falling. "You're bullshitting me, Cap. You're hurt bad. We have to stop the train and get you some help."

Cap pushed away from Nancy with a vengeance. "No! It's okay, really, Nanc. Just a cracked rib or somethin'. I'll get it fixed up after we launch the Whale. I promise, cross my heart, or whatever you youngsters say. If it makes you feel better, you can personally take me to a doctor."

Nancy was not so sure about this macho shit, bt she was pumped up about sailing the Whale. She really, really wanted to see the Whale afloat and knew that stopping now would surely doom the rescue operation. "Okay, if you really think you can make until then."

"I'm sure." He gave a little nod. Nancy turned to leave but Cap put a hand on her shoulder. "Look, Nancy, this is our little secret? No need to tell Phil or Jeffey. Just keep it between the two of us?"

"No big deal, Skipper. As long as you keep your promise about the doctor."

"You've got yourself a deal."

⌘ SHIPBLOCK

There is an obscure fact, known only to few people outside of Auto Club map junkies, that in our post-industrial country there are very few train routes that run in a straight line, completely unbisected by roads or other train routes. To the great misfortune of the entire rescue crew, the Southern Pacific line on which they traveled at great speed, backwards, was not one of them.

While Cap and Nancy made promises neither would keep, Jeff amused himself by harassing Salty. The dog was trying to keep his nose in the wind by resting his forepaws on the window sill. Jeff, at times as obnoxious as any other 13 year-old, slowly pulled Salty's hind legs back until the pooch was so spread out that he slid down the window back onto the seat. This game amused Jeff to no end but Salty tired of it very quickly. The view out the back window of the caboose (the leading point of the train) was boring in its consistency. The desert. The straight tracks. The empty road. A tunnel through which the train must pass.

Jeff grabbed at Salty's paw and Salty, his patience worn thin, snapped at Jeff. The game ended that suddenly. Jeff put his hands in his pocket and Salty went back to sniffing. With nothing else to occupy his interest, Jeff stuck his head out the window. If it was interesting to dogs maybe it would be for him.

With the wind ripping at his eyes, tears welled up. He blinked several times, his lids doing their windshield wiper thing. Finally, he could get the scene into focus. His eyes ran up the tracks to the east until they caught hold and refocused on the approaching tunnel. It looked big, dark and foreboding. Tunnels, in and of themselves were not a big deal, unless they were long and narrow and you were walking the wrong direction when a bright white light appeared at the far end. But this was a narrow tunnel, well lit, just wide enough to carry the east bound and west bound lanes of the highway over the railroad tracks. Jeff's normally active brain had shifted into hyper-drive as it digested this information flow. Thousands of trains had passed through this very tunnel and never, not ever, had there been a problem. But Jeff's eyes and Jeff's brain added two and two and two masts together and came up with a very tall problem. He screamed, "The masts!" Pulling his head back in the window, He frantically searched for something or someone to warn. He yanked on the emergency cord with all his might.

Train emergency cords, contrary to popular opinion, do not immediately cause a train to come to a grinding stop when pulled. Even when they are pulled frantically by a young boy trying to save his pride and joy from being splinterized by a railroad underpass. It does, however, set off an alarm on a control panel in the engine compartment. And that alarm jangled the nerves of both Fred and Phil.

Phil shouted over the engine din at Fred, "What is that? What is happening?"

Fred answered casually, too casually, "I don't know. One of your friends punched the alarm." With too many years of driving a train the right way, he checked the tracks in front of the engine. An obvious waste of time since this was territory that had been passed over already.

Phil with far less experience in the train business looked the other direction down the tracks and immediately saw a very large problem. The tunnel opening grew larger and larger like the mouth of Moby Dick ready to swallow up the Pequod. And Phil, not ready to become a latter-day Ahab, Jonah or Jepetto started screaming at the engineer, "Stop! Stop this damn thing. There's a tunnel up there!"

Fred, still thinking in the normal train-driving mode, failed to grasp the significance of a tunnel. It was the same tunnel he passed through early this morning on the way to Wendover. And there was no problem then so why should there be one now. He shrugged his shoulders, "So?"

In moments of high anxiety like this one, Phil's words fail him and pantomimed the issue at immediate hand. "Boat. Masts." He held his hands far apart. "Tunnel." He halved the distance between his hands. "Stop train!"

Having seen how crazy these people were just to steal an ugly boat, Fred couldn't even imagine what terrible tortures they would unleash upon his person in the event he destroyed the boat by jamming it through a tunnel. He threw on the brakes and bounced off the back wall of the compartment as the train's wheels locked. He was joined by Phil milli-seconds later as the squealing of the metal rims on metal tracks reached a crescendo and the train began to slow.

Cap and Nancy were thrown against the wall of the caboose and then down to the platform floor. Jeff and Salty rolled across the floor and out the door onto the back platform. The rusty iron railing was the only thing that kept them from rolling off the train and onto the tracks. From their scrunched up ball of mangy fur, dirty clothes, six legs and two heads, Salty and Jeff had a front row seat on the impending disaster. Being a light load freight-wise, the train's mass didn't generate as much friction as a normally weighted train and the march of one unbending object (train) toward another (tunnel) continued at a frightening pace. Jeff could only issue a multitude of silent prayers as the Whale skidded toward destruction.

The caboose entered the west end of the tunnel traveling at less than three miles an hour. As the shadow of the tunnel crossed over Jeff, he shut his eyes and waited for the inevitable crash of mast wood against reinforced concrete. He waited and he waited. No crash. Maybe he had passed out and wasn't conscious to hear the impact?

Unbeknownst to the conscious but closed-eared Jeff, the train had come to a complete stop with only a gentle tap of wood on concrete. In a vain attempt to protect the Whale, the guardian spirit of the ship had thrown itself in front of the mast. Alas, the density and cushioning power of the spirit was in reverse proportion to it's bravery. The mast sliced right through the spirit's form, easier than a hot knife through warm butter, and French-kissed the slab.

Salty, in a moment of pure joy, forgot his dignified upbringing and licked Jeff on the kisser—a moment he would look back on and shudder. Jeff opened his eyes and blinked twice and then twice again. While it was dark, and the train was halfway through the tunnel, he was absolutely certain that something that was supposed to happen did not happen. And with that realization he was incredibly overjoyed. He kissed Salty back and then leapt to his feet to congratulate the rest of the team.

ঞ A LIGHT AT THE END

Phil came whoopin' and hollorin' down the line from the engine. Having only seen that the glass was half empty (as in, a smashed ship is not worth talking about), he was ecstatic about the saving of the Whale. Nancy carefully helped Cap off of the caboose platform. They all met at the side of the flat car where they could look up and see just how close they come to the end of the dream. While Phil and Jeff were pleased, Nancy and Cap were looking at the fire after surving the frying pan. What good was saving the Whale from destruction when it was going to sit on the railroad track until Cinino arrived with reinforcements?

Cap spat in disgust. His bloody phlegm landed in the dirt and he brushed it into oblivion with his shoe before anyone else could see it. He was feeling bad, the hope of sailing the Whale serving as an anesthesia to the pain of his injuries. With the loss of hope came the real unmasked pain, and he wasn't handling it very well. "Damn," was all he could say.

Jeff's adrenaline rush faded and he, too, faced the discouraging predicament. Maybe they could head the other direction with a mad dash to the Pacific Ocean? Yah, and maybe the Whale could sprout wings and just fly over all the tunnels. Jeff stating the obvious, "We can't make it. It would wreck her."

Cap was the picture, and not a pretty one at that, of defeat. Physically and mentally demoralized, the best he could do was apologize. "I'm really sorry, Jeffey. I didn't use my pea-brain. Tunnels. I just didn't think about it." He looked up at the mast resting comfortable against the side of the tunnel and tried to visualize the Whale without the top 15 feet of its mainmast and 10 feet of foremast. Might as well hold up a bedsheet with your hands, that's how effective short masts would be. "Even if we were lucky and the masts just snap up high, she'd never go."

Nancy was not listening to the conversation. Instead, she was measuring off the distance between the side of the flat cars and the interior edge of the tunnel. Phil watched her, totally confused by her actions. She finished counting and then retraced her count by walking backwards, putting one foot right behind the other. Finally, she said to Cap, "How wide do you think this tunnel is?"

Cap was in no mood for jokes. "What the hell difference does that make? It could be as wide as the Golden, god-damn, Gate and the masts still wouldn't go through." See those teeny-tiny little poles sticking up way past the big bad tunnel." To accentuate his point, a car drove over the tunnel, paused as it passed the top of the mainmast and then continued on toward Salt Lake City.

Nancy could only take so much sarcasm, even from somebody with major pain in his gut. "Listen, old man, I am trying to save your butt and the Whale. So just answer a simple question, how wide are the YARDARMS?? Wider than the width of the tunnel?"

Phil, Cap and Jeff all eyeballed the tunnel and then the yardarms. Cap said "I don't see what difference that makes but since you got your bra in a twist about it, no, the good-for-nothing-now yardarms are shorter than the tunnel is wide. Are you happy?"

"Yes, and you will be too. If you just shut up and let a real sailor do her thing." She clambered back onto the flat car and then onto the

Whale. She shouted back down to Phil, "See if you can borrow Fred's toolbox. Make sure that he has a hammer in it."

Phil reluctantly jogged off to snatch a tool box. Cap, Jeff and Salty were left standing in the dirt scratching their heads and belly, respectively. Clearly Nancy had taken leave of her senses and none of them had the cajones to stop her. Jeff looked up at the Whale and then to the tunnel. He said to Cap, "What can she do with a hammer, Cap?"

Before Cap could answer, Nancy came to the railing and shouted down to them. "Unless you have something better to do, which I strongly doubt, you can come up here and help me lower the masts."

Cap and Jeff, spoke in unison, "What?"

"I said, come up here and help me lower the masts. Do I have to draw a picture for you. We lower the masts, we slowly drive the train through the tunnel and then we get the hell out of here."

Cap and Jeff, in harmony but not in unison, "How?"

ལྗུ A NUTS AND BOLT SOLUTION

Nancy smiled and beckoned to them. "Come and see, it is really quite simple." Yelling to Phil, "I need that hammer, now, Phil darling."

Fred, the engineer, had taken the near miss of the bridge as a sign from God that he, the Almighty One, was supporting this rescue operation. Given the celestial go-ahead, Fred assisted Jeff, Cap and Phil in slowly lowering the foremast support riggings when Nancy drove the pin in the rake adjustment bracket all the way out of the fitting. While originally designed to make a few degrees adjustment to the angle of the mast for ocean racing purposes, the rake adjuster was capable of pivoting through an 180 degree arc. A feature which Nancy made good use of. She directed the others to slowly release tension on the rigging until the top foremast gently rested on the top of the engine. While not completely parallel to the Whale's deck, it would easily slide through the tunnel. Since all of the crew, with the exception of Fred, had now been gifted with perfect hindsight, no one questioned the incredible vision Nancy had when she ordered the rake adjusters. Even though, at that long ago time, everyone thought it was the most foolish thing 'that girl' could have done.

Time being of the essence, and talk being cheap, the crew spent essentially no clicks of the clock on conversation as they repeated the lowering process on the mainmast. The mast came comfortably to a stop on top of the vertical stump of the foremast. Even before Nancy could rest on her laurels, Jeff raced up and hugged her. So passionate a move and an embrace that Phil felt a twinge of jealousy toward his 13 year-old competition. Jeff, still hugging Nancy tightly, said, "You are the most wonderful person I know."

Cap joined them, on deck, but not in the group hug. "Fickle kid. He said the same thing about me last week."

Nancy was still pleased with the compliment. "It was nothing, Jeff, really."

Cap, his eyes on the highway stretching to the west, "It will be for nothin' if we don't get goin'. I got a feeling the posse might be closing in on us." He turned to the engineer and said, "Any more tunnels between here and Saltair?"

"No, Sir."

"Then time's a wastin', Mister. We got a date with a lake, and I hate to keep her waitin'."

Fred, accompanied by Jeff and Phil, returned to the engine, leaving Cap and Nancy alone for a moment. Salty, realizing that everything was going to be okay had found a safe spot under one of the seats in the caboose. He had decided to remain there until the train trip came to an end. Cap, looking older than Methuselah but without the tan, gazed at Nancy with a growing respect. "You're all right, lady."

Nancy grinned. "Thanks, Captain. I could say the same about you." She winked. "But I won't." The train gave a lurch and began moving backwards, as usual, through the tunnel. With all eyes on the mast top and the yardarm ends, the train crept through the tunnel. The mainmast top brushed the apex of the tunnel and scraped a narrow channel in the cement. Cap yelled up to the engine, "Keep going! We'll worry about the damage later." He watched as the thick wood of the mast flexed as much as it could without cracking and finally sprang back as the Whale cleared the tunnel. "Step on it, Mr. Engineer!"

⚙ THE POSSE

The jiggley-headed L.A. Dodger doll which had graced Dave Caster's dashboard since his wild week in Los Angeles several years ago, had been cited for excessive speed in the great state of Utah. Or so said the citation stuffed under his plastic feet by Cinino. No Dodger before him, not even the great Maury Wills, had been clocked at a speed as great as that noted on the ticket. Even at the 65point9 miles per hour that Cinino was holding the car to, Mr. Dodger was rockin' out. With a silly grin painted on his kisser, he was the only one having a good time in the car.

With the speeding ticket and the loss of very valuable time, the two human occupants had lost any pretense of civility toward each other. Both stared straight ahead, a long and unwinding road ahead of them. Ditto for the train tracks to the south of the highway. Cinino finally spoke, "How much farther?"

"Farther to where, Billy Barty? They could be taking it to New Jersey for all we know." He crossed his arms across his abundant chest and refused to say another word. Cinino, figuring lightning wouldn't strike twice, stamped down on the accelerator. Mr. Dodger nodded his head in agreement, silently saying, 'go, go, go,' as the posse mounted their charge.

⚙ THE PLAN REVEALED

It seems like the train had just gotten up to speed when Fred started slowing it down. After checking down the tracks for any tunnels the engineer might have forgotten about, Jeff began to protest the slow down. Phil clapped a hand over Jeff's mouth and pointed out the window of the engine. Small clusters of people were standing alongside the tracks holding signs and cheering the arrival of the Whale. Fred slowed the train until it came to a gentle stop in the switching yard. More and more people appeared with home-made placards wishing the rescue crew good luck.

Nancy and Cap got down from the flat car and worked their way through the crowd to the engine. Nancy was in disbelief, Cap was pretty casual about the sudden appearance of Whale fans. Phil and Jeff hopped down from the engine and joined them. Phil beamed a smile at the crowd. His own self-acknowledgment for a job well done.

Nancy asked Phil, "Those people, why, how are they here? We didn't steal the boat until a little while ago." She couldn't have been more surprised if she had seen a prehistoric fish lizard doing flips over the railroad tracks.

Phil's smile broadened even more. The gas line on his helium-filled ego had developed a faulty cut-off switch, and his ego was in danger of over-inflating. "You mean you don't read your local newspaper every morning? How are journalists, like myself, going to keep our jobs?"

Nancy threatened to deck him with her clenched fist. "Can't you, just once, tell me straight and simple what's going on?"

Phil made a peace sign in front of Nancy's fist. "Far out." She grabbed his peace sign and squeezed hard. He grimaced, "Peace. Look, I made a wild leap of faith and gave the story to the Tribune last night."

"What story? We hadn't done anything last night. Last night there was no story!"

"Let's just say I took some journalistic license. I wrote the story just a little bit ahead of when it happened. Then I told everyone where they could see history in the making. Right here, as a matter of fact."

Cap interrupted, "History is going to get unmade if you keep yappin'. Get them to switch us over to the Garfield line out to the resort."

Nancy was incredulous. She had given some credit to Phil for deviousness, and a small measure of cuteness, but she never expected cunning from him or Cap. "You had this all planned out? How long have you known that you were going to steal the Whale?"

It was surprising that Phil did not have a splitting-head-ache. His ego had expanded beyond normal limits and was now pushing hard against the skull plates, restricting the blood supply. It made him a wee bit giddy. "Cap's known for quite a while. He let me in on it last week, and I managed the details. Not bad for publicity-hound reporter, eh?"

"I'm totally blown away. But how could you plan it? I thought Cinino only decided yesterday to move it by rail." This question was directed at either Phil or Cap, whichever one might have the answer. Phil was reveling in his little piece of skullduggery but Cap had his eyes on the horizon, namely the shore of the Salt Lake.

Phil opened his mouth to launch into a detailed explanation and Cap cut him off before he could utter a sound. "Later, Phil. You have a job to do." To accentuate his point, he looked over his shoulder. "Is that the sound of horses coming?"

"Okay, okay, I get the point." He jogged over to the local switching officer; a tidy, bespectacled man quite nervous with all these strange people milling around his switching yard. Phil pointed at the switch guard and then down the tracks toward the Lake. The officer vigorously shook his head 'no.'

This train was supposed to be going west to Wendover, Nevada and by God and Southern Pacific it wasn't going anywhere but. Phil gesticulated wildly, his effort drawing in all of his powers of persuasion. Even the Whale fans, hundreds of feet away, who could not hear his words were still moved to tears by his visual presentation of the Whale saga and its flight to safety. At the end of the passion play, the switching officer was unmoved. A simple shake of his head indicated a red light had been placed in the path of the Whale. Phil dug deep into his pocket and pulled out a wad of small denomination, tattered bills. He reached out with the hand containing the filthy lucre and the switching officer shook hands. When they released each other's hand, the moolah had moved. With an alacrity generated by wallet 'grease' the switch man went to the switch case, unlocked it, and threw the switch.

Phil hustled back to the train and rescue squad. He waved them back on board and yelled to Fred, "Move it out! Next stop, Saltair Resort." To Nancy: "Four miles and we're home free." The salt air coming off the lake had cooled his ego enough that he was focused, again, on the task at hand.

ঔষ THE CHASE CONTINUES

The Odd Couple of the desert were hot on the trail of their quarry even as their own relationship sank to a new low. Cinino was thinking of devious, maniacal ways of wresting control of Dave's motel away from him and then evicting the fat slob out into the desert. Better yet, he would make the rotund jerk swab the deck of the Wendover Whale when it was taken back from those Indian-giving Utes (it being inconsequential that neither Cap nor Nancy held state citizenships). Dave was thinking of the many surgical uses he could put the stiletto to, in making the Short One even shorter. Dave had always been a pacifist, secretly pleased with the anti-Vietnam war protesters he saw on the nightly news, but the thought of carving up a hunk of Cinino had him very excited.

The Datsun drove up an overpass, the railroad tracks ran beneath the tarmac. Cinino used the elevation gain to scan the eastern horizon. "You see anything, shit-for-brains? They can't be that far ahead of us." Dave had lost interest in the hunt and his head dropped down to the train tracks running beneath him. The caboose of the Whale train slid into the tunnel quickly followed by the Whale on the flat cars and the engine. The train was heading north and they were heading east. He glanced up at Cinino to make sure that he hadn't spotted the train and then closed his eyes. He couldn't talk about it if he didn't see it.

The car drove back down on the far side of the overpass and proceeded quickly toward Salt Lake City. When Dave felt they had driven far enough that the Whale was safe, he took a quick peek over his shoulder. Unfortunately, Cinino caught the look. "What is it, Caster?" He too looked back, thereby sending the poor, abused motor vehicle into a prolonged sideways skid.

"Nothing, Shorty," he smirked, "just a freight train."

"Freight, my ass. They got my little gold mine onboard." He pushed the brake pedal, adding more friction to the already overburdened brake system, and turning the tires into molten rubber. With only minimal control of the car, Cinino guided it, at an oblique angle, into the dirt median. With intentions of making a roaring U-turn, made famous in the early sixties by television's "Highway

Patrol," Cinino spun the steering wheel in a tight counter-clockwise motion as he passed through the midpoint of the median. "I've got their sweet little asses now." The Datsun fishtailed and, pretending to be a gopher, buried its rear wheels axle-deep in sand and salt. Cinino stripped his way through the gears hoping to find one that had enough torque to get the tires some traction. The auto gods were on coffee break and the wheels spun helplessly, sending a fine spray of grit into the air. Cinino threw the car into reverse, stripping the clutch plate and killing the engine. He climbed out, slammed the windowless door and watched the train chugging away. "Dammit!" He kicked the door and made a pretty good dent for a little guy.

Dave, from inside the car, "Hey, watch it, Squirt, this is still my car." He got out.

"So what?" Cinino kicked the door with his other foot and left a matching dent for Dave to complain about. He squared his shoulders and headed north. Dave watched him make it off the median and into the center lane of the west-bound lanes.

Dave asked, "What are you doing?

Cinino dodged a fast-moving car. The car honked and Cinino flipped him the 'bird.' He yelled back at Dave, "I'm going to get my boat."

"What about my car? You ruined it." Cinino kept on walking. Dave went after him, then remembered the keys in the ignition. He grabbed them and ran after Cinino. "You'll never catch them."

೧೮ THE WHALE DEBEACHES

Some mean-spirited and small-minded travelers have made reference to Wendover Utah as the armpit of the West. Disparaging comments about pass-through towns were appropriate and often accurate when spoken by people who really got around but the characterization of stately Wendover as a hole surely meant that the speaker had never been to the Saltair Resort. Comparisons to Malibu and Cote 'd Azur were meaningless once the traveler had seen the scum-flecked waves washing up on barren soil.

The Saltair anchorage, formed by a curve in the coast line and a man-made jetty, harbored no allusion of being anything but a run-down launching pad for pleasure boats and day sailors. The rail line led across the flats and ended at the base of the jetty, adjacent to a small boat-launching crane and concrete ramp for trailer launches. The Whale train arrived at the resort to the cheers of hundreds of well-wishers lining the small breakwater. Whatever Phil wrote in his story about the rescue had struck a responsive chord with the public. They were here to see good triumph over evil and the dreams of a small boy fulfilled. Better than a Disney movie but without the cost of a ticket.

The crowd let out a tremendous roar when the train came to a stop at the end of the tracks. The boat launch crane swung its cable and hook toward the Whale. The crane, while perfectly suited for lifting 18-foot Chris-Craft power boats, looked puny and fragile when it came up against the likes of the Wendover Whale.

The Rescue Crew climbed down from their perches on the train. Salty, given the opportunity to remove himself from the train, jumped off the back caboose platform, making a silent vow never, ever, to use this form of vehicular transportation again. Jeff was overwhelmed by the mass of people on hand to view the maiden voyage of his boat. He hugged Phil, acknowledging him as the mastermind behind this part of the plan. "You're the most wonderful person I know."

Cap couldn't help but shake his head in disbelief. "Jeez, Jeffey, that line is getting really old, really fast."

"But we made it, we really made it all the way." Jeff's face was glowing as bright as the day he hung the Whale banner on the top mainmast.

"I'll feel a whole lot better when we get her in the water and cast off. I smell Cinino around here and its making me want to puke." He was almost right but the transitive property of gastric upset didn't apply here. Cinino was close by and getting closer. Cap was feeling his internal organs were going to explode up his throat and spew like vomit out his mouth. But His Shortness was not the cause of Cap's internal distress. The cause was known but the cure, emergency surgery and several weeks in intensive care, was not forthcoming.

Phil had removed himself from the grasp of Jeff and snaked his own arm around the waist of Nancy. Nancy allowed herself to be drawn close to Phil. A feeling of euphoria had invaded the entire group with the exception of Cap (a lifetime of cynicism can't be undone by the Whale's proximity to water). Phil said to Cap, "Mellow out, fearless leader, there's no way he can stop us now."

The crane operator, almost the spittin' image of Cap, left the crane motor idling and joined the group.

"Which one of youse in charge?" The operator looked like he was plucked, fully costumed, off the Warner Brothers' back lot where he was in the midst of filming "The Old Man and the Sea."

Cap pointed to himself. "Me."

The operator eyeballed Cap, giving him the once over. Cap didn't look like a man capable of pulling this stunt off. "Hmm. That be the case, congratulations." He shoved a gnarly hand at Cap. "We didn't think you were going to make it."

Jeff jumped in with, "Neither did we." And then he laughed, because laughing came easy when you think the worst is over.

Cap shook the man's hand. He didn't quite trust the guy, something about him was too familiar and too unreliable. Just like the old Cap. The operator, looking up at the Whale, said, "We're all set for you. If you'll hook your ship up, I'll swing her over and set her down, real gentle-like. You won't even see a splash."

Cap looked at the size of the hook and then the cable holding it, and visually worked his way back down the cable toward the lifting motor and cable drum. The entire device was rusty and in need of an overhaul. Just like the operator. "Kinda' small, ain't she? What's the weight limit on your crane?"

"Now don't you go worrying your head about that, old-timer. Me and this crane will do the job." He stood tall, coming up eye to eye with Cap although the operator's eyes were a whole lot more bloodshot.

"Don't want to have a crash."

"Shit on shingle, neither do I. But, seein' as there ain't no other crane around, you don't have no choice. I'm the only crane you got."

Cap mulled it over, then smiled. "In that case, you young whippersnapper, what are you waiting for? Get our boat in the water."

◈ꙮ FORCED MARCH

The shortest route from the highway to the breakwater at Saltair was a line, obviously, but quick it was not. Once Cinino, with Dave straggling behind, cleared the north shoulder of the highway, he was forced to march through soft sand. Given the shortness of his stride versus the long stride of Dave, he wondered why the numbskull couldn't keep up. Cinino didn't get much time to worry about it because the sand gave way to mud shallows; the residue of a lake that was constantly shrinking from too much sun and sporadic rainfall.

Slogging through mud was slow going but the alternative, following the wide curve of the shoreline, would make the trip to the Whale a much longer one. He kept slogging onward, the briny water doing irreparable damage to the fine weave of his polyester trousers. Dave was in no hurry. While never a hard charger in life, he now saw the distinct advantages of stopping, smelling the roses and observing the humiliation of the short man in front of him.

Only a half mile in the distance, Cinino could see the crane lift the Whale out of its resting spot on the train and swing it toward the water. The fact that somebody had carelessly broken off the masts of his boat doubled his hatred of Cap and his friends. "Come on, Caster. Get your fat ass going."

Dave deliberately slowed his pace by half. He stopped and tied his already tied shoelaces for good measure. An unusual, time-consuming effort since both shoes were underwater. "Doing my best, oh greedy one." The distance between the two men lengthened since Cinino was unwilling to wait.

The crowd whistled and cheered as the Whale was gently placed in the calm waters of the Great Salt Lake. Cinino saw the crane swing back from the water's edge with the cable and hook dangling free. "I'm going to kill all of them. Every last one."

Dave fell further behind, apparently looking for something under the water. Finally, he stopped and scooped up a glob of Utah mud; a glorious mixture of sand, salt, mud and bird guano. He mounded it carefully, much like a youngster looking to make the perfect snowball. Unfortunately, Cinino kept trudgin and the distance between the two of them grew. Dave couldn't wait any longer. He flung his mudball in a high arc. The mud maintained its structural integrity surprisingly well but Dave's enthusiasm for the target sent it beyond and to the right of Cinino. The splash could not be mistaken for a fish rising to the surface, leaving Dave with no excuse when Cinino glared back at him. Dave casually washed his hands off in the water. "I'm behind you all the way, Mister Cinino."

ஒ஭ SO CLOSE

Where was Cecil B. DeMille when the Whale gently touched salt water for the first time? He would have been standing on a barge in the middle of the small craft harbor directing all of his extras lining the shore to begin chanting, "The Whale, the Whale, the Whale." He would have then leaned down and whispered to his cameraman to pull the focus back and pan toward the Whale, revealing the odd duck of a boat with masts pointing toward the horizon rather than the stars. Later, he would edit in a scene showing the dastardly villain, played achingly well by Cinino, struggling through the mud, perilously close to the jetty, ready to snatch the prize back from the sweet old man and the young boy. With C.B. dead, the scene went off as described without any direction or choreography.

Phil, Jeff and Nancy stood at the edge of the jetty holding their collective breath as the harness slipped off of the Whale. Cap and Salty were nowhere to be found. The ship, unencumbered, heeled slightly to port and then righted itself. Phil couldn't stand the tension, "She's not sinking!"

Not surprisingly, Jeff, the visionary, and Nancy, the builder, had their feelings hurt by this comment. Nancy said, "You had some doubts?" Jeff said, "You didn't really believe we could do it?"

Hurting a boy's feelings was one thing but hurting a potential spouse was a whole different matter. Jeff would have many years to have his damaged feelings repaired. Nancy was a once-in-a-lifetime opportunity. Phil, quickly replied, "No, Of course not. I was just glad to see her finally afloat. Where she belongs."

Jeff's feelings, at this very moment, could not be hurt by a sledgehammer, he only saw the Whale in the water. His throat was suddenly very dry. He was going to be sailing it in a matter of minutes. His dream of grabbing hold of a clipper ship and hanging on for his life had jumped out of his superego and landed right in his lap. "Let's go. We've got to get the masts up. And go out there." He pointed to the blue of the lake, stretching out farther than the eye could see. The Great Salt Lake, for those standing on its shore, appeared as large as the Atlantic Ocean did to Columbus, for those things that can't be seen, like distant shorelines, cannot be counted on until you reached them.

Phil locked into the same vision presented to Jeff. A small ship sailing smartly away on an enormous ocean. "He's right. Let's get cracking." He and Jeff headed toward the wood plank stretched between the jetty and the Whale. Jeff stopped to look for Cap. So intent was he on the launching of the Whale that he failed to realize his partner was not there to see it happen. Jeff said, to anybody listening, "Where's Cap? He was just here. Wasn't he?"

☜☞ A MAJOR HITCH

Nancy knew instantly that there was a big problem with Cap, one that she needed to take care of by herself. "I'll find him. You two start getting the masts back up. If you need help, ask a few of these folks. They got nothing else to do but stand around and cheer." She didn't wait for an answer, knowing that Jeff and Phil had waves in their eyes and wind in their ears. Anything they could do to get the Whale sailing, they would do it. She walked back up to the flat cars, now empty, and called Cap's name. She edged toward the caboose and called out for Cap, and then Salty. No answer from inside the caboose. As she reached the end of the train, she heard Salty whining. Nancy hurried toward the whine, knowing that Salty was not a dog to whimper lightly.

Cap was beyond pain, in fact, he was beyond consciousness, having collapsed against a wheel on the back side of the caboose. Salty was guarding him and looking distressed beyond words. Something Salty's close friends would have denied as being possible for the loquacious pooch. Nancy slipped down beside Cap and shook him gently. Why she did it gently was unclear, after all, if Cap was dead shaking him hard wouldn't mean a thing to him.

Cap was floating on a wave in a warm tropical place. The foaming curl of the wave tickled Cap's back as it carried him closer and closer to a pure white sand beach. The wave's power slowed and Cap felt he wasn't going to make it to safety on the beach. He reached out, extending his aching body until his fingers touched dry sand. He grabbed at it desperately like the anchor of a ship trying to gain a toehold on a soft seafloor. Suddenly, he was grabbed around the middle in the vise-like hold of a tiger shark and he was pulled back out into the sea. Cap clawed at the sand, leaving finger tracks in the wetness and then he was swallowed by the water. He screamed in pain and terror and then opened his eyes.

Cap saw the fuzzy image of Nancy and Salty hovering above him. He blinked away the cold sweat of fear that had blurred his vision and they came into focus.

Nancy was gripped by a different apprehension. She was witnessing a man die in front of her. "Cap?" she continued to shake him, perhaps unaware that she was doing so. Perhaps it was out of a fear that if she stopped, Cap would lapse back into unconsciousness. "I've got to get you to a doctor." She got up to leave.

Cap grabbed her arm and pulled it down hard. "No! Help me up. I'm all right."

"No you're not. You need to be in a hospital."

Cap pleaded with her. "Please, Nancy. Just help me get to my feet." He struggled to rise on his own but he couldn't do it. Nancy finally helped him up. His blurry vision returned and his body swayed in the breeze. A horrible wracking cough reverberated through his body and blood-mixed spittle dripped from the corner of his mouth. Cap brushed it off with the back of his hand. This was not a man ready to take his ship out into a treacherous sea.

Nancy, in an understatement of epic proportion, said, "That's more than a cracked rib, Cap." Salty re-evaluated his high opinion of Nancy on that one remark alone. But if she could physically force Cap to get medical attention, then Salty would gladly reinstate her in the pantheon of humans worth knowing.

Cap tried breathing a different way. Short shallow breaths didn't cause quite the intense shooting pains that normal regulated breaths brought on. "Yah, maybe you're right. Maybe its two cracked ribs."

"Funny, very funny." Nancy was in no mood to be joked with. Salty had to admit that it was a very good retort for someone with seven toes in the grave.

Cap took a painful step and stopped. "Come on, help me get on board the Whale."

"You can't go now, it'll kill you." She took his arm and supported a good deal of his weight.

Cap walked slowly around the caboose with Nancy's assistance. Salty led the way but kept checking to make sure they were following him. Cap softly said to Nancy, before they reached the crowd, "It might just do that. It might. But I know somebody who would definitely die if I didn't go." Salty barked at several people who closed in on Cap to wish him success. They backed away as Salty continued to bark at them. Cap continued, "You and Phil take care of Salty. Until we get back."

"Sure, Cap. Anything you say. Just come back."

ঙ⌀ BITING THE BULLET

By the time Nancy and Cap made their way down the jetty to the boarding ramp, Jeff and Phil, with many eager hands from the crowd, had succeeded in fully rigging the Whale. With the masts upright and the sails flapping loosely in the light breeze, the Whale had undergone a transformation. An ugly duckling out of water, it became a graceful swan once most of its hull lay beneath the water line. The sight of this newly-emerged beauty gave strength to Cap, who was badly in need of it. Cap stepped away from Nancy and walked toward the Whale. His eyes filled with tears, a combination of continued pain, and pride; an emotion he hadn't felt in a long time, if ever at all.

Jeff spotted him moving slowly from the jetty onto the boarding ramp and sprinted to meet him. In his excitement he literally skipped across the ramp. If he had to wait too long before they cast off, his heart would burst out from pure, unadulterated anticipation. "Where you been, Cap? We're all set to go."

If this wasn't the greatest day in Jeff's life, and he wasn't blinded by the brilliance of a dream fulfilled, he would have noticed something d(r)eadfully wrong with his friend. But children of all ages, pursuing elusive fantasies, slip on blinders, making sure the ugly things of day-to-day life are shut out. Cap's rapidly failing health went undetected. Cap spoke, barely above a whisper, "Sorry, Jeffey. Just had to make sure Salty was okay before we shove off."

Go without Salty, the final piece to the puzzle, the third part of the triumvirate? Jeff didn't understand. And judging from the whining Salty was doing in the arms of Nancy, the dog didn't agree with this Cap's decision. "Isn't he coming with us?"

"I don't think so. As a rattlesnake huntin' dog he's fine, but he ain't no sea dog. Get's seasick, turns green, it ain't pretty," He said with conviction. If Jeff had given it any thought he would have known it was a bald-faced lie. The only time Salty's was ever on a body of water was when he ran through a rain puddle in search of a steak bone.

Time didn't allow for the detection of the untruth. Phil whistled up from the deck of the Whale. "Let's go, people. I got a guy to tow us out of the harbor."

Jeff and Cap walked the rest of the way down the boarding ramp and stepped down onto the deck of the Whale. Nancy handed Salty to the nearest landlubber and followed. Salty squirmed in the landlubber's grip but to no avail. Cap stumbled and Nancy reached to help him. He brusquely pushed her away, glared at her and walked over to Phil. He reached for Phil's hand but Phil didn't know how to react. "Thanks for all yor help, Phil. I have to say we couldn't have done it without you."

Thinking the handshake was offered as a form of congratulations, not as the end of a relationship and a final farewell, Phil firmly took

Cap's hand. Even the slight movement of his arm from the handshaking caused Cap more grief. Phil said, "It was all my pleasure, Cap." And he sincerely meant it.

"We'll see ya' when we get back."

Phil's smile dropped like a bucket of lead over Hoover Dam. "Whatta' mean, 'when you get back?' I'm going with you. So's Nancy."

Cap stood aside to give Phil access to the boarding ramp. Or, in this case, the deboarding ramp. Exit, boat left. "Not this trip, Phil. Jeffey and I are going to sail her alone on this run."

Phil assumed his petulant stance, hands on his hips, feet spread. "You two can't possibly sail her by yourselves. It's too big." Like the addition of Phil, a total non-sailor, to the crew would make the difference on this voyage. Two novices sailing a home-made clipper ship could do just as badly as three.

"That may be so, but we're going to give it our best shot."

"But you can't. You just can't do it." Translated roughly into honest English, 'I worked for months and now you guys get all the fun.'

Cap got a little pissed off. Why couldn't Phil see the big picture just once? "My mind's made up. We go alone."

Phil turned to Nancy for support. "Aren't you going to say anything? You've got every right to be on the Whale for this trip."

Nancy responded in a voice that would have crippled lesser men, "I say, we'd better get off so they can get going."

"No," countered Phil, showing himself to be something between a 'greater' man and a 'lesser' man.

Nancy moved close to her future husband, thinking that this stubborn trait would have to be removed in the future for marital harmony. "It's their boat, Phil. Remember? They get to do what they want." Phil opened his mouth in protest, Nancy filled it with her fist. "You just don't know when to shut up." She removed her fist and shoved him toward the ramp. Then she knelt down to be at eye-level with Jeff. "Enjoy the sail, buddy. Enjoy it like it was going to be the only chance you ever get." Tears well up in her eyes and she struggled for emotional control. "You and Cap deserve every glorious minute." She hugged him and rose to her feet to face

Cap. Looking at his face, she lost the control she had desperately wanted to keep, a sob escaped her chest. "Good luck, Captain." She put her arms, very gently, around the old man and kissed him on the lips. A chaste kiss but one Nancy hoped would breathe an hour's worth of life into Cap. She released him, backed away and then turned away. She put her hands firmly on Phil's butt and pushed toward the boarding ramp and away from the maiden voyage of the Whale. He allowed himself to be slowly pushed onto the board and back onto the jetty. Jeff waved good-bye to his friends standing on the jetty. Cap was silent, mustering his strength for the journey ahead.

Now the two of them were alone again with the Whale. Just like in the good ol' days. "Okay, Jeffey boy, let's cast off and get her into the wind. If there is any."

Jeff asked the $64,000 question, the one on the minds of everyone who knew anything about Cap, Jeff and the creation of the Whale. "Do you really think we can sail her alone?" Cap didn't answer immediately because he was trying to answer two other questions, 'can this hunk of wood really be sailed,' and 'can it be sailed by two people who have absolutely no clue as to how to sail?' Finally he responded to Jeff's question (without answering his own internal questions), "We built her, didn't we? We can sail her!" He bent down and shoved the gangway off the deck. Normally, a push would send the ramp sliding back onto the jetty but Cap didn't have enough pushing strength to get it there, one end fell into the water. The board sank beneath the surface. An ominous start to their journey. The final connection to solid ground had been severed and they now depended on the Whale.

ଙ୍ଗ CLOSE IN

The creature from the black (salt) lagoon, a monster of Lilliputian dimensions, draped in the latest in wash and wear clothes, dragged his sorry ass out of the mud flats and onto dry land at the east end of the harbor. No one screamed as this gargoyle of the Great Salt Lake, completely covered in mud, pushed his way through the crowd. His low growl was sufficient to get people scurrying out of his path. While Cinino liked the effect his new persona had on these low-brow spectators, he was disgusted with himself for looking disreputable in public. Before the ranks of the civilian masses had a chance to close behind Cinino, Dave Caster came squishing out of the water in hot, make that, lukewarm, pursuit.

Looking past Cinino, and through the parted crowd, Dave could see the Whale, sails still flapping on the yardarm, being towed out of the breakwater by a small boat. The tow boat's severely under-horsepowered outboard motor was wailing in protest at having to drag this behemoth behind it. The crowd cheered as the Whale neared open water. Dave yelled to Cinino, "Give it up, Cinino. You can't catch them now. Relax. They'll take their little cruise and when they're done, they'll come back. Then the boat is yours."

Cinino only stopped long enough to fire off a verbal broadside at Dave. "That just isn't the way it's going to be, Caster. I'm going to bring my boat back now, even if I have to swim out and get it." As a stationary target, Cinino could now be identified by people in the crowd as the villain of Wendover, the malicious midget who stole the Whale from the boy. They booed and hissed at him as he pushed through them heading for the jetty. Dave shrugged, and followed after him. He didn't want to miss the final showdown, however it ended...

♋ UNDER SAIL

The little tow boat had managed to get the Whale out of the harbor. Cap and Jeff were near the stern of the Whale. Cap was flexing the tiller trying to assist the tow boat driver by keeping the Whale's bow directly in the wake of the tow boat. Jeff was fascinated by the water racing, at a mere three knots, past the Whale's hull. He couldn't take his eyes off of the foaming water pushing against his boat.

Cap watched him closely but Jeff's eyes never left the water. "Somethin' bothering you, partner?"

Jeff reluctantly looked up at Cap, a tinge of fear dappling a background of exhilaration. "Naw, it's not that important."

"Spit it out, big guy."

A light pastel of embarrassment blended into the fear and exhilaration on his face. "I just remembered something. Maybe I shoulda' told you sooner."

"How bad could it be? Can't be any worse than some stuff I've done."

Jeff sheepishly grinned, and for the first time, in a long time, he showed that there was a little boy lurking inside this veteran visionary and master shipbuilder. "I don't know about that."

"Out with it, already."

"I don't know how to swim, Cap."

Even knowing the risks, Cap broke out in a hearty laugh. One that he could feel from his feet all the way to the stagnating pools of blood in his chest cavity. When he finally managed to control his chortling, he, too, had a confession. "Since we're tellin' secrets, I got one, too. I can't swim a lick, neither."

Jeff didn't believe him, after all, this was Cap the mighty sailor, old enough to have taught Popeye how to eat Gerber's creamed spinach and still have time to teach him the Australian crawl. "You don't have to say that. You know, to make me feel better."

"I'm not. It's the truth as Davey Jones is my witness."

This just didn't jibe with Jeff's perception of Cap and Cap's carefully cultivated image as a man with seawater running through his veins. If Cap hadn't fessed up to this major flaw in his life skills until now, what other transgressions should Jeff know about? "How couldn't you? You're a sailor."

This was the golden age of dishonesty where all admissions of deceit were to be forgiven as long as the Whale plied the trade route between Saltair and oblivion. Cap felt that oblivion had just passed by on the starboard side and he needed to own up to other mis-statements. "Hold on there. I never said I was sailor. I said I built ships." He chuckled thinking about it. "Never did make it out on one. Come to think about it, this is my first chance at it." This declarative floated in mid-air between the two virgin sailors like a massive storm cloud appearing suddenly on the horizon and demanding the attention of all on board.

The man in the tow boat shifted the motor into neutral, climbed to the stern and yelled up at the Whale, "Ready to cast off, Mister?" He waited for a reply, the waves gently rocking his boat.

On board the Whale, Cap heard the question but wanted to finish his conversation with Jeff. It was one thing for a boy to build a ship with someone who knows a little about building, its a whole different can of tuna to sail a potentially non-seaworthy ship with someone who can't sail and can't swim. Cap said to Jeff, "We can call it off. Have him tow us back to shore?" It was a question asked but not with the impatience of someone wanting an answer. Cap had done what he's needed to do; build a boat and float it on an ocean (actually, a inland sea, but who was counting?). Anyone in his right mind, and Cap would have excluded himself from that group, would have given him high marks just for making it this far. No shame in going back home now. Right? It was Jeff's call and whatever he wanted, he was going to get.

Jeff was running the same questions through his mind. He had proven what he set out to prove. He should be satisfied. No one would fault him for going back to Wendover having shown the Whale was indeed a seaworthy vessel. But, and it was an enormous but, he kept seeing a slightly different vision in his mind. He couldn't shake it. This daydream had him making the leap out of the vast ocean and onto a flying clipper ship. The ship skimmed the water, fully rigged, and all sails taut against the wind. Jeff made his way forward until he was straddling the bowsprit, the salt spray streaming on either side of him, the entire ship straining against gravity which held it sea-bound.

The older vision had led him to this point and now Jeff succumbed to this new vision, forgetting the small things, like wrong ship, wrong body of water and no experienced sailors manning the lines, just to name a few. Jeff pulled himself up to his full 5 foot 5 inch height and said, "No! You and me are going to sail her. Right now."

Cap could only sigh. "Aye, aye, Captain. Full speed ahead." He left off the 'damn the torpedoes' since the enemy resided within. He yelled forward to have the tow operator cast off his line. The Whale was going to sink or sail on its own.

The operator untied the tow line from a cleat on the stern and tossed it up onto the foredeck of the Whale. He shifted the motor into forward and swung around, heading back to shore. As he passed by the stern where Jeff and Cap were standing, he shouted to them, wishing them godspeed and a stiff wind. Cap silently wished for less speed and more wind since the god of flotation had already shown a fondness for the Whale but the goddess of the wind had yet to reach a verdict. As an afterthought, the tow operator yelled "good luck" over his shoulder. Cap muttered, "I think we mighta' used that up already." And then to Jeff, he said, "All right, Jeffey boy, this is where we show them what sailin's all about."

"Right on." He gave Cap the clenched fist salute. A gesture that would have made the Black Panther Party proud if Jeff had been black, politically conscious, disenfranchised from the mainstream and distrustful of the entrenched white bureaucracy.

Cap looked up at the mainmast with its luffing sails, scratched his rough chin and, damn, if the wind didn't start to pick up. The white nylon sails slapped hard against the yardarms, causing the Whale to rock in the windchop. "If you can tie off the sheets, you know the ropes on the sails, I'll see if I can find a direction to sail in."

Jeff whipped off a snappy salute, of the nautical variety this time. "Permission to go aloft, Sir?" Cap smiled and flicked his hand at Jeff, as if to say, 'go on already.'

Cap retreated to the tiller, grateful to take a load off his feet. Jeff climbed the rattings of the mainmast ready to do battle with any knots that got in his way. He reached the first yardarm and shimmied out far enough to untangle the sail. Several times the pitching of the Whale forced him to grab the yardarm and wrap his arms and legs around it. The mainsail finally came free. Jeff tied it off as the wind continued to freshen. Jeff continued his climb up the mainmast toward the top yardarm. Cap watched him from below, appreciating the boy's courage and vigor. He allowed a small sliver of hope to creep into his psyche, a glimmer of the possibility of success. How hard could it be to sail on a lake?

ᘓᙉᦈ NAPOLEON GOES IT ALONE

Like a fireworks display at a Fourth of July event, each unfurling of a sail was met with a new and louder cheer from the crowd in the Saltair harbor. Even from a distance, the Whale had taken on the aura of a real live clipper ship (if a clipper ship could only have two masts and four square-rigged sails).

Phil and Nancy joined the just plain folks on the jetty to watch the unfurling of this special nylon-wrapped 'gift' ship. Arm in arm, they were the two young sweethearts, beginning the tunnel-of-love ride. Salty did not share this warm fuzzy feeling. He whined at their feet, hoping that all his senses were wrong, and the Whale would magically reappear at the jetty's side, a wholly healed Cap would jump off the side of the boat into the water and come wading ashore yelling epithets at his favorite dog. He continued to whine, knowing that one of his senses could be wrong occasionally but all of them wrong at the same time, never.

The epithets and invectives that he had hoped would arrive from Cap's mouth did arrive at his eardrums but with a timbre and tone unlike Cap had ever voiced. Cinino, mud caked and dried all over his clothes, shoved people aside looking for someone, anyone, from the rescue crew that he could vent his rage on. Spotting two prime targets in Nancy and Phil, he drew a bead and shot forward. "I'm going to sue your butts off. You'll be farting through straws when I get through with you." The crowd cheered, not for the cleverness of Cinino's repartee, but the unfurling of the last of the sails.

The Whale remained stationary in the water, the sail sheets loosely flapping awaiting First Mate Jeff's return from aloft. The motorboat that towed the Whale putt-putted back around the jetty.

Phil, refused to acknowledge Cinino's presence and continued watching the Whale. He talked to him over his shoulder. "Big deal. Sue us for every penny we don't have. You think that will get the boat back? Don't you see it out there? You're too late, way too late."

Cinino stopped pussyfooting around. He stripped off his grimy jacket and threw it on the ground. Salty saw an opportunity to let out some of his pent-up emotions and leapt on it. Never had a garment been given as thorough a chewing in so little time. Cinino kicked at Salty but the little dog was quicker than the little general. Cinino barked at Phil, "Oh yeah? We'll see about that." He stomped down the incline to where the motorboat was being beached. He passed Dave going the other way and threw a shoulder at the bigger man. Dave ignored the blow. Cinino tromped down to the water's edge and waited for the boat driver. Looking back at Dave, he said, "Aren't you going to follow me anymore?"

Dave was downright stoic. " Eat shit and die."

Cinino balled up his fists and snarled, "What did you say, scum?"

Dave took several steps toward Cinino and stopped in front of him. The slope accentuated how much bigger Dave was than Cinino. "I said, get out of my face, you little fascist. I am sick and tired of listening to your crap. The rest of Wendover may kiss your ass but not me, not anymore."

Dave's tirade knocked the little man down a few pegs, or, perhaps, he was just sinking into the wet sand. "I'll take care of you when I get back. I've got to get my boat back before it sinks."

Dave had really enjoyed letting go. Like a band of steel compressing his stomach finally being released, he felt liberated. Well, if a taster spoon of emancipation was good, a double dip of liberty had to be better. "I hope you drown your scuzzy little neck on the way out there. And if I had any balls, I would do the job right here." He mimicked a man twisting the head off a chicken, a small chicken.

Cinino didn't wait for the opportunity to feel Dave's hands around his neck, he turned away and bore down on the motorboat driver. He grabbed the bow line out of his hand, and when the man started to protest, Cinino shoved him to the ground. Before anyone could stop him, Cinino pushed the bow of the boat out of the sand, hopped aboard and took off. If Dave or Phil had been quicker, they might have stopped the ranting runt but there was no reason to do so. By the time he got to the Whale, it would, hopefully, be under sail. And the saga of the Whale would end happily for all concerned, except for one Italo-American with a Napoleon complex, massive greed and a desire to own the next Disneyland.

৩ড় THE WHALE IS FREE

Mariah, the goddess of the western winds, was having a field day on the Great Salt Lake. Having been summoned to a convention, above the hallowed halls of Las Vegas, of all of the gods and goddesses who had inflicted their personal visions on the Wendover passion play taking place beneath their feet (or whatever immortals have in lieu of feet), Mariah had been given a free hand (see parens above) to wrap this drama up, today, if not sooner. And with all eyes (ditto above) upon her, she was really strutting her stuff. She traded a few valuable gusts for some particularly pretty thunderheads and then cajoled Sol, a former lover, to knock the rheostat down a few watts on the sun's intensity; mood lighting, if you will.

Mariah grabbed the Whale pennant between her pearly whites and tried to yank it off the top of the foremast. The material slipped through her teeth and she bounced from one sail to another. A heavenly trampoline ride which, through mortal's eyes look like a driving wind. The furies blown up by a scorned woman in hell couldn't hold a candle to the blasts Mariah could summon up when she was having fun.

The wind goddess wasn't the only one having fun. The Whale, one of many inanimate objects to have feelings, was having a blast. Forgetting for a moment her poor design and shoddy workmanship, she felt the cold breath upon her bosoms and, titillated by the chilly touch, leapt from wave to wave. The combers of water thrust and gyrated in an effort to give her even greater ecstasy as her naked hull slipped and slid against its wetness.

Jeff, astride the bowsprit, was in the midst of a visionary's orgasm. That moment when a vivid dream collided with an even more vivid reality. The smack of wood against water and the salt spray splashing him in the face were several senses beyond what he experienced in his sub-conscious when dreaming his clipper ship dream. He radiated so much pure pleasure that Mariah was just about to chastise Sol for ruining the scene with too much light. Jeff screamed his rapture and gloried in the name of he who helped him achieve this moment. "Cap! Cap, we have done it. I can't believe it. We are sailing! No. No, we are flying. Don't you love it?" Mariah's heavy breathing through the sails was the only response. Facing forward, Jeff could not see if Cap had even heard what he shouted. He wouldn't let this moment get away with congratulating his captain. He slid off the bowsprit and started aft. "Cap, did you hear me? This is the greatest! I love you. I know I said it before to some others but I really mean it this time."

Mariah's was eavesdropping, hoping to get a little credit for the moment. She was too slow to react and Jeff's words 'I love you' tumbled through the air currents and splashed down far forward of the racing ship. She held her breath, the sails luffed, in hopes that the boy would speak the words again and they would be heard by the man in the back of the boat. Jeff saw that Cap had slumped over the tiller and did not repeat the three little words.

Cap could not hear Jeff's words. He faded in and out of consciousness, his eyelids fought to stay aloft.

The currents' push against the rudder was too much for Cap. He couldn't hold a steady course. The blood leaking up from his critically injured organs had flowed over his lips and streamed down toward his chin. There was enough volume and flow that it didn't coagulate before dripping from his chin. Even if he wanted to hide the obvious, and he couldn't, Cap was at death's door. Death had sized up his opponent and decided to go for the decision. A knockout punch was not an option when fighting an adversary of this caliber.

Jeff was on his knees, his arms around the dying man like a supplicant at the altar praying for the miracle that would not come. "Oh, Cap." He could do nothing but repeat his name, over and over. Cap worked enough saliva out of his mouth and onto his parched lips to get them functioning. He drew on his last ounce of strength, not that his trainer was picking up the white towel in the corner, and looked at his friend, "Don't you worry, Jeff, jus' a bad case a' seasick." He laughed, or what had to pass as a laugh under the circumstances. Jeff wiped the blood off the old man's face but it was a waste of time. Cap's heart kept pumping the red stuff through a big hole where there shouldn't have been one.

"You aren't dying, are you, Cap?" He knew the answer, he felt the answer, but he wouldn't believe it until he heard it from Cap's lips.

"It feels that way, Jeffey." There was no use in denying it. Everything that Cap wanted to accomplish with his life had been fulfilled in the last 24 hours. Living another 100 years wouldn't get him any closer to a complete life.

Jeff began to cry. And the tears flowed like the blood. Both hearts, the boy's and the old man's had been torn asunder. "You can't. I really, really need you."

"No you don't, Mister Cutter. We're finished. We made it all come true. Just you and me and the Whale." He struggled to open his shirt pocket. His hand, experiencing tremors, could not find the pocket opening. "Remember when all we had to show," he said as he pulled out the original sketch Jeff had drawn for his 'clipper ship', "was this drawing?" As he pulled the paper out, the book of matches from Jeff's pyromanaical efforts against the Whale fell to the deck. "And everybody thought we was two looneybirds?"

Through his tears, Jeff answered, "I remember."

"We showed them who was crazy, didn't we? You were the best damn partner I ever had." He coughed a deep, breaking cough and his eyelids fluttered shut. Jeff's heart felt like it was breaking open too. Then Cap's lids struggled upward once more. "You won't forget me, will ya, Jeffey?"

Jeff hugged Cap as tightly as he could. If Cap's spirit was attempting to leave his body, Jeff was there to capture it. "No, Cap, I'll never forget you. You're the best friend I'll ever have."

That's all Cap needed to hear, the one last resistant strand of life, frayed from the tension of the battle, unraveled. "I'm sorry to run out on you like this...you can make...you're tough...like me. He coughed and the last filament of life snapped. "Damn. There's never an Indian burial ground when you need one."

He died laughing, and nothing the gods and goddesses hovering over the sternpost could do about it—their powers had been diminished, regretfully, since the times of Zeus and his control over life and death.

The Whale hove-to with no one controlling the tiller. The bow settled down and the Whale no longer cleaved the water. Without its forward momentum, the Whale seemed to lose its vibrancy.

Jeff lay on top of Cap's body sobbing and shaking. He continued to talk to Cap between his sobs, "Please don't go. Please. Don't leave me alone." Grief was immobilizing. Jeff would have stayed with the body until hell froze over or until the soul of Cap reincarnated in a new body. Neither was likely to happen soon. But anger was invigorating and fury was overpowering.

Cinino arrived in his commandeered motorboat and circled the Whale looking to scream at someone. His choice of Jeff was a bad one. Jeff was a bundle of highly charged emotions with a short unlit fuse.

৻ৡ FLAMING JEFF'S PASSION

Cinino's ego was beyond bruised, it was pulverized, it was granulated and it was powdered. Nothing sweet about it. The theft of his boat right under his nose, the impudence of a-sack-of-shit like Caster and the humiliation of the Whale launching without him, had led Cinino to a point beyond reasonable and civilized. He was the Barbary Pirate of the Salt Lake Main, looking to rape and pillage, taking no prisoners and leaving towns in smoldering ruins. Since his position in the motorboat was low, he couldn't see anything that was taking place on the deck of the Whale. Since he saw no bodies in the water, he assumed that Cap and Jeff were still onboard, hiding from his wrath. "Where are you, you bastards? You are on my ship and you have no right to be sailing it." His voice carried across the stern of the boat rising high above the drone of the motor.

Jeff lifted his head off Cap's chest to hear the shouted words. Cinino continued his tirade, "Listen to me, Cap, or whatever your real name is. If you don't turn the Whale around immediately, I'm going to expose you as the senile old drunk you really are." He paused briefly waiting for a response from or the sight of his adversaries. Neither happened. "When are you going to tell the kid how you traded his boat away for a lousy bottle of booze? You hear me, Jeff? Your partner gave it all away. I'll bet he didn't tell you about that, did he?" Cinino's incendiary words, focused through a magnifying glass of a young boy's despair and anguish, lit Jeff's fuse. A very short fuse. "Come on, you cowards, show yourselves. You spineless sissies. You disgust me."

Cinino's diatribe only pushed the spark faster through the wick leading to Jeff's emotional detonation. Anger flooded his face, driving out the lassitude of sadness. His brain had sounded the alarm and his nerve endings were at battle stations. Without thinking, he crushed the sketch in his fist, then calmly collected the book of matches off the deck of the Whale. He stood and scanned the lake's surface for his enemy. Cinino was running the motorboat in a parallel course to the drifting Whale, within hailing distance but not boarding range. Jeff stood at the rail to get the measure of the man who would destroy the purity of the image Jeff held of his now-deceased partner.

Cinino interpreted Jeff's arrival at the rail as a sign that Cap was too humiliated to show himself. Since Cap had been the object of his anger, and Jeff only an accessory to the crime, there was no reason to continue the verbal attack. A patronizing approach, one he used with most people, would work, he thought, with the boy above him. "At least one of you is man enough to show. This fun little game is over, Jeff. Be a good little boy and turn the Whale around."

"The Whale is mine, and Cap's. You'll never get it." This was not an act of defiance in the face of overwhelming adult authority, but a simple statement of conviction. The boy possessed the ship and he was possessed by the ship. They were bound together.

FITTING BURIAL FOR A CAPTAIN

"Don't act like a child. You know the Whale is mine, and I am taking it now." Cinino turned the bow of the motorboat into Whale's port side. It struck the hull and glanced off. Without assistance, it was impossible for Cinino to board the Whale. Jeff turned away from the rail and walked amidships. Cinino called to Jeff but the boy disappeared behind the base of the mainmast. "I'm sorry, Jeff. Maybe that was too strong. A poor choice of words on my part. Help me get up there and we can talk about it."

Jeff was beyond the discussion point. The Jeffey-bomb went off, not with a boom, but with a small flicker of light. Using the mast as a windbreak, he had struck a match. The sulfur flared and then was extinguished by a puff of air from Mariah. Jeff heard Cinino shouting but his whole being was closed in and around the small cardboard matchbook. He struck another match. It was blown out as quickly as the first. He beseeched the gods and goddesses to be kind but something else—halfway between corporeal and immortal— reached out with two translucent hands to protect the third match. The hands, while unseen by Jeff, belonged to an old man, long exposed to the elements and suffering from years of hard work. The hands cupped the small flame as it blossomed on the end of the matchstick. Jeff transfered the flame to a corner of the crumpled sketch. Hungrily, the fire gobbled up the flattened wood pulp and pencil carbon. Like the torch runner at the beginning of the Olympic Games, Jeff held his ignited paper aloft, and touched the flame to his symbol of triumph; the mainsail of the Whale. He recited his own version of the Olympic Oath, "To my friend, Cap, may he rest in peace. And let the Whale keep him company."

Nylon was a very efficient material for sails, windbreakers and imitation silk ties. It wouldn't be a Boy Scout's first choice for building a bonfire or a funeral pyre. Unfortunately for Jeff, no one had offered him a cord of seasoned oak as an alternative. The nylon mainsail took a long time to accept the fiery offering from Jeff's hand. Once warmed to the concept of immolation, the nylon fabric wholeheartedly embraced it, like a born-again Christian to the New Testament. The flames shot up the slippery cloth faster than Cinino could shriek, "What the hell are you doing? That's not funny, Jeff. Put it out. Please." His shriek, like the flames, rose and fell with the wind currents, eventually turning into a plea. One that fell on deaf ears.

With the mainmast a towering inferno, Jeff returned to Cap's body to prepare it for its final campfire and cookout. Jeff acted quickly, operating on a simple statement that Cap had made many months before, that his burial be noble, like those of the Native Americans and their desire to return to the elements. He laid out Cap's body, parallel to the deck planking, then he arranged Cap's hat on his head and lay his arms alongside the body. Several wisps of molten nylon drifted down from the mast and settled on Cap's legs. Jeff quickly brushed them off. "I hope this is what you meant." The fire had eaten through the rigging and the mainsail yardarm dropped, crashing to the deck. "We don't have a choice now." The flames leapt from the mainmast to the foremast. The fire burned on the uppermost reaches of the mainmast, shooting flames high into the smoke-filled sky, scorching the derrières of all those celestial types who had stuck around. Was it the soot and smoke that singed their eyes or had they been moved by the tragic circumstances below to shed tears of sadness?

❧ RELUCTANT WITNESSES

Once the Whale had left Saltair harbor and taken up flight under sail there was not much for spectators to watch. A small ship, three-quarters of a mile out, could only hold the public's eye for a few minutes. Those with the shortest attention spans had turned their backs on the lake, preparing to return to their every-day lives. Those with a stake in the voyage and its ending; Dave, Phil, Nancy and Salty had watched until their collective eyes hurt. Phil was the first to spot the flames and he was certain that it was only an optical illusion caused by the sun on the water. It was only when the mainsail was fully engulfed could he loosen his tongue from the back of his throat and said, "Sweet Jesus, the boat is on fire." Dave and Nancy cupped their hands over their eyes to get a clearer look. Some of the crowd heard Phil's statement and returned to watch a different form of pyrotechnic display, courtesy of the Wendover Whale. Dave howled in pain. "That bastard set the Whale on fire. I can't believe it. He set the boat on fire with the boy and the old man on it. Just because they wouldn't give back." He was certain that Cinino had exacted the ultimate revenge on Cap and Jeff. Nancy was strangely unmoved by the spectacle in front of her. While she hadn't foreseen the destruction of the Whale by fire, she had anticipated that Cap and Jeff, or Jeff by himself, would not allow the Whale to fall into the enemy's hands. "You got it wrong, Caster. They're just making sure that Cinino doesn't get the Whale." The crowd watched in shock as if a giant lightning bolt had struck them deaf and dumb, the heat of the lightning welding their feet to the sand.

Dave wasn't satisfied. "Whether Cinino set the fire or not, there's at least two people out there who are going to die. Cuz Cinino won't help. He'd sooner let them drown than lift a finger. I know, dammit."

Phil had continued to watch as the flames leapt higher and higher. And for a moment, the journalist (aloof and independent) in him separated from his caring, human side. The vision of the ship on fire, the red and yellow tendrils of flame shooting skyward, the ship backlit by a screaming saffron sun on a cerulean blue platter was as awe-inspiring as the more simple vision he saw months before of an odd wooden skeleton, bleached by the same unmerciful sun and parched by the dry desert air. Phil was moved to tears and the sense that the story that connected these two images had become a tragedy. His caring side, the left side encompassing his heart, got control over the journalistic side. "We've got to get out there. Come on." The four of them ran down to the incline of the jetty looking for a way to get out onto the lake. As if the heat and flames from the Whale were an attractant, like a candle to a light-starved moth, the people who had come out to glory in the success of the Whale, now walked slowly to the water's edge to be close and bear witness to its death.

Phil managed to find a Boston Whaler with a small engine mounted on it. He helped Dave into the boat. Nancy carried a squirming Salty and handed him to Dave while Phil helped Nancy onboard. Dave yanked the cord on the motor, it caught and they raced out of the harbor on less than a wing and needing more than a prayer.

☜☞ RESCUING THE MEMORIES

Jeff waited with Cap for the end to come. The Whale remained afloat because the hull remained intact. As the flames ate through the rigging of the masts, the delicate balance that the ship once had was gone, any shift of weight would cause it to heel over. And that slight heel would become a roll and nothing would stop the roll from putting the bottom of the hull up into the air and the tip of the bowsprit into the water. A death roll that would leave the Whale on the bottom of the Great Salt Lake.

Jeff stared up at the top of his ship as part of the mainmast broke away and fell, a tangle of rattings ushering it down. He looked back down at Cap. "It's almost over." The dancing flames cast flickering shadows on the old man's face, giving it the appearance that his lips were moving. Jeff leaned close to hear the dead man's imagined whisper, 'You won't forget me, will ya?' Jeff responded with vibrations from his heart that passed through his skin and bones and out to where Cap's spirit hovered nearby. "No, Cap. I will never forget you." More of the mainsail fell away.

Through the smoke and the jagged top of the mainmast, Jeff could see the Whale banner fluttering in the rising heat currents. He blinked away the tears and saw the indistinct image of Cap accepting the banner in the shipyard and then turning and handing it to Jeff. That moment was freeze-framed on the retinas of Jeff's eyes until he heard Cap's voice urging him to go, to go and reclaim 'their' banner. And Jeff was up and running. Dodging the burning parts of the deck and the tangled riggings, he made his way to the port side foremast ratlines. All he could see was the banner and all he could hear was Cap urging him up. He grabbed the ratlines and pulled himself up. The Whale's center of balance, structurally flawed to begin with, to a swing for the worse as Jeff moved up the mast. The higher he climbed, the more the Whale heeled to port. Unfazed by the shift, Jeff continued to climb through the smoke and the heat. The fire leapt into the rattings below him, cutting off his escape route and leaving him only one direction to go; onward and upwards. Even on a good day, climbing aloft required skill and patience. Neither of these prerequisites was available to Jeff. His foot slipped out of the braided rope and his hands flailed away to maintain his balance. He reached the point where the riggings tied onto the mast and he was still ten feet below the top of the foremast, and the banner. He wrapped his hands and feet around the impossibly slender wooden post and inched his way upward. He repeated the mantra that Cap had given him, 'the banner, the banner.' He was within an arm's length plus two inches when the Whale began its final roll. Jeff released the mast pole with his hands and made a desperate lunge for the banner, forgetting that he was over thirty feet in the air and needed some physical connection to solid objects to keep from falling. His abrupt shift of weight caused the mast to snap below him and the Whale rolled beyond the point of no return. Jeff and the upper portion of the mast were flung off the side. Jeff hurtled through the air and hit the surface in a tremendous spray of water.

Another section of mast flew through the air and hit Cinino squarely in the head. He was catapulted into the lake, sinking beneath the surface faster than a card-counter got pulled from Cinino's casino. The Whale completely heeled over, the remaining fire extinguished in a cloud of steam and a loud sizzle. The Whale would not be destroyed by an element (fire) alien to its existence as a ship. Death by drowning was far more appealing than death by flame. The Whale's open hatch invited the lake's water to join it in a final dance. The brine obliged, coyly at first, creeping from the deck railing toward the uncovered hole amidships. The water, sensing no resistance, finally waltzed boldly into the darkness of the interior. And the death-dance was on. The hold filled with water molecules looking to boogie-woogie and the Whale slid sideways into the (relative) deep of the Great Salt Lake.

☇ A PRE-HISTORIC LIFE RING

An unconscious body floats in a highly saline solution, positive buoyancy keeps the unconscious from becoming the dead except when the body's organs used for oxygen exchange are face down in the water. As in Jeff's case.

The impact of his body splashing into the water had left him far from a reasoning position. If his would-be rescuers were able to see him, which they were not because of the steam and smoke, it would have been a simple matter of lifting him out of the water and resuscitating him. It was only simple when the boy in question could be found. And time was running out.

Far below Jeff, something quite old, even ancient, shook itself free from the mud of the lake bottom and began a second attempt at a new life. Through its rudimentary eyes, the wavering, watery image of a boy was nothing more than an odd refraction of the light and air. But this was all the creature needed to act. Faster and faster it climbed, knowing, this time, that a superfish-like effort would be necessary to overcome the physical properties securing him to his watery hell. He drove his body forward on a collision course with Jeff's body. The ichthyosaur struck Jeff just to the left and below his stomach driving water out in a forced exhalation and flipping the boy's body over so that he was floating face up in the lake. The impact of Ich's body with Jeff's broke the concentration of the ichthyosaur and he lost his edge. His long scaly body cleared the water but only for an (unseen by humans) instant before crashing back into the brine. For one marvelous moment, again, Ich was free of his liquid chains and then he splashed back into his dark watery prison. But this moment was enough to finally satisfy his primal urges and he allowed his body to be swallowed. He gave himself up to the pressure and slowly drifted down and away.

Dave, Phil, Nancy and Salty all heard the splash but could not see what made it. In light of the horrific scene around them, none was willing to speculate what caused it. Dave carefully moved the Boston Whaler closer to the smoldering hulk of the Whale. He bumped into Cinino's empty boat and Phil grabbed the railing. Dave cut the engine off for fear that the propeller would run over someone in the water. If he had been certain that person would be Cinino, he would have left it on full throttle. When the engine died, silence returned to the lake. The four of them sat in the drifting smoke waiting to hear something, or someone moving. Someone groaned on the other side of Cinino's motorboat and all three humans leapt toward the sound. Dave reacted the fastest, reaching down into the water. He felt cloth, closed his hand around it and hauled it up toward the boat. Nancy could not contain her fear, "Who is it? It's not Jeff, is it?" Dave continued to haul the body aboard until it flopped onto the floorboards like a recently gaffed fish. Dave didn't try to hide his disappointment. "It's only Cinino, the slime."

Phil hovered over Cinino's body as it shed water from the polyester. "He's not groaning anymore. Do you think he's dead?" Dave thumped Cinino's chest with both hands in a manner somewhat less genteel than a sumo-wrestling match. Cinino vomited a shower of water and partially digested food out of his mouth and started gagging.

Dave, somewhat disheartened, said, "No, unfortunately. Let's keep looking for Cap and Jeff."

Phil found an emergency paddle alongside the gas tank and started clumsily paddling the motorboat in a circle around the Whale. Nancy leaned over the side of the boat and paddled with her hand. She looked at Phil, "I can't see anyone. Do you think they could still be on the Whale?"

Phil answered, not wanting to dwell on the possibilities, "Not if they're still alive." The boat bumped into a piece of wood and Salty started barking up a storm. Nancy slid forward on her knees until she could feel the wood. Salty was barking with such intensity that his body was three-quarters of the way out of the boat. The only thing keeping him from falling in was his total focus on the object in the water. Phil asked, "What is it, Nancy? Part of the Whale?" Nancy leaned out over the railing, grabbing the wood with both hands.

"It's just a piece of wood. I'll get it out of the way." She lifted it up and out of the water. The wood was the topmost section of the foremast. And the Whale banner was still attached. Nancy pulled on the banner and Jeff's hand came up and out of the water, still grasping the banner. Nancy screamed, "It's Jeff!" She started pulling feverishly on Jeff's arm. Phil dropped the paddle and helped Nancy to pull Jeff onto the boat. She checked his breath and immediately started mouth-to-mouth resuscitation. Phil and Salty, wanting to help, could do nothing but watch Nancy work.

Phil asked, "Is he alive? Is he breathing?" As if in answer, Jeff coughed up water. The Whale responded to this positive life sign by hissing back at Jeff. Only a small portion of the Whale remained above the water line and that little bit was in imminent danger of disappearing. Jeff opened his eyes and pulled his fist in front of his eyes. His body sagged with relief when he saw that his fingers had not failed him—the banner was wrapped around his knuckles.

Phil was relieved that Jeff was alive but he continued to scan the water for a clue as to Cap's whereabouts. There was nothing out there to indicate another life was nearby, ready to be saved. He said to Jeff, "Jeff, where's Cap? When did you last see him?"

Jeff struggled to a sitting position that allowed him to see over the boat's side and out at the Whale. To no one in particular, he said, "He's still on the Whale."

Phil helped the boy stabilize his position as Jeff watched the Whale slide under the water, "He can't be. The Whale's going..." He didn't finish the sentence. The Whale did it for him. With a loud sucking sound, like a hungry patron of a restaurant slurping down a raw oyster, the Great Salt Lake swallowed up the great Wendover Whale.

Dave helped (maybe too strong a word) Cinino up in just enough time to see the lake's consumption of the boat. Dave was touched at the loss of the ship but pleased that it never fell into the hands of Cinino. Cinino watched it go down and then puked his guts out.

For a long, long time, Jeff stared at the spot where the Whale used to be. Salty had ceased to bark and he, too, stared at the patch of water ahead of him. Phil and Nancy, arms around each other, waited for something to happen. Anything to happen. It was just too damn uncomfortable to be doing nothing.

Finally, Phil said to Jeff, "I'm sorry, Jeff. I really am." Jeff pulled Salty close to him, stroking the dog's back. Salty, in a decidedly uncharacteristically submissive act for him, let the boy caress him. Jeff whispered to the dog, "It was what he wanted. He told me. He helped me do it." And then the words were replaced by sobs. Tears rolled down his cheeks and caught in Salty's fur. His shoulders sagged and life became all too real and all too cruel.

In Jeff's mind, each memory of the summer and the Whale was a group photo with one common element; an old man in a dirty captain's hat. Not all of the pictures in this memory album were pretty since Cap was not that photogenic but the sum total of the experience of looking through this scrapbook was that Cap had become an indispensable part of Jeff's life. It was this loss that now made Jeff realize how trivial most things in his life were and how irreplaceable his one friend was.

He unwrapped the banner from his hand and dropped it to the bottom of the boat where bilge water stained and discolored it. He stood and looked to the spot where the Whale went under and shouted, "Damn the Whale! I want Cap back."

౨ఠ AFT-ER-WORD

The elements of Earth have an unpleasant way of erasing the mistakes made by the pitiful human beings that populate its land. Not long after Jeff and Salty, Phil and Nancy, and Dave and Cinino returned to the harbor at Saltair, the sun had dried their clothes, the wind had blown away all the smoke and ash from the fire, the waves had dispersed the flotsam and jetsam to distant shores and the water had forced the skeleton of the Wendover Whale down, down into its tomb. There was no element that could eliminate the memories from all those who had participated in this event; the construction of a wild and fanciful vision into a living, breathing reality, decried by all manner of doomsayers.

Time, that guardian of all events, slowly and painfully began to wreck havoc upon the participants' brain cells that contained the fragments of this story, this fable, this tall tale.

Perhaps in time, even the visionary would lose his visions; the daydreamer would stop dreaming and the people who lived in the middle of nothingness would accept that life held no challenges and no adventures.

Until, that is, that fateful day when the molecules of an audacious fish lizard or the spirit of a cantankerous old yarn-spinner invaded the noggin of someone open to the possibility of being different. And on that day, somewhere between here and there, someone would take up the banner.

ACKNOWLEDGMENTS

To those with shipbuilding or nautical experience, I thank you for willingly, or reluctantly, suspending your disbelief while reading this novel.

To Mel Powers, for providing constant optimism in the face of many, many naysayers.

To Cliff Carle and Bert Lane (my father) for struggling through my mangled phrasing and unusual spelling. Any mistakes that the reader might find are surely mine and not yours.

To my co-workers at my 'other' job for picking up and completing the tasks that fell off my plate while I was messing around with a story about a boy, an old man, a clipper ship and the Great Salt Desert.

August, 1999

To the reader,

I sincerely hope that you enjoyed reading "The Wendover Whale."

Could you please take the time to send me your comments?

If, as it is my hope, you found pleasure in reading this story, could you please pass it along to a friend? Better yet, order them their own copy!

I can be reached at:

Shared Vision Books
c/o Wilshire Book Company
12015 Sherman Road
North Hollywood, CA 91605

Thanks, again, for taking the time to read my book.

Sincerely,

James R. Lane

A Personal Invitation from the Publisher, Melvin Powers...

Since we first published *The Knight in Rusty Armor,* we've received an unprecedented number of calls and letters from readers praising its powerful insights and entertaining style. It is a memorable fun-filled story, rich in wit and humor, that has changed thousands of lives for the better.

The Knight is one of our most popular titles and has been published in numerous languages. I feel so strongly about this unusual book that I'm personally extending an invitation for you to read it.

The Knight in Rusty Armor

The Knight in Rusty Armor is a lighthearted tale of a desperate knight in search of his true self. It's guaranteed to captivate your imagination as it helps you discover the secret of what is most important in life.

Join the knight as he faces a life-changing dilemma upon discovering that he is trapped in his shining armor, as *we* may find that we are trapped in *our* armor—an invisible kind that we use to protect ourselves from various aspects of life.

As the knight searches for a way to free himself, he receives guidance from the wise sage Merlin the Magician, who encourages the knight to embark on the most difficult crusade of his life. The knight takes up the challenge and travels the Path of Truth, where he meets his real self for the first time and confronts the Universal Truths that govern his life—and ours.

The knight's journey reflects our own, filled with hope and despair, belief and disillusionment, laughter and tears. His insights become our insights as we follow along on this intriguing adventure of self-discovery. Anyone who has ever struggled with the meaning of life and love will discover profound wisdom and truth as this delightful fantasy unfolds. *The Knight in Rusty Armor* is an experience that will expand your mind, touch your heart, and nourish your soul.

The author, Robert Fisher, has enjoyed a long and distinguished career writing for such comedy greats as Groucho Marx, Bob Hope, George Burns, Jack Benny, Red Skelton, and Lucille Ball. Mr. Fisher has also written hundreds of comedic radio and television shows.